STRABO IS NO[illegible] DECURION, BU[illegible] IS NOT W[illegible]OUT COST

Marcellus Strabo has transitioned from an unwilling legionnaire to a respected, battle-hardened decurion of the Tenth Legion, *Equestris*. His success is viewed with alarm by Raven, the Aeduan woman he loves, when Strabo begins to look and act more Roman than Aeduan. Strabo is aware of her growing detachment caused by a deep distrust of Rome. He resents her expectation he will one day have to choose between his Roman or Aeduan heritage while he questions why he has to choose at all. In the meantime, the wars in Gaul intensify with additional invasions by Belgae and Germani Tribes. The battles are many and bloody with considerable losses on both sides. While the legions generally prevail, there is one battle in which the legions come close to losing, an indication the tribes are learning how to fight the Romans. Apart from external threats to Gaul, Caesar is challenged by growing anger among the Gaulish tribes the legions are no longer transient protectors but are in Gaul to stay. The turbulent events leave little time or opportunity for Raven and Strabo to resolve personal concerns until a horrifying event becomes a consequential influence for reconciling their differences.

Praise for Strabo Book 1, The Unwilling Legionnaire from Goodreads

"Mr. Holtry's new Roman series set in the days of Caesar promises to be a worthy successor to his Arrius trilogy. Marcellus Strabo, the son of a Roman general and a Gaulish noblewoman is a wastrel and womanizer. His father has him "conscripted" into the Roman Army as a legionary. Marcellus proves his worth, rising to command a group of cavalrymen and to be Caesar's translator and that of Caesar's right-hand man, Tribune Setarius. He plays a large part in both Caesar's Helvetian and Suebian campaigns. Let's not forget a romantic interlude with a young Gaulish woman he has known from childhood when he had visited his mother's village. Marcellus still feels suspended between two worlds, Roman and Gaulish, because of his mixed heritages and really neither wholly either."—***Jane, Goodreads Librarian***

"Holtry's scholarship, military background and keen eye for historical detail are on full display in this compelling story centered on Caesar's ongoing campaign in Far Gaul. While Caesar seeks to increase his power and prestige in Rome through his conquests, Marcellus Strabo, a decurion in Caesars's service, is faced with a choice: continue his military service and honor the memory of his late father, General Lucillus Strabo, or be with the woman he loves, a fiercely proud Gallic woman who bristles at Rome's occupation of her home and Strabo's role in it. In *Decurion*, Holtry delivers a worthy sequel to *Strabo: The Unwilling Legionnaire* and whets the appetite for the next book in the series."—***W. Jeff Barnes, author of Mingo***

"Decurion is Preston Holtry's second book in his series about Julius Caesar's Gallic Wars. Through his main character, Marcellus Strabo, Holtry tells the story of Caesar's campaigns in Gaul, complete with a web of perspectives, relationships, and inter-connections that carry the story forward and engross the readers. His rich, multi-layered plot, smart dialogue and spirited action deliver not only a master class in the tribes of Gaul and war with the Romans, but also the life of Roman soldiers and the interpersonal relationships that existed between Romans and the tribes they governed. If you love historical fiction and Roman history, you won't be disappointed."—***Eric Schumacher, best-selling author of Viking Age fiction***

"Sired by a former Roman general and a noble Gaulish woman, Decurion Marcellus Strabo has a foot in two very different worlds. His continued battle successes and apparent intent to remain a Roman officer is increasingly at odds with Raven, the dynamic

Gaulish tribal woman he loves. She fears Marcellus is too committed to Rome in a way she can never be. Will he choose his mother's people and his beloved or his legionary weapon brothers? Their personal conflict and a fateful decision they will one day have to make is overshadowed by the events in Gaul. Julius Caesar is focused not only on making Gaul a Roman province, but expansion into Belgae, Germania and Britannia as well. This character-driven and action-packed novel rings with superlative historical and tactical detail far surpassing others in this genre. Ride along with Strabo into the hellish turmoil of Caesar's ancient battles."—***Thomas J. Howley, Author of Wolf of Clontarf - The Irish, the Vikings and the Foreigners of the World***

"Galloping into Caesar's Gallic Wars spear in hand, we follow Strabo and Raven on a host of adventures. A riveting jaunt into the brutal world of Rome that you won't soon forget. Highly recommended."—***Daniel Greene, author of the Northern Wolf series***

Marcellus Strabo

DECURION

A NOVEL OF JULIUS CAESAR'S GALLIC WARS
Book 2

Moonshine Cove Publishing, LLC

Abbeville, South Carolina U.S.A.

First Moonshine Cove Edition DEC 2022

ISBN: 9781952439452

Library of Congress LCCN: 2022921659

This book is a work of fiction. Names, characters, businesses, places, events, conversations, opinions, and incidents are either products of the author's imagination or are used fictitiously. Any resemblance to actual events, locales, conversations, opinions, business establishments, or persons, living or dead, is entirely coincidental and unintended.

Front cover image by Cindy Guare Paint & Design; cover and interior design by Moonshine Cove staff.

About the Author

Preston Holtry has a BA degree in English from the Virginia Military Institute and a graduate degree from Boston University. A career army officer, he served twice in Vietnam in addition to a variety of other infantry and intelligence-related assignments in Germany, England, and the United States. Retired from the army with the rank of colonel, he lives with his wife, Judith, and Max, a rescue Retriever in Oro Valley, Arizona. Read more about him and his published books at his website:

http://www.presholtry.webs.com

Historical Mysteries

Death in Emily 3
A Troublesome Affair
Seal of Confession
The Good Thief

Roman Historical Novels

The ARRIUS Trilogy:

Sacramentum (Oath) Volume 1
Legacy Volume 2
Enemy of Rome Volume 3

The Strabo Series:

The Unwilling Legionnaire

Modern Thriller:

Looking for Steiner (under the name Wayne Preston)

Acknowledgements

My grateful thanks to my wife, Judy and her sister, Ruthie, for the time and trouble contributing ideas, badly needed criticism and doing their best to make me a better writer and storyteller.

I created the terrain maps from a topographic map obtained on Google provided by Wikimedia Commons.

The original wall-size mural, **Boduognat Loses,** displayed on the jacket cover was done by the digital artist **Yannick De Smet ©Archeocentrum Velzeke, Belgium.** The scene depicts the aftermath of the Battle of the Sambre fought during Caesar's Gallic Wars. I appreciate the generosity of both Yannick and the museum for granting the one-time use of the mural.

My appreciation to Cindy Guare, digital artist and muralist for the cover design and Moonshine Cove for ensuring front and back covers are fully integrated for publication. And special thanks to Gene Robinson for taking on another Roman saga and helping me to "get the words right."

Dedication

For Barb, my sister-in-law, a loving, devoted mother and wife who, in spite of facing many challenges throughout her life, always remained cheerful and faithful to the McLeod Clan motto: *Hold Fast.*

Preface

Decurion follows the war in Gaul during the period 57-55 B.C.E. as Julius Caesar describes in books 2, 3 and 4 of his *Commentaries*. Apart from the events and battles in Gaul, Caesar continues to deal with political adversaries in Rome. His opposition is intent on removing him as governor of three provinces and command of the six legions in Gaul. Caesar is not without support. He has Pompey's political influence and the financial support of Crassus, the wealthiest man in Rome. He is also very popular with the *plebs,* the underclass masses in Rome with voting power. Caesar prevails and retains governorship of his provinces and command of the army in Gaul with two additional legions.

Caesar's objective in writing the *Commentaries* is less about recording an accurate history of the Gallic Wars than burnishing his reputation as a field commander and maintaining his position in the Republic's political hierarchy. His dispatches are high-level without the detail historians would have wished; consequently, I used my own experience as a career soldier to have the characters think and act in ways credible to historic events and battle actions. I use present day names for rivers and geographical features for the reader to have a better idea where the events and battles take place. All tribes cited in the novel are identified in the *Commentaries*.

In the Author's Notes preceding the glossary, I tell the reader where I took creative license to keep the narrative moving and the characters realistically engaged. The notes also include brief explanations concerning Roman organization, tactics and equipment. The glossary at the end of the novel provides a brief explanation of Latin terms and identifies modern-day geographical locations of settlements cited in Latin.

PWH, Oro Valley, Arizona

GAUL 57-55 B.C.E

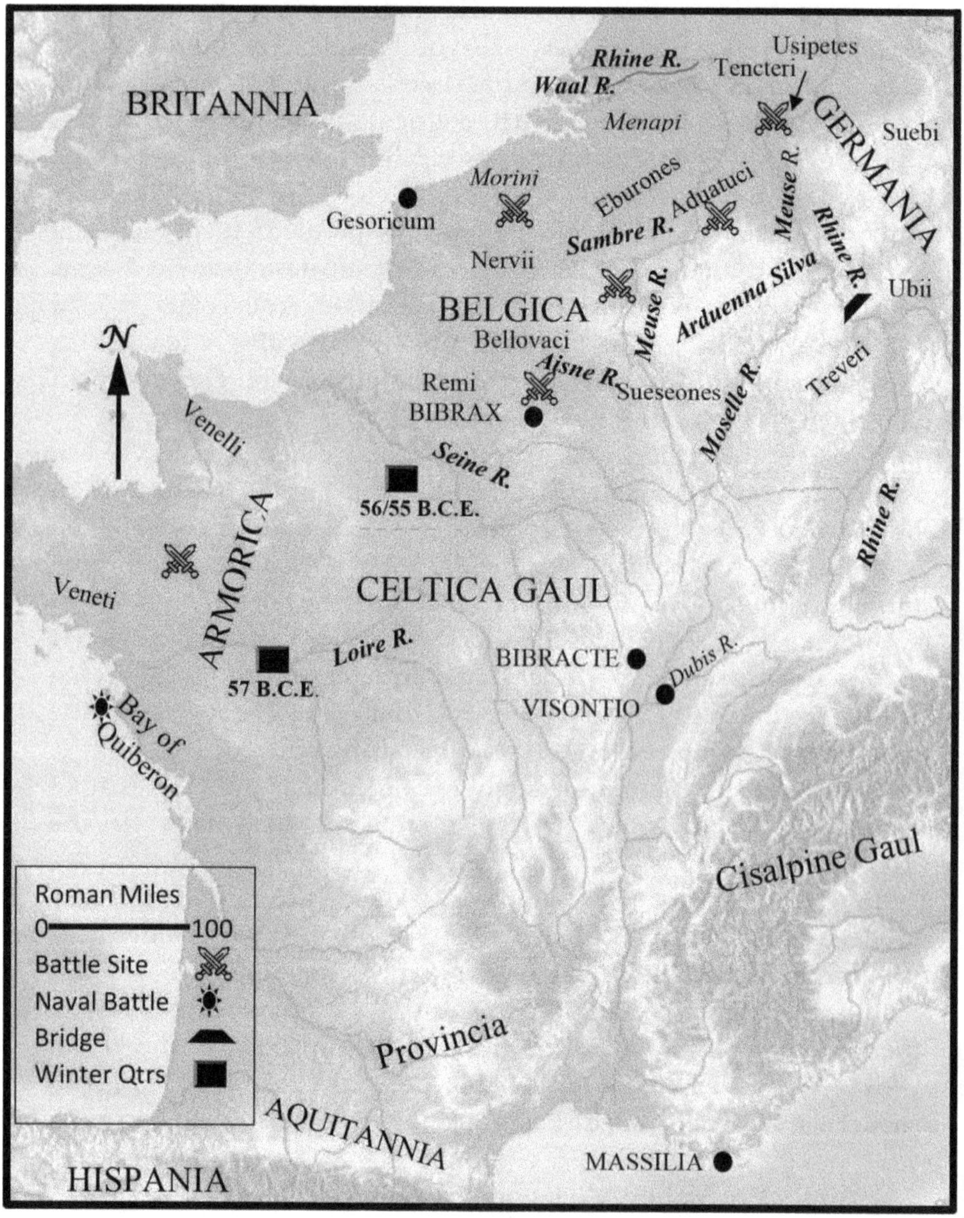

Main Characters

The Romans:

Marcellus Strabo, decurion, X Legion, *Equestris,* son of General Lucillus Strabo and an Aeduan noble woman
Brecius, *optio,* second century, first cohort, XI Legion *Claudia,*
Decimus Brutus, general and commander of Caesar's fleet
Gaius Marinus, centurion and commander, second century, first cohort, XI Legion, *Claudia*
Tulio, senior optio, XI Legion, *Claudia*
Rufus Valens, *primus pilus* (senior centurion), XI Legion, *Claudia*
Flavius Setarius, tribune and former *primus pilus,* X Legion, assigned to Caesar's staff
†**Julius Caesar**, former consul of Rome, governor of Provincia, Cisalpine Gaul and Illyricum
Quintus Servius, senior decurion, XI Legion, *Claudia*
†**Titus Labienus**, general, Caesar's Chief of Staff and commander X Legion, *Equestris*
Tarquin, senior decurion, X Legion, *Equestris*
Vinicius, legionnaire and Strabo's friend from Massilia
†**Publius Crassus,** cavalry general and son of Marcus Crassus, friend and benefactor of Caesar
Marcea Drusus, centurion, cousin of Publius Crassus
Ursinus, (Ur sin us) senior cavalryman, X legion, *Equestris*
†**Marcus Vitruvious Mammura**, *praefectus fabrum,* Caesar's prefect of engineers

The Aedui (I due):

Corius, childhood friend of Strabo, leader of the Aeduan scouts
†**Diviciacus** (Divi she ah coose), clan leader of the Aedui
†**Dumnorix** (Doom nor ic), younger brother of Diviciacus
Morgane, wife of Dumnorix
†**Liskus**, virgobret (chief magistrate) of the Aedui
Raven, sister of Corius
Talos, Aeduan scout

The Belgae Tribes:

†**Galba**, tribal leader of the Suessiones (Swee see onay), proclaimed king of the Belgic invasion into Gaul
†**Iccius** (Is see us), tribal chief of the Remi
†**Andecumborius** (Anday cum borius), senior elder of the Remi
†**Correous**, tribal leader of the Bellovaci (Bell o vah shee)
†**Boduognat** (Bo duen yaht), tribal leader of the Nervii and Belgae commander at the battle of the Sambre

†Historical character

DECURION

Prologue

58 B.C.E, early November, Bibracte Settlement, Central Gaul

Strabo approached the tribal leader's spacious dwelling and was surprised and pleased to see Corius coming out of the front entrance. He didn't expect to see his closest friend since their youth before returning to Visontio where the Roman legions were wintering. The Aeduan Tribe's chief scout looked both travel-worn and worried. Strabo knew Diviciacus had sent Corius north to assess the extent the Belgae Tribes were being threatened by the northern tribes along the border. His friend's expression alone suggested open conflict was no longer based only on rumor.

"Corius, I was afraid I wouldn't see you before I left. Is it as bad as we feared?"

"It may be worse. The Belgae Tribes are preparing for war, and it looks as if they're negotiating with some of the Germani Tribes across the Rhine River for warriors and forage. A few of the northern Aedui Tribes are considering support of the Belgae to drive the Romans out of Gaul. The tribes on both sides of the Aisne River have almost as much in common through marriage and custom than with their tribal clans. As we feared and warned, Caesar's decision to establish winter quarters in Gaul is the excuse the tribes on both sides of the border needed to form alliances and drive the Romans out of Gaul."

"Will the Aedui join or fight the Belgae?"

"That's for Diviciacus to determine and for you to be concerned about. What about you if the Aedui chooses to ally with the Belgae?"

"I'll never fight the Aedui. It's the one thing I'm certain of. I've been given the opportunity to leave the Roman Army of my own free will, and I'll choose to do so in the event I'm faced with the possibility. I'm committed to helping the Aedui if the tribe is threatened."

"As a Roman officer or a member of the tribe?"

The question was an echo of a recent conversation he had with Raven. He responded with a note of irritation in his voice. "You sound like Raven."

Corius hesitated before asking, "What did you tell her?"

"That I'm not ready to decide one way or other."

"I'm surprised. It wasn't that long ago you were ready to desert. You say you can leave without fear of punishment. What changed your mind?"

"Because I've been given a choice I didn't have before. It seems the more I'm being pushed to decide, the less inclined I am except for the one condition I mentioned. Why is it so important to you or anyone?"

Strabo saw his friend's jaw tighten. With a sigh of resignation, Corius said, "Marcellus, your question can only be answered by you when you understand and realize others will be affected by whatever you choose." Strabo started to say something. Corius cut him off.

"This is a matter for another time. I've been riding since yesterday, and I'm too tired and not in the mood to help you in a dilemma which one day you'll have to solve. I wish you safe journey back to Visontio."

Strabo watched Corius walk away and felt both offended and puzzled at the curt and unexpected rebuke. He would consider what Corius said some other time and instead focus on his father's imminent departure. Of particular concern was whether his father was capable of making the trip back to Massilia. He tried unsuccessfully to convince him to delay departure until he was physically more able to make the long trip. In the year since they were last together, he was shocked to see how his father had aged. During the last few years, Strabo had spent little time with him. The few instances they had been together were brief and more often than not unpleasant affairs occasioned primarily because of his own selfish behavior. In recent months, he'd begun to feel remorseful for past actions and words he deeply regretted. The distance between them had continued to widen since the death of his mother who had served as buffer and mediator while she was alive.

He wondered if it was too late to make amends. The decision he made a few hours ago to remain in the army might be a path to reconciliation for what little time his father had left.

Chapter 1
57 B.C.E. late March - Central Gaul

Ursinus stood on the high precipice and looked down at the camp of Visontio where Caesar's six legions were wintering. Three legions were quartered inside the walled settlement located within a near-circular loop formed by the Doubs River. The other three legions and the Auxilia were located east across the river.

His attention was focused on the almost four-mile outer bank of the river circling the settlement where the *fabri* were felling trees to widen the existing narrow road along the outer river bank. When completed it would be the track for two horseraces. The first race was for the nine cavalrymen representing each legion and the Auxilia. The second was for the decurions representing the same units and the final competition of the winter games General Labienus ordered. His reason was two-fold: provide a diversion in the slow days of winter and equally important, prepare for the forthcoming campaign season.

The pounding hooves caused Ursinus to turn and watch the three decurions coming toward him. The horses were being driven to their limit shown by their lathered sides and the roping saliva dripping from their muzzles. The riders looked no less strained from the rigorous course he designed to replicate the challenging race course below.

The taciturn cavalryman's lips twitched in a rare smile of approval as he observed the officers giving their best and demanding the same from their mounts. Strabo was clearly in the lead with Costa certain to come in second. Tarquin, the senior decurion of the Tenth Legion, was already too far behind to have a chance.

His smile faded as he observed the gait of Strabo's horse and his rapidly shrinking lead. Primus should have easily held or even increased the lead by now.

The three horsemen were close enough for Ursinus to hear the labored breathing of the horses. As Strabo's senior cavalryman within the *decuria,* Ursinus tried to remain neutral. He wasn't and privately favored Strabo. He always had a tenuous relationship with officers during his near twenty years of service which had much to do with why he remained a ranker, albeit a senior ranker. His experience and proven capability were the reasons the decurions he'd served under chose to look the other way for offenses any other ranker would have been flogged out of the legion.

Although young, Marcellus Strabo was showing signs he might be one of the few officers Ursinus could respect. He had genuine concern for his subordinates beyond viewing them as a means to advance his own career, and he never tried to exploit his father's fame to claim superiority and privilege. He had faults, but Marcellus Strabo had promise.

He was confident from the outset Strabo's mount, although no better than the other two horses, would prevail because of the rider's superior riding skills. He took a closer look at the way the horse was favoring the left foreleg and started to doubt Strabo would be first to cross the finish line. He held his breath as Strabo managed to cross a half-length ahead of Costa.

Strabo reined in and dismounted to examine the horse's foreleg. Ursinus joined him in the examination concentrating on the area above the fetlock. The swelling confirmed what he expected.

"It happened in the last sharp turn to the left," Strabo said. "It was my fault. I had a long lead, and I should not have taken the turn as fast as I did."

Ursinus scratched his jaw. "The tendon will heal. Unfortunately, not in time for the race. You need another horse, and Secundus," referring to Strabo's second mount, "won't do as well as Primus."

Grim-faced, Tarquin watched the two men and the limping horse coming toward him. Tarquin knew he had little chance to win today and probably no chance at all in the actual race. He expected Strabo to win and suspected Costa believed the same.

Tarquin looked at Costa, second in command. "It seems Marcellus is going to represent the Tenth Legion. I would have liked to claim the privilege. How could I? Both of you ride better than I do."

Costa laughed. "I agree with you. Having said that, I doubt I've ever seen anyone better than Marcellus. There is one problem. We've got to find another mount for him. Ursinus laid out the course today as close to what the competitors will face down there," thumbing over his shoulder at the activity below. "It's a tough course. A rider will need an exceptional horse to finish and a better one to win."

Strabo overheard the last. "I agree. There's not another horse in the turma that can outdo those we rode today."

Tarquin nodded. "You're right. Too bad there isn't another horse in the troop or the other decuriae in the legion any faster or tougher. I regret you persuaded me to give away Aquilo to your Aeduan friends, because it's a horse like him you need to win."

"As I recall, you once said, *the gray bastard could be the worst horse you've ever rode*. You were about ready to turn the stallion into horsemeat."

"Could be I was hasty. The truth is until you came along, I didn't think anyone could manage the beast including me."

"If you give me permission to go to Bibracte, I'm going to try and get him back."

"Are you sure the horse is there, or are you looking for a chance to seek comfort from a certain woman who lives there?"

"I'll have to see her — she's the one who has the stallion."

"All right, I'll grant you four days to get the horse back. It should be enough time to take care of personal business as well as getting the horse. There isn't much time left before the race."

Tarquin ordered the troop to mount then looked at Strabo with a smile. "It looks as if you have a long walk back on an easier trail. We'll leave you to enjoy it."

Strabo watched the troop begin its careful descent down the escarpment. The longer and less-demanding route to the river would require several hours to reach the barracks. He looked down at the four-mile race course being constructed around the near circular enclave of the winter quarters. The start line was across the north bridge with the race course following the river around the settlement and across the southern bridge to the finish line. Riders would be required to navigate uneven terrain and an occasional steep, precipitous river bank. Aquilo was capable of the challenge, and he was depending on Raven to loan him for a brief time. It was a race he wanted to win.

Strabo looked with misgivings at the overcast sky and the light rain soaking the countryside. Despite the early signs of spring indicated by the tendrils of grass shoots breaking through the melting snow, it was cold, and the ride to Bibracte was going to be miserable. He mounted Secundus and wrapped the woolen *sagum* around himself in a futile effort to remain dry and warm. It would be colder as he left the river behind for the windy and higher elevation above the escarpment.

Hours later and no less miserable, he kept his mind off the discomfort of the ride by thinking of Raven, Corius's sister. He had a close bond with Corius since childhood during his frequent visits with his mother at her Aeduan birthplace in Bibracte. Years ago, Corius's sister had changed her name from Elantia, which meant Doe, and chose the name Raven. She chose it to honor Morrigan, the shape-shifting goddess of fate and war symbolized by the black bird. The choice signified a conscious preference for spending her life in a male - dominated world rather than the traditional pursuits expected of her gender. On several occasions in the last year as a member of Corius's scout troop, Strabo was witness to how adept she was handling a bow and sword in a fight. She was equal to the best and far better than most of the other scouts.

The unconscious habits gained as a scout saved his life after he saw a flicker of movement in the trees. Instinctively he raised his shield in time to stop the arrow that imbedded with a thud, a sound he'd heard many times before. He reined Secundus to the right toward a shallow, stream-fed gulch. Before he reached it, another arrow missed him by a hands-breadth imbedding harmlessly in the muddy bank ahead.

He speculated his assailants might be Belgae based on the certainty the militant northern tribes were rumored to be preparing to cross into Aeduan lands. Previous indicators months ago of an incursion from the north was enough for Caesar to go there as soon as the winter weather abated. Strabo wondered if the Belgae offensive had started earlier than Caesar expected. It was disturbing to think the Belgae might be aided by Aeduan clans situated along the northern border. Corius recently confided some of the northern clans were sympathetic to the Belgae tribes. Intermarriage and commerce had softened tribal rivalry and encouraged mutual tolerance and the advantages it offered. Caesar's decision to winter the six legions in Gaul instead of withdrawing to Provincia as the Celtic tribes hoped had strengthened the possibility of formal alliances.

Strabo refocused his attention on the moment and considered his options. The gulch was curving southeast toward Bibracte in the direction where his attackers were coming from. The sound of horses splashing and laughter behind him confirmed whoever the assailants might be, they were confident of the outcome.

Mindful of the slippery stream bed and steep, muddy banks on either side, he resisted urging Secundus to a faster pace. He rode on looking for an opportunity to exit the gulch for open terrain and the chance to either confront or outpace his pursuers. He finally saw an opportunity. The left bank flattened out enough to risk the attempt. Halfway up, Secundus began slipping backward. Strabo swung out of the saddle. Without his weight, the horse would have a better chance of getting to the top. He realized while the horse had a better chance, he did not. In a desperate effort to keep from slipping back into the creek, he risked the animal's flailing rear legs and grabbed the horse's tail. As much on his knees as his feet, he held on until the horse finally reached the top of the bank and stood quivering, sides heaving from the exertion. Secundus was close to being blown and would require time to recover, time he didn't have.

The sounds of pursuit were growing louder, and to make matters worse, the tree-studded, narrow spine with dense underbrush above a crevasse was too steep for the horse to get down. Too late, he realized he would have been better off continuing down the gulch. The clatter of hooves on the rocky streambed below followed by excited voices indicated where they were as they neared the embankment. He had difficulty understanding what they were saying in a language that seemed a patois of Aeduan and what he assumed was a Belgae dialect. The gist was they were confident they were about to collect a head with disagreement who had the right to claim it.

He tethered Secundus to a small tree and shrugged out of his sagum. The sodden cloak would be a hindrance in the close fighting soon to take place. It wasn't until he let it fall to the ground that he saw the fletched arrow imbedded in the woolen folds. He picked up his shield and withdrew two of the four spears in the case strapped to the side of the saddle. The lighter spears were nothing like the heavier *pila* he had been trained to use as a legionnaire, but the concept of aiming and throwing them was the same. He counted on surprise and whatever accuracy he could muster would reduce the odds until he faced them using his *spatha,* the cavalry sword measuring a foot longer than a legionnaire's *gladius.* Today, on foot with the attackers coming up the bank, the longer, heavier sword would be an advantage, or so he hoped. Before losing his head, he intended one or more of them would see the gods first.

In a crouch, he made his way to a thick tree overlooking the gulch with bushes surrounding it. He knelt down. What he saw below was not encouraging. There were four riders dressed in metal-studded leather jerkins, colorful woolen trousers and calf-length boots not unlike what an Aeduan warrior would wear in Bibracte. The apparent leader wearing a cone-shaped helmet adorned with a horse-hair plume ordered the men to dismount. He gestured to one of the two warriors armed with bows. The warrior retrieved a bag of arrows from his saddle then using his bow to assist him, began climbing the steeper bank on the other side of the stream. With drawn swords and shields, the other three men started climbing up the bank toward him.

Strabo thought if the archer climbing the opposite bank gained the top, his chance of living long enough to engage the warriors would require timely intervention from whatever god or goddess he could summon. His mouth was so dry he couldn't summon the words to ask for help. His silent prayer would have to be sufficient to gain the attention of whatever celestial entity might be inclined to help him. He wished Raven was here. Her ability as an archer would have already taken care of the deadliest threat from the opposite bank. He saw a glimmer of hope. The archer was having difficulty climbing the steep bank. The three men directly below were doing better. The sure-footed youngest warrior who had left his bow behind was outdistancing the other two. The archer was almost halfway up the slope, and Strabo decided it was time to take the initiative.

Keeping low, Strabo moved closer to the point where the first warrior would reach the top. He quietly stood up and saw the archer was looking down instead of up. He launched the first spear. He missed. Fortunately, it was enough to cause the warrior to straighten up. Startled, he didn't bring his shield around fast enough. The second spear caught him in the right shoulder and knocked him backward into the nearest man. Both men slid to the bottom of the hill. Strabo's hope the man who wasn't wounded would remain below was dashed as he regained his feet and continued up the slope without his shield.

Strabo drew his sword and waited in a fighting stance for the warrior wearing the plumed, conical helmet and breathing hard from the exertion of the climb. He saw the hesitant look on the other man's face as he saw a confident adversary with the advantage of position.

With a savage cry, the warrior covered the last few feet to the top and managed to deflect Strabo's sword with his larger and heavier oval-shaped shield. Strabo wished he had the heavier and larger rectangular *scutum* he carried as a legionnaire instead of the small, round cavalry shield. The older warrior was equal in size and clearly confident shown by his broad smile. Strabo stepped back defensively feigning desperation, maneuvering in such a way to keep his opponent blocking the archer's aim on the other bank. He knew he didn't have much time to end this before the other man farther down the hill would reach the top.

The ploy worked. The warrior renewed a vigorous attack that forced Strabo back toward the trees near where Secundus was tethered and shielding him from arrows that posed the greater threat. He pretended to stumble and went down on one knee. Predictably his attacker saw his chance and with raised sword advanced to administer a killing blow to the head. Strabo stopped the hacking thrust with his shield and stabbed upward catching his opponent in the groin. The warrior fell screaming and writhing in agony. Strabo paused long enough to thrust the point of his sword into the man's throat before turning toward the remaining warrior. He saw movement across the draw and was surprised to see the archer tumbling down the bank with an arrow in his back. He had no time to think about it as he ran to meet the immediate threat.

Lungs heaving, the warrior gained the top and stopped a few feet from the edge. Strabo saw the warrior's eyes widen as he took in the dead man on the ground and Strabo running toward him. He started to turn as if intending to go back down the bank. Strabo reached him before he could and rammed his shield against the other man. Off balance and flailing in the attempt to keep from falling backward, he became vulnerable. With a sideways swing, Strabo decapitated him. Standing over the body, he watched the warrior's head roll down the embankment until it stopped a few feet from where Corius astride his horse was smiling and looking up at him.

Strabo felt his knees starting to shake and knelt down to keep his balance. "Better late than never," he managed to say in a voice that didn't quite match the bravado of his words.

"I think you seemed to be managing well enough as it was. Had I known you had the situation well in hand, I wouldn't have pushed so hard to get here. Come on down, and we'll see what the one still alive can tell us about who they are and why they came here. The one with the helmet, roll him down here so I can have a look at him."

Strabo stood up, sheathed his sword and hoping his shaky legs wouldn't betray him, approached the dead man. The effort of dragging the corpse to the edge and kicking him down the slope revived him. He walked over to Secundus, picked up his cloak and led the horse to the edge of the bank. He briefly considered mounting the horse. He decided he and the horse might be better off making their own way down. He gave Secundus a gentle slap on the croup and watched her stepping and sliding down with ease. He slipped and fell the last few feet. He regretted not staying on the horse.

Corius dismounted and walked over to help Strabo up. "Marcellus, how do you happen to be out here by yourself?"

"I was on my way to Bibracte to see Raven." He pointed at the broken arrow shaft in his shield. "I decided I better take a longer way to get there. Frankly, with all the patrols we've been sending out, I didn't expect to run into any surprises. I was careless. Who are they?"

Corius pointed to two of his scouts who were busy interrogating the warrior with the spear shaft still imbedded in his shoulder. Urged on by twisting the spear shaft, the wounded warrior appeared eager to talk to his interrogators. "We should know soon enough. I believe I have an idea why they're here and what they intended." Corius pointed to the dead warrior Strabo rolled down the hill. "I knew him but not well. His name is Cumboris. He's a minor clan chief of the Nervii, one of the Belgae tribes in northern Belgica."

The two men heard a desperate cry cut short and turned to see one of the Aeduan scouts wiping his bloody blade on the archer's woolen trousers. "It seems Tinnius thought the man had no more to say," Corius said.

Tinnius was brief and direct. "He confirmed what we suspected. Their party was one of several sent here to survey the Roman forts and assess the readiness of the Aedui tribes to fight the Romans led by King Galba of the Suessiones. Galba is forming a confederation of Belgae tribes and many of the Germani tribes across the Rhine."

"Did he name the southern tribe?" Corius asked.

"He's not certain, but he thinks it's the Remi."

Corius nodded. "That would be the most likely. The Remi are north of the Aedui tribal lands along the border with ties as close to the Belgae as the Aedui."

"How many warriors is King Galba expecting to lead?"

"He's heard as many as 300,000 will join the offensive particularly if the Germani tribes commit."

Strabo frowned. "Even though the number is inflated, Caesar will need considerable help from the Aeduan to confront such a threat." The silence and look on Corius's face were not reassuring. He turned to Tinnius. "Did he say when the campaign will begin?"

"As soon as the necessary forage has been gathered which he estimates will be in late spring. He said a high-level wealthy Aeduan has offered to help in providing additional forage."

Strabo and Corius exchanged looks, each knowing what the other was thinking. Corius waited until the scout left them to join the others stripping the four dead Nervii of gold arm rings and weapons. One of the scouts was wearing Cumboris's conical, horsehair-plumed helmet.

Corius continued. "Dumnorix has been up north for some time. I've no doubt your uncle is the Aeduan the prisoner was referring to."

"I'm afraid you're right, and if so, how much longer will Caesar be tolerant of his efforts to work against his brother? Diviciacus has proven to be constant in his support of an alliance mutually beneficial for both Rome and the Aedui."

"I'll inform Diviciacus as I assume you will do with those you must report to." Strabo nodded without comment. It was a matter for a level far above them.

Corius gave the order to mount up. The eight-man troop stopped what they were doing, collected the three Nervii horses that survived the skirmish and fell in behind their leader. Strabo guided Secundus up next to Corius wondering why the man who was close to being a brother had so far been distant. There should have been a welcoming embrace and the jocular banter typical of past reunions. He recalled the last time he saw Corius the morning he left Bibracte to return to Visontio. Corius excused his short-tempered comments with the excuse he was tired from spending days in the saddle. He thought there was something more behind it than fatigue.

Corius reined in at the entrance to the narrow gulch and looked at Marcellus. "Unless there's another reason to go to Bibracte than to see Raven, you may as well return to Visontio because Raven isn't there."

"What do you mean?"

"She left soon after you returned to Visontio and went north to a village called Bibrax in Belgica."

"Why did she go there? Is that where Talos is?"

"I don't know. However, we have relatives who live in Bibrax and that's where Leuca lives. She's Raven's favorite cousin, the sister she never had."

"I'm surprised she never mentioned leaving. How long will she be there?"

Corius hesitated wondering how best to respond, uncomfortable telling things Raven shared with him she should have told Marcellus.

"She didn't say. I think it may be a long time."

Strabo considered his last two days with Raven trying to recall anything he might have said or done that could have been the reason she left. What was most disturbing, she had given Corius no indication how long she would be away. He suspected Corius hadn't told him everything but resisted the impulse to question him further.

"You asked why I was going to Bibracte, and what I told you is true. There's another reason I wanted to see her. I was going to ask for the loan of Aquilo." He briefly summarized the winter games soon to be held at Visontio and the need to improve his odds of winning with Aquilo.

"Raven may not be in Bibracte, but Aquilo is. You can have him as long as you want."

Strabo was surprised she left the horse behind. His suspicion increased that there was more to her sudden departure than the reason Corius gave.

"Why didn't Raven take him with her?"

Corius embellished on what he'd said initially. "She may be reconsidering whether she wants to continue life as a scout and warrior. Time with Leuca could help her make up her mind."

"She never gave any sign she was dissatisfied with the way she lived much less any indication she'd leave it for a domestic life she scorned."

"I've never pretended to know the way women think, and that's particularly true with my sister. Let's go on to Bibracte and see how willing Aquilo is to go back to Roman ways. We'll meet with Diviciacus and tell him what we learned from the Belgic patrol. He will be interested in what you have to say and may have a message he wishes you to take back to Caesar."

For a time, they rode on in silence until Strabo realized there was a question he had neglected to ask. "You said Bibrax is in Belgica. Is it an Aedui settlement?"

Corius gave his friend a guarded look before saying reluctantly, "No, it's the main settlement of the Remi."

"That's one of the tribes the Belgae scout said was going to align with King Galba."

"True. I think it's likely they will not. The reality is the Remi are more closely aligned with the Aedui than any of the Belgae tribes. The Remi will do all they can to remain neutral."

"Is there a chance you can convince Raven to return to Bibracte?"

"Given what we've learned, I'll try."

The doubtful response did not convey assurance Corius would be successful. Strabo wondered whether he should reconsider his decision to remain in the army and go north with Corius to find her. By the time they reached Bibracte, he reluctantly decided he would depend on Corius to bring Raven back to a safer environment. He tempered guilt with a vow he would make sacrifices to keep her safe.

Chapter 2
Northern Gaul

Leuca noted her cousin's taut expression. "Raven, why are you here?"

"I couldn't bear to stay another day in Bibracte. I had nowhere else to go, no one else I could talk to."

"Even Corius?"

"Especially my brother."

"Was there no other woman you could confide in?"

"No, I'm looked upon by many as too different in ways they don't understand. There are occasions I'm not sure I do either. I tried once. I got married, and for a short time, I tried to be submissive and accept all the traditional things expected of a wife. It was a mistake and ended badly." Raven stopped aware she had implied what she didn't intend.

"Forgive me, Leuca, I didn't mean to judge your choice and other women who willingly choose marriage and consent to a domestic life I could not. I think I never will be able to choose the life you have."

"How many months since your last flow?"

Raven flushed and started to answer. Leuca interrupted her. "My guess is probably four months from the look of your rounding belly and an uncharacteristic emotional side of you I've never seen before. Trust me as the mother of two, I understand what you're experiencing for the first time. Who's the father, and does he know?"

"No, he doesn't, and neither does Corius although I think he suspects I'm with child. It's complicated."

"I doubt it. On the other hand, you were always the one ready to complicate your life with endless concern of who you are, what you wanted." Leuca rolled her eyes. "I'm sounding judgmental. Who is he?"

"You may remember him from many years ago when we were young. His name is Marcellus Strabo, the son of General Strabo, the former Roman governor of Provincia who was married to the sister of Diviciacus. As a boy, he came with his mother to Bibracte many times. I was attracted to him in a juvenile fantasy. After he came back to Gaul as a Roman soldier, I was attracted to him all over again in way a young girl could not be."

"It sounds as if your childhood dream came true."

"I thought so. The gods had taken a fanciful childhood dream and made it come true. I had feelings, urges I never had before and certainly never with the man I married several years ago. I wanted him to see me not as a younger sister, someone who he recalled long ago with a combination of tolerance and fondness. I tried to change that perception. I was shameless and pursued him. I think he began to see me in a different way, no longer a troublesome irritant. It was wonderful, a dream come true although not in the way I imagined."

"What happened to change it?"

"At first, he was the same only older. Gradually, I saw him beginning to look at me in a different way. He was conscripted against his will and planned to leave the army as soon as he could. Not long after, he changed from captive to a willing soldier. He soon became an officer both because of his ability and his father's reputation. The last time I saw him, he committed to remaining with the legions. It was then I decided to leave and come here."

"So, you thought his affection for you had waned in preference to being a Roman officer?"

"No, I was the one who changed. I accepted the Romans as long as they remained where they were, but I fear Caesar's legions are here in Gaul to stay. I accepted Marcellus because he is as much Aedui as Roman. I'm no longer certain I can if he becomes too much like a Roman."

"Are you certain that's the reason, or are you using it as a means to continue the life you've been living for so long?"

Raven hesitated before replying. "You may be right."

"Your concerns are much the same here. There's talk the Belgae tribes may challenge the Roman invasion. If so, the Remi may join them. Unlike his brother, Diviciacus, Dumnorix makes no secret he favors a friendlier relationship with the Belgae than the Romans. Dumnorix is here telling the Remi he's convinced Caesar has come to stay. We are much divided about where our loyalty lies. I fear there will be hard choices ahead, and life as we know it on both sides of the border will be difficult and dangerous. You would have been safer remaining in Bibracte."

"I'll take the risk. I need to be far away from Marcellus with time to think clearly about him," hesitating, she added, "and me. By the time the baby is born, or soon after, I hope I'll have answers to questions which help me determine the future for me and the child."

"When do you plan to tell Marcellus he's going to be a father?"

"Eventually I will, but not until I'm certain he won't take him or her away to raise as a Roman the way he was."

"I think you're being unfair and selfish. He has the right to know, and you owe him that."

The sharpness of Leuca's unexpected rebuke took Raven by surprise. Offended, she started to defend herself. She stopped. There was too much truth in the accusation.

Leuca saw the troubled look on Raven's face. "I'm sorry, I had no right to say that."

"No matter, you're my closest friend, and you can say whatever you want. You've given me something to think about in the coming months. It's late, and I don't want to dwell on it any longer."

King Galba's settlement north of the Aisne River

Wearing a crown, Galba considered Dumnorix's failure to address him as *King* unacceptable bordering on insolence. He would wait for a less public opportunity to put him in his place. He disliked Dumnorix as much as he liked his older brother Diviciacus who had recently reclaimed leadership of the Aedui tribe. Diviciacus may have reasserted his right as tribal leader, but in reality, he didn't have the financial and political ties his younger brother could claim. Dumnorix was the richest man in Gaul and could be instrumental in enlisting the help of the Remi. If the Remi refused to join the tribal confederation he was forming, the success of defeating the Romans was doubtful. He smiled and tried to look sincere and welcoming.

"Dumnorix, I'm pleased to see you. You've come far, and I'm most interested to hear what you have to say about the recent Helvetii and Suebi incursions. If my sources are correct, Caesar's legions defeated them decisively."

"Regrettably, whatever the worst you've heard is more likely to be the truth than not. Gaul has become ripe fruit, and Caesar is already picking it."

Looking thoughtful, Galba said, "You may be right. Caesar wants a triumph in Gaul to further his personal and political ambition to become first man in Rome. My sources in Rome report his ambition is to be like his uncle, Marius, who diminished the authority of the Senate by becoming a dictator. Has Diviciacus accepted the certain possibility he plans to make Gaul another Roman province?"

Dumnorix paused before answering. He had underestimated Galba by assuming he was a rustic, too far away to fully grasp the implications of Caesar's defeat of the Helvetii and Germani tribes.

"Possibly not. As for me, there's no question Caesar's objective is precisely what you've said. I've heard he's formed two more legions for a probable spring offensive. If so, it emphasizes the danger we may one day become a *togate* province like Transalpine."

"Your brother has always maintained a cordial relationship with Rome as a trusted, reliable ally. He believes diplomacy and trade will be the means for Gaul to remain independent of Roman dominance. I don't trust the Romans. What can you do to help stop them?"

"I've already accomplished a lot. I'm close to convincing the Remi to join you at the time you cross the Aisne to attack the Romans."

"I can say the same following my recent negotiations with the Remi."

"King Galba, I have leverage you don't." Use of the title king softened Galba's opinion of Dumnorix. "Although my brother recently reclaimed leadership of the Aedui, I have commercial and political power resulting from trade contracts with all the northern Aeduan clans including the Remi. My enterprises are becoming more persuasive than my brother's assurance to trust the Romans and their hollow pledge to protect us from the Germani."

"For the sake of discussion, I'll accept you have substantial influence with the Remi, but how will this leverage you claim benefit the confederation if we decide to fight the Romans?"

Dumnorix couldn't resist a scornful smile. "It's common knowledge it's no longer *if* the Belgae Tribes will enter Gaul but *when*. You delay for two reasons. You're waiting for assurance some of the Germani tribes will commit to joining you, and you don't have the food and forage you require. I have contracts in place to provide sufficient logistical support you'll need to be successful. Your chance of success is about to be challenged with two additional legions certain to join the six legions already in Gaul."

Galba remained composed following the Aeduan's last and startling comment. He knew Caesar was formidable enough with six legions. Eight legions could deter the Remi and some of the Germani tribes he was counting on from joining the confederation. He had to accelerate his preparations and prepare to launch the offensive sooner than originally planned. He needed Dumnorix's help without the Aeduan realizing how desperate he was to get it.

Galba gave Dumnorix a piercing look, leaned forward and said with an edge to his voice, "Dumnorix, before you think you're dealing with some primitive northern tribesman, I'm aware of how you helped the Helvetii and the Germani tribes under Ariovistus. You were going to profit regardless of which side you were on."

"I don't understand your insinuation. I didn't care which side prevailed. On the contrary, I was able to reduce the supplies to the

Romans to the extent they were put on half rations then quarter rations. My actions nearly caused the legions to mutiny. I did what I could to ensure a Roman defeat. Regrettably, I overestimated the tenacity of first Divico then Ariovistus who with superior numbers and my support were unable to defeat Caesar. Make no mistake, I've been outspoken in saying I will never accept the Roman boot on my neck. I would, if circumstances dictated, accept Belgae or even Germani dominance in preference to Roman occupation."

"We can reach an understanding, but do not try and take advantage of me. I expect you to profit from our arrangement." Galba pointed his finger and added, "If it's not reasonable, I'm not a forgiving man."

Dumnorix had difficulty concealing his satisfaction as he waited for the king to tell him what he wanted. As far as profit was concerned, it would be taken after Galba helped him become King of the Aedui.

Chapter 3
Visontio

Near the end of the second watch, Strabo rode up to the north gate of the fort where the Tenth Legion was quartered. The fort was quiet with the exception of the guards pacing the length of the walls. After a cursory stop, he was waved on and made his way to the stables where he dismounted painfully, grateful the long ride from Bibracte was done. To reduce the near two-day ride, he alternated riding Aquilo and Secundus without stopping except to water and rest the horses. It was imperative General Labienus be informed of the imminent Belgae attack. He was cold, his body ached and all he could think of was crawling under a blanket to get some sleep.

His report could wait a little longer and so could his comfort until he saw to the care of the two horses that had borne the hardship of the journey. He led Aquilo and Secundus over to the end of the tether line where Primus was tied. After securing the two tired horses, he knelt down to feel Primus's leg. The swelling had diminished although it would be a long time to full recovery. He felt guilty he was the major cause of the injury.

He was so concentrated on attending to the animals that he didn't realize Tarquin was standing behind him until the senior decurion spoke.

"Well, I see you managed to bring back the gray bastard earlier by a day than I expected." He looked at the travel-worn horses and added with a note of mild rebuke, "You rode them hard."

"I had a reason." Strabo summarized what had happened on the way to Bibracte. His terse report focused on the information gleaned from the Nervii warrior and the imminent Belgae offensive. Tarquin glanced at Strabo's shield hanging on the tack frame. The broken stub of an arrow imbedded near the boss indicated there was more to the fight with the Nervii than Strabo described.

"Marcellus, the gods must have something in mind for you, else why do they continue to favor you? General Labienus needs to hear this. Come with me, and we'll see if he'll receive you. General Publius Crassus is with him. Crassus and the Auxilia are about to be sent to Armorica to stop what may be a revolt in the making."

After Tarquin told the guard in front of the *principia* why they wanted to see the general, the guard ducked inside and reappeared with Tribune Setarius. Strabo had come to consider the scar-faced tribune with a black eye patch covering his left eye almost a surrogate father over the months since his conscription in the Roman army. The initial adversarial relationship between the two had developed into mutual respect neither one could have imagined months earlier. He gave a cryptic summary of what he had to report.

With an uplifted brow, Setarius said, "Your arrival is timely. It seems you may once again have something to say about what is happening in Gaul."

The tribune led the two decurions through the small vestibule to the spacious room inside where the two generals were seated. Strabo noted General Labienus's lined and tired face. It was a reflection of his unsparing and tireless dedication to fulfilling the heavy responsibilities Caesar assigned him. The square-jawed general was the commander of the Tenth Legion, and in the absence of Caesar, the senior commander of the other five legions and the Auxilia.

"General Labienus, Decurion Strabo has come from Bibracte with information that has a bearing on what we've been discussing particularly with regard to the decision to send General Crassus and the Auxilia to Armorica."

The general looked at Strabo with interest. "Decurion, you have my attention."

Strabo altered the circumstances and sequence of actions to avoid why he was alone on his way to the settlement.

"I was with an Aeduan scout patrol near Bibracte that encountered four Nervii tribesmen. There was an engagement. After it was over, one of the wounded tribesmen left alive told us why they were this far south. In preparation for a planned spring offensive, their patrol was one of several from Belgica sent to assess the capability of the legions. He claimed many of the Belgae tribes as well as Germani tribes across the Rhine have pledged their support under the leadership of Galba, tribal chief of the Suessiones. Galba has been crowned king by the tribes in recognition of his capability and willingness to fight the legions."

General Labienus asked, "Did the prisoner say how many warriors are in Galba's confederation and when he intends to come into Gaul?"

"He estimated around 300,000. He said there was a southern tribe that may join the confederation which, if it does, will add considerably to Galba's strength. The chief Aeduan scout thinks it is most likely the Remi Tribe he was referring to. The Nervii scout believed with or without the Remi, Galba will cross the border in about six weeks."

The general leaned back and looked at Crassus. "If the Remi decide to turn away from its close ties with the Aedui, we'll be significantly outnumbered. Caesar is bringing two more legions and replacements for the losses we suffered in the campaigns last year. He and the legions aren't expected to arrive until late spring. If Galba attacks before then, assuming the Aeduan tribes remain loyal to Rome with six understrength legions, the challenge will be greater than it was with the Helvetii. We were lucky then. If Ariovistus had joined the Helvetii instead of waiting until they were defeated, we would likely be wintering in Cisalpine or Provincia instead of here. We are going to confront a potentially greater threat than last year."

At the risk of incriminating his younger uncle, Strabo felt he had to add something else the Nervii scout reported. "The Nervii scout said a high-level Aeduan has been negotiating with Galba offering support of food and forage. Dumnorix could be the Aeduan he's referring to."

Labienus rolled his eyes. "I might have known. I wonder how much longer Caesar will tolerate the son of a bitch to retain your older uncle's support. Decurion, I'm aware Dumnorix is your uncle; however, unlike Caesar who's been forbearing, I would not have been." The general scowled and said with a note of resigned acceptance, "Caesar's right. The Aedui alliance is important. We're forced to overlook the bastard's treachery. He deserved more than forgiveness for helping the Helvetii."

Publius Crassus looked at General Labienus. "Caesar said I was going to Armorica to deal with reports the Veneti along with other tribes in the region may be planning an insurrection. Perhaps the trouble there is of less concern than what is happening on the northern border. If so, my immediate deployment with a legion and the Auxilia there to Armorica should be reconsidered."

"I agree. I'm going to delay your move west at least until Caesar gets here with the two additional legions due in May. I'll inform Caesar of my decision to delay your deployment. In the meantime, I want you to prepare your cavalry and the Auxilia for an immediate move to a position somewhere between Bibracte and the Belgica border. Once there, maintain close surveillance up to and along the border. Equally important, your presence in that vicinity allows a closer vigilance of the northern Aeduan tribes to discourage any possibility Galba will gain additional alliances. I want you to meet Diviciacus and tell him we suspect his brother may be colluding with Galba. If true, it's troubling and bordering on treachery."

In spite of Dumnorix being his uncle, Strabo disliked him for the same reason General Labienus did. Considering Dumnorix's past actions and possible involvement with Galba, the general was right to take steps to minimize the chance the Aedui would support the Belgae.

General Labienus stood up. "Thank you for the information you brought us. The hour is late, and there will be time enough tomorrow to consider what else needs to be done. It appears another battle is certain. The critical question left is when and where it will take place."

Outside the headquarters, General Crassus beckoned to Strabo. "I hear you're going to represent the Tenth Legion in the officers' race in the winter games."

"Yes, I plan to. Are you going to participate?"

"Unfortunately, I cannot. My role apart from organizing the games is to preside over the results. I've delayed the cavalry races four days. The two cavalry troops that arrived today for assignment to the Eleventh and Twelfth legions need to rest before competing."

"I'm disappointed. I was looking forward to giving you another chance to see if you could do better than the last time we raced."

Strabo recalled the day as a young boy he raced the young general and his cousin at the estate of Marcus Licinius Crassus near Rome. He won decisively. Marcus Crassus was then as now the richest man in Rome and Caesar's benefactor committed to whatever Caesar required to subjugate Gaul. In recent months, despite a considerable difference in rank, Strabo and Crassus had become friends based on a mutual passion for riding fast horses.

Crassus laughed. "I look forward to another time and place to see if I've improved."

Centurion Gaius Marinus, commander of the second century, first cohort, Eleventh Legion, *Claudia* stood a few steps behind General Sulpicius Gallius, the recently appointed legion commander. They and several other officers of the legion were waiting to review the three hundred cavalrymen assigned to the legion. He was indifferent to whether the long-awaited cavalry contingent ever arrived. He didn't think the missing cavalry troop had made any difference in how the legion had performed in defeating the Helvetii and the Germani.

With somewhat more interest, Marinus watched the first thirty-man troop approaching bearing the standard *Legio* XI-I indicating the first cohort of the Eleventh Legion. This would be the troop that would be placed under the cohort when it was detached for independent operations.

Rufus Valens, *primus pilus,* senior centurion of the *Claudia,* standing next to Marinus said in a low voice, "Gaius, the senior decurion of the first troop is Quintus Servius. He's going to represent the legion in the forthcoming cavalry races. He has a reputation for being a good rider and strong competitor. I doubt neither of the two other decurions in his turma were willing to challenge his right to represent the legion."

As the first troop passed by, Marinus took a closer at the decurion riding ahead of the two other decurions. There was something about the saturnine-faced, whipcord lean decurion that seemed familiar as did the name. The decurion had ridden past before it finally came to him. He last saw him nearly fifteen years ago.

Servius then was a ranker who was about to face a flogging tantamount to a death sentence. The offense was striking an officer. The optio was long past his prime and known for being abusive for no other purpose than exercising his authority. Being abusive was common and expected of optios and centurions. Ordering a young recruit to perform an obscene act was not within the range of abuses tolerated. Servius refused. Marinus had been the officer of the watch the night it happened and found the optio on the ground whimpering pleading for his life. He knew the optio's reputation, and the recruit's version of what happened was believable based on previous allegations. The problem of an assault on a junior officer was easily resolved in the legionnaire's favor when two witnesses spoke in defense of Servius. The optio was relieved and promptly discharged the next day. Servius thanked him, effusively grateful for his intervention and quick resolution after expecting a completely different outcome. Marinus disregarded the legionary's pledge that one day he would have an opportunity of showing his appreciation. He brushed aside the legionnaire's words thinking he had only done what was right. Now circumstances were different, and he had other thoughts about the passing comment years ago.

Two days ago, he had token interest in the forthcoming cavalry races until he learned Marcellus Strabo was going to represent the Tenth Legion for the officer race. His reaction provoked a fleeting wish the decurion would suffer some misfortune during the long and difficult race. Unexpectedly, he saw an opportunity to accomplish what Tertious failed to do the previous year. Anything could happen during the race. Quintus Servius might have a chance to show his appreciation beyond words.

Marinus left the ceremony in good humor. The uncharacteristic smile on the centurion's face was noticeable for those used to his customary sour expression.

Chapter 4

Carrying their saddles, Strabo and Ursinus went out into the large compound where a rail fence separated the horses of the Tenth and Eleventh Legions. Both men were going to ride east of the settlement to exercise Aquilo before the decurion race the next day. The reticent cavalryman rarely spoke except when responding to a question or if someone was not performing as they should. He made little distinction whether the individual in question was a ranker or an officer. Strabo was surprised Ursinus was the first to speak and at length.

"I rode the length of the track yesterday with representatives from the other legions, the Auxilia and the fabri. I wanted to identify any hazards that could be either reduced or eliminated in the time left before the races are run. While the track looked difficult from the escarpment above, it's much worse on the ground and more dangerous than I expected or should be. The fabri have done well to reduce the worst of the route; however, I pointed out several places that needed work to reduce risk to horse and rider. This is particularly so where the track narrows and the banks are steep to the river fifteen to twenty feet below. It won't be the swiftest horse that will determine the winner. It will be the rider who knows to slow down and accept the risk of momentarily losing the lead.

"There is one place approximately a mile from the southern bridge where the bank is particularly steep caused by a high hill. The hill will slow the horses. A game trail on the left leading down to the riverbank is close to the bottom of the hill. The river curves away from the bank leaving a dry area flat and wide for about three hundred paces before it rejoins the riverbank. If you use the trail, it will give you an advantage of a level course instead of a steep climb up and a dangerous descent on the other side. If you aren't already in the lead by then, there's a good chance when you reach the course, you will be."

"I would have preferred if General Crassus had allowed the contestants to ride the course to see firsthand what you described. Thank you for being my eyes. I assume the other representatives have done the same with the other contestants. I'll do my best to win, but I won't risk Aquilo the way I did with Primus."

Ursinus nodded in agreement. "The risk may be less going down the game trail than the hill, both up and down."

The two men saw Aquilo as usual separated from the other horses. The stallion's irritable and dominant nature kept the other horses distant. Strabo finished placing a halter on the stallion's muzzle when a voice behind complimented the horse.

"He's a handsome beast and looks prepared to take the lead in an attack and perhaps before the rider is ready."

Strabo and Ursinus turned to see who it was and saw a tall, lean, leathery-faced decurion striding toward Aquilo. The horse snorted, pulled on the halter then with bared teeth lunged toward the decurion as he came within reach.

"He's a prickly bastard."

"I've known friendlier horses, but we get along." Strabo replied.

"What's his name?"

"Aquilo, and like the north wind for which he's named, he can be unpredictable with a mind of his own. On occasion, we've had differences of opinion who was in control of the reins. So far, spirited as he is, I've managed to get him to do what I wanted when the situation required."

"I know what you mean. There have been times the horse knew what was happening faster than I did; otherwise I wouldn't be here. My name is Servius, senior decurion of the Eleventh Legion." Ignoring Ursinus, the decurion glanced at Strabo. "Who are you?"

Strabo started to greet the older man in a friendly manner then did not after perceiving the centurion's attention was focused entirely on Aquilo. He settled for an impersonal introduction.

"Strabo, junior decurion of the Tenth Legion."

"Are you any relationship to General Lucillus Strabo?"

"He's my father."

"You're fortunate to have a famous cognomen. You have advantage and opportunity whether you choose to remain in the army or pursue other alternatives."

Strabo found the note of condescension in the decurion's comment offensive. He'd been prepared to be cordial or at least neutral with the decurion. Now he wasn't sure that was going to happen.

Servius saw the frown on Strabo's face. "I meant no offense. Fortuna offers opportunity then it's up to the individual to go on from there."

Mollified, Strabo replied, "And she has a way of offering opportunity by a path not easy to walk. I spoke with General Crassus the other day. He said the horse races and other games were delayed to allow the Eleventh and Twelfth Legions to participate."

"We've had a long journey; nevertheless, the time he's given is enough to be ready. Will you be competing tomorrow?"

"I have the honor of representing the Tenth Legion."

"Then it seems we'll be competitors, and if this is the horse you're going to ride, I may have a challenge. Have you raced before?"

"Yes, many times in Massilia."

"Were you successful?"

"Usually. I planned on breeding and raising horses for both racing and for those who could afford a horse and able to stay on it."

With a curious expression, Servius asked, "It sounds as if the army was not your choice. If not, I'm surprised considering who your father is."

Nettled at the decurion's prying and tone of voice, Strabo concealed his irritation and decided it was time to end the conversation without going into why he came to be in the army. "Who knows when and why the gods will put you on another road to travel."

Servius understood the noncommittal response meant he was not going to learn anything else. "Well, I wish you good luck tomorrow. Take care, Strabo. You may find racing in the army is not gentle and friendly as you've been accustomed to."

Strabo watched Servius reach the east gate of the Eleventh Legion before asking Ursinus, "Do you know anything about him?"

"Aye, I served with him many years ago. He was a cavalryman assigned to the fourth cohort of the Tenth. He knew who you are. It was the horse he was interested in."

"How would he know who I am? He hasn't been here long enough to know anyone except the officers in the *Claudia* legion."

Ursinus huffed. "Decurion, the names of the officers who will race tomorrow are well-known by those who will be placing bets. Servius will make a point to learn something about the other five riders. He has a reputation for winning races. He also depends on more than a fast horse. Tonight, it would be better to bring Aquilo inside the fort to be sure the horse will be able to race tomorrow."

Before turning in, Strabo went to the stable area to check on Aquilo and the other two horses. A familiar voice called his name. It was Vinicius, his closest friend and riding companion from Massilia. Before his promotion to decurion, he and the legionnaire were assigned to the same eight-man contubernium in the second century, second cohort of the Eleventh Legion. Strabo's efforts to encourage Vinicius to request a transfer to the Tenth as a cavalryman failed because of Centurion Marinus's refusal. Both men suspected it was out of spite based on the centurion's intense dislike of General Lucillus Strabo.

"Marcellus, I was talking with some of the cavalrymen in the turma assigned to the *Claudia* Legion's first cohort. I wanted to see about the chance of transferring to the turma."

"It's good to see you, I haven't given up getting you transferred to the Tenth."

"And I appreciate it; however, I may have a better chance of getting on a horse sooner with the Eleventh Legion." The legionnaire, waved his hand impatiently. "I haven't much time. I'm due for guard duty in the second watch. The reason I came to see you is I heard your name mentioned several times. Centurion Marinus has offered a purse of 20 denarii in addition to the prize Publius Crassus has given if Servius comes in ahead of you and double if you aren't able to complete the race."

Strabo wasn't surprised about the centurion's offer. From the time he was conscripted, it was apparent Marinus resented the Strabo name for reasons he suspected was because of his father. Marinus coerced Tertious, another legionnaire in the legion, to harm Strabo in some way. The legionnaire's subsequent failures to injure him led the furious centurion to order Tertious to kill him. He learned of the centurion's efforts from Tertious before he killed himself rather than live with the serious injury that maimed him in the final campaign of the year.

"The bets already placed favor Servius by a wide margin in the decurion race, at least within the Eleventh. Evidently, he seems to have earned a record not just for winning but how he wins. He cheats. No other decurion who knows him will challenge him; consequently, he's the legion's champion by default. His horse will be among the largest, and he uses it to push aside smaller horses. If the size of his horse isn't enough, he has a barbed riding crop he uses to *persuade* a faster horse to get out of the way."

"What you've told me confirms the impression I formed, and what Ursinus said about him." Strabo briefly summarized his meeting with Servius earlier that morning. "I have Aquilo inside the fort instead of the outer corral as a precaution in case he might try something tonight. Thanks to you and Ursinus, I'll be ready for whatever Servius tries to do tomorrow. He may find I'm not the novice racer he thinks I am."

Chapter 5

Halfway between the two bridges crossing the north and south banks of the river, the seven decurions guided their mounts to the rope stretched across the ground marking the starting and finish line. The horses were skittish as if eager to see the formalities ended and the race started. Aquilo was no exception. Strabo stroked the horse's neck while holding the reins tight to keep the animal from getting too close to the riders on either side of him. He had drawn the seventh position on the right. The coveted positions were the lower numbers on the far left that put the riders closest to the river bank and less distance to get to the finish line – that is if they could maintain the position. In the center and two positions to his left, Servius was mounted on a hammer head bay whose size and muscular build was a match for Aquilo.

Strabo looked ahead at the narrow bridge three hundred paces ahead and only wide enough to allow three horses riding abreast. The first test would be which two or three riders would cross first and gain a slight advantage in the long race. The outcome was the potential for a collision in the narrow space that could end the race for any rider who took the risk and lost.

Strabo concluded there was an advantage in not trying to clear the crowded bridge first and instead depend on a cautious, long-distance approach to win. The cornicine blast signaled the start, and it was apparent Servius decided the same as both men made a conscious effort of holding their mounts in check. Their caution was verified when one rider ahead was edged out and forced into the river to keep from hitting the bridge rail and ending any chance of recovering the lost time. Servius and Strabo were the last two riders to cross the bridge.

The two men cleared the bridge riding abreast. The older decurion looked at Strabo and smiled. "It looks you have done some racing."

Gesturing toward the dripping rider crawling up the river bank, he said, "Now there's only five I have to beat. I'll soon see if you're good enough to finish. I wish you good luck because I think your odds of even finishing, much less winning, are not good. Let's see what you and your nag have that might make this race more interesting."

Both men kneed their mounts into a full gallop and remained neck and neck while slowly drawing closer to the five other riders. The course was the open space where the track narrowed abruptly, and the river started curving west. Strabo reined in slightly, content to remain in the back until an opportunity came to move up. Servius did the opposite and urged his horse on faster turning to the far right where the bank was steeper and less cleared.

Risking both himself and his horse where stumps and bushes presented obstacles on the track, Servius started gaining on the rider on his left. Out of the corner of his eye, Strabo saw the horse Servius was passing swerve out of control. The rider avoided a collision by reining in to calm the panicked horse. With no chance of doing better than coming in a distant last place, the rider turned his horse around. Strabo glanced back and saw the rider had dismounted and was examining the horse's croup. He thought of what Vinicius had told him about the decurion's reputation for how he won races and knew Servius was responsible for what happened. Already Servius exploited his advantage of an uphill position on the descent to gain speed. He swerved farther left still angling toward the riverbank. Despite condemning the decurion's unprincipled way of racing, Strabo admired the decurion's daring and expert horsemanship.

A mile later and a little less than half the race left, Strabo knew it was time to move up. Servius remained in front of him with three horses ahead and evenly strung out. Each rider had settled into an even pace waiting for the last quarter mile where the outcome would be determined by what each horse had left. He started to nudge Aquilo into a faster pace. It wasn't necessary. The stallion had already decided it was time. They passed the rider and were about to pass the rider behind Servius to go up the steep hill ahead when he recalled the game trail down to the river. He slowed Aquilo and moved behind the rider he was about to pass to get closer to the river bank. He almost missed the trail and had to rein in to keep from turning too fast. The bank proved to be as Ursinus described, hardpan and shale interspersed with clay.

He let Aquilo go full-out, took the low jump up off the riverbank and back onto the track without slowing down. Strabo looked to his right as Servius, 30 paces behind, reached the bottom of the hill and lashed his horse to a full gallop. Aquilo easily maintained the gap. In spite of the cool weather, the horse was beginning to sweat, and Strabo felt specks of foam and saliva on his legs. He deliberately forced the stallion to slow down in order to have enough left for the extra push in the final quarter mile fast approaching.

Above the sound of the pounding hooves, Strabo heard the labored breathing of Servius's horse slowly moving up along his right side. The decurion pulled abreast and slowed to match the speed of Strabo's horse.

Servius looked at Strabo long enough to shout, "Very clever, Strabo, but we have a long way to go. I'll still beat you!"

"I doubt it! Your horse is laboring to get you across the bridge much less to the finish line."

"I'll wager ten denarii you lose. Do you accept?"

"I do and gladly."

"Careful, Strabo, you may find a surprise or two that will prove you wrong. I'll have General Crassus's reward for winning, too."

Strabo looked behind to see the remaining three riders were strung out and if anything, farther back than before. Aquilo snorted and turned abruptly to the left nearly unseating him. He regained control and turned the horse back to the center of the track. Servius was already several lengths ahead and looking back with a broad smile while lashing his mount's flank with his riding crop. Ahead Strabo saw the quarter mile flag and unwilling to risk blowing his horse, resisted urging Aquilo to catch up. He glanced down at Aquilo's croup and saw the small, bleeding wound. He blamed himself for what he should have anticipated from Servius. Winning was not enough to pay the decurion back for what he did to Aquilo.

He passed the quarter mile flag nudging Aquilo into a faster gait. The horse slowly closed the distance. Soon he was two lengths behind and still gaining. Servius looked over his shoulder and saw the gray stallion a length behind. He started lashing his horse across the right croup. With the track curving to the left, the bridge was now in sight. Abruptly there was a roar as the thousands of legionnaires saw the approaching riders.

Strabo drew abreast of Servius on the right and attempted to maintain enough distance to prevent the decurion from using his sharpened crop. Servius swerved with the intention of shouldering Aquilo to break the stallion's gait. Instead of trying to avoid a collision, Strabo reined Aquilo into the other horse. The moment the horses came into contact, Strabo felt as if his face had been stung by a bee swarm. Instinctively, he grabbed the thongs of the decurion's riding crop and held on to them as he guided Aquilo to the right nearly pulling Servius out of the saddle. Servius let go of the crop and managed to stay precariously seated. His recovery wasn't fast enough to keep Aquilo from increasing the lead.

Strabo looked back and saw Servius steadily falling behind. The bloody froth coming from his horse's nose and mouth told him why. When he crossed the finish line, the rider wearing the cloth marked with the Seventh Legion crossed soon after followed by the decurion from the Auxilia. The horse Servius was riding collapsed well short of the rope. Oblivious to the roaring approval of the crowd and holding the crop, Strabo led Aquilo toward Servius.

"You owe me ten denarii, you son of a bitch!" he said between clenched teeth before lashing Servius twice across the face with the decurion's crop. "That's what you did to your horse." Strabo shoved the pointed end of the crop into the decurion's stomach. "And that's for what you did to the first horse you eliminated, and this," as he stabbed him again, "is for what you did to me."

Strabo felt arms grab him from behind at the same time he became aware of the growing silence. The legionnaires standing nearby watched with a combination of bewilderment and delight to see an officer treat another officer the way a couple of rankers might with too much to drink. Strabo was aware his public behavior was about to be questioned no matter the justification. The angry frown on General Crassus's face indicated he could be facing a judgment possibly more severe than what awaited Servius.

"Decurion, a rank you may not have much longer, what is the reason for this disgraceful behavior?"

"I regret letting my anger decide what would have been better settled in private. I cannot excuse my competitor's conduct during the race. He endangered the life of the decurion from the Ninth Legion early in the race and my own close to the finish line."

General Crassus noted the marks on Strabo's face. "Are you implying he lashed you?"

"No, sir. I'm accusing him, and this is the reason." Strabo held up the fringed crop and pulled aside the thongs to reveal the inch-long metal point, "If you examine my horse's croup and that of the competitor from the Ninth Legion, you'll find what this crop was designed for."

General Crassus looked at Servius. "Is that your crop?"

"Yes, sir, but he's the one who did that to his horse. I admit, I accidentally hit him across the face after he came too close to me while I was using it on my horse. He grabbed it out of my hand and nearly pulled me from the saddle. What he did cost me the race, and for that reason, he should not be declared the winner."

"You are certainly not the winner. Your horse never finished the race."

Strabo saw the rider from the Ninth Legion dismounted standing nearby with his horse then pointed to the wound on Aquilo's croup.

"General Crassus, if you ask the rider representing the Ninth, I'm certain he will show you a wound on his horse similar to the one on mine."

General Crassus gave Servius a pointed look. "If I examine the horse, will I find what Decurion Strabo claims?"

"If there is, I didn't do it." The worried expression on the decurion's face weakened the firm denial.

The general beckoned to the rider for the Ninth Legion. When the rider came forward, the general asked, "Decurion, what caused you to leave the race?"

Pointing to the riding crop in Strabo's hand then to the wound on his horse, "That was the reason. Decurion Servius did that, and it came close to costing me more than losing a race."

"I find the explanation of these two credible and your version the opposite. I'll turn the matter along with your riding crop over to General Metellus for him to consider what should be done with you. I will recommend your reduction to junior decurion for lying and for unacceptable conduct. It will be up to General Metellus to decide for a greater or lesser punishment. As for you, Decurion Strabo, General Labienus will consider the same for you. Your public display here hardly reflects the qualities expected of an officer even an inexperienced junior officer. In addition, I'll consider who is most deserving of the winner's prize, you or the decurion who finished second. You will be informed of my decision. Both of you are dismissed."

The general was barely out of earshot before Servius said through tight lips, "You privileged bastard, if it's the last thing I ever do, I'll give you reason to regret what you did. You'll beg me to send you to the gods."

"You will see them before I do, and I doubt they will be kind to you. I don't believe Centurion Marinus is going to be happy for what you failed to accomplish. In the meantime, I'll be very careful to avoid your *surprises* or what Centurion Marinus will try next."

The decurion's open-mouthed astonishment was enough to confirm Vinicius's suspicions why Marinus met privately with Servius.

As he walked away, he saw Tarquin and Ursinus coming toward him. Tarquin looked grim. In contrast, Ursinus was grinning from ear to ear. Tarquin was the first to speak.

"You are ordered by Tribune Flavius Setarius to report to him without delay. General Labienus witnessed what happened here, and he's not pleased; consequently, the tribune is unhappy. What in the name of Jupiter were you thinking of? You made a public spectacle about something that should have been resolved without six legions watching two officers acting like rankers."

Far from feeling chastened, Strabo wasn't sorry for what he had done, "Sir, before tomorrow dawn breaks, I may well be a ranker again or no longer answering to the drums, horns and demands of the Roman Army. If I had it to do over again, I would."

"Well, that may be true, and that's an explanation best saved for Tribune Setarius. I'm to take you to him without delay. Is Aquilo up to getting you to the fort without ending up a carcass like the one Servius killed?"

"He's got more and then some left. Better to get this over with sooner than later."

After Tarquin walked away out of earshot, Ursinus couldn't restrain himself any longer.

"Decurion, there will be many besides me who are hailing you for what you did and why you did it. That's particularly true with the cavalrymen newly arrived assigned to the Eleventh *Claudia* who know him well."

Strabo was grateful for the reassurance among the rank and file. He was aware of how his behavior of the moment had presented General Crassus and General Labienus with a problem. He was going to be punished, and he knew he deserved some accountability for his actions. The Strabo name made the adjudication that much more problematic, at least for them. Whatever Setarius had to say could be a deciding factor for how much longer he would be with the legions. How he would leave depended on the General's decision.

Strabo expected a stern, angry tirade when he reported to Setarius; instead, the tribune appeared only mildly irritated and even somewhat sympathetic to what he had done. He was told to sit which seemed surprising for the tongue lashing he expected he was about to get.

"The generals have left it to me to decide what to do with you. I saw what happened, and I was angry. It was an embarrassing spectacle no matter how much the decurion deserved it. However, I've come to the conclusion I'm at least partially to blame for you having been conscripted. Possibly Caesar deserves some blame as well for advancing you in rank without the seasoning necessary to mind your temper and moderate your actions. What you did should have been done in private."

The tribune paused, and his lips twitched in a brief smile. "Then I see by the marks on your face, I might have done worse to him than you did. I left Crassus and Labienus feeling they had similar thoughts. Well, there must be some reckoning, and this is what it will be. Both you and Servius are ordered not to race again as long as you're both serving the legions. In addition, you and your decuria are detached and assigned to General Crassus. The assignment will get you away from here and let memories fade, and the general has need of your language skills. You will leave tomorrow for Bibracte to see your uncle so he can prepare for the General's arrival and propose a suitable site north of Bibracte for the Auxilia to locate."

"What will happen to Servius?"

"General Metellus has accepted General Labienus's suggestion of reducing him to junior decurion with loss of pay commensurate to that rank. It's harsh punishment, and that's another reason to keep the two of you apart lest you both compound the trouble you've already created. He, too, has been ordered not to race."

"He bet ten denarii he would cross the bridge first. Under the circumstances, I won't attempt to collect what he owes."

"I think that might be best," the tribune said dryly while picking up a small leather bag he tossed to Strabo. "That's your reward for crossing the line first. I strongly suggest in the time left until you leave, avoid any contact with him."

Strabo left in complete agreement with the tribune. As for the winner's purse, he thought Tarquin and the entire decuria, especially Ursinus, deserved the largest share. He would include Vinicius for his warning concerning Servius. He considered what Vinicius said about the possibility Centurion Marinus may have had something to do with the decurion's actions in the race. If that was the case, Marinus had replaced Tertious with Servius. He would have to be careful.

Centurion Gaius Marinus eyed the dejected decurion and curbed his anger. Servius's failure to fulfill his expectations for the outcome of the horse race was frustrating. He silently cursed Strabo and his apparent support of the gods. He was tempted to give up on any further attempts to get revenge on the son for what his father had done to him. The repeated failure of Tertious and now Servius made him think the gods sided with Marcellus Strabo, and if he persisted, he would likely fail again. He was tempted to abandon the quest but couldn't. Servius was still his best prospect for getting revenge. At first, Marinus would have been satisfied with discrediting Strabo and shaming the family name. Now he wanted him dead.

"Had you been focused on doing what I wanted instead of winning a stupid horse race, I at least would be content with the outcome. I'm disappointed I didn't get the return on the twenty denarii I expected and you practically guaranteed." The decurion started to bristle.

"I don't want to hear excuses. I'll accept you tried. You failed. Next time I expect a better outcome."

"General Metellus has forbidden me to race again."

"Idiot, I'm not talking about a horse race and another opportunity to see you outclassed again. No, the objective has changed. I want him dead, and I don't care how you do it."

His face showing wide-eyed shock, Servius sat back, hands upraised in protest. "Centurion, that's going farther than we agreed. It's one thing for an accident to happen. Murder is another thing, and a risk I won't take."

Marinus calmly picked up a leather pouch and tossed it to the decurion. "I'm aware of the increased risk, and I'm giving you twenty denarii to mitigate it. You'll have another twenty when you get it done."

Servius hefted the pouch and smiled.

Chapter 6
Northern Gaul, early April

Leuca frowned and said with a hint of reproof in her voice, "Raven, why don't you get on the back of a horse. It might improve your disposition. Besides, it won't be too long before you'll be too big to ride."

Raven started to rebut her cousin's criticism. She had neither been good company nor very helpful to Leuca for the past several days. Contrite, she quickly apologized.

"You're right, I've been irritable, and I'm sorry. I've done little to repay you the past several days for putting up with me. It's that for the first time in my life, I don't feel I have any purpose except watching my belly getting bigger."

"I don't think you're being completely honest. Marcellus is on your mind. I believe you're beginning to understand you haven't been fair to him."

Raven started to deny the observation but knew she was right and nodded in assent. "It's true because I'm afraid. If I tell him, he may claim a father's right to take the child especially if it's a boy. I suspect the right is no different under Roman law as it is with the Aedui."

"I believe you're being unnecessarily concerned. You have no idea how he feels. For all you know, he may refuse to believe it's his child in which case you have no cause to worry."

The matter-of-fact comment was like a shock of cold water. The thought never occurred to her. Then she thought of the last time she saw Talos when he came to her house and found her alone with Marcellus. Talos had come to an obvious conclusion and left in the heat of anger. Marcellus may have come to a similar conclusion about her and Talos.

Stricken with a combination of guilt and anguish, she blurted out, "I never considered such a possibility. How could I have been so blind? I have to go back to Bibracte and tell him he's the father."

Ever practical, Leuca said, "Don't be hasty. It's a long way back there, and in your condition, not good for the baby. There's another reason you shouldn't. If he sees your swollen belly and you looking contrite, he may decide your sudden appearance is less about contrition and more about trying to convince him he's the father. If you're worried about him taking the baby away from you, don't ever tell him or see him again."

Raven heard the last, and as dour as Leuca's prediction was, it was a moment of truth. She needed to think about the consequences.

"You're right. I have some thinking to do, and there's no better place than on a horse."

Mindful of her condition, Raven kept the horse at a sedate canter while letting her mind clear of the worries and anxieties that had made her a prisoner for much too long. She was thankful for Leuca's frank counsel. The feel of the horse's easy gait beneath her was relaxing. Lost in her own thoughts, she was startled to see a rider cresting the hill ahead and shadowed by the morning sun. Too late, she suddenly questioned the wisdom of riding alone and unarmed except for a dagger. She considered going back to the settlement until her brother's voice called her name. She was curious why Corius had come this far north.

She stopped and waited for him to come down the hill. He reined in beside her and saw her rounded belly. His welcoming smile disappeared, replaced with a frown.

"You've saved me from having to go all the way to Bibrax to see you."

"What's happened for you to come so far?" She saw his uncertain expression, and she immediately thought it was about Marcellus. Momentarily she was speechless, afraid to ask the reason he had come so far.

“I wanted to see how you were doing. I was worried about you.”

“Why, because I’m with child?”

“Well, yes, that’s part of it...”

“Is Marcellus all right?”

Taken aback at her alarm, he responded, “Of course, at least, he was when I saw him a few days ago.”

He saw her visibly relax, and it confirmed Raven’s feelings for Marcellus were deeper than he thought. He didn’t think Marcellus felt the same for her in equal measure.

“He’s part of the reason I’ve come here. He’s worried about you.” He summarized the circumstances of how he encountered Marcellus several weeks ago and what they learned from the surviving warrior.

“It’s certain the Belgae will come into Gaul to challenge the Roman occupation. The entire border area is unsafe. All tribes along the Aisne River are vulnerable to what will happen regardless of which side they support. Marcellus asked me to persuade you to return to Bibracte.” She gave a sigh of relief pleased Marcellus was worried about her. “The unit the Romans call the Auxilia recently constructed a fort not far from here from which patrols are keeping watch along the border. Marcellus and his decuria are part of the cavalry contingent conducting the patrols. He has Aquilo.”

“I’m glad he does. It’s not good for the horse to be left in a corral getting fat. Did he win the race?”

“He did; however, there was some trouble with one of the other contestants who during the race stabbed Aquilo with a pointed crop and lashed Marcellus across the face. Marcellus apparently did the same to the other man. Because of that, he was punished by assigning him to the Auxilia.”

“I don’t understand why he should be punished at all. I’d be surprised and disappointed if he hadn’t done something to the other man. I would have only a lot worse.”

He shrugged. “Roman ways are different. They look upon us and think the same. Since Marcellus returned, I’ve come to understand what we didn't know long ago." He pointed at her belly and asked, "Are you going to tell him?"

"The next time I see him. Leuca thinks I should have told him when I first knew I was pregnant."

"She's right, and I wonder why you didn't."

"I was conflicted even before I learned of my condition. As much as I care for Marcellus, he's become more Roman than I can accept. I dislike the Romans as much as the tribes who would claim Gaul. I see him dressed like a Roman, and I wish he had never come back into my life. I worry after the baby is born, he'll take the child to Provincia and raise him or her as Roman."

"You sound like Dumnorix."

"I suppose I do."

"Diviciacus sent me to tell him he must return to Bibracte and explain why he's been meeting with King Galba. He's concerned his brother is providing support or at least preparing to support the king in opposition to the best interests of the Aedui and the Remi."

"There are many here who share the same views of Dumnorix including Talos."

"Talos is in Bibrax?"

"Yes, but I seldom see him. He spends much of his time away and makes no attempt to see me."

"Does he know you're pregnant?"

"I suspect he does, and that may be the reason he avoids me."

"Did you ever consider marrying him?"

"No. He's only a good friend, or he was. He may not think so anymore. I don't plan on marrying again including Marcellus. I tried it and lost my freedom. As soon as I'm able, I'll return to a life I prefer over a domestic existence I tried once and couldn't endure."

Corius's expression was a mix of surprise and concern. "What about the baby?"

"I talked to Leuca, and I think she's willing to care for it when I'm away. She knows a wet nurse that's available."

He was both disgusted and angry with her self-centered, selfish view ignoring the welfare of the unborn child or Marcellus.

"I don't understand you, Raven. You tell me you're afraid Marcellus will take the child and raise it as a Roman, yet you're ready to give it over to someone else. I'm disappointed in you. I'll sacrifice to Epona you'll come to your senses. Until you do, there's no place for you with the scouts."

Without another word, he rode away at a gallop to Bibrax. He left her hurt and angry at his unsympathetic reaction. She calmed, and her anger moderated after acknowledging his harsh comments were true.

Dumnorix signaled his steward to allow Corius entry. The chief of scout's appearance was not a surprise. He knew why Corius was here and was surprised Diviciacus hadn't summoned him sooner. It didn't matter. He'd accomplished what he intended, and the arrangements were made. He was ready to leave this desolate place and enjoy the generous comforts of Bibracte. Morgane would be disappointed by his return. She would be happier if he never came back. His beautiful wife had become tedious with her cold indifference displayed on the first day of their marriage. She accommodated his physical demands by ensuring there was a submissive slave available. His once promising alliance with the Helvetii by marrying her disappeared with the Roman victory in the battle of Bibracte.

"Lord Dumnorix, I bring greetings from your brother. He requests you return to Bibracte. He's eager to hear your assessment of developments along the border and with the Remi in particular. If the reports are true, there's reason to believe the Belgae are planning to come across the border into Gaul. He wants your opinion how best to prepare for it."

"There's always been trouble along the border, and there always will. You may tell him I see nothing unusual from what has always been the case, an occasional raid to steal horses and livestock. I expect no more than that. As for the Remi, they remain peaceful and friendly with both the Belgae and Aedui as they always have."

"I'm afraid that isn't what the Romans believe or what I've seen and heard about Belgae intentions. We passed near King Galba's main settlement of the Suessiones, and it appeared from the activity in the surrounding settlements attention is less on planting than preparing for war. The Roman Auxilia has constructed a fort thirty miles southeast of the Belgica border near the settlement of the Suessiones. The Romans are actively patrolling along the border."

Dumnorix struggled to maintain his composure wondering how it was he'd heard nothing about the Roman fort.

"The fort supports their fear the Romans are the ones who will cross the border. If so, the burden will be on the border tribes to defeat them; consequently, the Belgae have been preparing extensively for an imminent invasion. Reassure my brother he has nothing to worry about. I'll let him know in good time if it's the Belgae who plan to be the invaders."

Corius cleared his throat. "Lord, I used the word *request.* Your brother made it very clear he is not asking you. He expects me to escort you to Bibracte without delay.

"I see. I am to be treated as a prisoner."

"Not at all. I assure you I am your escort. You will be accorded all respect in accordance with your clan seniority."

"Very well, how can I possibly refuse my brother's invitation or disappoint Morgane by remaining here any longer. Is tomorrow soon enough to start back?"

"Then tomorrow it will be."

"Are you staying the night here in the settlement?"

"No, I have a troop of scouts camped a mile south. Given the tension on the border, I thought it best not to take any risks."

Dumnorix relaxed. By the time the sun rose tomorrow, he would be well toward the safety of the Atrebates north of Bibrax. "I'll join you at first light for an early start. In the meantime, I have some farewells to make."

Garos, second in command of the scouts, looked up expectantly as Corius rode into camp.

"I suspect Dumnorix has no intention of going back to Bibracte. He'll leave the settlement sometime tonight and go to the Suessiones or one of the other northern tribes. In case I'm wrong, you'll remain here with ten men to welcome him. I'll take the rest of the troop and circle a few miles north of Bibrax to intercept him. I could be wrong, but after talking to him, I've no doubt Diviciacus is right. His brother is helping the Belgae, and possibly to a greater degree than he was with the Helvetii. Diviciacus turned a blind eye to what he did to aid the Helvetii. Maybe he's decided enough is enough. It's time Dumnorix accepts he's no longer tribal leader, and the Aedui are allies of the Romans. If he doesn't, his brother won't be as forgiving."

Garos frowned. "There are some in the troop who are not supportive of an alliance with the Romans. The Helvetii and the Suebi are gone, and they wish the Romans would leave as well."

Corius was reminded of the testy exchange with Raven and silently conceded the point. Despite his close friendship with Marcellus, he was sympathetic to what she said about the Romans although not to the degree she and others were.

"I understand, and I, too, have such concerns. There could come a day when we'll have to fight the Romans should they change from protector to dictator. At present, we'll concentrate on what our tribal leader expects us to do."

A few hours later under a moon-lit sky, Corius led the rest of the troop north in a wide sweeping turn around the Bibrax settlement and stopped a mile away in a shallow ravine. Although the ravine concealed the horses, it allowed visibility across the comparative level ground toward the settlement. They did not have to wait long. Corius heard the muffled hoof beats before he saw the rider coming toward them. He quietly gave the order to mount up.

Corius led the troop out of the ravine and signaled for them to fan out. The rider saw them and reined in from a canter to a trot then a walk and stopped in front of Corius positioned in the center and slightly forward of the others.

With bemused resignation, Dumnorix said, “It seems I’ll be going to Bibracte after all.” He turned the horse around as the scouts fell in behind him. He felt a clutch of fear he may have underestimated his brother. Morgane would be the first to tell him so.

Chapter 7
South of the Belgica Border

It was Ursinus who saw the thin spiral of smoke in the trees a mile north and alerted Strabo. The smoke rapidly grew in size billowing dark and dense in the cloudless sky.

Strabo frowned. "There's something about this I don't like. I'm familiar with this area and place very well. There's no water here, and that's the reason there's never been a settlement. The closest one is farther north where some of the Boii settled last year," referring to the tribe that supported the Helvetii the previous year. Diviciacus granted clemency to them after they petitioned to remain in Aedui lands. "We'll continue east then circle around the trees and approach from the north."

By the time they were halfway past the trees, they heard faint screams and through a narrow gap in the tree line glimpsed horsemen and running figures. Strabo ignored the commotion and urged a faster pace. Behind him, there were muttered comments questioning his decision.

Ursinus riding on his left said in a low voice, "Decurion, are you certain this is the right thing to do?"

"Of course not, and if I'm wrong, I'll have to live with the consequences."

A quarter mile ahead, Strabo swung north where the trees had thinned out enough to maintain the fast pace. They were too far away to hear anything of what was happening behind them. He turned in the saddle and noticed the once dense smoke had already begun to dissipate strengthening his conviction caution was merited. It would have taken longer for thatched homes to burn down.

Soon after, he turned west and before long slowed the pace to a walk as the decuria began to ascend a low hill. Before reaching the crest, he reined in and spread his arms to signal the two sections to align on either side of him and remain in position. He handed his reins to Ursinus and dismounted. He moved up the hill at a crouch until the last few feet then crawled the rest of the way to the crest. Down the slope his suspicions were confirmed.

In the swale below, there was a score of dismounted warriors either standing individually by their horses or grouped together in idle conversation. Some sprawled on the ground looked as if they were napping. Farther down-slope men and women were huddled together under the watchful eye of several mounted warriors. A dismounted warrior was lashing a man held by two warriors.

As he moved back down, Strabo considered the wisdom of simply doing what scouts were supposed to do. Find the enemy, avoid unnecessary contact and report back what they found. They were considerably outnumbered and significantly more than he wanted to take on. Then the image of the settlers below intruded and decided the issue.

In a low voice, he described what he had seen to Ursinus and the two section leaders. “They outnumber us so we’ll have to surprise them. A downhill attack will give us an advantage. Walk your mounts to the crest then mount and attack on my signal.”

The decuria had already topped the crest and were partway down before the warriors below realized they were under attack. There wasn’t time enough for those on the ground to mount or to draw their swords as the disciplined decuria swept through their milling ranks with precision. Startled at the sudden din, many of the horses bolted down hill leaving their riders scattered and vulnerable. They were among the first to die. Those able to mount were too spread out and demoralized to counter the surprise attack. A few who were mounted fled galloping to the safety of the northern border. For those remaining to fight, it was carnage with spear and sword relentlessly cutting down the remaining warriors.

Strabo passed by the melee and headed for the dismounted warrior lashing the man on the ground. The bare-chested warrior turned and saw a man on a gray stallion bearing down on him with spear couched and pointed at him. He ran toward his horse. Strabo's short cavalry spear entered his back before he reached it. Strabo let loose of the spear and drew his spatha. While one of the two other warriors lashed his horse to escape them, the other stopped to engage. He wasn't quick enough to avoid the large stallion that crashed into his smaller horse with enough momentum to throw the rider out of the saddle. The unnatural angle of the man's neck was enough for Strabo to credit Aquilo for the kill.

Strabo looked back where the decuria was still engaged with the few warriors who remained to fight. He galloped up the slope and found Ursinus facing two opponents; he caught one of them across the back of the neck nearly decapitating him. He rode on leaving Ursinus to deal with the other. He sensed movement to his left and instinctively raised his shield in time to stop the sword wielded by a mounted warrior. Intending to deliver a chopping blow, the tattooed warrior left his torso exposed, an easy target for a quick and fatal thrust. Strabo looked around and saw there were no more warriors left in the swale except the dead or wounded pleading for mercy. A few survivors, some barely able to remain in the saddle because of wounds, were strung out heading north in complete disorder. He saw one of the wounded men start to fall out of the saddle but the timely assistance of another rider saved him. He looked closely at the rider helping the wounded man and thought there was something familiar about him. The way he rode with his left shoulder slightly lower reminded him of Talos. The distance was too great to be sure.

The action had been bloody, brief and surprisingly successful. Strabo credited the experience in the skirmishes and brief encounters over the past several weeks, although less daunting, had improved his willingness and the decuria's capability to fight even when the odds did not favor. He had Ursinus to thank as much as his intuitive ability to assess whether an aggressive response or withdrawal was called for. He was satisfied the harsh, occasionally punishing training he and Ursinus had put the decuria through had been worthwhile.

Strabo saw one of his men about to finish off a warrior with a minor wound and intervened to stay his hand. "I want to talk to him. In return for his life, he may be willing to tell what's happening across the border."

The cavalryman gave him a doubtful look and reluctantly sheathed his sword.

His attention was drawn to Ursinus kneeling next to one of the scouts sitting on the ground. Strabo guided Aquilo over to the two men and recognized the sitting man was Cletus.

Ursinus stood up and came toward him. In a low voice, he said, "Decurion, Cletus has a mortal wound. It would be good if you said something to him before he enters the next world."

Elation over the brief battle evaporated replaced by a sadness and the wish Ursinus had never seen the smoke and they were on their way back to the fort after an uneventful patrol. The youngest cavalryman was a favorite, ever jocular and willing to accept without complaint the onerous chores the older men were happy to escape.

Ursinus led him to where the wounded cavalryman was sitting, hands clutching his belly to keep his entrails from spilling out.

Strabo crouched down and grasped the cavalryman's shoulder, "Cletus, the gods will be pleased to take you. We're sad to see you go."

Through gritted teeth Cletus groaned. "Decurion, I think I would have been more pleased had they not summoned me so soon. Since they have, I would see them sooner than later to end this..." The cavalryman coughed and expelled a rush of blood with his last breath. Strabo knew the gods heard him.

"We'll take him back to the fort for a proper ceremony. Is anyone else hurt?"

"A few minor cuts, nothing serious. We lost a good man." Strabo gestured to the dozen wounded or lifeless warriors strewn about. "Whoever the bastards are, they paid dearly for it."

Strabo saw a gray-bearded man limping up the hill toward him with a younger woman walking beside him. The man stopped a few paces away, and Strabo realized he was much younger than he appeared at a distance. He was the one on the ground being beaten by the warrior he speared. The side of his head was bloody, and he cradled his broken left arm.

The bearded man looked over to where Ursinus was standing next to the dead scout. He then turned to Strabo and said something in a language he didn't understand. By his expression, Strabo assumed he was thanking them for coming to their aid. The woman then spoke in halting, barely understandable Aeduan and confirmed his supposition.

"His name is Tasco. He's my father and our village leader. He says he's sorry for the loss of one of your warriors. If you had not come, we would have suffered more than we already have."

"What is your name and what tribe do you belong to? Strabo asked.

"My name is Uinda, and we are Boii. We were allies of Divico. When you Romans defeated him, we asked the Aedui for permission to remain here rather than return with the Helvetti to their lands in the north." She paused, turned to Tasco and apparently told him what she said.

"How did you and the others come to this place?"

"We were taken early yesterday from our settlement near the border and brought here by warriors from the Bellovaci Tribe. The warrior you killed with your spear was their leader. He told us we were going to help him kill Romans, and if we did what we were told, we would not be harmed. Your men didn't come as expected, and my father was blamed and beaten because we weren't convincing enough."

"Ask your father if he knows anything about the Belgae plans to come south."

Tasco nodded and after a lengthy commentary, she said, "Many of the tribes across the border have pledged support to the Suessiones led by King Galba after he attacks the Romans. The attack was planned to begin soon. It's been delayed until the spring planting is complete. We learned the Germani tribes remain undecided whether to join King Galba. They, too, as we did, suffered losses when the Romans defeated King Ariovistus. The Boii were asked to join the assault, but our tribal leader refused. He told their emissary we had already suffered too many losses, and the Romans were too strong to defeat. We would not help either side. We wish only to live in peace."

"That is a wish unlikely to come true. No tribe can survive without alliances. My uncle is Diviciacus, and he granted the Boii a chance to settle in these lands. He would expect if the Aedui are threatened, your people will provide support. I will tell Diviciacus who may wish to talk of such things. Tell your father he may have the horses of the dead Suessiones to help you return to your settlement. He should take their weapons in case the Boii are unable to remain neutral."

Strabo walked away and beckoned to several scouts then pointed to the half dozen horses peacefully cropping nearby. "Round up as many as you can and turn them over to the Boii tribesmen." One of them was the scout he had told not to kill the warrior wounded early in the fight. "Where's the warrior you wounded?"

The scout shrugged and with a bland expression replied, "Sir, I couldn't stop the bleeding."

Strabo started to say something, thought of Cletus and merely nodded.

Except for the sound of creaking leather, the jingle of harness rings and the soft thud of the horses' hooves, there was no conversation. It was a silent departure. The feeling of exhilaration a short time ago for the success of the fight was moderated by the price paid and the sadness of losing a comrade. There was also guilty relief each of them had it was Cletus whose lifeless body was tied on a horse.

Riding to the left of Strabo, Ursinus was the first say anything. "Sir, you did well back there, and they," thumbing to the scouts behind, "say the same. You saw something we didn't and led us into a battle most, including me, would have refused to take on." The cavalryman cleared his throat "Your father would be proud."

Astonished at the surprising accolade from the taciturn cavalryman, Strabo responded, "I confess I had my doubts and wonder if it was worth the life of Cletus."

"It's a question for the gods to answer and not either of us. You are new to command. You will not always be as successful as you were today, but then who can ever be so? It isn't the gods who tell us what we should do in the moment. I think they leave that to mortals. Today you made a decision, and it was the correct one. Yes, we lost Cletus. Be satisfied it could have been much worse."

Strabo was speechless and merely looked at the cavalryman in astonishment for his eloquent, insightful comments. Most significant was Ursinus had addressed him as *Sir.*

Chapter 8

It was late afternoon when they reached the Auxilia fort. The guards at the gate looked inquisitively at the body draped over the horse. One guard started to say something then changed his mind after seeing the set, expressionless faces of the cavalrymen. Strabo quietly told Ursinus to take the decuria on to the stables. He turned Aquilo toward the principia to report the results of the day's events to Centurion Drusus, second in command of the Auxilia. Before he arrived, he saw the centurion and General Crassus come out of the entrance and walk to their horses. The two senior officers stopped and watched the body-draped horse being led to the stables.

Strabo dismounted and saluted. "Earlier today, my decuria engaged a score of warriors from the Catalaunni Tribe approximately 14 miles northeast of here. I lost one man and several others suffered minor injuries. The Catalaunni had nine confirmed dead; eleven were able to leave the field and rode north to the border."

The two officers looked at him with incredulous expressions. General Crassus was the first to speak. "And one man is all you lost?"

"Fortunately, yes. We had the advantage of surprise and a downhill attack on a dismounted, unprepared enemy."

"Why did you risk an attack against such odds?" Drusus asked with a frown. "Scouts should avoid needless risk."

"I agree, and I didn't plan on attacking until I saw what was happening to some villagers who turned out to be captured Boii."

By the time Strabo finished explaining what happened and what he learned from the Boii village chief, Drusus was somewhat mollified although skeptical. "I think you were fortunate it turned out as well as it did. I believe you acted impulsively without regard to what could have been a disaster."

Strabo controlled the slow burn at the patronizing comment from a superior who had yet to face an adversary or to confront a situation requiring a decision with little time to consider the consequences. It was at that moment he understood the difference of those who led from behind. Crassus sensed the tension and intervened.

"Had I been faced with a similar situation, I like to think I might have done as you did, and for that I commend what you and your decuria accomplished today. Your arrival is timely. I leave tomorrow for Bibracte to meet with Diviciacus to discuss what's happening along the border. What you learned today is one more reason I need to talk to him. You and your decuria will be my escort. We leave at dawn, and I expect by then you and your cavalrymen will be rested."

"We'll be ready, General."

Crassus nodded and reentered the principia.

Drusus cleared his throat. "I think my criticism was ill-founded as the general implied. Accept the apology of someone who is trying to understand what we face here in Gaul and how best to deal with it. I think you have a better insight than I do into what must be done."

"Centurion, your criticism was not unjustified. I've had concerns about the decision I made that cost the life of one of my men. I am new at this as are you. We may both have occasion in the days ahead to doubt the orders we give particularly when the outcome may not be what we expected."

Chastened by the pragmatic response, Drusus replied with an understanding smile. "Well said, and I will remember the wisdom of your words. Coincidentally, you have a replacement for the man you lost today. He arrived yesterday, and you'll find him in the stables."

His somber misgivings turned to pleased surprise to see a grinning Vinicius at the stables standing next to Ursinus.

"Marcellus!" his friend shouted, "I..." whatever else Vinicius was about say was stilled from the sharp jab Ursinus gave him.

"He is called Decurion. Decurion Strabo or Sir is how you will address him. The next time you address an officer in public keep that in mind, or you'll be mucking out the stables for the entire decuria. Understood?" With difficulty, Strabo suppressed a smile at the shocked expression on his friend's face.

"Yes, sir!"

"I'm not a Sir. The decurion is a Sir, you stupid shit. Didn't you learn anything when you were a legionnaire? I have a name, *Ursinus*, call me anything else, and I'll kick your ass until your eyes pop." Ursinus turned to Strabo with a wink and said, "This reject from the legions says he can ride, and he knows you. I'll be waiting in the stables as soon as you've finished with him. He's going to prove to me he can get on a horse and stay there without falling off. As for his potential, you have my sympathy."

Strabo and Vinicius watched the cavalryman, ramrod straight, stalk off toward the stables.

"One of these days, I'm going—"

"Until then, you're going to listen carefully to anything he tells you to do. The day may come sooner than you want and then you'll thank the gods you did. There's no better cavalryman in the legions or Gaul." Strabo chuckled and added, "Vinicius, with just the two of us, you can call me Marcellus. Otherwise, it will be as Ursinus promised. How did you manage a transfer from the *Claudia*?"

"Two days after I last saw you, Marinus inspected the century. He got to me and found about everything in my dress and kit unsatisfactory. He ordered Optio Tulio to give me ten lashes and ten days latrine detail for being sloppy and looking insubordinate. The bastard gave out almost no other punishment during the inspection. It was obvious to me and everyone else he singled me out. Maybe for being your friend. I finally had enough and went to see the First Spear.

"Rufus Valens and Tulio saw General Gallius and told him what had happened. It was agreed Marinus was punishing me out of proportion to the other legionnaires in the century. The only reason I can explain is for my repeated attempts to transfer to the cavalry. Valens may have talked to the general about Marinus before the latest incident. Evidently, Marinus has been the subject of complaints from other legionnaires in the cohort. He was called to the principia, and apparently it did not go well for him. The next thing I knew I was told to report to Tarquin, Decurion Tarquin," he amended, causing Strabo to suppress another smile. "That was yesterday before my punishment could be carried out."

Strabo nodded. "All right, there are a few things you need to understand and consider in joining the decuria. To be frank, I would have preferred your assignment to one of the other decuriae." Strabo raised his hand to stop Vinicius's surprised protest. "Listen to me. The reason I have reservations is because you're a close friend. I'm concerned it will be difficult for you expecting preferential treatment you won't get. I will require the same from you as I do from the others assigned to the decuria." He smiled to soften the effect of his words. "It will be awkward for both of us. I believe we can make it work. Do you agree?"

Vinicius scratched the back of his neck and said reflectively, "I admit I hadn't thought about what you explained. Your words are fair and make sense. I'll do my best to keep in mind what you said. I think my time in the *Claudia* has done much to change my resistance to rules and authority. I've no doubt there will be occasions to test both of us. If I make a mistake, I've no doubt you will do what you have to, and so will I."

"Then my friend, we'll speak no more about it. Report to Ursinus and do whatever he says. I got the same advice from Decurion Tarquin, and I was smart enough to follow it."

Vinicius came to attention and saluted. "Yes, Sir, Decurion." Strabo laughed and watched Vinicius walking to the stables.

Bibracte

Morgane looked with visible contempt at Dumnorix sitting across the table from her. Two years before, she welcomed a marriage to the tribal chief of the Aedui. The union would give her stature and influence. Since then, her favorable impression had turned to dismay and surprise. At the time, he was the leader of the largest tribe in Gaul. Their initial meeting, at least for her, was positive. He was physically impressive, handsome and well-spoken. It didn't take long after the rituals for her to see him differently. He wasn't as clever as he believed himself to be. His confidence was mercurial, and he reacted irrationally to sudden, unexpected setbacks. Soon after their marriage, his older brother, Diviciacus, reclaimed leadership of the tribe, and her opinion of him and any expectations deteriorated further. She concentrated on how to survive a situation she perceived was going to get worse. She was determined to survive one way or another. Distancing herself from her husband was the path to take. His clever attempts to subvert the Romans had proven unsuccessful and were viewed as duplicitous by the Romans and ineffectual by the Gaulish tribes he supported with promises he couldn't keep.

"My dear husband," she began sarcastically, "now that your brother has made you a virtual prisoner here in Bibracte, what do you intend to do about it?"

"Actually, dear wife, I plan to do nothing at all. I've already accomplished what I intended; therefore, I'm quite content to remain here and wait for the outcome I set in motion. It won't be long before my brother will be happy to go back to his druid incantations in a forest glade, and I will be tribal leader again."

"Is General Crassus planning to meet with Diviciacus?"

"Yes, Caesar is expected tomorrow. I imagine the meeting has something to do with me apart from conferring about what is happening along the northern border."

"Will you be invited to participate?"

He laughed without humor. "I expect an invitation to your bed before that happens. The Romans are fools for not attacking when the

Belgae are so unprepared to take the field. It suits me well they play the fool and delay while Galba is getting stronger."

"Are you confident Iccius," referring to the tribal leader of the Remi, "will join King Galba?"

"Yes," he said with more conviction than he knew was warranted. The reality was Iccius was tired of Galba assuming the Remi was going to acquiesce to whatever the Suessiones demanded. Iccius had made it clear he wasn't willing to accept Galba's dominance as did the other Belgae tribes. There was suspicion among the Belgae tribes his real objective was to rule Belgica, and he was using the Roman threat to accomplish it. Iccius was weighing the odds which side would dominate. He would decide and declare his allegiance to one or the other after seeing which one had the best chance to win. Iccius, the tricky bastard, was doing precisely what he would do in his place. His risk was the Remi would decide at the last minute to side with Diviciacus and the Romans. The latter would strengthen his brother's hold on the tribe further diminishing any chance to reclaim leadership of the Aedui. Until now, he never considered removing his brother in a way that was unthinkable. His wife's angry voice intruded.

"You're a fool if you're depending on a firm alliance between the Remi and Suessiones. I have my own sources that say Iccius will terminate the loose alliance between the Remi and the Suessiones. Iccius thinks Galba treats the Remi as if it's a subordinate tribe. I hear Galba is having difficulty getting many of the Germani tribes to join him in attacking the Romans. I don't believe you or Galba can depend on the Remi to join the confederation against the Romans. Galba may be fortunate if the Remi remains neutral."

Dumnorix's anger at her for calling him a fool cooled as he considered what she said. First, he was astounded how much she knew about the developments in the north. Second, much of what she said plucked at the strings of the loosely woven threads of his plan and his doubts it could easily unravel. Confined at Bibracte, it would be difficult to influence Iccius and Galba and provide his promised support to the northern tribes.

Morgane saw the effect her comments had on her husband by his vacant expression and sagging shoulders. She relented not out of pity but self-preservation. She needed him no matter what the outcome of events in the near future might be. She accepted the reality without him she was a relic of a past and promise fading away to nothing. Even diminished, he presented a strong possibility of becoming tribal leader again. Diviciacus was much older, and there was always an unfortunate outcome he might perish in the battles to come. She suppressed her contempt and any additional criticism.

"What you've done and the possibility you are tarnished by it doesn't necessarily imperil your future regardless of the outcome. Your brother has already shown tolerance of both your opinions and your hostility to the Romans. I see no reason he will change. He's aware that many of the Aedui clans share your distrust of the Romans and resent their presence in Gaul. In isolating you from the Belgae Tribes, he's done you a favor by removing you from the intrigues of the Belgae and their objectives with respect to the Romans. In fact, his action in bringing you here keeps you from being a target for the Romans had you remained in the north. You need to look less like an enemy of Rome. Be pragmatic and be ready to work with whichever side prevails. In so doing, you serve both the interests of the Aedui and your own. You realize, of course, this is not so different to what your brother is doing except unlike you, his objective is about preserving the Aeduan dominance in Gaul. You conspired with my father to become king of the Aedui and the lesser tribes in Gaul. You should not abandon that objective. Find other ways to achieve it."

He reacted with angry impatience. "You talk nonsense. It will be the Romans who will rule Gaul and one day the Belgae and the Germani."

"True, however, you can still achieve what you aspired to under the suzerainty of Rome."

"I won't kneel to Rome!"

"Then husband, I and the gods can't help you to keep from becoming a lapdog of whoever controls Gaul. Bend your knee when you have to if you want to live long enough to rise above the moment. Persevere and do whatever's necessary to remain influential in a future in which you, and, of course, the Aedui will benefit."

He looked at her as if seeing her for the first time. The clarity of her vision and the harsh logic of her analysis were both surprising and unsettling. He had underestimated both her intelligence and her potential usefulness. Until now, he regarded her as a tiresome irritant. Her constant criticism had reached the point his indifference turned to hate. It occurred to him her ambitions were the same as his except her vision how to achieve them could be better and more realistically grounded than his.

She noted his frown and brooding silence, hopeful her comments had some effect. She waited a little longer before asking, "If the Remi join Galba, do you really believe they can defeat the Romans?"

"Unless more Germani tribes join the effort, the outcome is far from assured."

"Then there's not much chance the Romans will be defeated?"

"No. Even if I'm wrong, it won't matter that much. It will represent a temporary setback that will make the Aedui stronger at the cost of the Belgae and Germani tribes becoming weaker. The day will yet come the Romans will realize too late the tribes within the borders of Gaul will be the ones to drive them out. I intend to be the one to lead them."

Surprised, Morgane considered she may have judged him too harshly. She would try to be less critical and confrontational in the future.

General Crassus halted his century-size escort a mile from the settlement, gave the order to dismount and beckoned Strabo to join him.

"We'll wait here while you ride ahead and tell Diviciacus we're here. I would give him at least a few minutes to prepare for our arrival. Please tell him I anticipate our visit will be brief, and I will not impose on his hospitality any longer than it takes to conclude our mutual purpose for the meeting."

Strabo saluted and remounted Aquilo. He brushed aside the formal way in which the general had addressed him. He knew it was a result of what he done to Servius. He didn't care what Crassus thought or believed. He was too busy masking his disappointment their visit would be so brief. He had relied on time at least to see Raven assuming Corius had convinced her to return to Bibracte. A short time later as he rode into the settlement and passed by Raven's small, conical-thatched dwelling, it was obvious no one had been there since his last visit. For whatever reason, Corius had not been successful in convincing her to return. He tried not to think Talos was the reason. It was becoming a recurring thought Talos might be more important to Raven than he was. Possibly it could be better for both of them if he distanced himself from childhood memories and a relationship too linked to the past. He wasn't sure he was connected to the Aedui and Gaul as he once was. The thought occurred to him the same could be said for his life in Massilia.

He stopped at the imposing rectangular, peaked-roof wooden structure where his uncle, clan and tribal leader of the Aedui, lived, presided and determined the tribe's affairs. Diviciacus came out of the entrance and greeted him warmly.

"I hoped you would accompany General Crassus. It is good to see you."

"And I say the same to you, Uncle. I had hoped to come sooner to see you and Raven. Events have not allowed much time for pleasure."

"I'm sorry. Raven is in Bibrax."

Strabo concealed his disappointment. "I suspect it's because she finds the company of someone there more to her liking. Perhaps that is as it should be. I give you greetings from General Crassus who wants to know if you're ready to receive him. He doesn't plan staying longer than it takes to talk of mutual concerns for the developments along the northern border. I had hoped for a longer stay with time to spend with you and the scouts."

"I understand. Tell General Crassus I welcome his timely visit."

Strabo nodded and mounted. "I'll bring the general to you momentarily."

Close to the settlement gate, he saw Corius riding toward him.

"Marcellus, I heard General Crassus was coming today and expected you might accompany him. I look forward to time with you after you've fulfilled your duties."

"It will have to be another time. I'm leaving with General Crassus as soon as he's finished meeting with Diviciacus." He hesitated and tried not to sound accusing. "My uncle told me Raven's still in Bibrax."

"I was unable to persuade her to return."

"Did she say why?" He saw Corius's hesitation and braced himself.

"She's enjoying her time with Leuca and claims it's a welcome break from living rough with the scouts. I told her where you were, and you had the gray stallion. She was glad the horse was getting exercised. She'll try to see you."

"Corius, is Talos in Bibrax?"

"I didn't see him, nor did she mention him at all."

Strabo considered telling him about his suspicion Talos was with the Bellovaci band that tried to ambush the decuria. He decided not to. He had no proof, and it might sound as if he was pursuing a vendetta against Talos.

"If you had said she was with Talos, I would not have been surprised. She once made a pointed reference to someone that *looks like a Roman* — that someone was me. It's time I returned to General Crassus. I hope the next time we meet it will be when we can speak of lighter matters."

Corius watched him ride away both sad and wondering who he felt sorrier for – Raven or Marcellus.

Diviciacus nodded after the general finished explaining his concerns about Dumnorix and the northern border. "General Crassus, my brother is no longer in the north. He's here at Bibracte where I can assure you, he will remain. He met with King Galba, and from what I've learned, his influence and capability to assist the king is considerably less than he thinks and Galba expects."

"While you reassure me concerning your brother, from all the reports I receive of activities in the north, I believe there's no longer any doubt Belgae will cross the border."

"I agree, and we, too, are very concerned; however, it may not be as imminent as you think. King Galba is having difficulty obtaining pledges from some of the Germani tribes critical to assure his success. Furthermore, some of the northern Belgae tribes are hesitant to support the king in fear your legions will prevail, and Caesar will keep on going north. Galba is worried about obtaining sufficient forage to sustain an invasion once it begins. He doesn't trust my brother's pledge I'm sure he made to help him, and he's worried the Remi won't join him. His concern is justified. Iccius will break with Galba. He'll try to remain neutral until he no longer can. I'm confident his choice will be to side with the Aedui."

"How can you be so sure?"

"I've been far north where I met with Iccius, and I've no doubt the Remi will remain a close ally of the Aedui and will not aid the Belgae. I met separately with King Galba." Anticipating the question to come, he added, "Yes, of course, he asked me to join his confederation. I told him I would not. I said it was not in the interests of the Aedui to fight Caesar who kept Gaul from becoming occupied by first the Helvetii then King Ariovistus."

"I speak for General Labienus who until Caesar returns commands the legions. Based upon what we know and expect, we'll plan for an imminent Belgae incursion or any other tribe threatening Gaul. Rome considers any threat to Gaul is a threat to Rome and will be treated as such."

Diviciacus remained silent and thoughtful. When he spoke, his tone was accusatory. "General Crassus, your comment is widely encompassing. I sincerely hope Rome and Caesar recognize there are tribes here prepared to do what is necessary to maintain peace in Gaul. The Aedui in particular have done much to encourage trade and a friendly relationship with Rome. Do not take my words as anything other than a gentle reminder not all tribes are an existential threat to Rome."

General Crassus responded with a slight note of contrition. "I understand and accept your cautionary remarks. I can assure you Caesar is well aware of the contributions the Aedui and a few other tribes have so far made."

Strabo flinched at the general's halfhearted clarification and use of the word *few* to convey Caesar's perception of what he thought of tribal support so far. The meeting ended with a noticeable coolness in contrast to how it began.

General Crassus stood up. "Lord Diviciacus, I thank you for your time and your very clear assessment of our mutual interests and the importance in maintaining them. We will continue to work closely with you to prepare for whatever the Belgae may do. Caesar is expected to arrive in Gaul in a few weeks. I'm quite certain he'll wish to see you soon after to benefit from your insight to counter the Belgae threat in the mutual interests of both the Gaulish tribes and Rome."

Diviciacus replied with a diplomatic smile. "May that be the maxim for how we will confront those who seek to separate the interests of Rome and the Gaulish tribes."

Chapter 9
Visontio, early May

The blare of trumpets and drumbeats announced Caesar's arrival. Mounted and waiting at the main entrance to Visontio, General Titus Labienus looked critically at the eight legions lined up, four on each side facing the route Caesar would soon take. The legions, even the newly formed and recently arrived Thirteenth and Fourteenth Legions under the command of General Pedia, looked impressive. There was no reason they shouldn't with the advance notice provided for the exact day and time he would arrive. They had ample time to thoroughly rehearse to satisfy Caesar's affinity for public ceremony planned and executed to the last detail. Fortunately, the weather was cooperating, for even had it been raining or snowing, a ceremony would be expected. He glimpsed the white horse, red cloak and the sun glinting off the gold circlet Caesar habitually wore on most occasions and always on a battlefield.

A few paces from the first two legions Caesar would pass, Labienus gave the signal. The cornicines blared and all eight legions came to attention. Each legion raised drawn swords and shouted, "Hail Caesar," as he rode past. Labienus sighed in relief. Caesar's broad smile indicated he was savoring the moment.

Inside the principia of the Tenth Legion, Caesar removed his cloak and laurel-leaf circlet and surrendered them to Otho, his ever-present chief secretary and steward. Otho was quietly accorded near equal status by the legion commanders and essential for assessing Caesar's mood before scheduling a meeting. Caesar accepted a cup of wine offered by one of the junior scribes and raised it to General Labienus.

"Titus, you never disappoint, and my thanks for it. It was a splendid performance. Are the legions ready to march?"

"We've been ready and waiting for your arrival. We have forage and provisions sufficient for the campaign and a pledge from Diviciacus for additional supplies should we need them. Tomorrow would not be too early to march."

"Excellent, then tomorrow it will be."

"How long do you estimate to reach the border?"

"We could be there in ten days. I suggest a slower pace. The baggage train is larger and slower than usual with the additional provisions we're taking. Twelve to fourteen days would be a better estimate. The Third Legion will secure the baggage."

Caesar frowned. "I'll settle for twelve days. Depending on how active the border is, I may consider moving forward with seven legions and leave the baggage train to catch up when it can. You mentioned in your dispatches Diviciacus believes Iccius, tribal chief of the Remi, will not join Galba. Is that still true?"

"Yes, but we need to prepare for the possibility he might change his mind before we get there."

"How many Belgae tribes are we likely to face, and do we have some appreciation of their strength?"

"With the Suessiones alone, King Galba has at least 50,000 warriors, the Bellovaci could provide upward of a 100,000, the Nervii 50,000, the Atrebates15,000 then another 40,000 combined from six to seven other tribes. If the tribes consolidate as one army, we may face over 250,000 warriors. Diviciacus doesn't believe Galba will be able to field that many."

"Why?" Caesar asked sharply.

"Galba has been having difficulty in convincing some of the tribes, most of which are Germani, to commit after what happened last year to King Ariovistus and the Suebi. Not all tribes have exchanged hostages to secure an alliance. It seems some tribal leaders are waiting to declare their intent underscoring their reluctance to fight Romans."

"If that's true, or even close to the truth, we have an opportunity to take advantage of their hesitation. We'll strike first while their caution or indecision reduces their advantage in numbers. I have a commitment from Diviciacus the Aedui will for once do their share of the fighting and improve our odds. If the Remi either join us or at least remain neutral, all the better."

"Do you want to see the legion commanders before we leave tomorrow?"

"I do, and Publius Crassus as well. From the current build-up of the Belgae and the probability they're belligerent, it was wise of you to delay sending him to Armorica. Depending on what happens over the next few weeks and the extent the Belgae are problematic will determine when I'll send Crassus to deal with the situation. He will command a legion with cavalry augmentation. The situation there has grown worse, and the wider threat of rebellion in the region warrants a stronger presence under an eagle standard."

Labienus's face showed his surprise. "Has the senate approved Publius's advancement to command of a legion?"

"This is Gaul, and here I decide what will happen and who commands one of my legions." Then with a smile and shrug, he added, "It seems promoting Publius is little enough in exchange for his father giving me two additional legions. Speaking of Marcus Crassus, you may have noticed the large contingent following behind the cavalry and legionnaire replacements."

"I did. They look like slavers."

"Which they are. Marcus Crassus was somewhat displeased by the few Germani slaves we sent back to Rome last year and expects a better return from his investment in Gaul during the forthcoming campaign. I assured him he can anticipate a significant improvement this year, a pledge I will make clear to the legion commanders they will do their best to support. To ensure their cooperation, the senior commanders will receive a share of the profits. I need to keep Crassus content. My plans for Gaul and Britannia will require more legions beyond the four Crassus has funded."

"Britannia? We haven't finished our efforts in Gaul."

Caesar's lips twitched in a humorless smile. "Gaul will soon become a province of Rome, and as it does, I'll keep the legions here until I find somewhere else to take them. Perhaps Britannia."

"Britannia?"

"Why not? I haven't been to Britannia. No Roman has. Well, that's a thought for another day."

Bibrax, twelve days later

The sun was rising when Andecumborius entered the tribal chief's lodge. By his haggard look and slumped shoulders, he knew Iccius had made his decision.

"You're going to support Caesar?"

"Yes, I'm told he will be here tomorrow. You and I will go to him and pledge our guarantee with hostages to support him."

Andecumborius sat down across the table with fatalistic acceptance. This was not the decision he wanted and feared, although it wasn't unexpected. The two men had been debating for days which side to take, each giving the advantages and disadvantages for whatever Iccius would eventually have to decide. The one thing they both agreed upon was whatever the decision, there would be far-reaching consequences for the Remi and Gaul.

"Does Galba know?"

"He will soon enough, but not before I've made my peace with Caesar and am confident of his protection in the future."

"Then at least we have a little time to prepare before he finds out."

"You think Bibrax will be the first objective Galba attacks?"

"Galba will consider your decision a knife in the back and a motive for other tribes to reconsider an alliance. He will make the Remi an example of what happens for any tribe helping the Romans."

"I suppose you're right. Curse the Romans for coming into Gaul and putting us in the position we're in now. On the other hand, I think it was only a matter of time our relationship with the Suessiones was going to change. Galba is ambitious and enjoys being a king. He's made no pretense he sees the Remi as a vassal under his rule. Inform the elders we meet here in one hour. We need to prepare for Caesar's arrival, the hostages each clan will provide, and consider what must be done for the defense of Bibrax. The outlying settlements have to be notified to have time to come here or go somewhere else."

Several miles from Bibrax, Raven looked east and saw a Roman delegation heading for the settlement. They were too far away to see detail, but a gray horse one of the riders was riding reminded her of Aquilo. The thought stirred her. She missed him and for the first time regretted her impulsive decision to leave Bibracte.

She rode on to the glade she'd been coming to for several weeks to maintain her archery skills and stopped the horse next to a low embankment. Carefully, awkwardly, she slid off the horse. It was obvious her time to come here was measured. She also enjoyed getting away from the bustling, intrusive settlement where she felt stifled and out of place. It was a quiet refuge until she could return to the life she desperately missed. Despite Corius's angry outburst the last time they saw each other, she was confident he would let her rejoin the scouts. She would first have to convince him the safety and welfare of the baby was assured.

After tethering the horse, she untied the bow and walked a short distance away to a cleared area where she could see the length of the glade. At the far end, targets of painted animal hide the size of a man's torso were positioned. At this distance, they appeared no larger than half size. Patience and perseverance eventually restored her skill and strength to a level close to what it was before. She pulled an arrow from the quiver hanging low from a shoulder strap on her left side and nocked it. In one quick, fluid motion, she pulled back the string and released the arrow at the farthest target. With the familiar act, all concerns were replaced with calm detachment and focus of a hunter. She watched the arrow in flight, confident it would strike exactly where she intended. The arrow had not yet reached the target when a twig snapped off to her right.

She reacted instinctively by drawing another arrow and had it nocked before the first arrow stopped quivering in the distant target. She turned where the sound had come from and saw three men emerge from the underbrush. She saw a fourth man with his back turned farther back in the forest holding the reins of four horses. He was too far away to note anything about him except his long gray hair. From the style of their hair and clothing, they were from one of the tribes north and west of Bibrax. Bellovaci she guessed. The tribes had generally been on peaceful terms in the past; however, with the rising influence of King Galba, the relations with the northern tribes were less friendly notably with the Bellovaci.

The taller man standing in the middle carried an axe in his right hand. His left hand rested on the hilt of his sword. He said something that caused the two other men armed with spears to nod and smile their appreciation.

She was aware of how vulnerable she was, a woman alone, far from the settlement and too pregnant to vault in the saddle had it been next to her which it wasn't. The taller man spoke and his accent confirmed he was Bellovaci.

"We're hunters looking for game, and it seems we've found more than what we are looking for. From your swollen belly, you've been plowed. In consideration, we'll treat you with care. It depends if you're reasonable and willing to drop the bow. Your cooperation will be generously rewarded with your life. When we're done, we'll leave you in peace."

Raven felt strangely calm. The man's words had the opposite effect of making her afraid. She accepted the stark reality no matter how much she cooperated the child may not survive even if they kept their word. She didn't trust they would.

"I prefer to shoot the first one that takes a step closer or lifts a weapon."

"Before you act rashly consider there are three of us, and your chances of resisting are not good. If you make the mistake of trying, there won't be any regrets for what will happen."

"I agree although it's likely only one of you will be lucky enough to tell what happened here. The other two will surely die, and you will be the first. If you doubt me, look where my arrow struck. If I'm able to hit a target that far away, I can easily put an arrow in whichever eye I choose," she stopped and smiled, "or between your legs."

She saw his hesitation and the dawning realization he did not have the upper hand as he first assumed. She saw the younger warrior on the left lift his spear and begin to pull his arm back. She drew and released. The arrow imbedded halfway into his chest. Without a sound he collapsed, dead before his body reached the ground. By the time it did, she nocked another arrow.

Raven focused her attention on the taller man. "If you want to live, we'll have a different discussion. From your accent, I think you are Bellovaci. Why are you here besides taking advantage of what you wrongly assumed was a helpless woman?"

The taller man raised his axe and started running toward her. His angry scream was choked off by the arrow in his neck. The remaining Bellovaci warrior stood frozen, wide-eyed after seeing Raven nock another arrow.

"What's your name?"

"Carrotacus."

"Listen carefully and do what I say, or you will die. Toss your spear away and get down on your knees."

"What are you going to do?"

"I'm going to take you to Bibrax. There you're going tell the elders why you came here."

"You may as well kill me. I'll suffer far worse with them than with you."

His fatalistic response surprised her. The difficulty of getting him to Bibrax by herself necessitated a practical solution.

"If your being here was peaceful, you wouldn't be concerned about talking to the elders. I'll give you an alternative. Tell me what I want to know, and I'll let you go back where you came from."

"I don't trust you. You'll kill me after I tell you."

"That's possible, but not as certain as what the three of you were going to do to me after you were finished satisfying yourselves. I'm giving you a chance to live which is more than I was going to have."

"Very well, I'll tell you. The leader of the Bellovaci wants to learn the intentions of the Remi if and when Caesar advances toward Belgica. Galba doesn't trust Iccius and believes he's going to help the Romans. If this is what happens then the Bellovaci will attack Bibrax and all other Remi settlements to prevent any aid to the Romans."

"How were you planning to find out? I knew you were Bellovaci tribesmen as soon as I saw you. You couldn't blend in and wander around Bibrax without attracting attention."

The tribesman smiled and said smugly, "We never planned to go any closer to Bibrax than here. We didn't have to because we had someone who could, as you say, blend in."

"Who is it?"

"Only Bannos knew, and you killed him. He was the one carrying the axe. I only knew the contact was an Aeduan recently come to live in Bibrax. He claimed he had his reasons for hating Romans and those who were ready to aid them. He's supposed to come here tonight."

Speechless, heart pounding, Raven looked away momentarily forgetting the tribesman kneeling a dozen paces away until she heard him move. He was already on his feet knife in hand running toward her by the time she reacted almost too late. Carrotacus took the arrow in his chest. At such close range, the arrow did not have the force to penetrate deep, but it was enough to slow him down. She swung the bow harder across the side of his head. He fell to his knees, and she hit him again. He sprawled face down on the ground, and the arrow point came through his shirt.

Even badly wounded, he managed to get up on his hands and knees. Without hesitating, she pulled her knife, grabbed a fistful of his hair and drew the blade across his throat. After wiping the bloody blade on his shirt, she walked to her horse without a backward look. There was the sound of someone running, and she remembered the fourth man. She nocked another arrow then relaxed after seeing a man with long flowing gray hair riding away leading three horses. The only thing she wanted to do now was find Talos.

Raven drew rein in front of Leuca's dwelling and saw Talos coming toward her.

"Raven, I need to talk to you." He hesitated when Leuca appeared in the doorway. "In private."

"I need to take care of the horse. Follow me to the corral, and we'll talk there." His sudden appearance surprised her after such a long time since they last saw each other. Then it was an accidental encounter. Their brief conversation was stilted, absent of the easy informality since their time serving in the scouts.

He helped her dismount then unsaddled the horse. An awkward silence followed as both busied themselves tending to the mundane tasks of caring for the horse each apparently waiting for the other to speak. Finally, Raven broke the silence.

"What is it you want to talk to me about?"

Talos took a deep breath. "You have to leave Bibrax. You're in danger here. Iccius met with the elders early this morning and told them he will support Caesar and not Galba. As soon as Galba is aware of it, the settlement will be attacked."

"I know."

Astonished, he asked, "How did you find out?"

"I learned about it a short time ago from a man by the name of Carrotacus before I killed him. He and another man were with Bannos, the man you were planning to meet tonight. You won't be meeting with him. I killed him and the other man, too."

Talos looked at her in open-mouthed shock. "What happened?" he finally managed to ask.

"I went to a place where I frequently go to maintain my archery skills. They evidently thought I was harmless and a welcome diversion. I killed the first one who lifted his spear after I warned them not to try anything. The second was Bannos. The third man, Carrotacus, wanted to live and told me they were there to meet someone from Bibrax. He didn't know his name only that he was Aeduan. I knew it was you. They were waiting for you and what you would tell them. I was going to let him go back to the Bellovaci after he told me everything. He made the mistake of attacking me with a knife. I put an arrow in him before I cut his throat. Talos, convince me it was someone else they were planning to meet."

He closed his eyes and slowly shook his head.

She started to shake, in part from delayed shock with what had happened in the glade and in anger at his mute confession. "Why?" she finally managed to ask.

"I came here because unlike the Aedui, I thought the Remi would resist the Romans by joining the Belgae. In time, it was clear to me the Remi were either going to remain neutral or likely support the Romans. I left here and joined the Bellovaci who were allied with King Galba and many other Belgae tribes who want the Romans out of Gaul. I went on several raids with Bannos. On one of them, I even saw your Roman and would have killed him if given the chance. In time, Bannos convinced me I could serve the Belgae better by returning to Bibrax and learn the true intentions of the Remi. I knew if the Remi decided to remain neutral or join Caesar what would happen to Bibrax. I came back a few days ago and didn't know you were still here until I saw you in the market place. I thought you had returned to Bibracte. This morning I learned Iccius met with the elders and told them the Remi would support Caesar. I wanted to warn you to leave Bibrax. Leuca told me you had gone riding and didn't know when you would return. Raven, you're in danger and must leave. As soon as Galba learns what Iccius decided, the Bellovaci will destroy the Remi settlements. I can't bear the thought of anything happening to you."

His last comment checked her anger. In a way she felt partly to blame for what he'd done.

"I don't excuse what you did, but I understand how you feel about the Romans. I want them out of Gaul, but I don't want the Belgae either. So far, you've done nothing to harm the Remi or to influence the Bellovaci. Had you met with Bannos as planned and told him what Iccius decided, I would feel differently. I worry I may have influenced your actions because of Marcellus Strabo, and if so, I'm truly sorry for that."

"At first you did. The last time I saw you with Strabo, I left Bibracte angry and bitter. It has taken time to realize I've been foolish. While I haven't changed my feelings about the Romans and Strabo, I've come to accept you see me only as a friend. Raven, as the friend I will always be, I beg you to leave before it's too late."

"I cannot. Bibracte is too far to go in my condition. There is nowhere close to Bibrax where I would be any safer. I will stay and help defend Bibrax. What will you do?"

"I'll tell Iccius what I did. If he doesn't have me killed, I'll stay here with you and fight the Bellovaci."

"There's no reason for you to say anything. Carrotacus told me what you confirmed; therefore, I'll tell Iccius what happened to me, and what I learned. I doubt what I say will change anything Iccius has already considered and prepared to do as a result of his decision. Say nothing and stay here and fight for the Remi."

Talos nodded. "I suppose you're right." He hesitated and added, "You are not like any other woman I've known. I wonder if your Roman sees how much you've changed. If he were to come here and take you away to a safer place, I would help him." He started to walk away then stopped. "That doesn't mean I won't kill him one day if he continues to look and be more Roman than Aeduan."

Chapter 10
Caesar's Headquarters near the border between Belgica and Gaul

Strabo heard what at first sounded like distant thunder, a continuous pulsating throb. He shaded his eyes and looked southeast where a dust cloud was rising in the late morning sky. The legions were on the march.

Over the next hour, the drums became progressively louder as did the accompanying trumpets. The first distinct movement was the cavalry screening the advance under the command of Tarquin. Strabo looked forward to seeing the decurion. Soon after, the first standard slowly rose above a hill. The *aquilfer* wearing the distinct leopard-skinned helmet finally appeared. Too far away to distinguish the number below the eagle, he was sure it was the Tenth Legion, Caesar's favorite legion he considered his personal bodyguard. Caesar's messenger two days before said he would be here midway between the fourth and fifth hour at which time, he expected Diviciacus and Iccius to be present for his arrival. Caesar wanted the tribal leaders he was about to meet to see the might of Rome on display.

The long serpentine column resembled a giant caterpillar moving over the low hills. The sun glinted off the standards and metal accouterments. Strabo had seen it all before. Almost a year ago, he had been another faceless legionary in those ranks. Even as a conscripted ranker, he was awed by the splendor of it. He still was.

Diviciacus was talking in low tones to Iccius and the other Remi clan leaders waiting for Caesar. In a small silent group behind the tribal leaders, the Remi hostages, sons, grandsons or close relatives of the elders, waited. They were hostages offered as surety Iccius would keep his pledge to support Caesar. A thousand paces north of the tent, General Crassus had positioned the Auxilia to secure the meeting site against the possibility of a rude interruption by the Belgae.

General Crassus said to Strabo standing next to him, "The messenger three days ago said Caesar would arrive today between the fourth and fifth hour. I was skeptical. He brought the legions here from Visontio two days sooner than I expected. I'll never doubt him again."

A quarter mile away the drums were silent replaced by several trumpet calls and the shouted orders of the centurions. The Tenth Legion halted and the cohorts began to move left and right of the standard while the legions behind moved obliquely in the same manner. The last cohort moved into position and the eight legions were arrayed in a silent line facing the white tent. A small body of horsemen cantered toward them with Caesar's flag prominently displayed. Caesar was easy to distinguish from the group. Unlike the plumed helmets of the other riders, he was bareheaded except for the gold circlet. There was speculation he wore it when he slept. His long, red cape, burnished cuirass and greaves alone would have drawn attention. If he been plainly accoutered, the imperious way he rode, chin up, left hand resting on his hip, his dignitas would have been enough to assert he was no ordinary man.

Caesar dismounted and with a broad smile greeted Crassus. "Publius, I bear greetings from your father. I told him he had good reason to be proud of you. He sends you best wishes and will make sacrifices for your well-being and continued success."

"Hail, Caesar, I bid you welcome to northern Gaul and give my thanks for the words from my father. Diviciacus awaits your pleasure as does Iccius, chief of the Remi. Hostages stand behind them as proof of their alliance to support you in whatever manner you require."

"I need to make clear my expectations without sounding harsh and too demanding."

Caesar turned to Strabo and smiled. "I see you've wintered well in Gaul." Then in a lower voice for Crassus and Strabo to hear, "Marcellus, I want my words to be clear and pointed without sounding like a threat. I want to emphasize my desire for a mutually beneficial partnership. We need the support of the Aedui and Remi particularly if the Germani tribes join the Belgae in greater numbers than they did for Ariovistus. Let's not keep them waiting any longer."

By the time the three men reached the tent, the legions had been dismissed to begin preparing the night encampment.

Caesar faced the consilium consisting of the eight generals, senior tribunes and senior centurions of the eight legions and wasted no time in telling them his reason and objective for advancing into Belgica the next day.

"Even though I've been assured of warriors from both the Aedui and the Remi, we are considerably outnumbered. We will go north at first light tomorrow. After crossing the Belgica border, we'll advance as far as the Aisne River and camp on the north side. I want the night forts completed well before nightfall. My objective for going into Belgica is to attack before they consolidate. I anticipate the Bellovaci, one of the largest tribes, will be the first we'll engage. Their strength is estimated to be more than twice ours. The Aedui have agreed to move against the Bellovaci settlements within a few days to split their forces. I don't expect to be attacked during the march; however, in case they do, we'll advance with two legions abreast as the terrain will allow.

"General Crassus, you will screen the advance with your cavalry and secure the north side of the Aisne River as the legions cross the bridge.

"General Labienus, The Tenth Legion will be the first legion to cross the bridge. Titus, I'll leave it to you to determine the order of march for the other legions. I invite General Crassus who has scouted the area across the river to describe the area and proposed location of the camp."

General Crassus nodded to two legionnaires who came forward, unrolled a large parchment and held it open facing the legion commanders and senior centurions. The parchment displayed a sketch of the principal terrain features of the proposed battle site and location of the encampment.

Using an arrow to point, General Crassus began. "The River Aisne in many places is too deep and swift to cross on foot and difficult by horse. There are fords west of the bridge and crossing is less difficult although variable depending on weather. Less than a mile north of the river, there's a low ridge extending a little over two miles southwest to northeast. The widest area on top of the ridge is of sufficient size to locate the main camp. The close proximity of the river and its depth in the immediate vicinity of the settlement and east for several miles will provide additional protection from a southern attack. The river is easily fordable two miles west of the bridge.

"The area north of the ridge is relatively open sloping down to a marsh beginning approximately 400 hundred paces from the base of the ridge. The marsh is created by a stream that curves like an oxbow at the base of a series of hills extending nearly five miles from southwest to northwest. The marsh is difficult to cross for both horses and infantry. West of the low ridge and left flank of the proposed camp site, the terrain narrows because of the marsh. Farther west of the ridge, the terrain is open and flat with fewer hills.

"The right flank of the camp is vulnerable and requires additional protection. I've recommended a defensive trench be constructed perpendicular to the northwest camp wall extending 300 hundred paces toward the marsh with a *castellum* at the end. The fortlet should be large enough for a century and six caroballistae. I've recommended a similar trench and fortlet perpendicular to the southeast side of the camp wall extending as far as the river bank.

"The most direct route to Bibrax, the main settlement of the Remi, is eight miles northwest from where we'll cross the river; it's easily accessible over relatively flat, open terrain. After Diviciacus told me the importance of the Remi, I went within sight of the settlement to locate it in the event the Remi joined Galba's confederation."

General Crassus stepped away from the sketch and looked at Caesar signaling he was finished.

"Thank you, General, the thoroughness of your assessment of the terrain will better prepare us for our advance into Belgica. Since I'm relying on the eyes of General Crassus and the scouts to describe the area we'll occupy and defend, some adjustments may be necessary to the deployment thus far proposed.

"Once in position and our defenses constructed, it's my intent to encourage the Belgae to initiate an attack. The reason is the marsh General Crassus described. Should they choose to cross it, they will be most vulnerable to our attack, and their advantage in numbers will be reduced.

"General Crassus, after we cross the river, the Auxilia will screen our left flank west of the road; it's our most vulnerable flank because the ground is open and, generally flat as you described.

"General Sabinus, the bridge is critical to securing and maintaining our supply of forage from the Remi. With six cohorts, one each from the six veteran legions, construct and command a defensible fort on the south bank near the bridge and maintain guards at the north end.

"General Metellus, while the other legions are constructing the main camp, the Eleventh Legion will dig the trenches and build the fortlets as General Crassus described.

"There's another detail that has a bearing on what may happen after we cross the river. Iccius, the senior elder of the Remi Tribe, learned the Belgae may attack Bibrax in retribution for his choosing to support Rome instead of the tribal confederation. That being the case, we need to prepare for that eventuality. If Bibrax is attacked and requires aid, the Auxilia will respond as needed.

"Otho, serve the wine so we may drink to our success in the days to come."

Tarquin noted the distracted look on Strabo's face. "Why the long face?"

"The tribal leader of the Remi told Caesar their main settlement at Bibrax is the first target the Belgae have vowed to attack because of their pledge to support Caesar."

Tarquin shrugged. "Why is that of any concern to us?"

"For Caesar, it isn't. I have reason to believe Raven is there. When I went to Bibracte to get Aquilo, I learned she went there to stay with a cousin. I asked Corius to persuade her to return to Bibracte. The last time I saw him weeks later, he said she was going to remain at Bibrax. I don't understand why."

Tarquin was sympathetic but chose to remain silent. It seemed obvious to him there was a reason for the girl to be in Bibrax other than visiting a cousin. He predicted Strabo would eventually come to the same conclusion.

"I expected after we arrived you and the decuria would come back to the Tenth Legion. Has General Crassus or General Labienus decided if you will?"

"No, I think for the time being, we'll probably remain with General Crassus. He's come to rely on us because the Auxilia consisting of cavalry, slingers and archers from Alexandria will do as they're ordered although without demonstrating any initiative or deep concern for the outcome."

"So be it. If the rumor is true, it won't be Crassus in command of the Auxilia much longer. I've heard a rumor General Cotta, commanding the Seventh Legion, may soon replace Crassus as commander of the Auxilia; Crassus is expected to replace him with command of the Seventh. There's speculation the Seventh may soon be sent west to Armorica to deal with an uprising there."

Strabo looked beyond where the legions were busy building the camp and saw a troop of cavalry heading toward the standard of the Eleventh Legion. As the troop drew closer, he was surprised to see Quintus Servius in the lead.

"I thought Servius was no longer a decurion for what he did to me and the other rider during the race at Visontio."

"General Metellus decided not to heed the recommendation of General Crassus to reduce him to cavalryman and was satisfied a fine equal to the prize money would be sufficient along with banning him from participating in any future competition as long as he was assigned to the Eleventh. He's a bad one. I advise you to stay away from him. He's made no secret he blames you for being disciplined. There are others besides him who do not hold you in high regard for not settling the matter privately."

"I regret what I did. I was angry and didn't think of the consequences. I'll follow your advice. In the days ahead, I'll keep in mind to watch my back in addition to the Belgae and Germani in front."

Chapter 11
The Bellovaci main settlement

King Galba regarded the dark-featured, sour-faced tribal chief and tried hard to present a calm, friendly appearance. He never liked Correous, and he knew the feeling was mutual. His dislike increased after he became leader of the tribal confederation, and Correous refused to accord him the respect and cooperation he expected. He disliked being dependent on a rival he didn't like or trust to halt the Romans long enough for him to convince the Germani to join the confederation. He silently cursed Dumnorix for his failure to convince the Remi to join the confederation. He knew he was probably more to blame for the condescending way he treated the Remi.

Galba broke the strained silence. "You've no doubt heard the Remi have pledged to the Romans yesterday. Caesar crossed the border early this morning with eight legions and his Auxilia. My scouts estimated his strength is about forty thousand. I want the lands of the Remi destroyed and Bibrax burned to the ground without delay. If Iccius won't help me, I don't want him helping the Romans. What's the strength of the Bellovaci, and how soon can you march?"

Instead of answering the question, Correous responded with a question. "What other tribes are prepared and ready to march?"

"My Suessiones are. My concern at the moment is my spies tell me the Bellovaci are Caesar's initial objective, and that's why I'm here."

"I think the main reason you came is because we and the Suessiones are the only tribes prepared and willing to confront the Romans. Is it true?"

Choosing to ignore he had been rudely addressed, Galba controlled his rising anger at the other man's probing and implied failure to forge a solid, responsive confederation.

"I concede the Romans have moved sooner and faster than I believed they could. The reality remains it's the Bellovaci about to bear the brunt of their initial assault. I've alerted the other tribes. How many warriors can you field, 50 thousand?"

"Near enough, 30 thousand by tomorrow; the rest will take at least a day longer. How many can you field?"

Galba relaxed. It was better than he hoped. "Fifteen thousand and another ten thousand in two days. I believe we can defeat the Romans with the strength we have; it will be certain when the other tribes assemble. My warriors are already on the march to meet the Romans with orders to observe and not to engage until after you've destroyed Bibrax and as many Remi whoresons as you have time to do in two days. I'll send scouts back to guide you where I'll be waiting."

He stood up to leave and considered whether he should say something and depart on a cordial if not friendly note. He decided he didn't have the words or the inclination.

Bibrax

The news the Roman advance was imminent traveled fast. The settlement was soon crowded with terrified farmers and livestock. Men and women capable of fighting were assigned places on the rampart wall. Except for enough guards on the ramparts to maintain surveillance, clan leaders were busy supervising the construction of makeshift shelters and covering trenches throughout the settlement to protect from the expected fusillade of missiles and stones. Others too old to fight were tasked to carry water and food to the wall defenders and help with the wounded.

Raven ignored the heated protests Talos made echoing those Leuca had made and claimed her place on the wall.

"How many who will defend the walls can launch an arrow faster and better than I can?"

"Not many, I suppose. In your condition, you need to be careful."

"I will, and I'll be just as safe watching missiles coming in than sitting under a flimsy shelter." To change the subject, she asked, "Where are the Romans?"

"They crossed the border this morning and stopped on the north side of the Aisne River. They're constructing a camp about eight miles southeast of the settlement."

"What about the Bellovaci? Any idea if they are coming here?"

"They're on their way." He gestured west. "If you go up on the ramparts, you'll see smoke from the farms they're burning. I expect they'll be here by first light tomorrow. Raven, there's still time to take you back to Bibracte or somewhere closer."

"It's too late for that, and I won't leave Leuca and the children." Indicating the villagers around them, she asked, "What would these people think of us if we left?"

Talos gave up. "Do you have a shield?"

"No, I left it in Bibracte."

"You're not going near the walls without a shield! You have no idea what it will be like in a siege. I do. Several years ago, before you joined the scouts, Corius and I were in one. We were in a village near Visontio when the Sequani attacked. We held out for almost a day under a fusillade during which a third of the those on the walls were either killed or so badly wounded, they could no longer fight. Eventually they were able to undercut the walls. The village chief finally surrendered to save the rest. Fortunately, the Sequani were satisfied to destroy the village and allow the survivors to move west." He stopped, gave her an angry look and walked away.

"Where are you going?"

"To find you a shield."

The night passed slowly with only the young, the seasoned and those unable to comprehend the threat sleeping peacefully. The rest remained anxious and awake.

Raven was no exception after listening to Talos describing what he and her brother had been through. She tossed and turned most of the night thinking of all the mishaps and mistakes she had made over the years. She looked for past instances when she made the right decisions and content with who she was and what she'd done with her life. The landscape of her recollections was bleak, and the future seemed no better. She had no paralyzing fear of tomorrow and considered an arrow or missile might be a justifiable end to what seemed an aimless existence so far. Unconsciously, she reached down to her rounded belly and waited for the sense of peaceful contentment others had described. She simply felt uncomfortable with an obligation to protect the life inside her.

The long, mournful sound of a carnyx signaling the Bellovaci had come was a welcome relief. The thought brought a smile of anticipation to her face erasing the melancholy thoughts of the past several hours. She stood up, slung the quiver of arrows over her shoulder, picked up her bow and the shield Talos had found for her and climbed the steps to take her place on the wall.

Talos was already there barely visible except for the dim light from the partially covered fire pots positioned along the wall. The carnyx stopped abruptly. The sudden silence was eerie, broken only by the faint sound similar to a light breeze blowing through trees or long grass, except there was no breeze. It was the Bellovaci moving into position. There was no sound at all. The silence was ominous, chilling. Time dragged and tension increased along the ramparts. She felt the urge to launch an arrow into the darkness in the remote chance it would strike someone and break the silence with a cry of pain. The drums and chanting started, and it was almost a relief. But there was a purpose to the noise beyond the unsettling effect it created.

Talos whispered, "Nock an arrow and get ready."

"For what?"

"Below us, they're digging at the base of the wall." He bent down and slid the cover off the fire pot and ignited the oil-soaked cloth. He waited long enough for the fuse to flare up and tossed it over the wall.

Raven followed the path of the glowing torch as it fell near several indistinct figures providing enough light to give her a target. She released the arrow and caught one of the diggers in the shoulder. Her second arrow buried in the chest of another. The third man had already disappeared beyond the range of the torch.

The results of the brief encounter caused a ripple of chuckles and praise along the wall. "Good job, Talos," said someone close by.

"It wasn't me. It was Raven. If it had been me, I would've wasted two arrows." The reply elicited another appreciative round of laughter. "Better duck and get your shields up for what's about to come."

Raven ducked down and barely raised the shield over her head in time. Rocks began to smash against the walls or pass overhead to land with a thud or the sound of splintering wood.

As quickly as it started, the brief fusillade stopped. After a few dire warnings shouted from the darkness for what was going to happen to the Remi defenders, there was silence beyond the walls. Within the settlement below, the murmur of quiet conversations was interspersed by occasional cries from frightened children or nervous livestock.

Gradually, the sky lightened. Those on the wall saw the silent, shadowy lines of Bellovaci warriors surrounding the settlement a bowshot away. Raven heard gasps and curses along the wall. The Bellovaci and whatever other tribes had joined with them dwarfed the Remi defenders. Raven wondered if she'd been mindlessly obstinate in refusing Corius's offers to take her away. She shivered and touched her belly silently invoking Epona to protect the growing life within. The spontaneous act surprised her as so unlike the prevailing indifference she had felt thus far during the pregnancy. The loud chanting from the enemy lines reinforced her decision to stay.

When the chanting stopped, the drums sounded, and the fusillade began. From all sides of the settlement, there was a steady rain of near fist-size rocks. Holding shields over their heads and to their sides, bands of warriors raced to protect the diggers who would attempt to undercut the walls. Behind them a line of shielded warriors protected the archers who added to the volley of missiles being launched. Raven heard a choking sound from the man on her left. She turned and saw him as he fell backward with an arrow protruding from his mouth.

With Talos covering her head with his shield, Raven and other archers similarly protected managed to find enough targets to cause some of the digging teams to turn back. Others who managed to reach the walls found the surrounding trench a potential death trap for the large, shield-smashing boulders dropped on them. One by one, the diggers abandoned their efforts and returned to their ranks leaving dead and wounded behind. The wounded were quickly dispatched by either arrows or boulders.

The fusillade began to slacken then ceased altogether. There was cheering and jeers along the wall. Raven looked on either side of her; the defenders had sustained casualties. The dead and wounded being carried off the ramparts would be difficult to replace.

"It could have been worse," Talos said. "The weather is clear, and the ground is hard and dry. They might have been more successful by attacking when it was dark. Let's hope it doesn't rain to make their digging easier and our bowstrings useless."

Raven looked up at the clouds forming. "What are our chances?"

Talos started to answer truthfully then decided an optimistic response was better.

"Good. We're better prepared to defend than they are to attack. We're well-provisioned, and I doubt they are. Their strength is intimidating, but it doesn't guarantee victory against a walled settlement such as this. Much will depend on what the Romans do. Galba can't afford to spend too much time here while the Romans are so close. The legions are his primary objective. A victory here may satisfy his revenge against the Remi, but he risks intervention by the Romans." He hoped he sounded convincing. In reality, he wasn't sure they could last until nightfall.

The drums signaled the next assault, and Talos thought they would be lucky to last the morning.

Chapter 12
The Roman Camp

Caesar stood on top of the wall near the northern gate of the nearly completed camp and surveyed the terrain ahead. Crassus was right. The site was well-chosen. An attack across the marsh would result in unacceptable losses for either side trying it. Diviciacus said King Galba was more bluster than clever. If so, he might be foolish enough to take the chance. The fortlet on the right was already completed, and the eight caroballista operators were launching four to six-foot practice bolts. The open ground below the ridge where the six legions would deploy provided ample space for maneuver on both flanks.

He turned to Labienus. “It’s a waiting game. Patience and the excellent terrain Crassus selected would offset Galba’s advantage in numbers.” He eyed the sun about to drop below the hills. “We were fortunate today that Galba didn’t contest our river crossing. Had he, we would not have the advantage of preparing the strong defense we have. He made a mistake by allowing us to cross the river unopposed. If our positions were reversed, I would have destroyed the bridge and defended this side of the river. It would have been costly for us to get across without unacceptable casualties.”

Labienus saw movement in the direction where Bibrax was located a few miles away and recognized a decuria of scouts top a low hill galloping toward General Crassus standing next to his standard. “I think we’re about to hear where and what Galba and Correous are doing.”

Crassus mounted and with the decurion riding beside him, cantered up the slope toward the camp.

“Praise to the gods, the news will confirm we are well-positioned to meet their intentions. If not, the game has newly begun, and we’ll adjust as necessary.”

Crassus reined in and saluted. "Decurion Tarquin has information concerning the Belgae Army."

Caesar looked at Tarquin and nodded an invitation to speak.

"Sir, the Belgae are attacking Bibrax with an estimated force of 50-60 thousand warriors. So far, they seem to be holding. How much longer is questionable."

Caesar smiled. "By seeking revenge on the Remi, Galba's risking unnecessary losses and allowed us to cross the river unimpeded with time to prepare for him. Any losses he suffers improves our odds."

"What about Bibrax? Should we consider helping them?" Crassus asked.

"I'll wait to see how the situation there develops and the extent the Remi can hold out. I've no intention of leaving here and marching in a rescue effort that favors Galba. In the event Iccius asks for help, the Numidian archers and the Belaric slingers are all I'll spare."

Crassus and Labienus understood the Remi along with the Auxilia were about to be sacrificed.

For the first time, Labienus was doubtful the man he so much admired was right. It wasn't so much about the cavalier treatment of the Remi and auxilia infantry. It was about not taking a more aggressive action when the Bellovaci was preoccupied with a siege. Caesar believed staying in a strong defensive position was sound considering the size of the Belgae Army. He was not as convinced. The Belgae had taken the initiative and gained time to increase the size of the confederation. There was one factor that made the difference regardless of what tactics were decided. Many believed Caesar was favored by the gods including most of all Caesar.

Bibrax
Nightfall

The light was fading, and the Belgae lines had pulled far back out of bowshot. Their fires were burning bright, and the festive air of the warriors sitting around them indicated they were confident of the outcome tomorrow.

Raven sat down with her back to the palisade wall and massaged her left arm struck by a ricocheting missile that left it too sore to use the bow with any predictable accuracy. She was too tired to think or care about what daylight would bring. Except for an occasional curse and groan, the men at the walls were silent. The most seriously wounded were being evacuated below. If you were wounded and had the capability to lift a boulder or shield an archer, you stayed on the rampart. She knew the situation was serious and no longer asked Talos about their chances. Here and there, the Belgae had successfully collapsed some of the palisade logs. The damage so far wasn't enough for even a determined assault to take the settlement. The defenders knew time was on the side of the Bellovaci unless the Romans came to improve their odds.

She missed Talos and wondered why he had been summoned by Iccius to join a council of the elders. It didn't seem likely he would be asked to provide insight for improving the defenses. While bright and battle-tested, his experience was in no way close to the elders and those who counseled them. She started to drift off too exhausted think about it. She came wide awake. Had Iccius somehow learned of his association with the Bellovaci? She'd been careful to avoid mentioning Talos when she warned the elder what she learned from the Bellovaci leader.

Talos whispered her name and sat down beside her. "I'm leaving the fort soon. The elders have asked me and several others to contact the Romans for help. Without them, we can't survive another day."

"How will you get past their lines? We're completely surrounded."

"No, we aren't. On the southside there are wide gaps in the ranks where they've gathered together. They're confident and celebrating an easy victory tomorrow. Several of us will make the attempt to reach the Romans. The odds favor at least one of us getting through. It's a shorter distance overland from here to the bridge where the Romans crossed the river than by the road. I know the way very well and should be able to get there in a few hours."

They talked quietly until she fell asleep and was oblivious to the shouting from the Bellovaci ranks.

Talos heard the clamor behind him and knew at least one of them had been discovered. It had been easier than he thought. Rather than trying to snake through the enemy lines, he chose to brazen his way through wearing the wooden headdress and cloak he took from one of the dead attackers killed below the wall. With the dead man's shield hanging from his shoulder, he strolled casually past the campfires. He was stopped by an inebriated warrior who insisted on sharing his wineskin. He was forced to listen and pretend he was impressed by the warrior's bragging and what he intended to do to the women after the fighting. Barely overcoming the impulse to plunge his dagger in the man's throat, he managed to move on with the excuse he had to piss. Once far enough away, he pulled the headdress off his head, discarded the shield and started running. It was going to be a long night.

He crossed the shallow ford southeast of the bridge and headed east along the river bank. Two miles later he smelled horses and saw the dim silhouette of the Roman fort a short distance east of the bridge. He slowed down, apprehensive for how he was going to be received by the guards and cavalrymen near the bridge. His rudimentary Latin presented a greater risk than getting through the Bellovaci lines a few hours before. He called out with what he hoped was clear enough Latin to stop a spear or a charge from the cavalry.

A voice shouted in Aedui, "Come forward and tell us who you are and why you're here."

He breathed a sigh of relief. "My name is Talos. I've come from Bibrax with a message from Iccius, elder tribal leader of the Remi."

"Come forward," someone shouted in Aedui.

Talos started walking to the dismounted cavalrymen. He didn't get far before one of the shadowy figures came running toward him. He stopped and started to pull his dagger, believing he was being attacked. Then with a mix of anger and relief, he recognized Strabo.

"Talos, is Raven all right?"

"She was when I left her a short time ago. Iccius, senior elder of the Remi, sent me here with a message for Caesar requesting help. If we don't get it, the settlement will not survive another day."

The two men reached the bridge, and Strabo pointed to a saddled horse.

"Mount up. I'll take you to General Crassus, commander of the Auxilia; He's been tasked by Caesar to provide assistance to Bibrax if it was requested."

With Strabo in the lead, the two men cantered over the wooden bridge and up the long slope of a low ridge. A mile later they reached the southwest gate of the huge Roman camp. After a brief conversation with a man wearing a cuirass and crested helmet, they were waived on. At a trot, Strabo headed to a large tent in the center of the camp.

Strabo and Talos dismounted. "This is Caesar's headquarters. General Crassus and the other generals will be here for the evening council."

Talos watched as Strabo saluted and talked to a guard who shook his head emphatically. Strabo spoke again, and the guard finally nodded, disappeared into the tent and returned with a man not much older than Strabo. Talos didn't think the individual's frown was a good sign.

"General, his name is Talos. He's an Aeduan scout. He came from Bibrax and has a message from Iccius.

"Talos, this is General Crassus. Tell him what you know about what's happening in Bibrax. I'll translate as you speak."

"Iccius sends greetings to his Roman friends and tells of the grave conditions the Remi are suffering. The Bellovaci and Suessiones attacked Bibrax at first light this morning on all sides. We believe he has an army of over 70 thousand warriors. We've suffered many casualties and our walls have been partially breached in several places. Iccius doesn't think we can hold much longer unless we are reinforced by early tomorrow morning. When I left the settlement a few hours ago, all was quiet and no attack seems imminent. The Bellovaci are confident and are already celebrating the victory they are certain of tomorrow."

"Ask him how he managed to get through their lines."

"Talos says he dressed like the attackers and walked through their lines."

"Amazing. Is he able to guide the reinforcements we'll send?"

"He can lead them back the way he came. It's shorter by several miles than the road from here to the settlement and isn't guarded as the road is. The route he came is not good for horses. Reinforcements will have to go on foot."

"Marcellus, Caesar will send the Numidian and Cretan archers and the Balearic slingers."

Strabo tried not to show his surprise and concern when he responded. "General, seven or eight thousand men is not enough to make a difference against so many."

"It will have to do. That's all Caesar will spare. Don't forget, we're badly outnumbered here as well. Caesar is encouraging an attack here to avoid an open battle we might not be able to win. Ask him where the reinforcements should assemble."

"Talos says it's best to gather on the east side of the river near the bridge. He'll take them west on that side of the river to a ford two miles away. From there, it's another three miles to the settlement. The forest is not thick, and if they leave without delay, they can be at the settlement well before dawn."

After Strabo finished translating, Crassus said, "Centurion Drusus will command the reinforcements. He knows the commanders of all three contingents. I want you to accompany him since you're the one who can communicate with the guide. Go to the bridge and wait for him. You won't have to wait long. The archers and slingers have been on alert in the probability Bibrax would have to be reinforced."

Correous leaned back with a self-satisfied smile, belched and said to Galba, "It went well today as I expected it would. The men deserve to celebrate the victory certain to be ours tomorrow."

"The victory should have been achieved by now. You underestimated Iccius and the will of the Remi to resist. We've wasted enough time here. We'll leave this place at first light and attack the Romans. My scouts report they've had time to construct a large fort near the bridge."

"We'll leave after I'm finished here," Correous responded with a flash of anger. "Let me remind you, it was your wish to burn Bibrax to the ground *before* attacking the Romans which I wanted to do. Tomorrow you get what you wanted. After that I get to kill Romans."

Galba restrained himself, the son of a bitch was right. He depended on the Bellovaci more than Correous needed him. He replied with a conciliatory smile.

"You're right. I wanted to make Iccius pay. I do not mean to question what we achieved here today. You planned and executed the attack very well, and the victory here is yours by right to claim. I'm merely in a hurry to fight the Romans. What you accomplished here today is what I wanted for the Remi."

Mollified, Correous relaxed. "I think you'll get what you want when you see the heads of the Remi elders on pikes and the burning ruins of the settlement."

Galba was speechless. He wanted to make an example by burning the settlement, but heads on a pike? That was not at all what he wanted. He needed the Remi in the confederation, and the destruction of Bibrax was the means to convince Iccius to reconsider his decision.

"Tomorrow I'll offer Iccius a chance to surrender and join the confederation as an alternative to what you have in mind. I'm ready to accept a lesson has been well and truly taught. Our efforts are better spent uniting against a common foe."

Correous yawned. "I'll give you enough time to ask Iccius and for him to tell you to piss-off then I'll finish what I came here to do."

Strabo was impressed by the way Talos, using a hastily drawn sketch in the dirt, explained to Drusus and the three Auxilia leaders where they were going, the final approach to the settlement and location of the hostile tribes. He went on to offer suggestions for the pre-dawn assault. Strabo was then equally surprised and pleased Drusus accepted the recommendations causing him to moderate his opinion of the two men for the better. The slingers spread out between the archers. They were close enough behind the Belgae lines to hear the quiet murmur of men preparing for the assault on the settlement and unaware their plans were about to change.

Drusus gave the signal as the sun was about to come up. Strabo regretted the smaller, round cavalry shield he had instead of the larger rectangular scuta he carried as a legionnaire. He regretted not having a shorter gladius better suited for close contact on the ground than the long spatha he carried.

The long, drawn-out notes of the ram's horn stopped and scores of Belgae warriors were down by either arrow or stone. The rest were in a state of pandemonium. Warriors fled mindlessly away from the deadly onslaught creating additional panic with those who were not immediately threatened. The din aroused the settlement defenders who added to the confusion.

Drusus ordered the advance, and both archers and slingers moved forward pressing the devastating surprise attack. Strabo heard cries of jubilation from the settlement walls as the nearest gate opened, and a throng rushed out with sword and shield to join the battle.

Unlike the organized relentless advance of legionary ranks he was used to, the slingers and archers avoided close contact with the Belgae who were starting to slow their withdrawal and turn on their attackers. Strabo soon found he was alone when the auxilia archers and slingers were quick to fall back. He was as vulnerable from the missiles being launched behind him as the Belgae warriors were focusing on him.

Three warriors converged on him at once. He felt the swish of an arrow passing by his left ear then saw it catch the leading Belgae warrior in the face. The odds had narrowed somewhat, and he concentrated on the remaining two running toward him. The larger of the two wielding an axe reached him first with more zeal than experience. His momentum and size were his undoing. Before the two collided, Strabo ducked down with a knee on the ground, shield upraised, and the unsuspecting warrior tumbled over him to land on his back exposed to the spatha that sliced across his neck. Strabo stepped back in time to avoid a killing slash to his head by the remaining warrior. The warrior recovered and renewed the attack. The light shield splintered leaving him dangerously exposed. He dropped the useless shield and drew his pugio with his left hand. The warrior's confident smile widened. The two men stepped toward each other at the same time. Strabo feinted with his sword, and the warrior casually moved his shield to stop it. The move was enough to leave his left side open for the dagger Strabo thrust deep into the warrior's side. The wounded man took a step back. His smile was replaced by shocked surprise. He dropped the shield and clutched the dagger's hilt in a vain attempt to pull it out. Strabo swung the spatha in an arc that sent the warrior's head tumbling to the ground even before his body had finished voiding. With a quick promise for sacrifice to Epona, he retrieved his pugio, picked up the warrior's shield and moved on after the panic-stricken Belgae running for their lives.

A mile north of the settlement, Drusus halted the advance and formed a defensive perimeter against a counterattack. Winded and tired, Strabo was grateful the Belgae didn't look as if they were going to stop.

Correous was furious, and Galba was relieved they were headed for the Roman camp even though the way they left Bibrax was closer to being a rout than an orderly withdrawal. It had taken too much time and wine to get Correous to agree to lift the siege and be satisfied with what they'd accomplished. Galba thought the porcine-featured tribal leader had himself to blame. His warriors had not met his expectations in comparison to his Suessiones. He hoped Correous and his warriors would be more resolute with the Romans. They had to fight the Romans before Correous learned the Aedui were on the march. If the scouts were right, Diviciacus was headed to the lands of the Bellovaci. Once Correous learned of the threat behind him, collective resistance to the Roman offensive would collapse. Galba had an uneasy feeling events over the next few days weren't going to favor the Belgae.

Strabo saw Talos with several others on horseback ride out of the settlement and head toward him. The Aeduan scout reined in at a trot as he passed by.

"We're going to see where they're going, or if they intend to counterattack."

Strabo nodded and continued walking to the settlement to see about Raven. He hadn't gone far when Drusus hailed him.

"Come with me." He saw Strabo's bloodied left arm and said with dry humor, "Well, I can see you weren't standing by and watching. I also see you seem to have acquired a new shield in the process."

"If I'd been thinking clearly, I would have stayed back and watched. The next time I fight, I want either to be on a horse or a legionnaire on foot with weapons and a shield suitable for the occasion."

Drusus laughed. "I'm looking for Iccius. Before we leave, I want to be sure we're finished with what we came here to do and confirm there's no probability of a counterattack. I'm going to encourage him to send out scouts to find out what the Belgae are doing and if there's any indication they'll return."

Strabo thumbed back in the direction Talos rode. "Those are the scouts Iccius sent to find where the Belgae are going and see if Galba has any intention to come back." After Drusus gave a non-committal nod, he asked, "Sir, how long are we going to be here?"

"Until Iccius and I are confident the Belgae aren't coming back. The men can rest for a couple of hours before we leave. I want to get back to the encampment as soon as we can in case the Belgae get their courage up and attack the legions."

The two men walked in silence until Strabo said, "The men fought well. I didn't think we would be successful. I thought at best we would force them back long enough to get inside the settlement and strengthen the Remi defense."

"I agree. It has me wondering if Galba may have attacked Bibrax less for punishing the Remi than attempting to draw Caesar to a place better suited to him than where the legions are now positioned. That would explain why Caesar sent less reinforcements than warranted."

The two men neared the settlement and saw the dead Belgae directly beneath the walls and the amount of damage to the palisades, silent and grim testimony to how close the settlement came to falling.

Strabo's concern for Raven mounted with each step he took closer to the nearest gate. He found himself murmuring a prayer to Epona in Aedui causing Drusus to look at him quizzically. Strabo noticed the centurion's expression and was both discomfited and irritated at the silent question he didn't want to answer. He resented the time he was going to spend with Iccius and Drusus, time he preferred looking for Raven. He remained silent and walked on without saying a word prompting Drusus to speak.

"What's wrong? This should be a moment to rejoice for our success."

Strabo silently cursed and accepted he had no choice except to answer the question. "There's someone here I know, and I'm concerned about her welfare."

"It sounds to me as though she's someone more than just a friend. After we find out what Iccius wants from us, you'll have time to look for her. Iccius might want to have someone stay here in case the Belgae return. If so, you can stay for a day or two to coordinate any assistance he needs." The supportive offer made him regret his initial reaction.

"She's someone I've known for a long time. Since my return to Gaul, she's become more than a childhood friend. I thank you for the offer. I would be willing to remain if there's a valid reason for it and not as a pretext to serve a personal concern. If the Belgae are likely moving toward the legions, we can't delay here any longer than necessary."

"Well said like a true Roman. I'll tell Iccius we'll leave here as soon as we're certain the Belgae aren't coming back."

The centurion's reference to a *true Roman* made him wonder if he was. He didn't think so or even that he wanted to be. The thought caused him to consider if the same was true about his Aeduan heritage.

Drusus noticed Strabo's puzzled expression. "What's troubling you?"

"Nothing that has anything to do with what happened here. It's a matter for another time and place to resolve, and I'm in no hurry to get there. Perhaps, I never will."

It didn't take long to find Iccius and gain immediate agreement for a quick departure. "Please convey my deep appreciation to Caesar for his timely response without which we would be at the mercy of King Galba."

"I'm going to allow a few hours of rest before we leave. The night was long for us. Certainly not as long as it was for those here in the settlement."

After a few conventional exchanges, Drusus and Strabo left Iccius to deal with the aftermath of the attack.

Before they parted Drusus said, "I hope you find she survived the ordeal. Listen for the signal to assemble. We'll go back the way we came and avoid the chance of running into the Bellovaci."

Strabo gratefully hurried off to find Leuca, the woman Corius had identified as Raven's cousin. Unfortunately, the name was common, and his search was taking longer than he anticipated. He saw Talos ride through the western gate and wondered if he knew where she was or even would tell him. The unfriendly expression on the scout's face wasn't encouraging.

"I'm looking for Raven. Corius told me she came here to visit a cousin by the name of Leuca. So far, I've found three women with that name. None of them have heard of her. Can you help me?"

"She doesn't live with Leuca anymore. She has her own place."

"Will you take me there?" Strabo saw the hesitation and added, "I don't have much time. We're leaving once the men have rested a few hours."

Talos's inclination was to refuse in part for his dislike of Strabo and the slight chance Raven would change and regard him as more than a friend. Reluctantly, he had to accept friendship was all she had for him. It was petty to deny Strabo the chance to see her.

"Come with me. I'll show you where she lives."

After a short and silent walk, Talos stopped in front of a small dwelling close to the settlement walls and the ramp that led to the ramparts.

"She lives here." Strabo started to enter the doorway. Talos stopped him. "If you harm her in any way, I'll kill you."

Strabo looked at Talos in astonishment. "Why would I possibly want to harm her?"

Neither man was aware Raven was standing in the doorway until she spoke.

"Because I'm with child, and he's worried you may believe the child is his or someone else is the father."

Strabo froze before slowly turning toward her. She appeared calm until he saw her eyes welling. A moment later without a word spoken, they were in each other's arms and unaware that Talos had gone.

Inside lying together on her bed, Raven said, "I should have told you the last time we were together in Bibracte, but I was afraid to."

"Afraid of what?"

"In part for the reason I already said. You wouldn't believe you're the father." She hesitated, uncertain how to explain her greatest fear.

"That's not all, is it?"

When she finished, he remained silent thinking about her concerns for the child's future and Gaul under the domination of Rome, concerns not too different from his own.

"Raven, the difference between us is I believe Gaul will be better served under Rome than by the Belgae or Germani. My belief is why I remain in the Roman Army. The day could come I'll change my mind. I've experienced what you haven't. Life under the Romans is benign and–"

She interrupted sharply. "True if you're a Roman. The Romans look down on us. To them we are primitive people who become civilized after being conquered and living, dressing and speaking Latin like a Roman."

He accepted there was some truth to what she said.

"Let's not debate the point in the short time I have. Under the circumstances, there are other important things to consider. Are you going to remain here or go back to Bibracte after you give birth?"

"I haven't decided. Here I have Leuca who can help me. I don't have any women friends in Bibracte."

"Good," he patted her arm and felt her flinch. "What's the matter?"

"I hurt my arm."

"What happened? How bad is it?"

"It's nothing. It will soon heal."

He knew why she didn't answer the first question. "You were on the walls."

"And so were many others who shouldn't have been. Our situation was desperate, and my skill as an archer was needed."

"I should have expected you would be. In fact, I'm proud you were doing your part. If I had I been here, I wouldn't have let..."

"And I would have gone anyway. I'm not a wife obliged to obey a husband's every command." She added in a softer voice, "Nor will I ever be a wife again."

Her last comment was pointed and not surprising. It gave him a sense of relief in resolving a matter he had thought about without knowing what to do about it.

"It wasn't until my father had me conscripted against my will that I understood the value of choice. Your answer might have been different had I chosen to leave the Roman Army after being given the opportunity. I'm staying because I believe it serves the Aedui as well as the Romans. One day, I may choose to leave the army, and when I do, I want it to be *my choice* and not one made by someone else. If I believe this, how can I fault you for believing and doing what you want? Our child will be registered as a Roman citizen. It will be his or her right to choose whether to live as a Roman, an Aedui, or both as I do."

Her silence became prolonged. He wondered if he had clouded rather than clarified his feelings and his understanding of her choice to be independent.

She reflected on what he said. For the first time since he came back into her life, she felt at peace. It explained everything without the need to resolve anything.

Strabo wondered about her silence expecting she would have something to say, a rebuttal, denial, rejection. She said nothing. Mystified, he sought to clarify and simplify how their future together would be and decided to risk a question the answer to which he already feared.

"Since it seems we will not be hand-fasted, does that mean I will no longer be welcome in your bed?" He was surprised after a brief silence she started shaking. She giggled followed by laughter eventually subsiding to hiccups. He was at a loss what to say and irritated over her reaction.

She eventually regained control. "I'm sorry, it's that you managed to bring serious matters back to a simple and practical level." He started to protest, and she covered his mouth. "Of course, you will always be welcome and without the conventional ceremony and public approval, which I care nothing about."

He relaxed and ventured, "Are you, can you...?"

"Are you asking me to undress? If so, the answer is yes. I'm not so far along ..." The raucous sound of a ram's horn intruded.

"Shit." Strabo muttered. "I have to go. That's the signal to muster." His resigned acceptance caused her to laugh again which proved infectious.

"Before you go, I'll bandage your shoulder."

"It's nothing."

"It's nothing until it begins to fester." She got up and told him to do the same. In the light of the oil lamp, she made a cursory examination. "You're right, it isn't much. It needs washing and a proper bandage."

Despite her making light of the wound, she prolonged her ministrations until he finally said, "Raven, I have to go. Tie it up, or else I'll have to run to catch up."

"Why do you have to leave at all? Stay here with me."

"I wish I could, but I have to do what I think is right. Whether I'm Roman or Aeduan doesn't matter. At the moment, I'm defending my mother's heritage as much as my father's."

They parted both as lovers and friends willing to accept each other as they are with possibilities neither one of them had envisioned a few hours before.

Talos saw Raven's serene smile as she watched Strabo disappear through the settlement gate.

He approached her with genuine concern. "Are you all right?"

"Of course, why do you ask?"

He fumbled for a response, undecided what to say. "About the child, is he convinced it's his?"

"Yes."

"What will you...," he stopped, wondering if he had the right to be concerned about her well-being. He wished he was somewhere else.

She looked at him and realized she'd never comprehended the depth of his feelings for her.

"I'm sorry," she said in a low voice, "I didn't ..." she stopped when he held up his hand.

"I assumed too much and wished for more. What will you do?"

"Marcellus said he wanted the right to choose who he is and the time to find the answer. It's an answer I can better understand now because I feel the same."

Chapter 13

From the north wall of the Roman camp, Caesar and Labienus stood apart from the other generals watching the Belgae army beginning to appear on the higher hills on the other side the marsh. There were no recognizable formations. It was more a human tide resembling a swarm of ants with less organization. The warriors began to spread out across the lower slope of the nearest hill in multiple ranks.

Labienus saw the calm expression on Caesar's face and wondered if he had any qualms about the fate of Bibrax and the relief force that may no longer exist. He broke the silence.

"The appearance of the Belgae and the absence of our archers and slingers does not bode well for Bibrax or them."

"It's early in the day to assume the worst. If we haven't seen or heard from Centurion Drusus by early afternoon, I'll share your concern for the outcome. Until then I remain optimistic."

"Will we form the legions outside and invite battle tomorrow?"

"No. We'll remain in the fort. I'm depending on what Diviciacus said about the possibility Galba's confederation is not a cohesive, reliable force. Galba may be worried his confederation won't hold together. If so, time is not on his side. I'm willing to wait and see what he'll do. If Galba believes we're afraid to leave the fort, it could prompt him to make the mistake of attacking through the marsh."

Shouts from the west wall caused them to turn and look for the reason. Caesar relaxed when he recognized Centurion Drusus and the relief force crossing the bridge.

"Titus, Drusus either did better than I could have hoped, or Galba decided Bibrax had been punished enough. Send word to General Crassus I want to see him and Drusus."

Caesar looked expectantly at General Crassus and Centurion Drusus. "I presume Bibrax has been spared at least total destruction."

"I'm happy to confirm as much as I do the thanks Iccius asked me to convey to you for sending us. Iccius was right to call for reinforcements. They couldn't have held out much longer. We launched our attack as they were assembling for their next assault. On reflection, I'm not certain it was in preparation for an attack as it was for a departure. The reason I say that is the way they left the field. I wish I could believe it was entirely because of our unsuspected arrival and the ferocity of our attack, but I have doubts. There was light enough to assess our numbers. A competent leader would have rallied his army against an obviously smaller force."

Caesar nodded. "Interesting observation. What do you conclude from this?"

"Galba decided enough time had been invested at Bibrax to make a point. It was time to move against the legions here without wasting time and warriors there. Iccius gave Galba losses he didn't expect. The way they left the field in panic suggests his army is more rabble than an organized foe."

"What are your thoughts, Titus?"

"Thus far, there's been much reported about the Belgae tribes coming together along with various Germani tribes to fight us. Some of the reports indicate reluctance based on what happened to the Helvetii and the Suebi. Galba's numbers may be real, but his confidence he can keep it together might be his paramount concern."

"A fair assessment and further confirmation of my intention to let Galba make the first move. He needs a decisive victory to keep the tribes he has and an inducement for the other Belgae tribes waiting to see if he's successful. The Germani may be of similar mind. Time is our ally. Here's what we will do. Publius, tomorrow your slingers and archers will have a well-earned rest. In the meantime, we need to see what the cavalry can find out about their intentions. A prisoner or two might be helpful to learn what happened at Bibrax and their current morale. I want the legionary cavalry to scout to the east. Publius, concentrate in the area west of the encampment."

Crassus stood up to leave. "I commend both Centurion Drusus for his command of the relief force and Decurion Strabo for providing the means for him to successfully accomplish the mission."

"Just so, Publius. Centurion, General Crassus has spoken of your capabilities on past occasions, and I believe the action at Bibrax is further confirmation you have ability I can depend on. You've earned more than my appreciation. I've approved a phelora for your superior performance while in command during a major action. Otho, ensure the commendation for Centurion Drusus is entered into the record."

General Labienus said to General Crassus. "It's time for Strabo and his decuria to return to the legion. Enough time has passed since Visontio to cool hot tempers.

"Of course, I'll see to it immediately. Decurion Strabo will be missed. He has served me extremely well these past several months."

The Belgae campfires flickered over a near eight-mile expanse across the low mountains opposite the camp. The sheer number of fires was intimidating, and the usual sound of almost 40,000 legionnaires preparing for the night was muted. The battle in the Vosges mountains months ago was the last time the legions fought. The veterans were ready and fatalistic; Strabo knew most of the legionnaires in the two newly arrived legions would not sleep tonight.

Strabo found Ursinus rounding up the horses in the penned enclosure outside the main camp in preparation for bringing them into the camp. He saw Aquilo and wondered if the horse had missed him while he was gone. He was worn out, and the idea of a horse thinking was a testament of how tired he was.

"Sir, I was beginning to wonder what had happened to you." Ursinus noticed Strabo's bandaged shoulder, frowned and added, "It looks as if one of them got past your shield. How bad is it?"

"It's sore but not worth talking about. As of a few minutes ago, we're no longer with the Auxilia. We're back with Tarquin and the Tenth. General Labienus probably thinks I've been punished enough. I'm too tired to care one way or the other. I need sleep. Tomorrow we're going to be busy. While the legions sit on their ass inside the camp, the legionary cavalry will be out to get prisoners and try to goose the Belgae into a fight. Let's find Tarquin and give him the good news we're back."

Strabo grabbed Aquilo's halter and was pleasantly surprised when the fractious horse nickered and gave him a friendly nudge. He looked at Ursinus. "Today I think I realized given the choice, I'd rather be on a horse in a fight than on foot. At least on a horse if things go bad, you've got a better and faster way to get somewhere else."

He remembered his promise to Epona that morning for a sacrifice. Perhaps he could find a priest who'd be satisfied with something small, maybe a chicken. The legions were almost a month overdue to get paid, and the cost of a pig required an alternative. He was glad he was only thinking so Epona wouldn't get the impression his faith in the celestials tended to be in proportion to how deep the shit was.

The sun was nearly full coming over the mountains when the two turmae from the Eleventh and Twelfth Legions leisurely walked their horses out of the southwest gate.

Decurion Tarquin shook his head. "Jupiter's golden balls," he muttered to Strabo and Costa standing next to him. "So much for getting started at first light. We might as well have had the drums and cornicines here to give us a send-off so the Belgae bastards can see which way we're going. Marcellus, are there any fords in the river northeast of the bridge? If there are, can you find them?"

"Yes, there are two I know of, possibly others we didn't find. The first one is at least four miles from here, and the second one is farther."

"Good. We're late, and I'm changing the plan." He saw Quintus Servius and gave Strabo a sharp look. "Take care you keep your distance from Servius and your mind on what we're going to do."

"I will although I can't speak for him."

"The one who starts anything will answer to me first and Caesar afterward." Tarquin beckoned to the six decurions from the two legions to come to him.

Strabo noted the humorless smile on Servius's face as the decurion pointed an upright thumb to his throat, the *pollice verso*, sign of death for defeated gladiators in the arena. He responded with a wide-eyed grin and an extended thumb and forefinger.

Tarquin cleared his throat. "We're starting later than I expected; therefore, we're going a different route than I planned. Instead of staying on this side of the river, we'll cross the bridge and follow it northeast. We'll cross the first ford we come to come back to this side. Decurion Strabo has scouted the river before and knows where two of the fords are.

"Our mission is to scout the left flank of the Belgae Army to learn what we can about them and the terrain they occupy. Within reason, we'll attempt to get them to engage. Caesar wants to see how eager the Belgae are to fight and how well they do. At Bibrax yesterday, the Belgae left the field with the odds in their favor which raises questions why. Finally, if we do find some Belgae to fight, kill as many as you can but spare one or two. Caesar wants to find out about their intentions and strength. I'll lead, Servius, you'll follow me, and Livius you take the rear. If we form for battle, my troop will take center. Servius, you'll form on my left flank. Livius, you take position on my right. Questions, complaints?" After no one spoke, he gave the order to mount up.

Not long after, the three troops clattered across the bridge to the accompaniment of jeers from the fort for heading away from where a battle could occur at any time. A mile later, Tarquin turned farther northeast and motioned for the outriders ahead and on both flanks to move out and screen the advance. The trees and foliage along the river provided ample cover to conceal their progress as they moved along at a canter to preserve the horses for what was likely going to be a long day.

Strabo guided Aquilo closer to Ursinus and said, "I think I recall where the fords are. I'm counting on your eyes if I don't."

Several miles later, Strabo saw a lightning-struck tree and recognized it was close to the path leading to the first ford. Pointing to the tree, he said to Tarquin, "The trail leading to the first ford is by the dead tree over there. I recommend holding here until I make certain. If it is, I'll check to see if the river is fordable and secure."

Tarquin agreed and Strabo led the troop to the tree. Before they reached it, he was certain this was the path leading to the ford.

"Ursinus, the path was barely recognizable and not well-traveled the last time we were here." He took a closer look at the numerous hoof prints going in the direction they were. "The prints are fresh."

Ursinus nodded in agreement. "At least 50 horses, maybe more. The way the grass is starting to come back up, I'd say within the past couple of hours."

Soon after easily fording the river, the decuria followed the trail to an intersection with a road that curved from the northeast to the southwest in the direction of the bridge they had crossed an hour ago. The trail they were following turned in the direction of the bridge.

Strabo beckoned to Vinicius. "Ride back to Decurion Tarquin and report the ford is secure and about 50 horses crossed within the past few hours. Tell him we're following a probable Belgae reconnaissance patrol heading southeast toward the bridge. The decuria will continue to scout in the vicinity of the intersection while awaiting his arrival or order to return." Strabo then said to Ursinus, "I'll take Paulus and ride a mile or two toward the bridge. Send Mercea in the other direction. Remain here with the rest." Strabo saw the frown on Ursinus's face. "You have a better idea?"

"It would be better if I go toward the settlement, and you remain here to wait for Decurion Tarquin."

Strabo considered what the cavalryman said and reluctantly accepted Ursinus was right. He still had much to learn.

"Very well, I'll remain here."

Mercea was the first to return and reported no sign of any Belgae activity in that direction. Strabo heard the faint hoof beats of the three turmae nearing the intersection from the south. His attention was drawn to the louder sound of galloping horses from the direction of the bridge. He kneed Aquilo out of the trees and saw Ursinus and Paulus riding toward him with several mounted warriors close behind and closing fast. He drew his spatha and called the six other cavalrymen to join him. As soon as the three warriors saw the seven cavalrymen fanned across the road, they drew rein and galloped back the way they came.

Ursinus reined in next to Strabo. "Sir, about two miles from here we saw a dismounted cavalry force of at least 100, could be more."

Strabo saw the forest ahead and frowned. "They're likely in there." He pointed south to a low hill. "That's where we should fight them. There are no trees, and they'll have to attack uphill. We'll go there and wait for Tarquin to agree or decide something else."

Ursinus smiled and nodded in approval a few minutes later after Tarquin led the three turmae to the higher ground Strabo pointed out. He thought the young decurion was learning fast.

The three turmae formed across the slope in three ranks facing south toward the ford and two miles northeast of the Roman camp. Tarquin gave the order for the first rank to dismount. The Tenth turma was in the center flanked by the Eleventh on the left and the Twelfth turma on the right. The size of the Belgae cavalry they were about to fight was unnerving and dampened the usual undercurrent of humorous, often dark banter normally heard before an engagement.

As the junior decurion in the troop, Strabo was in the third rank. He glanced to his left and saw Servius facing his turma and talking to his troop. He was too far away to understand what he was saying. The older decurion was smiling, and whatever he said caused the cavalrymen to smile and raise their swords in response. He envied and admired the decurion's way of projecting a confidence he wasn't sure he shared as much or was able to convey as convincingly. Before turning to face down-slope, Servius saw Strabo looking at him. The decurion smiled and lifted his spear in a casual salute. Strabo recalled the *pollice verso* sign the decurion signaled less than two hours ago and wondered if he had more to deal with in the forthcoming battle than the Belgae.

There was a flicker of movement at the edge of the distant tree line ahead and several horsemen appeared. There was no sign the scouts had seen the Romans as they continued on. The main body of Belgae cavalry came into sight, and it, too, was oblivious of the three troops watching them. By the time the last of the Belgae cavalry left the trees, it was obvious the earlier estimated strength was three times as much.

Strabo closed his eyes and prayed the Belgae would keep on riding. He hoped if they did, Tarquin would order their return across the ford to wait for another opportunity with more reasonable odds. Aquilo's ears pointed forward, and he stamped the ground with his right hoof, all signs the gray stallion anticipated a fight he didn't. Apparently, Tarquin felt the same as the stallion by beating his spear shaft against the shield, an audible invitation to battle. The beat was picked up by the cavalrymen behind him. Trying to look enthusiastic, he joined in.

The rhythmic sound finally reached the Belgae cavalry. The result was surprise and confusion. Strabo heard the faint sound of trumpets, audible indication the legionnaires were watching.

Tarquin stopped and faced the three Turmae. "I think we got their attention. The bastards think because they have the numbers, they're going to own the field." Tarquin gestured in the direction of the Roman camp. "In case you haven't noticed, the legions are watching what happens here; let's make certain we give them something to cheer and for us to brag about afterward.

"This is what we're going to do. First rank, when they come in range, pick your target and launch a spear on my signal then mount and take up your shield. Second and third ranks, be quick and do the same. When they're halfway up the hill we close ranks and charge. Use your charging spear for the first contact then draw your sword. For Rome and Caesar!"

Strabo felt the familiar adrenaline rush before a battle accompanied by an urgent need to dismount and piss, a shared distress along the ranks, each wondering if he would soon kneel before the gods. He looked to his left and saw Vinicius looking uncharacteristically calm and intent. He had misjudged his companion from Massilia. His friend was adapting to the harsh life in the legions better than he would have supposed. He did, too, much to his surprise. It wasn't long ago all he wanted was a fast horse under him or a winsome, willing woman. He patted Aquilo, smiled and amended the thought. He had both.

The distant sound of a horn blew, and the Belgae cavalry led by a long-haired, bare-chested warrior on a white horse leading a disorganized swarm galloped toward the disciplined Roman ranks. Surprisingly, a considerable number of warriors remained behind. Tarquin gave the order, and the first rank launched their spears with deadly accuracy. The warrior on the white horse was the first casualty. The impetus of the Belgae charge faltered as falling warriors and wounded horses impeded the progress of those behind. With lowered spears, the disciplined Roman cavalry smashed into the Belgae ranks and caused further disarray.

Strabo guided Aquilo toward a warrior brandishing a long-handled axe riding a smaller shaggy-coated horse. He saw the warrior's fierce expression turn to alarm as he saw the large gray stallion bearing down on him. The downhill momentum coupled with the stallion's size overturned the horse and rider as well as the mounted warrior behind him. A warrior adjacent to the fallen horses turned aside to avoid the collision and became an easy target for Strabo's spear that struck him in the chest. Strabo dropped the splintered shaft and drew his spatha in time to stop a plunging sword meant to split his head in two. The warrior made the mistake of raising his arm for another attempt and exposed his neck long enough for Strabo's spatha to end his life in a spray of blood.

He felt something hit his left shoulder and warm liquid splashing on his neck. He glanced left and saw a headless warrior beside him fall from his horse still clutching a sword. Servius passed him and said with a cold smile, "You ought to be careful or you could end up like him."

Considering the decurion had probably saved his life, Strabo was going to thank him. Servius rode on before he could say anything. His attention was immediately drawn to the two warriors coming toward him. The warrior on the right armed with a spear was the immediate threat over the one on the left with a sword. He pulled Aquilo sharply right and concentrated on him. Strabo avoided the spear by twisting aside. The warrior was momentarily exposed and unable to miss Strabo's slicing stroke across his back. The warrior rode on, and Strabo turned his attention to the swordsman. He used his shield to blunt the warrior's downward thrust and buried his own deep into the warrior's exposed upper arm. The warrior dropped his sword and clutching the nearly severed limb, fled the battlefield.

A warrior with his back to him exchanging sword blows with Vinicius never saw the blade that decapitated him. Strabo turned sharply and caught another warrior unprepared on his shield side. Distracted, the warrior looked away from Ursinus and died for his mistake. The cavalryman nodded his thanks and pulled his sword from the warrior's chest.

Strabo felt a sudden tug and on his left side and looked down at a spear shaft lodged between his chain mail armor and his *submaralis,* the padded tunic providing both additional protection and chafing from the ringed cuirass. He turned Aquilo to the right, pulling the spear shaft from the warrior's hand. The Belgae warrior reached back, fumbling for the sword sheathed on his back. Strabo raised his sword for a killing blow, and the man froze, eyes wide in fatalistic acceptance he was about to die. Strabo hesitated, lowered his sword and prodded the warrior in the chest.

"Get off your horse and live as my prisoner or die on your horse."

"You'll kill me anyway. Why should I trust you?"

Strabo lowered his sword and nodded. "No reason you should although my mother was Aeduan and that may make a difference in trusting me. If you answer my questions, you'll have a better chance of living."

The warrior dismounted and said with undisguised contempt, "The Aedui are dogs kneeling at the Roman knee and ready to shit whenever they tell you."

Strabo winced and considered from the prisoner's point of view the comment was probably too close to being true. He looked around and saw the battle was over. For every Roman cavalryman lying motionless on the field or wounded, there were ten times the number of Belgae. Most of the surviving Belgae were fleeing back where they launched the attack. A smaller number headed north toward the Belgae encampment.

Ursinus rode up next to Strabo shaking his head. "We have two injured in the decuria, and they're minor. In all my years, I never saw anything like this. Before they attacked, I wasn't sure any of us would survive to tell what happened here."

Tarquin joined them with the rest of the turma. Three cavalrymen were draped over their saddles, a few others were nursing various cuts and bruises. "It looks to me most of them were in their first battle. They didn't want this fight."

Strabo dismounted. "Maybe I can find out why from him," indicating the prisoner sitting dejected on the ground.

"What's your name?"

"Sagomaros."

"Are you Suessiones or Bellovaci?"

The prisoner slumped and with a resigned expression replied, "I'm Suessiones."

"Were you with the Bellovaci when they attacked the Remi settlement?"

"No, the Suessiones are close to the Remi. My wife is Remi. Most of us did not want to join the Bellovaci."

"But your king is allied with the Bellovaci?"

Sagomaros frowned, turned aside and spat. "He calls himself king because the Suebi and other Germani tribes do as well. There are many like me who call him other things."

"I was there yesterday and saw the Bellovaci running from the Remi settlement. They could have easily taken it. Why didn't they?"

"I'm told the Remi fought harder than expected. Galba persuaded Correous to lift the siege after learning the Aedui were moving toward the Bellovaci settlements. He was concerned if Correous found out, he'd turn away from the Romans and fight the Aedui."

"What about today? Your warriors had far greater numbers, yet you fought poorly — the outcome should have been in your favor."

The prisoner looked down and slowly shook his head. "Most of us didn't want to be here. We were told many Germani tribes pledged to join Galba. They haven't come. We no longer believe they will because of what the Romans did to the Helvetii and to King Ariovistus of the Suebi. Other Belgae tribes are choosing to remain within their domains hoping the Romans will not venture into them and leaving us to face the legions alone. You Romans are an army of soldiers, and we fear you. We are mostly farmers who fight when our borders are crossed without permission or if another tribe raids for livestock and slaves."

Strabo looked at Tarquin and summarized what the prisoner said. "I think he's being truthful, and it explains what happened yesterday and today. The coalition Galba expected to form doesn't seem as if it has happened."

Tarquin nodded. "Caesar needs to hear this. I've ordered Servius to take the dead and escort the wounded and prisoners back to the fort. Take your prisoner to Servius and tell him what you learned so he can inform General Labienus."

"I gather you intend to continue on the patrol with the rest of us."

"Of course. Our casualties are comparatively light, and my orders were to investigate the Belgae left flank which we have yet to do. What happened here might have been the end of us; instead, it turned out to be a skirmish. I want to find out why we survived, and they fled. Your prisoner has probably told us, but I want confirmation. We'll leave as soon as we've accounted for everyone."

Strabo led the prisoner to where Servius was organizing the detail for the return to camp. The decurion listened impassively to the summary of what the Belgae warrior said, nodded in dismissal and started to turn away.

Strabo stopped him by saying, "Servius, I owe you my thanks for what you did. Otherwise, I probably wouldn't be alive. I'm in your debt."

The decurion regarded Strabo without expression, "You owe me nothing. I didn't want some Belgae son of a bitch depriving me of what I intend to do to you. One day you and I will have a reckoning, and it will be your head on the ground."

Chapter 14
Caesar's Headquarters

Otho parted the curtain separating Caesar's private quarters and announced, "Caesar, the generals and senior centurions are present for the consilium."

Caesar nodded, lifted his cup and took a generous swallow of wine, more than he normally allowed himself. The truth was he was undecided on what to do following the surprising Belgae actions or better described as inactions He expected and assumed the risk that crossing the river into Belgae territory would precipitate a strong, aggressive resistance. He wasn't sure how to interpret the passive response so far. He stood up and followed Otho into the larger tent chamber.

"Generals, Senior Centurions and Decurions, you may have wondered why I've so far remained in camp and on the defensive. The primary reason is the size of the Belgae Army which I believed would grow larger when the Germani tribes joined Galba. I was reluctant to leave a place as defensible as this to confront a much larger army with the potential of growing larger. The success of our cavalry over the past two days and the information they obtained from captured prisoners have changed my perception. The Belgae are less prepared with fewer allies than I anticipated. Therefore, it is my intent to invite battle tomorrow. General Labienus will explain how and what we will do."

"The objective is to provoke the Belgae into launching a frontal attack through the marsh between us. If they attack as we hope they will, a substantial part of the Belgae Army will be delayed as they try to go through the marsh. This will give us the opportunity to engage their army a little at a time thereby reducing their numerical advantage.

"The six veteran legions will form north of the camp in three ranks beginning at sunrise tomorrow morning. The legion cavalry consolidated under the command of Decurion Tarquin will depart the camp first to screen forward and the left flanks as the legions depart camp to take position. The Seventh Legion will lead followed by the Eighth, Tenth, Eleventh and Twelfth. Caesar will be with the Tenth Legion. The Thirteenth and Fourteenth Legions will remain within the camp to defend it and reinforce the engaged legions as necessary. The Auxilia infantry with the archers and slingers will screen the open and broader left flank. The auxilia cavalry will protect and screen the right flank.

"The Belgae may not make the mistake of attempting to go through the marsh opting instead to envelop our flanks. If this is the case, the cavalry will engage and slow their advance long enough for the legions to adjust appropriately to whatever the Belgae may do. Our departure from camp will be announced with drums and bugles loud enough to wake up the sons of bitches. Then we'll see if they're ready to fight and die or run back to their villages and farms."

The sun was well above the horizon, and the only signs of human occupation on the opposite hills were tendrils of smoke drifting upward through the trees. The Belgae displayed neither alarm nor urgency to react to the Roman Army waiting in disciplined ranks below. Time stretched on and the legionnaires were becoming restless prompting optios and centurions to admonish verbally then with vitis and hastile as the morning stretched on.

Gradually the Belgae camp started to come alive. Flashes of movement in the dense trees high on the hills quickly became a steady stream of Belgae tribesmen swarming down the slopes. The Belgae stopped in the treeless open space overlooking the marsh. The formless mass of warriors stretched nearly three miles. A spontaneous murmur rippled through the legionary ranks and dismounted cavalrymen standing by their horses.

Strabo muttered to Vinicius standing next to him, "Jupiter's golden balls, they've finally decided to fight."

Vinicius responded with dry humor, "Aye, and maybe I should have stayed in Massilia."

"Considering you nearly killed the son of the richest man in Massilia, if you hadn't left, you'd probably be spending the rest of your life either digging in the mines or pulling an oar in a galley."

"He started the fight, and it was his fault he fell out the window. At least in a galley I'd be alive which every day looks more doubtful."

Their conversation was interrupted by the sound of galloping horses on the distant right flank. Tarquin gave the order to mount and draw swords. Strabo saw the Auxilia cavalry mounted and ready to engage a large Belgae cavalry force.

Before the two forces met, the cart-mounted caroballistae in the northern fortlet began releasing four-foot arrow bolts into the densely packed Belgae ranks with deadly results. The close range and high torsion of the catapults easily passed through any rider hit or imbedded halfway into a horse. The densely packed cavalry horses were easy targets. Wounded and dying horses threw their riders under the hooves of the horses behind. Although a comparatively small number of riders and horses were killed or wounded, the shock and lethality of the catapults effectively blunted the attack. By the time the outnumbered Auxilia cavalry smashed into the Belgae, the enemy force had descended into a milling, demoralized mob. The majority of warriors turned and fled back the way they came. Those few who remained to fight were slaughtered. The battle ended so fast and decisively there was a momentary silence before the ranks of legionnaires broke into loud cheers.

The cheers died down when another force of Belgae cavalry came down the road leading to Bibrax to threaten the Roman left flank.

Tarquin shouted the order to form in three echelons to meet the attack. The first echelon consisting of the six decuriae from the Seventh and Eighth legions wheeled left in line to face the Belgae cavalry; the second echelon consisting of the six decuriae from the Ninth and Tenth Legions followed behind; the two decuriae of the Eleventh and Twelfth formed the third echelon.

As Strabo led the decuria to position on the far right close to the marsh, his pre-battle tension from the hours of waiting disappeared. He looked ahead as the two cavalry forces came together in a tumultuous sound of ringing swords, shouting and the agonized cries of both men and horses. The Belgae cavalry was showing a vigorous tenacity lacking in the days before.

Roman and Belgae met in a tight melee with neither side appearing favored. Those behind the hotly contested front lines on both sides looked for an opportunity to move up through the densely packed combatants. Gradually, the flanks began to widen giving those in the rear a chance to join the contested battle.

A warrior with blood streaming down his face from a slash across his right cheek rode toward Strabo with his sword raised. Strabo lifted his shield and stopped it then shoved his sword into his opponent's exposed belly. The momentum of the badly wounded man falling backward off his horse pulled the blade free. He rode on to meet the next adversary.

Strabo lost track of time as the battle raged on. He was beginning to doubt how much longer they could hold their own. Waves of fresh warriors easily replaced those that fell or rode away too badly wounded to remain on the field. His left arm was feeling the strain of warding off axe or sword blows. His shield was beginning to splinter apart. A cut on his right shoulder while not serious was bloody enough to make it difficult to grip the hilt of his sword. Imperceptible at first, he sensed the pace of the battle was beginning to slacken. A carnyx wailed, and the Belgae cavalry began to withdraw. He assumed it was also the signal for the infantry assault.

He took a moment to assess the strength of the decuria and was dismayed to see Calvus lying on the ground writhing in pain. The rest of the decuria remained in the saddle. While at first glance the number of dead and dying Belgae appeared to far exceed Roman casualties, it was apparent the legionary cavalry had suffered, too. He anticipated a trumpet call to sound recall to clear the field for the legions. The signal didn't come. After looking at the marsh, he saw the reason. The Belgae infantry remained in place with no indication of an attack.

Eventually the bugles sounded recall, and the cavalry turmae began to assemble in front of their respective legions accompanied by the admiring cheers of the legionnaires. Any sense of elation by the cavalrymen for having won the battle was dampened by the number of casualties amounting to a quarter of the three hundred men who fought.

For three hours, the legions remained in place waiting for an attack that did not materialize. In mid-afternoon, Caesar gave the command to return to camp leaving the cavalry to maintain surveillance of both flanks.

Caesar remained beside the north gate with Titus Labienus watching the legions marching up the slope to the camp until the last cohort passed by.

General Labienus shook his head and said in disgust, "This reminds me of how difficult it was to get Ariovistus to fight. I wonder if Galba has the same reason he won't, maybe superstitious nonsense about the moon." He was referring to the reason the Germani king avoided battle after the seers said he would be defeated if he fought before the new moon.

Caesar smiled and chided, "How many times have we delayed battle after a priest proclaimed the bull's guts didn't look or smell right. I'll give Galba credit for not crossing through that marsh which I would never do. I think the game is on our side. Their cavalry did well enough although ours did better. If what we've learned from the prisoners is true, Galba is running out of time and forage, and so far, his troops don't seem to have the stomach for a fight."

"What do we do in the meantime?"

"Why we'll stay where we are and wait until they either fight or leave. If they withdraw, we'll march on. Eventually we'll either have a battle or their surrender."

As the last legion entered the Roman camp, Galba turned to the Bellovaci tribal leader Correous with a resigned expression and said, "Evidently Caesar has no intention to cross the marsh for the reason I won't. We can't remain here until he decides otherwise. It's obvious the forage I expected Dumnorix to deliver was based on a false assurance and treachery. In any case, our provisions will be gone in two days."

"There's another reason to leave," Correous said. "My scouts report Diviciacus is approaching my border. If he crosses, he's a greater threat to me than the Romans. I'll leave here as soon as he does."

Galba's jaw tightened. "If you go, the Suessiones will have no chance against Caesar."

Correous shrugged. "From what's been reported, the Bellovaci has the same problem with Diviciacus. Would you be willing to come to my aid if I fight Diviciacus?" Galba's silence was his answer.

"We have the choice of attacking the Romans now or slinking away with the result Caesar can defeat the Belgae tribes one at a time. Well, I'm not ready to do that without at least showing the Romans what they face if they go any farther."

Correous looked across the valley at the settlement and bridge a short distance from the Roman camp and said, "I have an idea." By the time he finished, Galba was smiling.

Strabo was feeding and brushing down Aquilo when the trumpets blared the signal to arm and form ranks. The Roman camp immediately came alive as legionnaires and cavalrymen donned armor and rushed to their assembly points. He looked with approval as Ursinus with prods and rebukes readied the decuria minus Calvus whose wound would keep him off a horse for at least a month.

Tarquin assembled the decuriae and tersely explained the reason for the turn-out. "The Belgae are moving with a large force of cavalry and infantry heading toward the river and ford two miles west of the camp. The assumption is their objective is to cross the Aisne and destroy the bridge and fort to prevent the Remi from supplying the camp. Caesar will lead the legionary cavalry and a part of the Auxilia consisting of mounted archers and slingers to reinforce the six cohorts guarding the bridge and nearby ford. Two legions will follow. We'll form outside the southwest gate in the order we did earlier today and wait for Caesar and the Auxilia contingent. I'll command the legionary cavalry."

Tarquin had the cavalry formed and ready by the time Caesar arrived accompanied by Tribune Setarius and several aides with the Auxilia contingent following behind. Looking calm and confident, Caesar was smiling as he rode past the line of cavalrymen to the front of the column and headed for the bridge four miles away.

By the time they reached the bridge, Strabo saw the Belgae cavalry force had almost reached the ford two miles west of the bridge. Some of the Belgae would be across the river by the time they got there. Four of the six cohorts and General Sabinus were outside the fort in a defensive position protecting the bridge. Caesar ordered General Sabinus to send one cohort to the ford behind the mounted attack.

Tarquin signaled an open attack formation a quarter mile from the ford where the Belgae cavalry had formed a protective screen to allow the last of the cavalry and the infantry to cross. With a clash and hoarse cries, the opposing cavalries met. Caesar's presence in the vanguard did much to add encouragement and momentum to the Roman advance, and the Belgae cavalry was slowly pushed past the ford. The archers and slingers moved in and commenced a deadly barrage of missiles at the vulnerable infantrymen moving slowly in the waist high water. Despite the carnage in the river, those waiting to cross were not deterred and entered the water with some using dead bodies as shields.

Strabo thought the intensity of the battle was greater than a few hours before. The Belgae seemed more determined bordering on desperation. It wasn't enough to compensate for their inexperience against a well-trained, organized adversary. He credited Aquilo's higher and larger size as well as the horse's belligerent nature for significant advantage over the Belgae cavalrymen riding smaller horses. The battle became a blur as he slashed and stabbed one opponent after another. In a brief pause, he saw Setarius nearby and admired how at his age he was able to hold his own in battle. Soon, the few Belgae who remained mounted were throwing down their swords or spears in surrender.

Caesar turned his attention to the ford and saw no reason for concern. The Auxilia mercenaries had dominated, and the surface of the slow-moving river was covered with dead bodies. The Belgae on the far bank turned and fled after seeing their cavalry surrendering.

After Ursinus finished rounding up the decuria, Strabo was relieved to see all appeared to have survived the battle although two of his cavalrymen were on foot carrying their saddles; one of them was Vinicius. Ursinus pointed to the captured Belgae horses and told the two men, "Unless you want to walk back to camp, get over there and pick a couple of the best before the other decurae get around to it."

Tribune Setarius reined in beside him. "The legionary cavalry with some help from our mercenaries have won the day. I'm glad you survived both battles." He paused and noted Strabo's bloody shoulder. "At least you're in better shape than the gods might have decided."

"Sir, from the cut on your face, I could say the same."

Setarius laughed. "Serves me right for not having a shield, but then Caesar didn't either. It would have been unseemly for me to have one. Marcellus, when you have time from your duties, come and see me tonight."

Strabo saluted and walked Aquilo over to Ursinus wondering why he'd been summoned. Until the brief exchange a moment ago, it was the first time they had spoken since the aftermath of the race in Visontio several months ago. He reflected on how their relationship had gradually transitioned from mutual dislike to grudging respect. Surprising for him considering the tribune's confession he was the one responsible for his forcible conscription in the Roman Army. He thought about his initial days as an unwilling recruit spending nearly every waking hour plotting his escape. In the course of a few months, he had changed from a privileged, dissolute idler to a respected Roman soldier and a soon-to-be father. He credited the tribune for much of his transition. Then perhaps it was the gods who were responsible for reasons of their own.

Chapter 15

In his tent, King Galba worried about the increasing restiveness of the camp. Usually no more than a soft, indistinct hum had risen occasionally punctuated by loud angry voices. The news the scout brought concerning the Aedui advance had spread quickly throughout the camp. He was about to call for Correous, but the tribal chief entered the tent without being announced. The worried look on the face of the Bellovaci leader mirrored his concerns. The fiasco of the cavalry battle in the morning followed by the subsequent and humiliating defeat in the attempt to destroy the bridge foretold the possibility the campaign was in jeopardy. That was before the scout arrived. He'd been thinking what he would say to Correous and his own clan chiefs to rally flagging morale and carry on the offensive until hearing the Aedui had started their advance. The campaign was finished.

"Galba, I'm leaving to deal with Diviciacus who is expected to attack as soon as tomorrow with the assistance of the Remi. My tribesmen are preparing to leave, and nothing I can or will say is going to stop them."

Galba nodded in reluctant agreement. "I understand. I was about to call for you after hearing about the Aedui. From the sound of unrest outside my tent, my Suessiones are actively debating the inevitable end to a campaign that until today, I was confident we would win. I was overly optimistic. Dumnorix failed to provide the forage I counted on, the chicanery of the Remi choosing to ally with Diviciacus and the Germani never came as promised." Galba shook his head with fatalistic acceptance. "The main reason we lost is the Romans are better than we are. They're professional warriors in contrast to ours who are accustomed to small seasonal raids against neighboring tribes to acquire livestock or slaves."

Disgusted at the defeatist tone of Galba's comments, Galba bristled. "You sound as if you're ready to cross the marsh and surrender to Caesar tonight. Because we lost a couple of battles doesn't mean I'm going to stop fighting Romans."

"You're the one who's leaving. Without the Bellovaci, I have no choice except to do the same. Stay here. We'll fight them tomorrow and avoid the dishonor of slinking away in the dark."

Correous slumped and came as close to looking contrite as he was capable. "I can't fight the Romans while the Aedui are coming in my back door."

"I suppose it would be the same were the Suessiones in the same situation. All right, I want a quiet, orderly withdrawal without the Romans aware we're leaving."

After Correous left, and while waiting for the clan chiefs to arrive, Galba heard the intensity of the clamor outside escalating. The chance of a quiet unopposed withdrawal was as dismal as ever defeating the Romans.

Close to the end of the first watch, Strabo entered the tribune's tent. "My apologies, Sir. My duties delayed me from coming sooner."

Setarius put down the scroll he was reading. "I understand, the duties of a commander whether a decuria or a legion never end. Marcellus, sit down." He indicated the camp stool opposite the desk. "I regret the reason for you being here is to inform you that your father was called before the gods almost six weeks ago. The dispatches this morning included the news of his death. Caesar, as do I, extend our sympathy for his passing. As I told you not long ago, Lucillus Strabo was more than my commander. Our friendship grew long before he took command of the Tenth Legion and remained following his time as governor of Provincia. The last time we spoke, he thanked me for how you had changed. I told him I regretted my suggestion to have you conscripted although you survived the experience well enough."

Strabo looked away and remained silent, throat too tight to speak. He recalled how his father looked the last time he saw him at Bibracte and wasn't surprised. He felt deep remorse for all the things he had done and said to cause the rift between them. His regret was softened by the way they parted.

"Thank you for your kind words. I wish I could have enjoyed the warm relationship with him you had. I am profoundly sorry I failed him for so many inexcusable years."

"In the end and where it really counts, you didn't." The tribune picked up a sealed scroll and handed it to Strabo. "This is from your father; it was included in the dispatches."

Strabo broke the seal and found there were two sheets of parchment. The first was a letter which he read with eyes threatening to betray his feelings. Somewhat stilted, it conveyed a warmth and gratitude for the gods giving him a son of whom he was immensely proud. The second parchment with official seals appended was his father's will. With a catch in his throat, he said, "My father has bequeathed his estate to me."

"Congratulations. You're a very rich man with the capability to do anything you want. You have the wealth and status to leave the army with political opportunities to advance as your father did."

Strabo glanced sharply at the tribune and saw there was an underlying challenge.

"One day I will. This is not the time."

"Why not? You could leave tomorrow with Caesar's blessing as I told you in Bibracte." Again, there was a note of challenge behind the question.

Somewhat nettled, Strabo replied with an edge to his voice. "Tribune, we're on campaign. I'd be called coward for leaving before the campaign ended, and if others did not, I would think it so. Besides, there is something else to consider."

"You're referring to the Aedui woman — I believe her name is Raven."

"Yes, and our unborn child."

Setarius smiled in relief. "My congratulations again both for becoming a father and your willingness to see the campaign to an end. You're becoming more like your father every day, and that may be the highest compliment I can give you."

Strabo found himself unable to speak, overcome by both the words and unexpected sentiment the aging tribune voiced. He was relieved when an orderly burst into the tent and spared him from responding.

"Tribune! Caesar requests your presence at the headquarters."

Setarius stood. "Very well. Marcellus, I must go."

Strabo followed the tribune outside the tent and heard a muffled hum coming from across the shallow valley. Torches winked like fireflies on the slopes where the Belgae were encamped. All around him there was quiet speculation with no consensus to account for the strange activity. He left the tribune and headed back to the stables anticipating there was a good chance whatever was happening across the valley would have the cavalry in the saddle to find the reason. By the time he reached the stables, Caesar had already been told by Auxilia scouts the Belgae were leaving.

Caesar shook his head in disbelief and said to General Labienus, "Why in the name of Jupiter would they retire? It makes no sense. True, they haven't done well, but the battles so far have been minor. It's hard for me to believe Galba is giving up without fighting a major engagement. They far outnumber us and at least have the capability to keep us from moving farther into Belgica."

"It could be the Aedui are threating their rear faster than we thought possible."

"You could be right. It may also be his confederation is even weaker than we believed. We'll wait until dawn to verify they are really leaving. I cannot discount the possibility the Belgae are not withdrawing at all. They may be dissembling to provoke us into a risky night attack across the marsh. At dawn, when it's confirmed Galba is leaving the field, you will pursue with the Tenth, two other veteran legions of your choice and all the cavalry. Assuming they are as disorganized as reported, we have an unexpected opportunity to destroy the Belgae Army."

Led by five legionary decuriae, 5000 Auxilia cavalry under the command of general Publius Crassus left the camp at dawn and headed northwest around the right flank of the Belgae position. With General Labienus and the Tenth Legion in the lead, the Seventh and Eighth Legions followed. The other three Roman decuriae and remaining 2000 Auxilia cavalry under the command of Centurion Drusus advanced northeast around the Belgae left flank.

Strabo glanced behind at the dusty cloud the horses were creating and didn't envy the legionnaires marching behind. He recalled during his time in the ranks the dust stirred up from the legions ahead was a choking torment.

Three miles later, the route of the retreating Belgae was plain to see. It was evident the retreat was a disordered stampede shown by discarded shields, personal belongings and men too badly wounded to keep up.

The Belgae rear guard with an estimated strength of ten to fifteen thousand was eventually sighted two miles away and positioned across the slopes of several small hills. General Crassus ordered a halt and sent a rider back to inform General Labienus then waited for him to arrive. General Labienus appeared with the commanders of the other two legions. After a hurried exchange, General Crassus ordered the Auxilia cavalry to split into two wings, one wing on each flank, in preparation to envelop the Belgae; the legionary cavalry remained in the center.

The three legions, with the Tenth Legion between the other two, moved forward in three ranks abreast and halted. General Labienus nodded to the *primus pilus,* senior centurion of the Tenth, who began pounding his sword against his shield. The rhythmic sound was taken up by the other legionnaires in all three legions. The thunderous noise continued after a bugle signaled the attack.

Tarquin waved the legionary cavalry forward at a trot. Strabo was relaxed, reassured for once the enemy strength was less than what they expected and usually confronted. The two sides drew closer, and he admired the bravery of the hopelessly outnumbered Belgae cavalrymen riding toward them. The warriors showed both courage and resolve far different than he expected based on what they had showed during the past three days. The two sides met in a clash of flashing blades. Strabo easily deflected the sword of the first attacker and delivered a slashing and mortal cut to the warrior's neck. His next adversary was experienced and Strabo found himself using all his skills to defend the warrior's attack. Fortunately, Aquilo's aggressive nature became the deciding factor. The stallion bit the other horse on the neck. The horse reared, and the warrior dropped his sword in a desperate effort to remain in the saddle. Breathing a sigh of relief, Strabo rode on expecting to engage another that with any luck would be less of a challenge. But there weren't any left. The enemy warriors left on the field were either dead or lying on the ground too badly wounded to be a threat. What little remained of the Belgae cavalry had gone back behind the infantry. The bugle sounded recall. It was time to leave the field for the legionnaires.

During the cavalry fight, the legions had moved close enough to launch the first volley of spears. Observing from behind, Strabo saw the second volley was already in the air before the first one struck with horrific results. Unlike the Roman defense against such an attack when a testudo formation provided both side and overhead protection, the Belgae didn't have a cohesive, effective defense. Each warrior either crouched down behind his shield or tried to dodge the oncoming spears. By the time the third volley struck, there was no time for another. The first line of legionnaires met the diminished Belgae ranks with a ferocity that pushed them back a dozen paces before they briefly held. Slowly the Belgae gave ground against the relentless attack. In minutes it was over. The defenders still standing dropped their shields and weapons and pleaded for the mercy which for most was never given. Strabo heard later less than 500 Belgae warriors were left alive for sale to the slaver.

Before General Labienus finally gave the order to return to camp, Strabo saw the slaughter repeated time and again throughout the day as the demoralized Belgae fled. By then, even the battle-hardened were beginning to tire of the carnage.

After brushing and feeding Aquilo, Strabo sat down next to Vinicius and Ursinus and massaged his sore shoulder. After a moment of reflective silence, he said, "This isn't a day I want to remember, and I don't look forward to tomorrow if it's going to be the same."

"Aye, they were like sheep, and we slaughtered them like sheep. While I was killing them, I didn't think about it. I just did it. I wonder if I'm always going to feel this way."

Ursinus responded, "Don't think about anything except how you're going to kill the next bastard — that's what will keep you alive. If you think too much, you won't be ready for the one who's about to take your head."

Strabo recalled Scevola, the veteran legionnaire and his tentmate in the *Claudia* Legion, saying something similar last year after his first skirmish in the Alpes Mountains.

The conversation ended when Tarquin returned from the principia and told Vinicius to find Costa.

The other decurion arrived a few minutes later, and Tarquin said, "Caesar is leading the legions north tomorrow after the trenches are filled in. Auxilia scouts report the army is in total disarray. His intent is to pursue what's left of the Belgae Army. He's pleased with what happened here and the few casualties sustained compared to Belgae losses. He believes the confederation Galba planned for was wishful thinking on his part. Well, we've had a long and successful day. It's time to celebrate by getting some sleep."

Chapter 16

Raven thought the brief stabbing pain that woke her was another cramp possibly gas until it came again, sharper and persistent. After a few minutes, it stopped, and she decided it was probably nothing to worry about. By her reckoning, the baby wasn't due for another month. On the other hand, she could be wrong. Instead of staying in bed and worrying, it would be better to talk to Leuca. She sat up on the edge of the bed and massaged her lower back to relieve the pain. She stood up and quickly sat back down, doubled over in pain. Then the contractions began, and there was no longer doubt what was happening. She needed Leuca.

Raven slowly made her way to Leuca's dwelling stopping several times to grit her teeth and suffer contractions painful enough she wasn't sure she was going to be able to go any farther. She was grateful at least it was early, and few people were stirring. The last thing she wanted was the birth to become a spectacle. The thought of it kept her going. She regretted not taking precautions to avoid having a child. Almost every woman she knew, especially Leuca, believed giving birth was a woman's supreme fulfilment. She never felt that way and with the pain getting stronger by the minute, she still didn't.

She reached her destination at the same time her water broke. All her stoic resolve disappeared in an instant, and she called out in desperation for Leuca whose husband came to the doorway and saw what was happening. He stayed long enough to help her inside before making a hasty departure.

Leuca looked at the large, fully-formed baby Raven was suckling and said with conviction, "He isn't early. You miscalculated. What are you going to name him?"

"I haven't given it much thought."

"You haven't decided on a name?" Leuca exclaimed with a mix of disbelief and exasperation. "You've had months to think about it. Well, it's Marcellus who has the right to name his son. Did he tell you the name he wanted?"

"We didn't talk about it." Raven flushed. "When last we were together, there wasn't time. Other things were more important."

Leuca rolled her eyes. "I seem to recall you spent several hours together before he left."

"Anyway, I don't accept Marcellus has the right to choose. He can give him any Roman name, or names, he wants. I'll give him a Gaulish name. A name which reflects his heritage and hope for the future of Gaul. Something like Caturix would be fitting. Yes," she said thoughtfully, "with such a name he may be the *battle king* who will one day rid Gaul of the Romans."

Leuca didn't respond in her conviction it was best to accept the Romans were here to stay. She changed the subject. "Some time ago you considered getting a wet nurse. Are you so inclined?" She was encouraged when Raven delayed answering the question.

"There's no hurry. It will be a week maybe longer before I can ride. I'll consider it then."

Leuca sighed and accepted the reality Raven probably wasn't going to change. Why did she expect she would? Her attention was drawn to the sound of scratching on the door curtain. She left to find out who it was.

She pulled the door screen aside and saw Talos standing there looking tired and travel-worn. "I thought you were with Diviciacus fighting the Belgae." Then she noticed the bandage on his right hand.

"I was scouting with Corius until this," holding up his hand. "There wasn't much point in staying with him. I won't be holding a sword or stringing a bow for some time. I came back here to see your husband about a horse. Mine broke a leg. I stopped by to see how Raven is doing. She wasn't there. Do you know where she might have gone?"

Her inclination was to tell him to come back later and was about tell him so until Raven asked, "Leuca, is that Talos you're talking to?"

"Yes, he's looking for you. Considering your condition, I'm going to send him away, and he can come back when you're feeling better."

Talos in an urgent, hoarse whisper asked, "What's wrong with her?"

Exasperated, Leuca replied with a note of irritation. "She's just given birth and not ready to see anyone. Come back tomorrow or better in a few days."

It was obvious from Raven's response she'd heard the conversation. "I'm fine, and I want to see him. Talos, come in here and tell me what's happening with the Romans and Belgae." Leuca gave up and waved him in.

Raven handed the sleeping infant to Leuca who then left with a scowl showing her disapproval.

Talos watched her leave and began to have second thoughts about coming to see Raven. He covered his discomfort and asked about the baby without caring about the answer. The terse response and the question she asked made him wonder if Raven cared either.

"It's a boy. Have you seen or heard anything about Marcellus?"

"No, but your brother is fine and hopes you're doing well."

Her contrite expression indicated she understood his pointed answer.

"With the baby's arrival, Marcellus has been much on my mind. I trust the other scouts are well?"

"Yes, we've done little other than watch what both armies are doing. Until a few days ago, there were no major battles. The Belgae made one attempt to seize control of the bridge crossing, and it ended in a bloody defeat for King Galba. The Belgae withdrew that night. The Bellovaci and Suessiones separated with each tribe returning to their own lands. The Romans pursued and prepared to attack King Galba's settlement first; however, the Suessiones saw the huge siege machines the Romans were moving to the walls and surrendered. Surprisingly, the Remi interceded in their behalf. Two of Galba's sons are among the many hostages Caesar accepted. King Galba apparently left the settlement before the surrender was agreed to. It's been rumored he went to Germania."

"Are the Romans moving against the Bellovaci?"

"Not anymore. Before the Romans ever reached the main settlement, the Bellovaci surrendered as well. Diviciacus met with Caesar before he accepted the surrender and requested leniency for the Bellovaci. Caesar agreed and took six hundred hostages and no slaves. His intervention increased his stature among the Belgae tribes. Many of the Bellovaci leaders who encouraged the hostilities fled to Britannia. Caesar moved to engage the Ambiani, but they surrendered peacefully."

"Where are the Romans now?"

"They're getting ready to advance against the Nervii. Caesar is going to find the Nervii are a greater challenge than he's faced so far."

Raven's expression and voice reflected a mix of awe and regret. "The Roman gods must be more powerful than ours for them to succeed against numbers so much greater than theirs. Why do you think the Nervii will do better?"

"They're primitive and fierce. They live simply, and their contact with other tribes, primarily the Atrebates and the Viromandui, is limited. Traders have no access to them. They don't drink wine or want other goods of no practical use. They believe reliance on such things will make them dependent and reduce their strength and courage. They have very little cavalry and use horses mainly for domestic purposes. Primitive they may be, but they will not bow to the Romans as the other tribes have done."

Chapter 17

Strabo led his decuria to the bank of the Sambre River and stopped to survey the other side of the river where several Belgae cavalry pickets were observing them. At first, he planned to cross. He reconsidered after seeing the vegetation close to the river and the possibility the few cavalrymen were decoys.

"We need to know the depth of the river. Vinicius, go get your feet wet."

Warily eyeing the Belgae cavalrymen, Vinicius muttered an oath and nudged his horse into the wide, slow-moving river. He was surprised to find the water came up only as far as his ankles. The revelation eased him somewhat. At least if the Belgae decided he was an easy target, his chance for a faster escape had improved. He tried to look as if he was unconcerned, silently grateful with his back turned no one could see his shaking hands. He reached the other bank with the urge to turn around and get back as fast the horse could go. He overcame the impulse and with foolish bravado urged the horse up the bank. He breathed a sigh of relief when the Belgae cavalry showed no inclination to come after him. By the time he was halfway back, he was heartened his hands no longer shook. He managed to assume a calm expression while beseeching the gods to prevent him from ever being so stupid again. Maybe the gods could help by getting him promoted to decurion?

The decuria reached the top of the hill to join Tarquin and the rest of the turma. Strabo saw Caesar and General Publius Crassus talking to Tarquin. He rode over to them and saluted Tarquin. "The river is about three to four-feet deep."

"Did you see any indication there were Belgae in the trees behind the pickets?"

"No, sir. Could be the Belgae want us to think the pickets are all that's over there."

Caesar broke in. "That's what I think, too. General Crassus, take the cavalry and Auxilia infantry over there and see what they're up to. Decurion Tarquin, your turma is now under the command of General Crassus."

From the top of the densely wooded hill facing the river, Boduognat watched the Roman small cavalry troop on the opposite side of the river. They walked their mounts down the slope and stopped at the river's edge. A cavalryman left the formation and cautiously entered the river probably to test the depth. After reaching the other bank, he climbed it, took a quick look at the Atrebates cavalry pickets and went back across the river.

Behind the troop and ranging across a wide almost treeless hill, other riders, appeared and fanned across the hillside for a distance of one mile. Under the supervision of officers wearing side to side plumes on their helmets, the riders dismounted and started planting stakes 200 paces from the river bank. He nodded in satisfaction presuming the stakes marked the walled camp the Romans planned to build. The location the Romans chose was almost as if the Belgae gods had directed them.

The Bellovaci prisoners who escaped the Romans warned him three days ago the Romans were coming. In the interim, there was sufficient time for the Atrebates and Veromandui to join him. He expected the Aduatuci would get here before the Romans. It would be better if they didn't come. Their arrival at this point might be more problematic than useful. The prisoners' description of how the Romans were organized on the march and camped was useful in planning where and how he would engage them for the battle to come. The length of their marching column with baggage trains behind each legion suggested a vulnerability he intended to exploit.

He was satisfied in the intervening days he had ample time to prepare. Holding them at the river was critical. If they did manage to cross, the bastards wouldn't get much farther. The dense vegetation alone would be a formidable obstacle. The barriers he had constructed of bent saplings tied together and interlayered with thorns made them challenging for infantry and virtually impossible for cavalry to pass through.

He scowled as the six legions he expected arrived without their baggage trains The Belgae prisoners had been wrong, and the vulnerability he expected to exploit was gone. He expected to attack when the six legions were spread out and separated by their baggage trains thereby reducing their capability to reinforce each other. He cursed. He had to adapt. There was no time to change the battle plan.

The legionnaires lined up in ranks 50 paces behind the stakes and dropped their packs, covered their shields and stripped off their armor and weapons. With small picks and baskets, they moved to the stakes and began digging a long, lateral trench across the hill. The loose dirt was piled uphill to form the beginning of a wall. He was dismayed how fast the large rectangular walled fort was progressing.

The baggage train came into view in the distance, and he was shocked to see two legions he didn't expect. The situation was not what he planned for. He considered withdrawing until the Aduatuci could join the other tribes then decided against it. There would never be a better time and place to defeat the Romans than here.

He watched the Roman cavalry and light infantry force on the hill moving toward the river and cross over on his right flank. He discouraged King Commius from bringing his cavalry. He had little use for it. He would have preferred more infantry. Yet the Romans had taken the bait, and Commius was pushing the Romans back. He was beginning to think the cavalry might be more useful than he thought. He was disappointed the Romans didn't press the battle into the dense forest.

Over the next few minutes, he watched the Roman cavalry and light infantry being pushed back. It was time to launch the attack. He stood up,walk ed over to his principal leaders and gave the order.

From the hill above, Caesar, General Labienus and several staff officers watched the legionnaires digging the night encampment. The walls were less than ankle high. A carnyx blared across the river and Belgae infantry flanked by cavalry came out of the tree line in a wide front heading toward the river. Caesar's jaw tightened.

"Gentlemen, Crassus has stirred up a hornet's nest. Unfortunately, sooner than I expected or wanted. Boduognat has stolen the moment at the time we're most vulnerable with a fortified camp barely started and the last two legions still on the march. I pray Jupiter will help General Crassus hold the Belgae until the other legions get here." He was shocked by how fast the Auxilia was pulling back across the river in complete disorder, and the Belgae were following with little resistance. The legionnaires working on the wall closest to the river were running up the slope to get their weapons. Many died before they could.

Strabo saw the densely packed ranks of infantry flanked with cavalry rushing toward them. It was going to be a hard fight. The Auxilia showed signs of faltering, and General Crassus ordered recall. Strabo was astonished believing the recall was premature. Despite the general's frantic efforts to maintain an orderly withdrawal, it became an ignominious scramble to get back across the river.

With an expression of total disgust, Tarquin managed to keep the turma together and shouted above the din, "The general wants to reform at the baggage train."

Publius Crassus was listening to an angry Tribune Setarius, and from the tribune's furious expression, Strabo was certain he thought the withdrawal was premature as well. He saw Ursinus watching the exchange and noted his narrowed eyes and angry expression. Ursinus said what he was thinking.

"We're dishonored. In all my years of service and all the battles I've fought, I've never seen or been a part of anything so disgraceful. The gods above are laughing at us. I didn't even have the chance to get blood on my blade". He pointed to the Seventh and Twelfth Legions on the Roman right flank. "Look what's happening down there. They're getting slaughtered!" Strabo saw the Eighth and Eleventh legions in the center were being hard-pressed.

He didn't rebuke the cavalryman for saying what he was also thinking. He prayed Scevola would survive the bloody onslaught. He saw Caesar behind the Tenth Legion attempting to restore the line. Minutes later he was with the Ninth Legion doing the same.

Trumpets blew, and the two legions advanced to the river. Caesar turned his attention to the crumbling center and right flank. Caesar's presence was timely, and the beleaguered legions began to rally. The Belgae attackers started to give way and were slowly forced to the river bank. Additional warriors came across the river, and the Belgae rallied pushing the legionnaires back to the line of stakes. All four legions were becoming separated when the Belgae warriors enveloped the flanks of each of the four legions in the center and on the right flank.

Strabo felt guilty he was only observing the developing battle. Surely the Auxilia and legionary turmae would be ordered to go back over the river and attack the Belgae right flank.

It was as if someone read his mind. One of the tribunes rode up to General Crassus, and after a hurried exchange, General Crassus signaled to Tarquin and the other three subordinate commanders of the Auxilia cavalry.

Tarquin returned and said with determined emphasis, "The Ninth and Tenth Legions are going to attack the Belgae right flank and push them back across the river. We've been ordered to support by screening the left flank."

The Atrebates cavalry protecting the Belgae flank was less tenacious than the infantry and gave ground. The Roman cavalry crossed the river ahead of the Ninth and Tenth and continued uphill. The higher up they went the less opposition there was until finally there was no longer any Belgae to fight.

Strabo stopped at the top of the hill and dismounted to examine Aquilo. The horse had not been spared. There was blood on the left shoulder and on the right croup. He was relieved both wounds looked worse than they were, and the horse was not showing any sign of distress. Fresh cuts on his right upper arm and wrist were making it difficult to grip his sword. He undid his neck cloth and wiped the hilt then looked around and saw makeshift shelters and smoldering fires of the deserted Belgae camp.

He mounted Aquilo and looked downhill to see the progress of the battle below. The first wagons of the baggage train were coming over the hill to occupy the flat area above and to the left of where the Ninth and Tenth Legion were located. The two legions had crossed the river and forced the Belgae into the trees. Although the Eighth and Eleventh Legions in the center were holding their ground, he saw warriors moving up the hill behind the legions to attack the baggage train. The Twelfth and Seventh Legions on the far right were again in serious trouble.

Viewing the unfolding battle from part way up the slope, Caesar saw the widening gap along the front created after the Ninth and Tenth Legions crossed the river and the Eighth and Eleventh Legions were slowly being forced back uphill. The densely packed and faltering lines of the Twelfth Legion on the extreme right flank threatened being enveloped by both cavalry and infantry. The closely packed legionnaires were too close together to fight effectively and increasing the threat of being enveloped. He saw at least six centurions on the ground. Most of the other centurions throughout the ranks were missing, presumably dead or too badly wounded to fight. Bucelus, the *primi pilus,* was badly wounded and would have fallen if he hadn't been holding on to the legion's eagle standard. The loss of the centurions had created a leadership void, and the legion was on the verge of panic. The Legion's effectiveness was disintegrating before his eyes. The Seventh Legion on the right flank were holding despite heavy losses. Worse, the Nervii on the right flank were moving into the widening gap in the center that threatened to split the Roman lines. With chilling clarity, he thought, *By the gods! I underestimated Boduognat and may well pay the price for it. If the two legions guarding the baggage don't get here in the next few minutes, all is lost.*

Caesar dismounted, unbuckled his cloak, drew his gladius and ran toward the lines of the Twelfth Legion picking up the shield of a dead legionnaire on the way. He met fleeing, demoralized legionnaires moving uphill.

"Legionnaires! The fight is down there." Most turned and returned to the ranks. He made his way through the rear lines toward the front shouting to the remaining centurions and optios to extend the lines. The cheering legionnaires gave some assurance there was a renewed determination to hold the position. He reached the front line and stepped between two legionnaires who glanced at him in startled surprise to see him in the frontline. They cheered as he quickly lunged forward and attacked a careless warrior. After pulling his bloody sword from the warrior's bare chest, he was pleased he could still hold his own. It was time to move on to the Seventh Legion and see what could be done there to stiffen the front line.

He found the Seventh in even worse shape tightly bunched and close to breaking. Among the many dead was General Antonius Pavius. He had a brief moment of regret he had not replaced him with Crassus before the campaign began as he originally intended. Then again, it might be Crassus lying there instead, a greater loss than Pavius. He pushed all other thoughts away as he plunged in to fill the leadership void as was necessary with the Eleventh. Gradually the legion rallied. The Nervii pressure had shifted to the Eleventh and the gap in the center left. The line was holding, and the flank assault was not as grave.

He made his way back through the ranks and reached the rear line. He looked uphill. There was panic and confusion within the baggage train caused by the Nervii passing the Twelfth Legion's flank and coming uphill. The staunch, always reliable Treveri Cavalry assigned to protect the baggage train were fast disappearing back the way they came. There was still no sign of the Thirteenth and Fourteenth Legions. He looked toward the Belgae camp and prayed. *Jupiter, I served you faithfully as High Priest at your temple in Rome, and now I ask for your help. Tell General Labienus to come back to this side of the river!*

General Labienus had every reason to be satisfied. The Belgae cavalry and reserves were defeated, and Commius had surrendered the Atrebates. The Ninth Legion below on this side of the river appeared to have successfully stopped the Viromandui. He looked across the river beyond the Ninth and saw a disaster in the making. It was clear the Roman right flank was in trouble and in danger of being enveloped. The Nervii were going past the Eleventh Legion on the center left flank and moving up hill toward the baggage train. He beckoned to the nearest tribune.

"Find the primus pilus and tell him we're disengaging and going back to the other side of the river. Send someone to tell General Crassus the same, and he will lead the way with the cavalry. He must be quick as the legions across the river are about to be surrounded."

On the way down the hill, Strabo prayed Scevola would survive the desperate battle across the river. He felt some guilt he wasn't there beside his former tentmate in the Eleventh; however, it was less than his relief for not being there.

By the time the turma reached the river, the Ninth Legion had turned around and was crossing the river. Strabo felt the cool water splashing on his legs and wished there was time to dismount and lead Aquilo to the other side. They reached the other bank and heard faint trumpets sounding and becoming progressively louder. Once past the trees lining the bank, he saw a cavalry turma and the standard of the Thirteenth Legion crest the hill above where the baggage train was located. Soon ranks of legionaries were trotting down the hill behind.

Crassus signaled for an oblique turn to attack the Nervii right flank. The Nervii advanced in the direction of their new attackers with a savagery unseen before in previous battles with the Belgae. Their ferocity did not make up for their inexperience with cavalry. Instead of pulling together with spears extended to confront the charging horsemen, they were spread out and vulnerable.

Strabo aimed his spear over the shield of his first opponent and the three-pointed metal point went into his face. He rode on and let the forward momentum and the weight of the dead warrior pull the spear free. Aquilo claimed the next one by rearing and with a kick crushed the warrior's head. He jabbed the spear into the chest of another warrior so deep he couldn't pull it out. He let go of the shaft and drew his spatha then looked for another adversary. However, the Nervii in front and on the flank were beginning to pull back to reduce their risk of being overrun by the cavalry.

General Crassus signaled a halt in place and far enough away to avoid the spears the Belgae launched to allow the Tenth Legion to pass ahead of the cavalry ranks. By then, the Ninth Legion had finished crossing back over the river and was attacking the Nervii rear ranks. Seeing the hopeless situation, some of the Nervi were turning back across the river.

The Nervii who remained to fight were gradually being enclosed on all sides into a killing zone in which there was no escape. The warriors a short time ago about to win the field were falling in droves where they stood felled by arrows, slinger stones and spears. The Nervii ranks had been so compressed the remaining warriors were standing on the bodies of the dead and retrieving the Roman spears to throw back. Gradually the Roman ranks stopped closing in looking at the few hundred exhausted and bloody survivors in awe as they stood or kneeled, no longer with enough strength left to fight. Silence descended on the battlefield. One by one, the Nervii warriors cast away their swords and shields.

Those close to Caesar saw his hard expression soften and heard him say, "By the gods, they are the bravest men I ever saw. Those warriors will not be killed or given to the slavers. I want to earn their trust and make them allies of Rome. The one wearing the torque must be Bodougnat. If he's still alive, I want to talk to him."

"Caesar, I hear you, and I agree they fought well. I don't care. I would put them to the sword to prevent having to fight the bastards again. We have suffered much including the loss of a legion commander and far too many centurions. I would rather see all of them dead or in the galleys."

"No, Titus! Find me someone who can help me talk to him. He's worth more to Rome alive than a headless corpse only the vultures will value."

Tight-lipped, the general managed to control his anger and responded in a neutral voice. "It will be as you have ordered." He motioned to a centurion and pointed to the man with the torque and relayed Caesar's order.

Relenting, Caesar softened his voice. "Titus, I nearly lost this one. I would have if you hadn't come back here with the Tenth and Ninth and the two new legions had delayed any longer."

The centurion returned leading two legionnaires carrying the badly wounded Nervii and dropped him face down at Caesar's feet. "From the looks of his wounds, he's about to see his gods."

"Lift him up so I can see his face. Perhaps he speaks enough Latin to tell me who he is." The legionnaires pulled the dying warrior to his knees and held him up facing Caesar. Slowly the dying man lifted his head and stared at Caesar with an expression of calm acceptance."

"Are you Boduognat?" At the sound of his name, Bodougnat gave a slight nod.

"For your bravery I will spare you and your…" He stopped when he saw the dying man's eyes close, and his body slump lifeless.

The legionnaires released their grip on his shoulders, and the dead tribal leader was now nothing more than the hundreds of other warriors and Romans dead in a costly battle in which he privately conceded had come too close to losing. His reflections were interrupted when Labienus spoke.

"Does the campaign end here?" Labienus asked.

"No. We march against the Aduatuci after a few days of rest. The first priority is completing the fort and seeing to the wounded. After the camp is secure at the end of the first watch, I want to meet with the legion commanders, senior tribunes and senior centurions to praise what we did right today and highlight the occasions we did not. I've no doubt after our losses today particularly with the Seventh and Eleventh, I will see new faces among the centurions who will attend. I've ordered Publius Crassus to turn command of the Auxilia over to Centurion Marcea Drusus and take command of what's left of the Seventh. Before Crassus takes the legion west to deal with unrest in Armorica and along the coast, we'll have to levy the other legions for replacements."

It was nearly dark when Strabo left the picket line and saw Quintus Servius coming toward him then stop and face him. The decurion's usual hostile demeanor was replaced with a quizzical expression. He was surprised and caught off guard when Servius asked an unexpected and surprising question.

"Strabo, what did Gaius Marinus have against you?"

Perplexed, Strabo responded. "Why are you asking?"

"Before we raced at Visontio, Marinus paid me to see you had an *interesting* race. He made it very clear, *interesting* meant something other than making sure I won and gave me sestercii to make it happen. If I had any doubt what he meant, following the race I didn't. He offered more sestercii, to try again."

"What did you tell him?

"I told him I would." Servius saw Strabo's angry expression and added defensively, "It was the way you humiliated me at the finish line I can't forget or forgive. I don't like you, Strabo, and I hate losing a horse race. I admit it. I seldom lose because I'm not particular how I win."

"Why are you telling me this?"

"I'm curious why Marinus hates you."

"Whatever he had against me may have been because of my father. I have no idea what it was. Marinus served under my father when he commanded the Tenth Legion years ago, and he may have disciplined Marinus in some way. You haven't answered my question. Why do you care?"

Servius shrugged. "I'll never have the chance to ask Marinus." The decurion saw Strabo's questioning look. "You apparently don't know the Eleventh Legion lost several centurions and one of them was Marinus. From now on, the Belgae are all you have to worry about." He hesitated then with a slight curve of his lips, added, "I suppose that's not entirely correct. Relax, you can sleep easy at night. I'm no assassin. The day we settle what's between us, however we do it, you'll have time to prepare."

"Thanks for the warning, but as far as I'm concerned there's nothing to settle. I got my satisfaction at Visontio for what you did. I don't think you'll ever have the chance to do what you want while we're both in the army. The severe consequences for settling a personal matter having nothing to do with the army while we are actively serving the legions is not worth it."

"I take risks others don't without worrying about the consequences, and that's why I win races. You were lucky at Visontio. I was clumsy and not up to my standards. There will come a time you and I will race again, and I'll do better."

Strabo watched the decurion walk away with a feeling of hopeless resignation Servius intended to find a way and the day to get his revenge. He shrugged and continued on to where the Claudia Legion was encamped. He wanted to find out if Scevola had survived and dreaded the possibility he hadn't, particularly after learning about Marinus.

He found Scevola alive and with a *hastile* in his hand inspecting the tent area of the first century, second cohort.

"Salve, Scevola. I'm relieved and pleased to find the gods decided you haven't yet served enough time in the legions. I trust the optio staff is a sign you've finally been recognized for promotion and not because something happened to Brecius."

"I'm glad you, too, have not been called by the gods. Brecius has taken Tulio's place as senior optio of the cohort; Tulio is acting commander of the century. I was promoted not because I wanted to be. I accepted out of conviction there was no one else as qualified. It may say more about the inadequacy of most of the surviving veterans than my capability to be an optio."

Strabo changed the subject." I heard Centurion Marinus was killed during the final minutes of the battle. I think the second century is better led than before."

"He had his faults, but the gods may forgive him for being brave and dying well. I was near enough to see him during most of the battle. I'll not speak ill of the man now he's dead."

"I'll try to do the same. I doubt I can for what he paid Tertious to do to me."

"Aye, you've got reason enough. What have you heard about what we're going to do? The tribes we fought today are no longer a threat."

"Tarquin said Caesar is going to rest the legions here for three days to reorganize, tend the wounded and bury the dead. After that he's going after the Atrebates who evidently were supposed to have joined Bodougnat here today. For whatever reason they didn't, I'm grateful."

"This will be my last campaign. When the legion goes into winter quarters, I'm going back to Massilia where I will stay whether my wife likes it or not. If she doesn't, I'll find another woman more agreeable." He paused with a speculative smile. "She might be pleased if I did find one. What about you? Have you decided what you're going to do?"

"No. Since we last talked at Visontio, I learned I'm going to become a father, and I'm less certain than I was before what my future will be. Not long ago my father died; consequently, I have the wealth to do what I want. I need to consider the child and the problem the child's mother dislikes everything about Rome. She wishes Gaul free from Roman rule and influence and possibly me as well. I suppose, for the time being, I'll continue as I am."

Embarrassed, Strabo laughed self-consciously. "I apologize. I'm chattering on about personal things that are inconsequential to what happened here today. The legions have been battered. The Belgae, especially the Nervii, suffered grievous losses. I heard a delegation of the Nervii senior tribal members told Caesar the tribe has been almost totally destroyed and reduced from sixty thousand to less than five hundred left alive."

"The slavers will have to be content at least some survived to profit Rome."

"Not so. Caesar was so impressed with how well the Nervii fought, he spared the survivors from slavery and declared their territory and settlements will not be touched. He commanded the neighboring tribes to refrain from taking advantage of the tribe following their severe losses. Rumor has it, given our losses, some of the legion commanders resent his clemency."

Chapter 18

Three days later, General Crassus led the Seventh Legion away from the camp southwest toward the coast. Caesar took the remaining seven legions northeast to where the principal Aduatuci settlement was reported to be two days march away.

The once large fortified camp at the Sambre where so many died was now a partially filled rectangular depression. A mile away were three long mounds marking the graves of the Roman dead. The unclaimed bodies of the Belgae tribes were taken two miles away and left to rot. Depending on the wind, the stench hastened preparations to leave. The mood within the ranks of both diverging columns was subdued. Victory had been costly. Although the three-day respite provided physical relief, it did little to lift spirits over the loss of so many. There was no anticipation for another battle with an enemy potentially as resolute and savage as the Nervii had proved to be.

Strabo halted the decuria and looked at the rugged hill several miles away upon which the walled fortress and principal settlement of the Aduatuci was situated. The tribe had chosen the site well. The steep rocky slopes directly below the walls of the fortress made it impregnable to assault on three sides. On the fourth side of the rectangular stronghold where the main entrance was located, the land fell away in a gentle slope. The vulnerability of this side was in the process of being mitigated by a deep trench in front of a nearly completed high, double wall. The wall joined at both ends to the settlement wall was being topped with sharpened stakes.

"Ursinus, what do you think?"

"When Caesar sees this, he'll regret the extra time spent at the Sambre instead of getting here sooner. It will be a siege with little for cavalry to do."

Strabo heard the faint sound of galloping horses west of the settlement. The number of yelling horsemen riding out of the tree line, half-mile away coming toward them was not what he wanted to see. There were too many, and they were too close.

"It's time we left." Strabo turned Aquilo eastward and kicked the grey stallion into a gallop cursing his inattention and worried about their tired horses.

Strabo looked at Ursinus riding next to him and said, "If you have any suggestions, I'm willing to hear them."

"Ride faster than they are!"

"Is that all you've got to say? The horses can't keep up this pace much longer."

"Pray, and pray hard. Maybe they'll pay more attention to an officer than they will me."

Strabo cursed instead. Whatever god or gods he asked for help would laugh at him for being stupid enough to get into such a situation. He had nothing to lose by trying. His mouth was too dry, and he hoped either Epona or Jupiter, maybe both, would hear a silent prayer. Part way through his desperate plea, the narrow, steep gorge they passed by earlier that day came to mind. The foot path down and up was too treacherous to risk the horses; consequently, he led the decuria on a long detour to avoid it. The gorge was less than a mile away, and circumstances dictated a second thought.

"Ursinus! We're going through the gorge we passed by this morning."

The cavalryman's expression was one of shocked disbelief. "Is that your idea or the gods?"

"It must have been. Either way, it doesn't matter. We don't have a choice." He signaled a turn toward the gorge while asking Epona if it was her idea, give them time to get across before the Aduatuci cavalry caught up with them. He spotted the familiar tree line ahead where the comparatively level ground dropped off precipitously and looked behind. The turn had shortened the distance in favor of the pursuers. It was going to be close with the additional risk of negotiating the narrow trail faster than if they'd chanced it earlier.

"Ursinus, when we get there, lead them across and have them dismount on the other side with all their spears. If the Aduatuci take the risk and follow, they'll come up slow, and the odds will be in our favor."

"Let me be the last one, and you lead them across."

"You have your orders, follow them!" The cavalryman's silent disapproval was plain to see. Vinicius continued cursing and complaining loudly behind him as they drew close to the gorge.

"Shit, I'd rather turn around and fight those sons of bitches than go down there. We'll get to the bottom sure enough, and that's where our bodies are going to stay."

Over his shoulder, Strabo said, "Fine, Vinicius, you can stay with me and remain on this side to fight while the rest cross."

Whatever Vinicius may have been considering changed abruptly as the sound of the horses behind became increasingly louder. Cursing even louder, Vinicius was the first to follow Ursinus down the steep incline.

Strabo turned around and saw the oncoming Aduatuci cavalry less than a quarter mile away and closing fast. He looked down into the gorge relieved to see Ursinus and those who were making the descent were doing better and going faster than he expected. Vinicius's loud cursing rose above the shrill protests of the horses and the sound of hooves sliding down the loose scree. Finally, he alone remained above as the Aduatuci closed within spear range. If they had archers, even Epona would have her hands full trying to get him across safely. He judged there was enough space behind the last man to make the attempt.

He was halfway down the path when the first spear flew past him and ricocheted off a boulder a few feet on his left. Another followed on the other side and close enough it brushed his shoulder. He heard the sound of a horse starting to descend as Aquilo reached the bottom. He crouched low in the saddle and urged the stallion to a pace as fast as the uneven ground would allow to reach the ascending path a hundred paces away. He dropped the reins long enough to reposition the shield to protect his right side as more spears came toward him. Most were stopped by foliage or rocks except for one that hit and penetrated the shield far enough to strike Aquilo in the withers inches in front of his right thigh.

The stallion snorted, reared then bolted at a faster pace. Strabo pulled on the reins enough to keep the horse from going past the path leading up to the other side. His efforts dislodged the spear point. He glanced down and saw the wound, although bloody, was shallow and not serious. He dropped the unwieldy shield and concentrated on getting the horse under control. He saw the path to the top and took it with a sigh of relief.

He looked up and saw two of his cavalrymen on the path ahead of him. The others were ranged along the rim above with javelins poised. He risked looking behind and saw a line of Aduatuci riders pounding on up the path. Seconds later, the one in the lead fell backward with a javelin protruding from his chest. The warrior's body caused the horse following to lose its footing sending it and the rider crashing off the path and down the steep slope. With no way to turn around, the other riders on the path either had to choose between stopping and backing their horses down, or continuing upward. A fusillade of javelins brought two riders down, and the rest turned their mounts around.

Aquilo gained the top and stopped, lungs heaving, mouth foaming. Strabo saw Ursinus looking at him with a broad smile.

"I was right, the gods always pay more attention to officers than they do rankers."

Caesar observed the legionnaires from all eight legions in the early stages of constructing a wall to circumvallate the five-mile perimeter of the settlement. He admired the choice to locate it there. It was going to be a daunting task.

"Titus, the scouts were right, it will take time. We'll have them out of there one way or another." He turned to Praefectus Mammura and said, "Marcus, I need your engineers to help crack this nut."

"What do you have in mind?"

"In addition to the wall the legionnaires are building, I want watchtowers constructed on top of the wall at places where it would be most likely the Aduatuci might attack. I think three on the shorter end walls and three times that on the longer walls. The legionnaires will build a ramp between our wall and the one the Aduatuci are constructing. I want a siege tower built to roll up the ramp.

The prefect of engineers nodded. "When do you plan to attack?"

"As soon as you've completed what I've asked for."

"Will three days be acceptable?"

"It will, sooner if you can. For whatever additional labor you need, see General Labienus, and he'll determine which legions will support you."

The two men watched the stocky and muscular praefectus ride away. Once out of earshot, Caesar, laughing, turned to Labienus and said, "Back in Rome, I read an amusing poem by Gaius Catullus. There was little doubt the object of his ridicule was none other than our own prefect of engineers. Apparently, he's done more than build siege machines. He's *built* a reputation for licentiousness to the extent Catullus refers to him as a *mentula.*"

"It must come as some relief Catullus is focusing on Mammura and sparing you."

Caesar's frown turned to a smile at the reference to his own and similar reputation for womanizing. "Well, admittedly there's truth in what you say. I repaid Catullus by widely praising his poem. I've been told his attempt at ridicule has been blunted by laughs and envy of me. I'm grateful Cutullus is not well read among the plebs. As for

Mammura, I don't care what he does in Rome. He's an engineering genius. May he continue to be sharp in the eye of Catullus."

The general's laugh was muted; he was ready to move on to serious matters. "After we finish with the Aduatuci, what are your plans for the legions? No other tribes appear to be a threat, and Publius Crassus reports success in easing tensions on the coast."

"If the coast remains quiet, the legions will go into winter quarters along the borders of Belgae and Germania. Gaul is a simmering cauldron always on the point of coming to a boil. The legions will stay in Gaul for many years to fight the next king of whatever tribal confederation decides to challenge the destiny of Rome."

"And to add another province to the others you govern?"

Caesar's jaw tightened. The aides nearby noticed Caesar's changed demeanor and quietly kneed their mounts away to avoid being a close witness to the storm about to break.

"Careful, General, do not presume to intimate my motives in Rome are inspired by personal ambition alone lest I find your words accusatory and questioning how I deploy the army. My actions in Gaul serve the Republic by giving it another and very profitable province. Our successes in Gaul have won widespread acclimation with the plebs as well as providing additional security to the three provinces you made reference to. If by pacifying Gaul, I also gain, you and many others will profit as well."

"I apologize. The question was both improper and uncalled for."

"Very well, apology accepted." Caesar looked away for a moment, his expression thoughtful before he faced the general.

"I may not have the three provinces I govern much longer. My brief time in Rome before coming back to Gaul was spent doing more than reading Catullus. The triumvirate I instigated with Pompey and Marcus Crassus made the pacification of Gaul possible. The triumvirate has become fragile. I hear Pompey is concerned I've become too successful in Gaul, and there are signs he may withdraw his support. If he does, the political support needed to maintain the peace in Gaul will erode and the financial support Crassus provides will not be enough to keep the legions in Gaul. The dissolution of the triumvirate will give my detractors the power to end my governorship of my provinces. I'll be fortunate if all I have left is a small estate in southern Italia.

"I need to get back to Rome and stop those who oppose a Roman investment in Gaul. If the legions do not remain here, Rome will keep on fighting every tribal bastard who wants to be a king. Rome will benefit from a peaceful Gaul. The legions are the means to make it so." Caesar smiled and said, "I should take Marcus Mammura with me to Rome. Let the attention remain on him and not me. For the moment, we'll focus on the Aduatuci. The sooner we get this done, the larger concerns concerning Gaul can be attended to."

Accompanied by his aides, Labienus watched Caesar ride up the slope where the legionnaires were digging and heard their rousing cheers as he approached. He envied the vocal adulation Caesar received whenever he appeared without any prompting by the optios and centurions. He cursed his impulsive question which Caesar was quick to perceive as both too critical and too judgmental. He had let his growing concern for Caesar's unbridled ambition to take over his tongue. He had to be careful to conceal his uneasiness for the future of the Republic. He shook his head and thought the Gauls have less to fear of Rome than Rome has of Caesar.

Strabo woke up. His mouth was dry, and his head ached. He vaguely remembered the return to camp and the celebration that followed after the narrow escape from the Aduatuci cavalry patrol. To a man, the cavalrymen attributed their escape to the ingenuity of the decurion first and the gods second. The gods weren't visible. Decurion Strabo was, and he was the focus of their appreciation. He tried initially to pass off their accolades with an admission their predicament was the result of his inattention. After too many cups of wine, he stopped disagreeing because he was too drunk to debate the matter further. His last memory of the night was hanging on Ursinus's shoulder, as the senior cavalryman helped him to his bedroll. The next thing he knew the sunrise was blinding him, and he felt like shit. He regretted the night before. He gave it a second thought — it may have been one of the best nights and sunrises he could remember ever having. If he could remember the thought and his promise to Epona and the other gods. He resolved to make sacrifices for surviving a near hopeless situation. May the gods remind him of the promise when he felt better able to make good on it.

He felt someone shaking him rudely as he was about to enter into a golden haze of contented remembrance. A harsh, unrelenting voice kept interrupting a dreamscape he wasn't ready to leave.

"Sir, the sun's coming up, and it's time to meet the day."

The voice faded as his favorite, buxom whore in Massilia began to come into focus, and he started to drift off until the voice intruded again and louder.

"We've been ordered to scout north of the settlement where the Aduatuci cavalry have been interdicting the legionnaires building the siege wall."

Strabo opened his eyes and saw Ursinus peering down at him with an unsympathetic smirk on his face. He groaned. In all the many times he'd caroused in Massilia, he never recalled feeling worse. He sat up and struggled to lace up his boots with five thumbs then stood and immediately regretted it. A wave of dizziness made him retch what little was left in a stomach emptied several times during the night. After fumbling on his cuirass, dagger belt and sword baldric, he was beginning to think he might survive. He went to where Aquilo was tethered and already saddled to inspect the wound on his withers. Satisfied it was no longer bleeding, he lifted his helmet off the right pommel and pulled it on. Starting to mount, he hesitated and saw a wooden box which offered an easier, safer way to get in the saddle. The gods were helping, and he was grateful.

Once in the saddle, he stared balefully at the nine grinning cavalrymen lined up watching him. He tried to look stern, failed and smiled back.

“I had a good time last night, and now I ask a favor. If any one of you sees a spear or arrow coming toward me, don’t get in the way. It will be Jupiter’s way of putting me out of my misery after drinking that fermented horse piss you found last night.”

Tarquin led the legionary cavalry force numbering nearly five hundred out of the east gate and past where the siege tower was in the final stage of completion. The fabri were busy shaping and rounding the logs to roll the tower up the completed earthen ramp that reached halfway up the settlement wall to the gated entrance. Their work was accompanied by the raucous jeers of the confident Aduatuci thronging the ramparts for what they believed was a hopeless effort to breach the walls.

For Strabo, the first couple of miles was agony. Gradually, the throbbing in his head began to lessen. He became conscious of his surroundings, their mission and his doubts for his capability to make a substantial contribution to its success.

They saw the dust first then heard the faint sounds of battle growing louder the closer they approached the settlement. Strabo estimated the small number of Aduatuci cavalry present was only a nuisance to the legionnaires building the wall.

The legionnaires saw the Roman cavalry and cheered. The attackers immediately pulled back and headed away from the settlement toward a distant tree line west of the settlement. Tarquin signaled to pick up the pace to catch them before they reached the safety of the trees. Any seasoned cavalry leader would avoid a forest where a mounted cavalryman was disadvantaged and vulnerable to infantry, and Tarquin was not going to be an exception.

Well short of the tree line, Tarquin signaled to the three other troop leaders to follow him away from the settlement toward higher, open ground northwest to avoid the dense trees ahead. The four turmae had gone barely a quarter-mile when Strabo heard drums pounding behind them. He turned and saw a tightly-packed horde of mounted warriors charging out of the trees far outnumbering the Romans. The time they faced a large Belgae cavalry at the Aisne River, it turned out to be only formidable in size. Perhaps the Aduatuci cavalry would be the same.

Tarquin reined in at the top of the hill and swore. The hill ended abruptly with a near vertical drop into a wide ravine.

"We'll fight them here. The decuriae from the Eighth will remain here in reserve. My decuriae with the Eleventh on my right flank will go halfway down the hill and form a crescent. From the top of the hill on the left flank the Thirteenth and Twelfth Decuriae in that order will curve downhill and close in with the Tenth. The Fourteenth and Ninth Decuriae will do the same on the right flank curving downhill to close with the Eleventh. When the bastards get close enough, use your javelins as we did at the Aisne River. Kill the horses first to create obstacles for those coming behind. If I think we can push through them, the bugle will be the signal to ride toward the settlement. If you don't hear a bugle, this is where we stay.

"With Jupiter's help, we're going to show the sons of bitches how Roman cavalry fights. After we're done here, you, Caesar and Rome will know we fought well."

Strabo felt his stomach tighten at the decurion's last words. He regretted the reality he may never see his son or daughter. He patted Aquilo's neck and hoped the stallion would be spared if he wasn't. The last thought jolted him. He withdrew three javelins from the saddle quiver and gripped two of them in his shield hand with the remaining javelin in his right hand. He watched the Aduatuci gallop up the hill with fatalistic calm refusing to concede an inevitable outcome he wasn't willing to accept.

The tightly-packed warriors rode knee-to-knee with no room between them to fight effectively. Any javelin reaching them was certain to find a target. Warriors in the rear were aggressively pushing through the ranks ahead in their eagerness to reach the front line. The jostling resulted in collisions that caused tempers to flare with some warriors lashing out in anger with the flat of their blades or spear shafts. Here and there a horse stumbled or went down causing others behind to fall adding further confusion to a chaotic attack.

Observing the disorganized Belgae cavalry, Ursinus said to Strabo, "If they keep on killing each other, there will be fewer to fight when the rest get here. It might be a good idea to ask the gods for another favor. It worked yesterday, and they may be willing to help again. Better tell them we need it now. The odds don't look good."

"I did and pledged a bull to sacrifice in gratitude if they do."

The Aduatuci cavalry separated in three parts with the main effort continuing directly toward the center of the Roman defense. The flanks separated and swept around the Romans on all three sides.

The volley of javelins raining down on the Aduatuci below did not discriminate between horse and rider. The results were deadly; however, those who fell were few in comparison to those who remained urging their froth-mouthed horses up the hill eager to kill a Roman while there were some left. At first, the Romans easily met the Aduatuci vanguard with a defense inspired by the reality there was no choice except to fight or throw down their swords in shameful defeat.

The Roman horseshoe-shaped defense slowly contracted from the continuous, unrelenting assault. Strabo felt his sword getting heavier in the continuous onslaught. His sword arm was bloody from both the wounds he was receiving and the blood of the warriors he killed or wounded. Strabo knew there would be no signal for a breakout. He looked to his right and perceived a widening gap. His attention was drawn to a horseman coming toward him with a sword raised that exposed his chest. Confident the mistake was about to cost the warrior his life, Strabo raised his shield and leaned forward for a killing blow. The warrior was faster and blunted the sword with his shield while splitting Strabo's shield down to the boss. Strabo raised the broken, almost useless shield to blunt the next strike and knew before the sword struck, he wasn't going to be successful. He felt a sharp, blinding pain on the left side of his head followed by the sensation of falling into darkness accompanied by the deep, drawn out sound of a cornyx.

Mammura watched the tall siege tower come to life trundling slowly, almost majestically, toward the open gates of the twelve-foot Roman wall surrounding the settlement. The raucous jeers and laughter by the Aduatuci defenders common during the construction of the tower, turned to gasps of horror and wails of desperation. Until then, the defenders perceived the tower as a futile endeavor built too far away to be a threat.

Standing next to his prefect of engineers, Caesar saw the sudden change in the behavior of the defenders and said, "It looks as if our opponents have never seen a moving siege tower. My congratulations for completing your task in so timely a manner."

The siege tower had barely traveled another fifty feet with a long way to the ramp when the settlement gates swung open. An entourage of older men preceded by a solitary individual carrying a sheathed sword in both hands above his head approached the smaller group of mounted Romans.

"By Jupiter, Titus, I think they're ready to talk. Where's Strabo, he may be able to make sense of this."

"Caesar, he left hours ago with Decurion Tarquin and decuriae from the other legions to stop the harassment along the west wall. From the distant sound of battle, I think Tarquin is dealing with the trouble. Since the Treveri cavalry never returned, I'm not certain we have anyone left who knows whatever dialect they speak."

Caesar frowned and said peevishly, "I thought Strabo was going to be available when I need him instead of wasting time in inconsequential skirmishes. Too bad Diviciacus isn't here. I hope one of them speaks enough Latin to tell us they're surrendering and if so, what I'll demand. We'll stay mounted to hear what they have to say."

The young warrior carrying the sheathed sword stepped aside, and a stooped, white-haired man older than the rest came closer and stopped several paces in front of Caesar. The two men studied each other without speaking. In spite of his careworn face and withered frame,

Caesar was struck by the other man's demeanor. From his shrewd, unblinking eyes and gravitas, he didn't think the Aduatuci elder, or tribal leader, was a supplicant about to plead for mercy. The surprise came when the man spoke in slightly accented but otherwise flawless Latin.

"My name is Drusalos, Magistrate of the Aduatuci, and these men are my council of elders. Are you Caesar?" After Caesar nodded, Drusalos said, "We've come before you to surrender and avoid needless bloodshed. My counselors have asked for this meeting in the belief your recent victories and the capability you have to build such machines are proof you are favored by gods more powerful than ours." Lifting a shoulder in resignation, Drusalos added, "Well, that's what they believe."

"Do you also believe that?"

There was a hint of sardonic humor in the response. "I have seen such towers before and know well how they move. My councilors and people have not. As for the gods, my experience is the gods tend to favor those who are resolute...and stronger."

Caesar couldn't help smiling and nodded in agreement. "I accept your surrender with the following conditions. Signal your cavalry now engaging mine to withdraw. You spoke of avoiding needless bloodshed. Let it be so in order to accomplish what you propose. It's time to stop any further needless bloodshed." Caesar waited while Drusalos spoke to the young warrior with the sheathed sword. The warrior turned and ran back to the settlement. Caesar resumed.

"All weapons will be thrown over the walls. I will send a legion into the settlement to verify you have truly surrendered and there is no cause to doubt your peaceful intentions. The legion will be withdrawn from the settlement before nightfall to avoid any incident by either side that could jeopardize a peaceful end to this matter. If my requirements are met as I've specified, I will leave the settlement as it is and no harm will come to your people."

"You are generous, Caesar,"

"I am because it is the wish of Rome and my responsibility to establish mutual and beneficial relationships with the tribes of Gaul, Belgae and perhaps in time Germania. Such can only occur if there is peace instead of war in which the young are sacrificed for little purpose except to satisfy the curiosity of the gods." A cornyx blew from the settlement, and the faint noise of battle slowly faded away. Caesar nodded in satisfaction. "I hope the end of that battle marks the last time there will be hostility between us."

"Caesar, you spoke of *the curiosity of the gods*, and I think that may be true of our gods as well. I'm old and have come to believe there may be less to be feared from the gods than what men will do while invoking the gods to justify what they do."

Caesar smiled and responded, "I concede your point and admit the possibility of having done so from time to time. Where did you learn to speak such excellent Latin?"

"I was an unwilling guest of Rome for many years. My owner was wealthy, and while not kind, he was not a bad master. He thought I was more intelligent than the others; consequently, he had me tutored to become his scribe. He traveled to many places, and I had the opportunity to learn and admire much about the Romans including the things they build such as your siege tower. I came to fear them for their belief in the destiny of Rome to dominate the world. I hoped after I escaped and made my way back here, I would be far enough away never to see these lands conquered and subjugated by Rome. It seems my hopes were in vain."

"It's unfortunate you don't see the potential of how Rome can benefit the Aduatuci."

"You are correct, Caesar, I do not. I lost my freedom once before, and I do not welcome its loss again."

With a frown and pursed lips, Caesar watched Drusalos lead the elders back into the settlement. There was something about the benign countenance and particularly the last words of the magistrate that struck him.

"After we see their weapons come over the wall, send in the Thirteenth Legion into the settlement, and we'll see if our new friends are something other than what they appear to be."

"You suspect the magistrate is dissembling?"

"Without a doubt. By his own words, the son of a bitch betrays himself. He admits to knowing how we attack a fortified settlement and the means we employ. I think the display of deference to the power of our gods based on a moving siege tower is a charade. He has a plan and intends to go on the offensive when we least expect it. That's what I would do if our situation was reversed. Probably tonight, sometime in the third watch I'd guess. Tell the legion commanders to double the watch just in case."

General Labienus had long since seen too many occasions in which Caesar's intuition was proven correct to doubt him. His immediate concern was for the Thirteenth Legion.

"Caesar, I suggest instead of sending in the Thirteenth, a more experienced legion would be better."

"Ordinarily, I would agree; however, in the event Drusalos intends mischief sooner than I expect, I don't want to risk losing a battle-tested legion."

Strabo drifted in a void filled with fleeting images. Occasionally he heard muffled voices. He didn't understand what was being said or who was speaking. It was during such episodes he felt an intense, unrelenting pain relieved only when he drifted off into a dark, featureless landscape.

Standing in front of Tarquin and Ursinus, Tribune Gaius Setarius watched the medical orderly finish bandaging the terrible wound on the left side of Marcellus Strabo's face. He looked at the grim-faced senior doctor supervising the orderly. "Will he survive?"

The doctor shook his head. "The gods will decide, not me. If he does, there's no way of knowing if he'll ever be the same again either physically or mentally. He may be this way for hours, days or forever. The next day or two are critical."

The doctor reached over to a table and picked up Strabo's badly-dented helmet with the left cheek guard missing. "He's fortunate the sword or axe that struck him glanced off the rim of his helmet. If the strike had been more direct, he probably would not have survived. The cheek guard saved him. He will have a scar for a lasting reminder of how close he came to a fatal blow, that is assuming he lives. There is undoubtedly some swelling in the brain typical with head injuries. His left eye is damaged or destroyed; I can't really tell because the swelling is too great to examine it. Time will tell. He's young and strong and may recover with only a sore head and a scar."

"Whatever it takes, do everything you can."

"Tribune, we already are and will do what we can. Best talk to a priest and see what he thinks is a sacrifice worthy enough for the gods to help him."

The one-eyed tribune nodded. "It will be done. In the meantime, keep me informed how he's doing. There are others concerned. Caesar has asked about him. Thank you for what you've done."

Setarius left the tent and headed toward his own located near Caesar's headquarters. Steps behind him were followed by a gruff voice. "Tribune, I would speak with you about the sacrifice the medici spoke of."

Irritated at the distraction and impertinent tone of voice, Setarius stopped and turned to see the cavalryman who had been standing behind him in the medical tent. He looked closely at the aging, lantern-jawed cavalryman and thought he looked vaguely familiar.

"What do you want?"

"Decurion Strabo and I talked before the battle began. We didn't think any of us were going to see anything afterward except the gods. He told me if we did, nothing less than a bull would satisfy Jupiter for our survival. I want to be sure the sacrifice you make will be at least a bull." The cavalryman stopped and regarded the tribune's scowl with narrowed eyes. "If you're unable to afford the cost, I'm willing to make a contribution."

Setarius was about rebuke the cavalryman's disrespectful manner for his impudent offer. His stern expression softened after perceiving the bluntly spoken offer reflected a genuine regard for the young decurion.

"What's your name?"

"Ursinus, Sir."

"Your offer is generous, and I'll accept a modest contribution — a sesterce will be satisfactory."

"I had in mind something much more than that," Ursinus replied with an expression bordering on a sneer. "I'll bring five denarii to your quarters."

Setarius was both surprised and humored by the generous offer. "Very well, I'll arrange the sacrifice and inform you when and where the priest will perform it in the event you wish to be present."

"I'll be there with the rest of the decuria."

"It seems Decurion Strabo is looked upon with high favor."

"He is. He reminds me of his father."

"You know of General Strabo?"

"Aye, I served under him both when he was the primus pilus of the Tenth and later after he took command of the legion. I was a legionnaire in the first cohort at the time you were the legion's aquilfer."

"By the gods, Ursinus, I remember you. That was a long time ago. I recall you got into trouble with an optio and nearly killed him."

"That was me. My regret is I didn't succeed."

Setarius threw back his head and laughed. "Yes, that was General Strabo's opinion, too. Ursinus, tell me about the battle."

"We were expecting to engage a few hundred. It turned out to be closer to a thousand and twice what we expected. There was nothing left except to do the best we could. Unlike the cavalry we faced so far, the Aduatuci were better and didn't give up. We lost many. They lost more. I saw Decurion Strabo go down and thought he was gone. Soon after, we heard a carnyx blowing from the settlement, and the Aduatuci below the hill started yelling to the warriors fighting on top. At first, we thought the trumpets meant the Aduatuci were being reinforced. But the warriors we were fighting started to disengage and turn their horses downhill. We gave thanks to Jupiter."

"The Aduatuci surrendered the settlement, and Caesar ordered them to recall their cavalry. The surrender was unexpected. Caesar thinks it's a trick, and they're going to try something. We'll see."

Chapter 19
Midway through the third watch

The settlement gates showed only briefly and dimly under a crescent moon covered intermittently behind scudding clouds. The bleary-eyed optio of the guard walked back into the watchtower after finishing his periodic inspection of the guard. His watchtower overlooked the closed Roman gates below and the siege tower nearby. He thought the flickering torches along the Roman parapet revealed more about the presence of the Roman sentries than what might be happening in the silent blackness of the settlement.

The guard looked across the gates and saw the dim silhouette of his counterpart from the Twelfth Legion and suspected he was likely as tired and bored as he was. His optio said Caesar suspected treachery, and the guard had been doubled as a precaution. The legionnaires in all seven legions were sleeping fully armed. He started to drift off overcome by fatigue after the recent battle with the Nervii, the forced march here and the construction of the circumvallation. He prayed the Aduatuci was the last tribe they would face this campaign season.

With leaden eyelids, he put out the annoying torch and leaned back afraid to close his eyes in case the centurion of the guard appeared and accused him of sleeping, a fate only slightly less severe than cowardice in battle. A faint rumble woke him. He looked toward the newly-constructed gated wall distant from the settlement where the sound was coming from and saw nothing. The sound abruptly stopped replaced by the hollow rattle of wooden shields and low voices, and he saw moving shadows. He kicked the sleeping trumpeter awake.

"Wake up, you son of a bitch, we're under attack. Signal the alarm, and it better be loud and clear, or I'll throw your sorry ass over the wall."

Whether out of fear of the optio or the sudden sound of splintering wood from the gate below, the trumpeter managed a credible alarm echoed from the four Roman camps three hundred paces behind. Illuminated by the torches above, the optio looked down and saw a score of men below using a tree trunk to batter the gate while a restless mass of warriors waited silently behind. The gates crashed open, and accompanied by loud, almost maniacal shouting, the Aduatuci warriors ran toward the Roman camps unaware the legionnaires were assembled and waiting.

Flanked by General Labienus and Tribune Setarius with a dozen other officers and orderlies standing behind, a scowling Caesar surveyed the quiet battlefield and said to no one in particular, "Even though I expected something like this, it's not what I wanted."

General Labienus responded with unconcealed satisfaction, "They got what they deserved. I estimate they suffered at least four thousand killed while our numbers were a fraction of that."

"I would have preferred a peaceful resolution and another alliance to reduce the chance of the Germani coming back into Gaul. They pissed on my generosity, and I'll show no mercy for it. We will attack the settlement as soon as our wounded are taken care of. I doubt they have the means any longer to pose a credible defense. When the settlement is ours, the survivors left alive will be given to the slavers for auction in Rome. Those too injured or infirm will be put to the sword. The Aduatuci Tribe will cease to exist. I want the consequences of the Aduatuci treachery to serve as a lesson for any tribe that ever does what they did. If Drusalos still lives, I want him crucified. A quick death is too merciful for him."

Setarius cleared his throat and said, "His gods have shown him mercy. From where he lies dead, he must have led the attack."

"Too bad, but I'll credit the treacherous bastard for the way he died."

Ever practical, Labienus interjected, "There will probably be more than forty thousand people left in the settlement after we take it. The slavers will have difficulty getting so many to Rome."

"They'll find a way. They always do. By the way, I want all the slaves shorn before the slavers have them. Their profits will be great enough as it is without the addition of Gaulish hair so much in demand by the wig makers in Rome."

Strabo struggled to come out of a black well of silence as if awakening from a deep sleep. He was becoming aware of a painful, throbbing headache worse even than the one he had that morning before the battle. He wasn't sure the battle was real or the terrible images of a bad dream. Gradually he became aware of voices and snatches of conversation he began to understand. It took a while longer to realize he was the subject they were talking about. He started to drift off until someone began shaking him. A voice urged him to wake up. He tried to open his eyes but found he couldn't open his left eye. He managed to open his right part way and saw shadowy faces peering down at him although not clearly enough to recognize who they were. He closed his eye and tried to go back to a gray world where there was less pain. The effort to leave it was too great.

"Marcellus, can you hear me?" The question was insistent, intrusive, and the voice was vaguely familiar.

With his eyes closed, he answered in a resigned, hoarse voice, "Water."

"Orderly, he wants water!"

He felt his right cheek being patted, and the unrelenting shaking resumed. He had enough.

"The next son of a bitch that touches me without giving me water better be ready to kneel before the gods when I get my hands on a sword."

The laughter made him angry. He tried to sit up and see who was mocking him. He didn't have the strength to do it. He finally recognized the voice.

"Ursinus, for the love of Jupiter, get me some water. I feel like shit!"

"And you look like it, too, maybe worse," the cavalryman said belatedly adding, "Sir."

Unseen hands lifted Strabo up to a sitting position, and he felt a cup touch his lips followed by cool water filling his mouth. He kept swallowing until the cup was drained.

"I want more."

An unfamiliar and stern voice said, "Decurion, I'm the senior doctor, and that's all I'm going to allow. You can have more in an hour or so and some food as well. Open your right eye and tell me what you can see."

Strabo tentatively did as he was told. The light of a flickering lamp was so bright he quickly closed it.

"Try again."

He did as he was told, and this time managed to keep his eye open long enough to hear, "Good, you have a slight concussion, better than I expected. You may be luckier than you thought, and I believed."

"What about the left eye?"

"We'll see in a few days after I take the bandage off. Then it will be a test of how lucky you really are."

Strabo reached up and realized the left side of his head was bandaged. He felt the whiskers on his face that prompted him to ask, "How long have I been here, and where am I?"

"Four days, and you're in my hospital. Lay back down and rest." The doctor looked at Ursinus and said curtly, "I'll let you have a few minutes. If you're here when I get back in half an hour, I have several very large orderlies who will help you leave."

"Ursinus, what happened? How did we survive what should have been our last battle?"

"About the time I saw you go down, a carnyx sounded in the settlement, and they rode away. After we got back here, we learned the Aduatuci had surrendered to Caesar, and the tribal magistrate stopped the fighting."

"I think I heard a carnyx just before I blacked out. Aquilo, what about him? Is he all right?"

"He's fine. He's got a few minor cuts, that's all."

After a brief pause during which the cavalryman remained silent, Strabo said, "I think I saw Vinicius go down."

"Vinicius was one of the three we lost. Costa was wounded almost as bad as you; he's in the other tent."

Strabo gritted his teeth even as he felt his right eye watering. Vinicius was his last real contact with Massilia and a life already feeling distant.

He was finally able to speak without fear his voice would break. "I was the one who encouraged him to become a cavalryman. If he'd remained a legionnaire with the *Claudia*, he might be alive."

Ursinus was quick to respond. "He did what he wanted. And maybe with another campaign, he might even have made a reasonably capable cavalryman."

Strabo started to bristle at the implied criticism of his friend. He knew there was much truth in the observation. "Or maybe two or three more campaigns under your close supervision."

"Are you saying it would take me that long to make something of him?" Strabo glanced at Ursinus and saw his lips twitching in a rare display of humor.

He changed the subject. "What else happened since the surrender?"

"Caesar had the town sacked. Those who survived and were worth taking as slaves are on the way to Rome. I've heard it said it may be the largest auction ever — 53,000."

"How are the slavers going to guard that many?"

"The campaign season has ended, and many of those who have served their annual commitment have been hired by the slavers to help guard them."

"Are we in winter quarters? Where are we?"

"You'll be happy to hear the Tenth and Eleventh are collocated 20 miles north of Bibracte which should be convenient for you."

Ursinus saw Strabo's disappointment. "What's wrong?"

"Raven is with the Remi settlement. It's at least a hundred miles north of here. She may have already given birth to our child, and here I am in a medical tent with one eye that barely works and the other maybe worse. In spite of what the doctor said, I don't feel lucky at all."

"What a shame, the gods allowed you to live so you can wallow in self-pity. Considering what happened to so many others, you're luckier than you think. Maybe we should have settled for a rabbit to sacrifice instead of the bull Tribune Setarius and the decuria bought to persuade the gods to save you."

Strabo sighed as he realized what his lament sounded like. "You're right. You probably talked that way to my father."

"He and the gods would say you're right."

Chapter 20
Winter Quarters north of Bibracte

Strabo was apprehensive. He was trying to take his mind off what was about to happen by currying Aquilo. He would have preferred an easy ride. The doctor warned him riding a horse would be the worst thing he could do. Even the sedate, even-tempered Secundus was ruled out. Normally, brushing down a horse had a calming effect on him particularly after a battle when nerves were on edge. Today was different.

It had been ten days since the doctor thought he might be blind or have permanent damage in the left eye. The time had come to find out. It was less about how he would look than how the loss of an eye would make it difficult to judge where the sword or spear coming toward him really was. He wasn't encouraged after Tribune Setarius told him in time, he would adjust to it. His mood took a further downward turn after hearing Servius call his name.

"Strabo, I said the first time I saw you with that horse he was a standout. If I had been riding him, I wouldn't have bothered with any of my racing tricks."

Without turning around, Strabo said, "Even so, you wouldn't have won. You don't ride well enough to control a horse like Aquilo."

"Implying you're a better and more experienced rider than I am? I've been racing before you had hair between your legs."

Strabo turned around with a look of mock surprise. "More than ten years?"

"Almost that many."

"Well, there you are. I've been riding almost before I could walk. I won my first race and a purse of 50 denarii a few years from having hair between my legs. I owned a stable of racing horses in Massilia and raced several times a week. I occasionally lost although it wasn't often."

Servius's eyes widened. "Fifty denarii, that is impressive. Who did you race against?"

"General Publius Crassus and Centurion Marcea Drusus. They were several years older than I was. At the time, I was eight years old."

"A father who was both a general and governor and friendly with a son of the richest man in Rome, I'm surprised you're not a general or at least a centurion. By the way, I heard your father died recently. As a former ranker in the Tenth Legion, I saw him at a far distance and knew of his widely respected reputation. I might even have respected him except for the woman he married. I may be the son of a legionnaire and a whore, but at least they were both Roman."

"I'm disappointed. I thought you came here to offer your sympathies."

"No, I wouldn't go that far, I wanted to see how your wound was doing, or if you're going to look like that old fart Setarius."

"Could be. I'm about to go to the medical tent to find out."

"I wish you good fortune in the outcome." This time Strabo's surprised expression was genuine. Servius smiled. "No, don't get the wrong idea. My sentiment is based on having both of your eyes able to see my sword which will be the last thing you may ever see and feel again. In the meantime, I bid you farewell. I hope while I'm gone, you'll manage to stay alive. As I said before, I won't be happy if somebody else deprives me of the satisfaction of killing you."

"In that case, I'll certainly do my best. Where are you going?"

"You've spent too much time in the medical tent. The Twelfth Legion has been ordered to establish a camp somewhere between Genava and the Rhone River to protect the supply route between Gaul and Transalpine Gaul. We leave tomorrow. General Mettellus was quick to offer my decuria to the Twelfth to meet General Gallius's request for additional cavalry. Ever since the race at Visontio, Metellus has looked for an opportunity to get rid of me, as he made very clear, for *embarrassing* the legion." Servius laughed and said with unrepentant candor, "Well, I suppose I did at that. What really bothers me is losing the race."

Strabo watched the decurion walk away with regret. Even though he didn't doubt one day he and Servius would likely have a reckoning, there were things he respected about him. He recalled how Servius calmly prepared his men for battle at the Aisne River, his fighting ability during the battle and most of all, his help for Strabo during the battle.

The small tent was dark with both entrances closed up. The only light came from the flickering oil lamp on the table next to where Strabo sat, fists clenched, right eye closed tight. The orderly began slowly unwrapping the bandage while the doctor looked on.

"When the bandage comes off, don't open your eye until the orderly cleans up around it. You have dried blood and some discharge around it. When he's done, try to open it."

The orderly finished and stepped away. Strabo waited for either the orderly or the doctor to say something. He opened his right eye and saw the doctor leaning toward him, legs spread, hands behind his back, staring at him with pursed lips and a deep frown. Finally, the doctor cleared his throat and said matter-of-factly to the orderly, "Paulus, you did a good job sewing him up, maybe the best you've done so far." Strabo started to relax until the doctor continued, "Decurion, for the rest of your life anybody who sees you will wonder what the other fellow looks like. Now, let's see about the eye." The doctor chuckled, and Strabo felt like kicking him in the crotch until he repeated, "see about the eye" and realized that was as close to humor as the medici was capable. "Open slowly and don't look directly at the lamp until I tell you."

Strabo took a deep breath and did as he was told and immediately felt dizzy. He resisted the urge to vomit. "Everything looks double and blurry." He closed both eyes resigned his worst fear had happened.

With sudden animation, the doctor exclaimed, "My boy, I thought you might be lucky, and I've been proven right."

"Doctor, I can't even open the other eye without being sick."

"It will go away in a day or so and faster if you use it. Your good eye will help make it clear up. There's nothing wrong with it. You're experiencing the effects of the blow you received and the resulting concussion. The blade cut across your eyebrow to the left of the eye. If it had been any closer, you would have lost the eye. As soon as the double vision clears, you can start riding again. I recommend using a mounting block to get in the saddle. As for the scar, it will look better when it fully heals and the swelling's gone down."

Strabo thanked the medici and left the tent reasonably optimistic the diagnosis was better than he expected. A few days later, he ignored everything the doctor told him not to do.

Chapter 21
Bibrax

Leuca and the wetnurse watched Raven wrap the baby in a long cloth across her chest from her right shoulder down her back where the two ends of the cloth were tied at the waist. It was a routine the two women watched many times with silent disapproval. She picked up her quarrel of newly fletched arrows, bow and saddle and went to the back of her small, rounded shelter where the horse was tethered. Leuca had given up cajoling, pleading with her to give up her near obsession to rejoin her brother as a scout. She was dismayed Raven seemed unconcerned for what would become of the child if she did. She resented the unspoken acceptance Raven was going to depend on someone else to take on the responsibility of looking after the infant. She was on the verge of disliking her for her single-minded, selfish behavior.

Oblivious to her friend's tight-lipped disapproval, Raven checked to see the baby was secure, stepped up on the mounting block and climbed into the saddle. She kneed the horse into a walk and headed for the settlement gate and the forested glade a few miles away from the settlement. She didn't think it would take many more trips to achieve the range and accuracy she had months ago.

Raven stopped the horse next to a tree stump she used as a mounting block. She dismounted and saw a middle-aged woman and an older man with long gray hair sitting in the shadows of a nearby tree. Face expressionless, the man stared at her with an intensity that made her vaguely uneasy. While the man remained sitting, the woman stood up and approached her holding an arrow.

"I found this in a thicket. By any chance, is it yours?"

After a quick glance at the crudely made arrow, Raven shook her head. "No, but thank you for asking. Are you from Bibrax?" knowing from the woman's accent she probably wasn't. Possibly Bellovaci, she believed.

"No, we come from farther north to get away from where the Romans have been fighting. How old is your baby?" the woman asked as she watched Raven lift the carry-cloth over her head and cradle the sleeping infant.

"He's three months old. Would you like to see him?"

"Yes, please." Raven pulled the cloth away from the baby's face and turned to let the woman see him. "He's beautiful," the woman said softly. "What's his name?"

"Caturix."

"It's a good, strong name."

Raven leaned down and placed the swaddled infant on the ground in the shade of a sapling. As she straightened up there was a primal scream behind her. She started to turn, felt a sharp blow to the back of her head then nothing.

Occasionally the blackness faded to gray, and she heard muffled voices too distorted to understand what was being said. The plaintive cry of a baby was clear, and she moaned at the realization the nightmare she thought she was having was real. It was Caturix crying. She opened her eyes and screamed. The beatings began.

Gradually, the voices were back and even though they were speaking in the Bellovaci dialect, she understood them well enough. She felt a throbbing pain throughout her body and particularly in her chest. She was certain some of her ribs were broken.

"Enough!" a man's voice said. "You'll kill her."

"I want to, she deserves to die," a woman's voice replied.

"And I told you I want her to live."

Because of the swelling, Raven could hardly open her eyes. Her arms were stretched upward, wrists tied to a tree branch above, and her legs were tied to the trunk of the tree. She saw the woman she'd been talking to. The older, gray-haired man standing next to the woman looked at her with such hate it brought a chill to her. A younger man, tall, muscular and expressionless stood behind them. The woman was holding at her side what appeared to be a stick. She identified it as part of her bow. Her arrows were broken and strewn about. Too busy arguing, they didn't notice she was conscious. She turned her head in the direction of the crying, reassurance Caturix was alive. Blinded by her tears, she couldn't see him.

The woman started to reply then saw Raven looking at them. "She's awake!"

The woman started to walk toward her lifting the bow stave to begin the brutal beating again. He was quicker and snatched it from her pushing her roughly to the ground where she remained cursing bitterly.

Standing over her, the man shouted, "I said no, and I meant it."

He left her and limped toward her dragging his left leg. She noticed his right hand was missing. His threatening look indicated he might have changed his mind and was the one who was going to beat her. If he was going to kill her, she hoped it would be quick.

He stopped inches from her face and in a low, barely controlled voice said, "Not long ago on this very spot you killed our son. His name was Bannos." She vaguely recalled hearing the name before, and a hazy image came to her of a man carrying an axe and running toward her.

"For that, you will remember us as the ones who replaced our son with the son you will never see again. I want someone to find you here alive. I'm going to release your horse to ensure you're found. I'll release it far enough away from here it will take time to find his way back to you or his stall. By then, we'll be far away. If I let her, my wife would be kinder. She would kill you. Whether you're awake or asleep, the loss of your son will burn in your mind forever. He will live to become a man and will never know you."

"Please, don't, I'll do anything you want. I'll serve you without complaint for the rest of your life."

The man limped away shaking his head. He walked past his wife and didn't see her jump up and run toward Raven clutching a broken arrow shaft. By the time he saw what she was going to do, it was too late to stop her from stabbing Raven in the chest. Raven screamed in agony and started to fall into a gray world that rapidly darkened. Her last conscious thought was praying she would never wake and relive the horrifying nightmare.

It was near sunset Leuca saw the saddled mare trotting past Raven's dwelling to the paddock behind. She assumed Raven had returned hours ago. She covered her mouth certain something had happened to her and ran over to Raven's dwelling. It was empty, and she imagined the worst. Could the normally docile horse have been frightened and thrown Raven off? The day was nearly gone and so was her husband, spending the next several days guarding the horse herd. Talos! He would know what to do.

She found him sooner than expected in the gathering place where the men frequented at the end of the day and where beer and women were available. Thankfully, he had his hands around a cup and not around a woman.

"Talos, I need your help!" Talos regarded her with bleary-eyes.

"What's the matter?"

"Something's happened to Raven. Her horse came back to the stable a short time ago without her or the baby. This afternoon, she went to the glade several miles south of Bibrax where she's been sharpening her archery skills. She should have been back long ago."

Talos stood up somewhat unsteadily. "I know the place. I'll take one of your husband's horses. Mine is with the herd and too far away."

The sun was an hour from setting when Talos found her. At first, he thought she was dead. There was no sign of life until he came closer and heard her, a mewing sound an injured animal might make. In the last minutes of the day, there was enough light to see how bloody and swollen her face was and the arrow shaft protruding from her chest.

He cut the bindings around her ankles, and holding her body with one arm, he reached up and cut her free from the branch above. She sagged in his arms and moaned. He laid her gently on the ground and left her to search the immediate area for the baby. He didn't find any trace of it. It gave him hope Caturix may have been spared and taken away.

He sat down and gathered her in his arms torn between his love for her and the bitterness for her choice of the half-Roman instead of him. For the moment and holding her, she was his. He knew he couldn't prolong the moment. If she had any chance of surviving, he had to get her back to Bibrax.

The ride back to Bibrax was slow. He was afraid to go faster than a walk and risk making her injuries worse. Each time the horse lurched, she stirred and cried out in pain. Terrible as it was for him to hear her suffering, it assured him she was alive.

Leuca came to the door as soon as he called her name.

"Leuca, she's hurt bad."

"What about the baby?"

"She hasn't been able to talk. I looked all around where I found her. There was no sign of it. It's likely he was taken by whoever did this to her. Right now, she needs a healer."

"We'll put her in my bed then I'll get the healer."

With Leuca's young and wide -eyed children watching silently, Talos laid her down on the bed and stood looking at her in the semi-darkness of the room. There was enough from the dim oil lamp to show her bruised and badly-swollen face. Leuca gasped when she saw the broken arrow shaft. She was so still they thought she was gone until she cried out. Leuca knew pain wasn't the cause. It was for Caturix.

After Leuca left to get the healer, Talos sat beside her and couldn't think of anything to do except hold her near limp hand and invoke every god and goddess he could think of to spare her.

He must have drifted off. The next thing he knew, someone was shaking him and a gruff voice said, "Wake up and get out of the way. Leuca, bring more lamps and get the children out of here, and young man, that especially includes you."

Talos went into the next room while Leuca left briefly to get the children in bed. On her way back to assist the healer, Talos said, "I should go. The healer is right I'm in the way. I need to get some sleep to look for Caturix. It could be a long day tomorrow."

"I understand. I'll make offerings you will be successful."

He left without feeling optimistic about tomorrow and finding Caturix. He had no reason to expect the infant was alive. He couldn't imagine any reason why he would be. What happened to Raven couldn't have been a random encounter. If it had been, he would have found their lifeless bodies. There had to be another reason.

After another and more thorough search of the immediate area around where Raven had been tied, Talos found no trace of the infant suggesting he might have been taken alive. It didn't make sense. Why wasn't she killed to keep her from identifying her attacker? He mounted and headed deeper into the glade. He wished Corius was here. He was by far better at tracking than he was, but then so were most of the other scouts. Unfortunately, all of them were far away in Bibracte.

In a clearing behind a dense stand of trees and past where Raven had positioned her farthest targets, he found where horses had been tethered. The amount of dung present and the degree of freshness indicated several horses had been there for many days. Across the clearing, he found a rude shelter, a fire pit, and detritus left by a careless camper or campers. He saw two pallets of leaves close together and a single pallet across the clearing. There was no way to tell if the campsite had anything to do with Raven; however, there was at least a possibility it did. Raven was known by many for her skill with a bow and how often she came to the glade to maintain it. Did her assailant, or assailants, camp here while waiting for her? If that was true, what happened to her could have been planned and not a random sadistic act. He considered the possibilities as he followed a trail made by at least four horses going west out of the campsite.

The trail soon intersected the road circling Bibrax. Observing the well-used road, his first thought was this was as far as he would be able to follow the trail. He was about to give up and return to the settlement until he saw the trampled grass directly across the road. He walked the horse over to take a closer look. It was the same trail continuing west. Three miles farther on, he saw a circular dwelling and a corral with three horses inside. He walked his horse close enough to announce his presence and remained in the saddle, hand resting on his sword hilt.

A man with a quizzical although friendly expression came out of the dwelling followed by a woman with two young children clinging to her legs. He was unarmed except for the usual working knife tucked inside his belt. Instinctively, Talos didn't think they were the ones he was tracking.

"My name is Talos, and I live in Bibrax. One of my horses was taken yesterday, and I've been following a trail made by four horses, one of which I believe could be mine. Whoever took the horse came this way. Have you seen anyone passing by here late yesterday?"

"I'm called Ciel. My wife is Eda. We've seen only the parents and husband of Nahtaira who stayed with us for several days while they went to Bibrax to find their daughter's baby. Another man claimed the baby was his and took it away in the middle of the night. Since he was a Remi, they believed he went to Bibrax and came here to find him. Apparently, they did because the older woman was holding a baby. They left yesterday and headed west. No one else has passed by since."

"Did her parents have a fourth horse with a saddle on it?"

"Yes, they did. I wondered about it since their daughter has her own horse and saddle. She and her horse remained here while her parents and her husband were gone. Not long after they left, we saw the saddled horse gallop past here in the direction of Bibrax. I think that may be the horse you're looking for."

He was certain the single horse was Raven's. It made no sense. Why would they release a perfectly good horse unless the horse simply got away from them?

"Yes, I think the horse is mine. I'll go back and look for it." He feigned a curious look and asked, "Did they say where they were going?"

"No, and Nahtaira didn't talk about where they came from or much about anything. Eda felt sorry for her. Her baby was missing, and her parents treated her more like a slave than a daughter. She had bruises on her face and arms. And her husband seemed to have little interest in either her or the baby. We thought her parents and husband were upset with her for being the cause the baby was taken. After her mother gave Nahtaira the baby to nurse, she didn't seem particularly excited to see it or grateful. Eda thought Nahtaira was a wet nurse and not really the baby's mother. She appeared reluctant to leave here, and we were sorry to see her go even though the man paid us to look after her. She helped Eda with the chores."

"What did Nahtaira's mother and father look like?"

"Both were old — we think too old to have a daughter as young as Nahtaira. They weren't very friendly. He was missing his right hand, and he walked with a limp; his left leg was stiff as if he had been injured. There was nothing about the woman to tell her from any old woman anywhere except she looked like she never smiled. From their accent, they could have been Bellovaci or from one of the other tribes farther north."

Talos felt his throat constrict. He knew who the man was. In a hoarse voice, he mumbled his thanks before guiding the horse back the way he came, too numb to think clearly. Ciel's description was too close to fitting Bannos's father not to be the same man he met briefly in the Bellovaci settlement. He didn't remember the father's name although he did recall the bitterness the man had for the Romans who had maimed him in battle. Now that he knew the identity of her assailant, he felt indirectly responsible for what happened to her. As the shock wore off, he realized he owed her more than feeling remorseful. He would find Caturix if it was the last thing he ever did. Momentarily, he considered turning around to go after them. The thought was fleeting. The odds of going alone into Bellovaci lands and successfully getting her son away safely were too poor to make the attempt. He needed help, and Bibracte was a long ride to get it.

Chapter 22
Three days later.

With her eyes closed, Raven struggled to come awake wondering as she did why she hurt so much. For some reason she didn't understand, she didn't want to open them, nor did she want to sleep and fall back into the nightmarish world in which she had been drifting. She slowly opened her eyes and realized the terrible dreams had been real. She screamed.

Leuca heard the scream with a mix of relief Raven was going to survive and despair for how her friend would be able to cope with what had happened to her. In her place, she might have already lost her mind. Raven's cavalier attitude since the infant's birth had not shown she cared deeply for the child.

She rushed into the bedroom and found Raven breathing in short, shallow gasps and staring wide-eyed at the roof timbers.

Leuca laid down beside her and pulled her close. "Raven, it will be all right. You will see Caturix again, and he'll be fine." She felt Raven begin to relax and saw her eyes close. She thought she had fallen asleep again until she spoke.

"It's all my fault. I should not have taken him with me. They took him because I killed their son. The man said he wouldn't let his wife kill me. He wanted me to remember what happened to him for the rest of my life. Caturix will grow up without ever knowing me. He was right. Living with what happened is worse than death."

"Talos knows who did this to you, and where he might be. He's gone to Bibracte to get your brother's help to find Caturix and bring him back."

Raven sighed and a moment later from her regular breathing, Leuca knew she had fallen asleep. She stayed with her a little longer until it was clear she had. She stood up and wiped her eyes overcome with sadness and convinced Raven would never be the same. Despite telling Raven it was going to be all right, she didn't believe it would be. The possibility Talos and Corius would be successful in rescuing the infant seemed too remote. She wondered when Marcellus Strabo would be told what had happened or if he even knew he had a son.

With two horses, Talos was able to reach Bibracte late at night on the second day. It was too late to wake Corius; consequently, he quietly put the horses in the corral behind the dwelling Corius shared with his wife and daughter. After feeding and watering the horses, he put his bedroll down outside the corral. Exhausted, he fell into a deep sleep.

Talos felt someone shaking him. He opened his eyes and saw Corius kneeling beside him. "Why didn't you tell me you were here?"

"It was the middle of the night, and I didn't want to wake you." He took a deep breath and said, "Something terrible has happened to Raven. She was assaulted and badly hurt. She hasn't been able to tell us who did it or why. Whoever it was took her son, Caturix, born several months ago. I think it had something to do with what happened in a glade near Bibrax where she often went to practice her archery before and after she gave birth.

"Several weeks before the Bellovaci attack and the birth, she told me on one of the occasions, she encountered three men. They intended to take their pleasure with her; however, they weren't prepared for her skill as an archer. She killed all three before they could harm her. Before one of them died, he told her Bannos was one of the other attackers. I met this man once before. She glimpsed a fourth man who saw what happened and rode away without getting involved. From her brief description of him, he could be the father of Bannos. He's missing his right hand and lame. After seeing what happened, he rode away knowing he had no chance against Raven.

"How did you happen to know Bannos and his father?"

Talos skirted the truth. "I met Bannos and his father at the Suessiones settlement some time ago. It was before the Remi decided not to join King Galba as the Bellovaci had already done. There were many Bellovaci there celebrating the alliance and why I had occasion to meet them." He avoided questions by omitting the time he had gone to the Bellovaci settlement afterward when he agreed to help them and why. He was relieved Corius didn't pursue the matter despite his frown.

"Talos, there's more to this tale than you're telling. I'll let it go. I'll go with you although unlike you, I'm not willing to ask any of the scouts to risk their lives in what will be a dangerous and likely unsuccessful effort to get the boy. Marcellus needs to know about this and have the chance to help."

"Why involve him? He doesn't care about Raven, and he wasn't anywhere near enough to protect her."

"He's the boy's father! The reason Raven and Marcellus haven't been hand-fasted is my sister's refusal. He has the right to decide what to do about it. He's in winter quarters not far from here. We'll leave tomorrow with an additional horse for the two of us and another for Marcellus."

The two men rode up to the nearest entrance of the fort and dismounted. The surly guard eying them with suspicion was not an encouraging sign. Corius pointed to the open gate and with a beckoning motion said, "Strabo."

A flicker of interest replaced the guard's unfriendly expression. A man wearing a cuirass and plumed helmet, clearly an officer, strolled out from the shadows inside the gate and came toward them.

"Guard, what's this about?"

"I don't know, sir. The only thing I understood the bigger one said was *Strabo.* Could be they've come here to sell horses."

"Well, if it isn't Strabo they want to see, at least the decurion speaks the language. He can find out who and what they want. I'll send an orderly to find him."

Corius watched the officer walk back inside the fort and started to relax hopeful he may have succeeded in making clear his intent. The minutes dragged. The baleful looks of the guard were a reminder for most Romans, Gauls were nothing more than barbarians. Marcellus finally appeared and his puzzled expression immediately turned to a broad smile of welcome as he walked to Corius and embraced him while ignoring Talos. Corius was shocked at the fresh, livid scar running diagonally from the left side of Strabo's forehead across the eyebrow and cheek down to the lobe of the ear.

"The orderly said there were two men asking for me, possibly to sell me some horses."

"No, we're not here to sell horses."

Corius's somber demeanor and cryptic comment caused Strabo to step back and regard his friend with a sharp look. "What's wrong?"

Strabo was stoic and silent while Corius told him what happened to Raven and his son. After Corius finished, Strabo nodded, "I'll go with you. I need time to get permission to leave."

"Permission?"

"If it isn't granted, I'll leave without it. Wait here, I won't be long."

"You can't go with us looking like a Roman. We are of a size, and I have clothes and weapons that will make you look less Roman."

After Strabo finished, Tribune Setarius said, "You have permission for however long it takes. I wish you success in finding your son, and I pray to the gods after you do, you'll come back to the legions." The tribune stood up and came around the table to clasp Strabo's arm. "May the gods be with you and give you success."

He stopped long enough to tell Tarquin and Ursinus why he was leaving. Asked if he was going to return, he shook his head. "I'm not certain I will. Tribune Setarius told me I was free to choose."

Tarquin asked, "When will you decide?"

"After I find my son."

Chapter 23

The three travel-worn men dismounted in front of the dwelling. Each one hesitating to announce their arrival and reluctant to confirm their worst fear Raven had died of her injuries.

Strabo handed Aquilo's reins to Corius and walked alone to the entrance. Leuca's sudden appearance indicated she must have heard them arrive. She looked tired, sad. Her expression gave no indication of Raven's condition. Strabo felt his jaw clench, afraid to ask the question.

Leuca's face softened. "Are you Marcellus Strabo?" He nodded. "She lives. She suffers less from the wounds than the loss of Caturix. If you're able to find and bring back the baby, it might not be enough to bring her back the way she was. She blames herself for not caring enough for the baby or looking after him the way she should have. She isn't blameless. She was too focused on getting back to a life she preferred."

"Is she well enough to see me or Corius? Does she want to?"

"I'm not sure. If she does, don't stay too long, she's weak with a long recovery ahead of her."

Leuca was gone longer than he thought she would be. She finally returned, and what she said wasn't encouraging. "She will see you. At first, she refused to see any of you. I talked her into it. Be patient. It would not take much to push her into the next world where she's said many times she deserves and wants to be."

He followed Leuca to a small room in the back of the dwelling. From a few toys in a corner, it was a child's room. The room was dark except for an oil lamp hanging from a rafter near the small bed where Raven was lying, a blanket covering her to her waist. Prepared as he was from the description Talos had given, he was shocked to see the extent of the bruises and lacerations on her face; her left arm was in a splint. He wouldn't have recognized her if he hadn't known it was Raven.

He couldn't speak and knelt down and took her hand. Her eyes were closed, and she started to pull away, stopped, opened her eyes and pulled him down with a choking sob.

She spoke in a faltering voice barely above a whisper. "I'm sorry. I cared more for what I wanted to be than for our son. I wish he let her kill me instead of leaving me with a wound that will never heal. I wish I had died before Talos found me."

"Don't talk about dying! We know who did this and where they are. I promise when I return, I'll have Caturix with me."

Contrary to what Leuca told him, he remained with her until she finally fell asleep. He left dreading the possibility he wouldn't be able to keep his promise. He didn't want to think about coming back to tell her he failed.

Grim-faced and silent, Strabo mounted Aquilo. "She's asleep. There's no point in wasting time." Equally impatient to leave, Corius and Talos mounted and fell in behind.

It wasn't until Strabo reined in to rest the horses a few miles from Bibrax that Corius asked about his sister. After a moment of silence, Strabo responded.

"Her injuries are severe, and it will take a long time for her to recover; however, Leuca is right the wounds are not what threaten her life. Her spirit is broken, possibly forever. She blames herself. If we aren't able to rescue the boy, I don't think she'll want to live. I promised we would find him and bring him back. They were words I felt I had to say without any confidence I, we, would be successful."

Corius saw his friend's torment and replied. "You speak for us. We know the odds. With what Talos knows, I believe we have a good chance. You have the strongest reason for what we are going to do, and you should lead us."

"No, Corius, both you and Talos are familiar with where we're going. I agree I may have the strongest reason for this, but it's also the reason I shouldn't. I may have us taking needless risks. Corius, you have led us well in the past, and you will be more objective in deciding what we should do than I can be." Talos was quick to agree, and Corius nodded his acceptance.

To break the brief silence that followed, Talos said, "They probably returned to the Bellovaci settlement believing no one would be foolish enough to come after them. The man we follow was once a clan chief. After his injuries, he stepped aside. He remains a clan elder and is influential with a strong following."

Frowning, Corius said, "Talos, we have to assume they do think they're going to be followed and be prepared."

"I agree," Strabo said. "If he does expect to be followed, he may think a larger force will come than the three of us. If he does, it will come from the direction of Bibrax. We should go north and circle back."

Talos was quick to respond. "We'll save time if we go directly west to the Bellovaci settlement."

Strabo shook his head. "Time is not as much a concern as making sure we get there without anyone knowing who we are and why we're there."

"I agree with Marcellus. We're too few to march in there and take Caturix by force. We're scouts, and we need to use the skills we've learned as scouts. We have to find where Caturix is and take him away with the least notice. The Bellovaci were never on the best of terms with the Aeduans, and since Diviciacus supported the Romans, the relationship has gotten worse. We cannot afford to look and act like Aeduan or worse, Roman. If we fail to do that, our chance of success will be at greater risk. Marcellus, in spite of being dressed to look like us, you look too much like a Roman with your short hair and shaved face."

"My name is not Marcellus. I'm Cilurnos, a Roman slave for many years until I recently escaped to the Aduatuci. I was wounded during the fight with the Romans. With the help of my two Aeduan brothers, I managed to keep from becoming a slave again."

Corius smiled his approval. "Well, met Cilurnos."

For the next two days, they traveled at night to avoid the occasional travelers they might meet and the usual curiosity where they were going and why. Even at night without the help of Talos, Strabo was able to identify where they were from the recent progression of the legions. Their indirect route to the Bellovaci settlement had brought them back to within a few miles of the northern gate as the sun was about to rise.

Corius stopped at a small stream. "We'll camp here, rest for a few hours then go to the settlement. Talos, is there any risk you'll be recognized by any Bellovaci you met at the Suessiones settlement? If there is, stay here with the spare horses."

"I don't think so. I met only with Bannos and his father who didn't talk much. He was mainly interested in what was in his cup instead of what Bannos was proposing. I have a better chance of finding where the father lives than either of you by asking about him in a way neither of you can by finding Nahtaira."

"What does she have to do with it?" Strabo asked.

Corius responded with disbelief in Marcellus's apparent ignorance of why the infant was dependent on Nahtaira for survival.

"Marcellus, she's a wet nurse and critical to keeping Caturix alive. If we can find her, we'll find your son. Talos and I will go in the settlement and learn where Bannos's father and mother live or anyone who knows where a wet nurse by the name of Nahtaira can be found. I know you want to ride in there and get your son. It will take more than boldness to achieve this. We need to be cautious and deliberate first to find him then to take him away safely."

Strabo saw the resolute expressions on the two men and leaned back with a sigh. Corius was right. He had to control his impatience.

Over the next two days, Strabo struggled to hold on to his resolve when there was nothing Corius or Talos had to report. It wasn't until late in the third day when the two scouts came back and told him they knew where Caturix was. Strabo was ready to go that night and get him. Corius restrained him.

"Patience, we're not ready. We need to confirm what we learned and who else is living there besides Bannos's mother and father and maybe the man who was supposed to be Nahtaira's husband. Most critical is to find out if the wet nurse is living there or somewhere else. She is key to keeping the infant alive until we reach the safety of the Remi settlement. Finally, are there clan members guarding the dwelling or close enough they could intervene if they heard a disturbance?"

They were valid questions, and Strabo agreed the two scouts were the ones to learn the answers.

Two days later, Corius and Talos decided they learned enough to plan how they were going to accomplish their mission. Corius drew a map of the settlement in the dirt.

"There are four entrances to the settlement. Bannos's father, whose name is Bragimoros, lives with his wife and Nahtaira in a large dwelling befitting a clan elder located near the southern gate." Corius drew a circle to indicate the approximate location and drew another smaller circle next to it. "The smaller circle is where Toccus lives. He's a bastard son of Bragimoros and serves his father as a personal bodyguard. He is likely the individual who was identified to Talos as Nahtaira's husband. From what I've learned about him, he's devoted to his father. He has earned a reputation for being both fearless and an accomplished fighter. The two dwellings are located about 200 paces from the gate and close to the settlement wall. Fortunately, they are somewhat distant from the other dwellings surrounding them.

"The gates are closed and guarded after sunset. Anyone entering the settlement after they're closed is questioned. That's not the case for those leaving. Tomorrow afternoon, we'll go in the settlement and remain there after the gates are closed. There's a large open area in the center of the settlement and close to the market place. It's where visitors and vendors camp with their horses and wagons for a few days. Marcellus, you'll have a chance to become familiar with the settlement and particularly where Bragimoros lives. We'll stay there just long enough, a day or two at the most. We'll go after Caturix on foot. Six horses moving about at that hour will be too noticeable. After we get Caturix we go back for the horses and go to the south gate. Coming from the direction of the market place, the guard may be less interested in why we're leaving at such an hour. If he gets too inquisitive, my sword will silence him.

"Marcellus, it's important you remember you are Cilurnos. Your wound and story are believable. Make sure you act the part as you move around the settlement. Talos, tell him what you learned about Nahtaira."

"I happened to be at one of the market stalls when a young woman was buying vegetables. The woman selling the vegetables knew her and greeted her by name. Nahtaira is well-known as a wet nurse and servant of Bragimoros and his wife. The couple back at Bibrax thought she wasn't being treated well. I can confirm that by her appearance. By her comments to the merchant, the wife is particularly abusive. Nahtaira may be willing to come with us."

"If she isn't, we'll take her anyway. We need her and a cart to get Caturix safely back to Bibrax."

Strabo saw Corius stand up and shake Talos awake. Strabo breathed a sigh of relief it was time to get his son. Despite a sleepless night and the anxious days since leaving Bibrax, he was calm and ready for whatever was about to happen and the possibility they would fail.

The settlement was quiet except for the muted sounds of a distant dog barking, the soft whicker from one of the tethered horses and muffled snoring of nearby campers. Under an overcast sky, the market stalls and wagons were dark shapes. The air had the smell of rain.

At the edge of the camp area, the three men separated each taking a separate route to their destination. Assigned the shortest and most direct route, Strabo headed for the south gate at a leisurely pace. He was almost at the gate and stopped. He had passed the small trail on the left he should have taken. He cursed, turned around and with a quickened pace found the narrow trail meandering among the circular dwellings. He was relieved to see a dark figure standing silently where several trails intersected. It was Talos. They heard the soft pad of footsteps coming from the trail on the left Corius had taken.

There was no need to talk. Each one knew where he was going and what he would do when he got there. Strabo drew the sharp double-sided dagger and followed Corius and Talos. The two dwellings were near the intersection, and the shapes were visible. Strabo stopped at the entrance of the smaller dwelling and waited until Corius and Talus took position on either side of the entrance of the larger dwelling a few paces away. They were in agreement killing Toccus was key to getting inside the larger dwelling to take care of Bragimoros and his wife. The unknown was Nahtaira. Would she scream and resist being taken before they could silence her? It was a risk they had to accept. They had to take her willing or not, and that was Strabo's task.

Strabo's first concern was the flicker of light outlining the skin doorway of the small dwelling. The light was not unusual. Nocturnal needs obliged an oil lamp to guide the way where relief could be satisfied.

He stepped closer to the doorway with the intent of looking through the narrow gap between the animal skin and the door frame. Suddenly, the animal skin was ripped aside, and Toccus, naked except for the long sword he carried, burst through the doorway. Surprised at the sudden and disastrous turn of events, Strabo was caught off guard. The choice of using daggers was his idea for quick, silent kills to avoid the possibility of a swordfight and the loud ring of metal on metal. He hoped he would live to regret an idea that seemed practical at the time.

Holding the sword with both hands, Toccus swung the blade laterally. Strabo stepped back in time and the sword only sliced through his leather shirt above the dagger belt. Stunned surprise transitioned to thinking how he could survive the one-sided match.

Toccus was formidable in size and better armed. The advantage was lessened after realizing his adversary was not a skilled swordsman. He also appeared unaware Corius and Talos were behind him. Unfortunately, they were too far away to help in the few seconds he had left to live. He had lasted this long only because his opponent's unimaginative back and forth swings were intended to disembowel for a slow, painful death. Relaxed and confident, Toccus was in no hurry. He saw Talos beginning to move slowly toward Toccus, and he had a glimmer of hope. It was a fleeting hope that disappeared after he backed into the cart he'd passed earlier and forgot it was there. Toccus smiled broadly and taunted him with a slow sweep across his stomach which he purposely missed. In desperation, Strabo saw the opportunity he was looking for. He stepped inside the back swing of the sword and plunged his dagger deep into the left side of Toccus's throat. He let the bodyguard fall before he pulled the dagger out to avoid the bloody fountain that erupted.

In the dim light of the doorway, Strabo saw the worried looks on the faces of Corius and Talos turn to smiles of relief.

Strabo sheathed the dagger and bent down to pull the dead man into the dwelling. Before he left, he blew out the oil lamp. He left the dwelling and paused listening for any indication the brief encounter may have been heard. Relieved there was no apparent outcry, he followed Corius and Talos to the larger dwelling.

Similar to where Toccus lived, there was a faint glow illuminating the interior. Corius entered first with Talos close behind. Strabo was focused on where Nahtaira was. He saw a young woman lying on a pallet to the right of the door. She sat up with a startled expression.

Strabo put a finger to his lips. Surprisingly, she didn't cry out at the sudden appearance of the three men with drawn daggers. The woman had to be Nahtaira, and Caturix would be near her.

Strabo sheathed the dagger and walked toward her. She looked past him and said in a soft voice, "Please, let me kill her!"

Astonished, all three men stopped and watched her while she retrieved a small knife from under her pallet and went to where the clan elder's wife was sleeping. Before she got there, Corius had already slit the throat of her husband. With calm detachment, she held the dagger at the woman's throat and shook her awake.

Strabo understood enough of the Bellovaci language to understand what the young woman said that explained why she ended the woman's life silently, slowly and painfully.

Strabo looked away searching for the one thing that mattered. He saw the small basket near where Nahtaira had been sleeping. He looked down at the sleeping infant unsure what to do next. Nahtaira appeared at his side and picked up the baby. Before he realized it, Caturix was in his arms, a small almost weightless form that he couldn't see clearly for the tears stinging his eyes.

Chapter 24

The departure from the Bellovaci settlement at dawn was unremarkable as was the four days it took to reach Bibrax. The journey could have taken longer, and Strabo wouldn't have cared. The time spent with Caturix was an experience he couldn't have imagined before seeing and holding him for the first time. Until then, Raven's condition was just an occasional thought for what it might be like to be a father. In truth, he wasn't sure after Raven told him she was with child that he was particularly looking forward to being a father. He was saddened to recall how indifferent he had been.

In sight of Bibrax, Corius recommended someone ought to ride ahead and prepare Raven. Strabo didn't waste any time giving Aquilo a sharp knee and galloped the rest of the way.

He saw Leuca outside the dwelling bent over a tub washing clothes. She looked up as he reined in and gasped, both hands pressed to her face. She saw his broad smile and burst into tears.

"Is he...?"

"Yes, he'll be here in a few minutes. I came ahead to prepare..." There was a joyous cry behind him, and the next thing he knew Raven was in his arms sobbing. The emotions of the two women touched him, and for a moment, he couldn't trust himself to speak.

He found his voice. "We have a wonderful, handsome son who's missed his mother as much as I have."

His comforting words caused both women to cry even harder. He was relieved at the sound of the cart pulling to a stop behind him. Raven pulled away. He saw her bruised face was no longer grotesquely swollen. Her left arm was in a sling.

It was then Raven saw the scar on Strabo's face. Her eyes widened, and she reached up to touch it. "When did...?"

"It's nothing. It happened before Caturix was taken. Come, see your son."

Nahtaira stood next to the cart holding Caturix busy playing with a lock of her hair.

Strabo gestured to the young woman. "Raven, this is Nahtaira who has been caring for the baby. She has done so extremely well."

Raven managed a nod and a wan smile as she held out her right arm and took the baby carefully. Strabo found his eyes watering again. He saw Corius and Talos similarly affected, looking down, looking away.

Raven broke the emotional tension. "Nahtaira, I owe you my son's life. Please come and stay with us, I," she hesitated as if embarrassed to explain why she had asked. "I cannot nurse my son. Will you do that?"

Nahtaira smiled then started to cry. "I will and gladly. He is god-sent, and while not my son, he has helped me recover from the son I lost at birth."

"Then you are very welcome, Nahtaira. Marcellus, come, it's time for us to start again." With Strabo beside her, she walked with a slow but determined stride across the road to her small dwelling by the settlement wall with Nahtaira following behind.

The next few days for Strabo and Raven were quiet and serene. By tacit agreement, they avoided talking about the recent past or the future, content to live in the moment. Raven's wounds obliged Strabo to restrict his physical attentions to careful hugs and the use of a separate sleeping pallet.

Corius left immediately for Bibracte puzzled why Talos chose to remain in Bibrax. Raven was the first to understand why. In the pretext of seeing Caturix, Talos visited often. Finally, even to Strabo it was obvious he really came to see Nahtaira; she seemed pleased that he did.

It was Raven who precipitated a change in the peaceful interlude by abruptly announcing she wanted to go back to Bibracte citing her main reason was to leave a place that had too many unpleasant memories.

Strabo was surprised. He assumed her close relationship with Leuca would be reason enough for her to remain in Bibrax. He suspected there was something else and asked her if there was.

"You're right I'll miss Leuca, but I would miss you more when you leave here."

Astonished, Strabo was quick to say, "I'm not going anywhere. I told you I've been given the choice to leave the army or return should I choose, and I've decided to stay with you."

"You aren't ready to make a choice as you've often said. You are too much Roman, and in spite of coming here as a conscript, you've come to accept the army. By returning to Bibracte, you'll be closer to me and Caturix, and I'll have a better chance of seeing you than if I stayed here."

Strabo shook his head in denial, yet she could be right. He hadn't consciously thought about it until she voiced it.

"I'll take you back to Bibracte, and that's where I'll stay."

His somewhat over-emphatic reply confirmed she was right. She managed a smile to conceal her sadness.

Raven and Marcellus weren't surprised after Nahtaira agreed to go with them, and Talos announced he, too, was going. His excuse was a desire to rejoin the Aeduan scouts.

The emotional farewell with Leuca days later left both women in tears with fervent promises to meet again and soon. The tumultuous events in Gaul in the following years were such it was never to be.

Chapter 25

Late winter, 56 B.C.E. Illyricum Province

Caesar read the reports from General Publius Crassus and General Labienus and shook his head. He'd been naïve thinking the recent successes against the Belgae and the defeats of the Helvetii and Germani the year before gave some promise Gaul might be peaceful. Three weeks into his first visit to Illyricum as governor of the province, and his focus was on Gaul.

General Labienus reported indications of unrest in Eastern Gaul with the Germani east of the Rhine and some tribes west of the river. Most alarming were the concerns about the Remi.

Crassus was writing of concerns for what was happening in western Gaul with the coastal tribes, notably the Veneti in Aquitania. Six tribunes sent to six separate tribes to arrange for a supply of corn had been detained. The officers were being held captive until Crassus released the hostages the tribes surrendered to guarantee peace. It was an outrageous act of defiance that could not be ignored.

Caesar closed his eyes, and considered what steps needed to be taken to deal with problems that could easily spark a widespread rebellion. He called for his secretary and trusted assistant.

"Otho, get the scribe in here." While he waited impatiently, he began to frame the orders to General Labienus to deal with the latest problems. Eight legions were beginning to look insufficient although he wasn't certain Marcus Crassus would agree to finance one or two more. The scribe arrived, and Caesar began to dictate.

General Titus Labienus, Legatus Pro Protare, Roman Forces, Gaul

General Labienus, I share your concerns for what you have reported concerning the tribes in eastern and central Gaul. I applaud your vigilance in keeping abreast of potential instability. Your report is particularly significant given General Crassus's description of events along the coast where the Armorican tribes are on the verge of hostilities. I believe circumstances require active measures to discover any latent or overt actions for rebellion. I therefore direct the following actions be taken.

Accompanied by a significant cavalry escort, I request you meet with each of the major tribes, beginning with the Treveri, the Sequani, the Boi and the Germani tribes west of the Rhine. Although the Belgae tribes in the north were recently defeated, we cannot assume they are pacified. The purpose is both to verify continued peaceful intentions and remind them with a show of force Rome's capability to maintain peace in Gaul. Upon completion of your mission, rejoin the Tenth Legion in Armorica

General Publius Crassus has been ordered to take the Seventh Legion with two other cohorts from a legion or legions you select and with a large detachment of cavalry move to the Valley of the Loire. His objective is two-fold: to prevent the dispatch of auxiliaries from the tribes in Aquitania into Gaul and to build a fleet of galleys in an estuary of the Loire River. When completed, the fleet will be commanded by General Decimus Brutus. A successful offensive against the coastal tribes in Armorica necessitates the capability to confront them on both water and land.

General Titurius Sabinus has been ordered to take his three legions and move to the territory of the Venelli, the Curiosolite, and the Lexovii. His objective is to prevent these tribes from joining the Venetii and their allies.

You have my approval to modify any of the above orders as circumstances may require. I will depart Illyricum soon to join the legions in western Armorica.

Gaius Julius Caesar

Strabo set a leisurely pace with no reason to be in Bibracte before they wanted to be. There was the practical consideration Raven was still in the early stages of recovery both physically and mentally. Except for an occasional drop in temperature accompanied by snow showers, the weather was clement for that time of year and added to Raven's recovery. Gradually she relaxed, confident she and Caturix were safe.

Strabo began to see another side of Talos he wouldn't have considered before. His selfless, constant attention to Nahtaira was reciprocated in a way Raven had never shown for the scout. He was glad Talos may have found someone who returned his affection in kind.

The five days to reach Bibracte gave Strabo ample time to reflect on what Raven told him at Bibrax. He tried to forget what she said and her implied acceptance he wasn't going to stay with her. He couldn't, yet the possibility she was right made him try harder to concentrate on enjoying the present. He enjoyed being a father holding Caturix, feeling his warm body in his arms. That is until a strong odor signaled it was time to hand him to Raven or Nahtaira, whoever happened to be closest.

Talos rejoined the scouts soon after they reached Bibracte. Strabo was tempted but decided against it. He'd become used to being a leader, and the thought of being relegated to being something less was not appealing.

As the days passed, he found himself increasingly restless. He spent time riding Aquilo to keep him and the horse fit. From their resigned expressions at his clumsy attempts to help with chores, he guessed they would have preferred he spent more time with the horse. The prospect of more aimless days ahead eventually forced him to acknowledge the truth. It was time to leave.

That night, Raven saw his worried expression and interrupted his clumsy attempt to tell her what he was planning to do and spared him.

He left the next morning for the Tenth Legion's winter quarters. He wasn't certain, but suspected or at least hoped, Raven's calm acceptance reflected an equal mix of relief and regret.

Looking more like an Aeduan than a Roman, Strabo stopped at the gate and identified himself. He wasn't surprised or offended at the surly optio's unfriendly skepticism. Fortunately, he saw Ursinus inside the fort and called to him.

"Sir, I can vouch for Decurion Strabo." The optio nodded and with a sour look waved him on.

"Well met, Ursinus. The optio must be a replacement."

"Since you've been gone, we've had many. The turma is back to full strength with most replacements coming from the ranks. Decurion Tarquin hoped you would return and didn't replace you. Did you find your son?"

"Yes, he was taken to the Bellovaci settlement. It ended well enough, and he's with Raven in Bibracte."

"I'm surprised you didn't stay with her. I wasn't sure you'd come back."

"For a time, I wasn't either. During the past several weeks, Raven didn't believe I was ready for domestic life. I tried to convince her she was wrong. She was right. I never thought the day would come I'd miss the legions."

"You came back in time. The tribes in Armorica are either in rebellion or thinking about it. General Titurius Sabinus with two legions is already positioned in the Loire Valley. Under temporary command of Felix Valerian, the Tenth Legion leaves for the coast tomorrow to join the two legions. General Labienus is visiting the eastern and Belgae tribes to assess the rumors the tribes there are showing signs of unrest. Decurions Tarquin and Costa and their decuriae are with the contingent of auxilia cavalry accompanying General Labienus.

"If you're ready to quit looking like a native, you're now the senior and only decurion in the legion. There's little time and much to be done. You might want to tell the paymaster you're here." Ursinus paused and said with a mocking grin, "Considering who you are and a decurion's pay, you may not want to bother. Welcome back."

Strabo made his way to the leather tent the three decurions shared and saw his personal effects carefully gathered and covered on his pallet in expectation he was coming back. He was touched. In contrast to his doubtful opinion he would return, Tarquin, Ursinus and Raven expected he would. He felt somewhat guilty he left Raven and Caturix and rationalized Raven was as responsible for his departure as he was. He couldn't, and it dampened his relief in rejoining the legions.

Chapter 26
The coastal plain of Gaul early spring

On a bluff overlooking the estuary of the Loire, Caesar surveyed the river and boatyards where the fleet of triremes were in various stages of completion.

"Publius, I congratulate you and the legions for what has been accomplished here. You've exceeded my expectations."

General Crassus nodded appreciatively for the compliment. It didn't erase his concern the difficult task ahead might not be successful. His primary responsibility was to build the galleys and make sure they were seaworthy. Building the galleys was one thing; learning to sail them was another. He was privately relieved General Decimus Brutus would be responsible for that phase.

"It's an impressive sight, yet the difficult task ahead is daunting for General Brutus. He will have to train the legionnaires how to sail and fight on water treacherous enough for veteran seamen. We've identified enough local seamen who are experienced and willing to teach them how to sail the galleys. The crews are first taught here in the harbor to learn the basics of propelling, steering and maneuvering. They are then taken out to sea to practice what they've learned in rough water." Crassus pointed to a pair of three-tiered triremes moving slowly down river to the open sea. "Those two galleys are taking the crews out to sea for training."

Caesar thought the galleys resembled giant water spiders. Above the noise of the ship builders directly below, the two men heard the rhythmic beat of the drums controlling the pace of the two ships.

"How many legionnaires can each ship carry?" Caesar asked.

"Each ship requires a legionnaire for each oar. If the winds are favorable, the two square sails will spare the rowers. In addition to the

170 rowers and crew to sail and maneuver the ship, 150 hundred additional legionnaires with another 50 slingers and archers will fight from the ship. The reason we can take that many is the ships won't be burdened with supplies beyond what's needed on a daily basis."

Caesar glanced at Crassus and his worried expression. "I have a feeling there's something else you want to tell me."

"There is. Our triremes are swift and maneuverable compared to the Venetii if there's no wind. That is our only advantage. Our ships have keels; consequently, they can't go as close to shore as do their flat-bottomed ships. The Venetii ships are larger in length and higher in the bow and stern. It gives them the advantage of launching missiles down on our lower ships. While the galleys have the advantage of greater speed necessary for ramming, their ships built of oak are too strong to suffer any serious damage. The Venetii also know how to navigate the sea in stormy weather. We don't. We'll keep on training and looking for ways we can successfully overcome our disadvantages. I regret if I sound overly pessimistic."

"I see. What you're telling me is a land attack may have a better chance of success." Caesar brightened. "Take heart, Publius, all is not as gloomy as the picture you paint. Fortuna will favor us, and we must be confident she will. When do you expect the fleet to be ready?"

"Two, possibly three months."

"Very well. In the meantime, we'll see what we can accomplish on land."

The two men walked to the town below, one more somber than the other. Caesar was satisfied. Whether the fleet would be needed in the land campaign about to begin was not important. He preferred to defeat the coastal tribes without having to risk destroying a fleet he had other plans for. He was going to be the first Roman to invade Britannia, or at least, the first on record to do so. He was annoyed at Publius Crassus for making a brief trip to Britannia two months ago without his permission or knowledge. Publius Crassus would be cited in his accounts of the campaigns in Gaul for the many things he had done well; his brief incursion into Britannia would not be mentioned.

The Eleventh Legion arrived in the Loire Valley a day after the Tenth and built a fort a quarter mile away. Strabo was returning from patrol and saw the standard. He considered stopping long enough to see Scevola and Brecius but decided not to after seeing Decurion Quintus Servius leading his decuria coming toward him. His inclination was to ride on and avoid an unnecessary confrontation. He expected Servius would do the same. He was wrong. The decurion halted his decuria and waited for him. He felt he had no choice so signaled a halt.

He drew rein and was struck by Servius's gaunt features. He felt guilty. In comparison to the way he had spent the intervening weeks since the last time they saw each other, it was obvious the reports the Twelfth Legion had endured harsh conditions and fought a determined adversary were true.

"Strabo, I see you're looking remarkably fit. I'm glad you are. While I was away in the far mountains freezing my balls, I thought about you."

"I'm flattered and sorry to say I didn't think of you at all. We heard the Twelfth did well. I've no doubt, as always, you and your decuria acquitted yourselves well."

"We did. General Metellus was so pleased he recommended to Gallius we should be suitably rewarded. In addition to awarding a service torque to the decuria, my seniority has been reinstated."

Strabo turned to his decuria and said, "For what these cavalrymen did, they deserve our respect and congratulations." There was a chorus of appreciative shouts genuinely given. He saw Servius's mocking expression change to a thoughtful frown.

"Strabo, I would speak with you alone. I suggest, if you're willing, we dismiss our decuriae and talk privately."

Strabo nodded and said to Ursinus, "Take them on in. I'll be back soon." The two decurions waited until they were alone then Servius spoke.

"I said I thought about you in the mountains, and I spoke the truth. I told you once not to worry about your back because that's not my way. You and I will never be friends; there's too much between us that can't be overlooked or forgotten. You were right when you said if we settle our differences with swords, it would not go unnoticed or unpunished. That time will have to wait until one of us is no longer serving the eagle. In the meantime, I thought of another and less terminal way to confront each other. What about another race, just the two of us?"

"I don't have any inclination to *confront* you in either hostile or friendly circumstances. Let it go, Servius. I'm not interested. And you would probably lose again unless you can find a better horse than Aquilo."

"I'm disappointed but not surprised. You're not tough or brave enough to race me on another horse against a rider like me, and rules don't mean shit."

Strabo watched him ride away resigned to the prospect Servius was not going to give up trying to find a way to salve his humiliating defeat. He didn't trust his assurance not to worry about his back. The comment had the opposite effect. However, he started having second thoughts. Maybe a race was a practical way to end what would otherwise would be a continuation of pointless hostility. He had reservations. At Visontio Servius showed the kind of race he favored — do whatever is necessary to win. He shook his head and rode after Servius. What he was about to do was probably a mistake he was going to regret. The concern was balanced with the urge to beat him again and do it decisively.

For the Romans, the next several weeks became a monotonous blur as the legions pursued first one tribe then another across southern Armorica without an opportunity to achieve a decisive battle. The Venetii proved particularly elusive, and the terrain favored their attempts to avoid concentrating their forces.

The settlements were located at the end of long narrow ridges which at high tide became islands. The legionnaires spent days building moles at low tide to the height of several settlements. It was a time-consuming back-breaking endeavor and succeeded twice. Thereafter, settlements under siege waited until the moles were nearly done and a high tide to offload population and everything of value onto ships and sailed to another settlement along the coast. Caesar had enough. He ordered the fleet to be deployed.

General Brutus tried to look confident as he surveyed the tribunes and centurions commanding the four divisions of the fleet. In spite of weeks of training, the legionnaires were a long way from being good sailors. While oar handling had improved, there were too many occasions when one or more rowers missed a stroke decreasing the ship's speed and forcing the ships behind to slow down. At least maneuvering had been improved after experienced helmsmen from the local Pictones were brought in to work the steering oars. Individual ships managed to do quite well. The main problem remained melding the ships into a confident, cohesive force.

"We leave here at the end of the third watch tomorrow to attack the Venetii fleet. Their fleet is somewhat larger than ours." He waited a moment, frowned and said with a philosophical shrug, "Well, it's a lot larger. At last count, they have a little over 200 ships." Brutus heard groans accompanied by nervous rustling and said, "Consider this, the odds are no worse than what we've had to deal with thus far."

A gray-haired, scarred centurion muttered loud enough to be heard and draw snickers and a smile from Brutus, "Except this time we're on ships and trying to look like we know what we're doing."

Brutus let the noise subside and continued. "According to the reports I received a few hours ago, the fleet has shown no sign of leaving harbor in the Gulf of Morbihan. The entrance from the gulf to the Bay of Quiberon is narrow. There's a possibility if our fleet can reach the entrance first, we can prevent their ships from entering the bay where they have room to maneuver. The chance of getting there before they leave the gulf is not good. The entrance is about 40 miles from here.

We can reasonably expect as soon as the first galley leaves here, the Venetii will know it. We will most likely engage them in the bay about halfway to the gulf.

"I realize there are some among you, as one of you has already indicated, who ask what is an army doing on ships and about to fight an enemy with so many advantages? The Venetii are used to spending their lives on water, and they have twice the number of ships in their fleet than we do. The difference is we're Romans, and they aren't." The muted chuckles did not sound encouraging.

"We do have one important and significant advantage. They're dependent on the wind, and we are not; it could be their undoing. The pole-hooks are the tools by which we'll take the wind away from them. If we can bring down their sails, they'll be helpless. Any ship dismasted can be surrounded and overwhelmed. Make no attempt to ram. Their oak timbers are too thick for our small triremes. After a ship has been dismasted, three or four triremes can surround and board it. The fighting then will be no different than on land.

"Once in the bay and a mile distant from the coast, we'll form three columns. When the Gaulish fleet is sighted, I'll give the signal to form in three ranks abreast. Their fleet will have to spread out and separate wide enough to keep the wind in their sails. It's my intention to attack their center in a wedge formation and pass through them. They'll have to tack, and it will slow them down, making them vulnerable to our greater speed and capability to maneuver faster. May Jupiter look down with approval and guide us to success for Caesar and the glory of Rome."

Several miles south of the Gulf of Morbihan, the Tenth Legion was deployed on a promontory overlooking the open sea approximately where the two fleets were expected to meet.

Strabo was standing close enough to hear Caesar mutter, "We should have seen them by now."

Unperturbed, General Labienus said, "The wind and choppy seas are the reason. The fleet is rowing against the wind." General Labienus looked north where the Venetii ships were moored. "The Venetii don't look concerned. Their sails are furled and there's no sign of activity. With luck, they may not see our fleet until it reaches the entrance to the gulf."

Ursinus rode up to Strabo on a lathered horse. "Decurion, the fleet is about twelve miles away from here. It should be in sight in a few minutes."

Strabo approached Caesar and reported what the scout said. Caesar nodded and appeared to relax until a carnyx sounded faintly south of them repeated closer and louder then by another on a hilltop overlooking the Gulf.

Caesar cursed. "So much for surprising them."

During the next half hour, the leisurely preparation of the Veneti to leave the estuary harbor and enter the gulf reflected how little they were alarmed. Strabo thought the Venetii were justified in being confident from the challenge General Brutus had in transforming infantry army into some semblance of a navy.

The sky was cloudy, and the sea remained choppy with a persistent brisk wind. The triremes finally came into sight. It was also obvious the ships were having difficulty maintaining a disciplined formation. Strabo saw Tribune Setarius's frown and Caesar's expressionless face and surmised they had the same misgivings he had. Imagining how sick the legionnaires must be, he was thankful he wasn't on one of the galleys.

With billowing sails, the Veneti ships moved out of the harbor close together and headed for the entrance to the bay. In contrast to the galleys, their superior seamanship was displayed by a tight, disciplined formation after the fleet entered the choppier bay formed in two lines abreast. With the wind behind them, the ships raced toward the Romans at a speed that caused the galleys to appear almost motionless.

A bugle sounded on one of the lead Roman ships and was repeated back through the fleet. The triremes slowly transformed from three columns to a wedge half as wide at the base as the one-mile front of the Venetii fleet. The closer the convergence of the two fleets, the larger size of the Gallic ships was emphasized compared to the diminutive galleys. The lead ships met with a resounding crash of splintering timbers easily heard from where Caesar and the Tenth Legion observed. A dozen triremes were crushed or capsized by the larger Venetii ships.

The initial contact a little less than a mile away was met by groans and curses from the officers and legionnaires watching what appeared to be a Roman debacle in the making. Gradually, most of the galleys were north of the Venetii ships and turning back to the south in small clusters. The Venetii ships found the initial advantage of wind at their back had suddenly become a disadvantage. With a favoring wind, the galleys raced after the slower turning sailing ships. The time to tack and reverse course left the Veneti ships momentarily vulnerable to the more maneuverable galleys. Three or four galleys converged to attack an individual ship. Watching, Strabo was reminded of wolves attacking a deer. The sails of the beleaguered ships were pulled down by long hooked poles, and the becalmed ships were ensnared by grappling hooks, boarded and overcome.

The battle continued apace for several hours with each side attempting to exploit the wind to their advantage. A conclusive outcome for either fleet remained uncertain. To Caesar's and the collective astonishment of all watching, the Gauls decided their losses were becoming unacceptable. A few ships turned and made their way out to sea. Soon, the rest of the ships not engaged did the same. The slower Roman galleys were rapidly left behind.

Later, Caesar was convinced Fortuna finally intervened in favor of the Romans. Abruptly the wind died, the sails of the Veneti ships went slack and the vessels came to a halt bobbing gently in the now calm waters. The Gauls had become the defenseless prey. Bugles sounded, and the galleys went after the stationary ships. The fighting continued until sunset when the wind returned and gave what was left of the Gaulish fleet the chance to sail away.

Chapter 27
The next day outside Caesar's headquarters

Stone-faced, Caesar stared at the group of men kneeling and shackled representing the Veneti and the three allied tribes. He wasn't in a forgiving mood in spite of the victories General Sabinus and Publius Crassus had reported earlier that morning which assured both Aquitania and Armorica were kneeling to Rome. The coastal tribes were subjugated at least for the moment until another minor tribal chieftain decided otherwise. The rebellion cost the lives of too many legionnaires the extent of which Rome would never know. The message had to be clear. Defy Rome and suffer the fate of the Venetii.

Caesar pointed to the tribal chief and seven elders of the Venetii Tribe. "You started a war with Rome and encouraged the other tribes to join you. Your pleas for leniency require more than providing treasure which is already mine to do with as I will. Many lives on both sides have been lost and to what purpose? For the Veneti to claim sovereignty in Armorica? You are the ones I hold most accountable in convincing your tribal members and allies to pursue war. You spurned friendship and chose war, a choice that will cost the Venetii and serve as a warning to other tribes who might consider following a similar path. All eight of you will be executed here at this place. I will spare the lives of the rest of the Venetii who will spend the rest of their lives in slavery."

The tribal chief spat in the direction of Caesar. Two of the elders remained stoic while the others began to wail, pleading to be spared. The tribal chiefs and elders representing the allied tribes shifted nervously. Some began to weep, but most looked resigned and cursed the Venetii.

Caesar pointed to a cleared area surrounded on three sides by three centuries of the Tenth Legion. Eight legionnaires, each with a drawn gladius, stood waiting in the center.

"Centurion Aeimelius, have the guards take the condemned over there and get it done." He motioned to the slaver. "Stand the rest of them up. I want them to see what will happen. If they or any other tribes should ever challenge Rome again, this is what they can expect."

The headless bodies had been taken away, and the leaders of the other three tribes were escorted back to their domains with the understanding they had three days to deliver food and forage to supply the legions for 30 days. Failure to do so would be considered an act of rebellion.

Later that day, Generals Sabinus, Brutus and Crassus arrived at the headquarters and were welcomed with effusive praise for their significant actions in quelling the rebellion. It didn't take long for the generals to understand the real purpose of the assembly.

Caesar started by saying, "We're not done with the coastal tribes." He saw the perplexed expressions on the generals' faces. "I'm not talking about the tribes we defeated. The Menapii and Morini north of the Somme in coastal Belgae remain under arms. They've refused my invitation to send embassies to discuss how to assure peace in Gaul. It's my intention to leave here and persuade them to stand down before the winter ends the campaign season. If they've taken note of our recent successes in Belgae and Armorica, it could encourage them to negotiate rather than fight. In the event they're not ready for a friendly relationship with Rome, I have to convince them with more than words."

General Labienus was the first to object strongly, an uncharacteristic response to his normal quiet, objective manner.

"The legionnaires are worn out. They expect after a long and difficult campaign to stand-down for the winter. They need to rest and recuperate. I suggest in the spring would be a better time to deal with the two tribes."

There were murmurs of agreement although low enough not to draw undue attention. Let Labienus be the focus for objecting to another campaign. Caesar had prepared for opposition.

"My purpose in going north is not to fight and subjugate. I don't anticipate the need to do more than a show of arms. I assume by the time we get there, they will have heard of our victories here in Armorica. It might encourage them to consider a friendly alliance. I anticipate a brief stay then we'll go into winter quarters south in the vicinity of the Loire Valley. It's a practical location. At this time, the local tribes here do not have the capability to provide the support we need during winter quarters. Remaining close to the Menapi and Morini is a passive reminder to think of peace if they haven't already agreed to it."

Labienus persisted. "The tribes you speak of are peaceful now. They showed no interest in supporting any of the tribes we've fought."

"You're right, still they represent an existential threat to our friendly occupation of Gaul." Caesar ignored the suppressed chuckles and continued. "We've come a long way in taking a barbarian wilderness to the threshold of making Gaul into a new and rich province of Rome. Our gains thus far must be maintained to achieve the latter goal. I want the legions ready to march in two days."

The last comment ended any further debate although not the speculation Caesar had another reason for going north than the ones he gave.

Caesar asked General Labienus, General Brutus and Tribune Setarius to remain and waited until the others left.

"Titus, you and I should have had the conversation we're about to have before I spoke of going north. Your argument for not leaving here has merit for the reasons you gave. The rationale I gave was reasonable and true especially about not burdening Armorica with the expense of another winter here. We need forage which is no longer sufficient here, and they need time to recover. I don't think the tribes we'll face in the coastal region of Belgae will pose any difficulty. I could be wrong and accept the possibility we'll conduct another campaign where the gladius will be the instrument of persuasion.

"What I'm about say goes no further until I'm ready to tell the legions. Later, I'll let the sons of bitches in Rome know what I'm going to do *after* I've done it. So far in Gaul, I've had almost as much opposition as approbation to what we've achieved. I have political adversaries who misrepresent our victories as defeats and lament the undeserving hardship the poor, defenseless tribes of Gaul are experiencing. I need achievements to keep my detractors in the minority. I want to go to Britannia." He waited for the surprised officers to absorb the proposal's historic significance.

"I'm aware General Crassus made a brief trip there several months ago. It was not done with my approval or knowledge. Had he consulted with me, I would not have authorized it. He didn't have either the strength or the logistical support to do anything except step ashore and claim he had; I've been told he did not. He only sailed near the shore and said he did more. I have greater ambition. I see Britannia under Roman authority. One day it will be another extension of the Republic."

Setarius noted the expression on General Labienus's face, a mix of exasperation and frustration in being required to carry out Caesar's destiny-marking declaration. The latter without the reality of how to make it happen and without the belief it was even realistically achievable. The stunned silence ended with General Brutus risking a challenge to the ambitious proposal by focusing on the practical means of how to achieve it.

"I gather the fleet we've built here is about to take on a different imperative."

"Up to a point you're right. The triremes so instrumental to our success against the Venetii are not as significant in getting to Britannia and landing there. I'm told the natives there do not have fighting ships. We'll require only a few triremes; the specific number I'll leave to you to define at a later time. The important vessels are the larger cargo ships to carry supplies, legionnaires and horses. The cargo ships we have here are insufficient. We'll build and get more in or near Gesoriacum on the northwest coast of Gaul. It's the largest and closest harbor to Britannia."

General Labienus asked, "When do you plan to make the incursion, and what size force do you foresee?"

"Next spring on the assumption by then Gaul is peaceful. That's why it's imperative to ensure the Morini and Menapii are allied or at least neutral. As I said earlier, I have hopes it will be the former outcome, in which case we'll go into winter quarters that much sooner. Titus, you used the word *invasion* implying a larger force than I'm considering. Crassus was not able to remain long enough, if he ever went ashore in Britannia, to gather sufficient information of the land and people to plan for a major incursion. Consequently, my objective is to explore with a larger force consisting of two legions to assess the feasibility of returning later with an army. I have in mind the Seventh and Tenth Legions with slingers and archers from the Auxilia. I expect only a nominal cavalry contingent — a few hundred. Since the Seventh has been there, it's a logical choice to have it as one of the two legions."

Caesar waited to see if there were any other questions. Their silence and expressionless faces confirmed his suspicion he had work ahead to generate enthusiasm for the plan and his reason to march on two more coastal tribes.

Chapter 28
Northwest Gaul three weeks later

The sullen mood of the legionnaires was due in part to the extended campaign season and aggravated by the near constant rain and soggy landscape. The usual marching chants and good-natured banter in camp were missing. Strabo knew the morale within his decuria wasn't much better and neither was his. It was difficult to muster enthusiasm for what was a miserable campaign without any indication it was going to get better. He was having second thoughts about leaving Raven and the boy and the comparatively dry comfort of Bibracte.

Also missing was any sign of the tribes they were there to confront. In the villages and isolated farmsteads, abandoned houses and litter indicated hasty departures into the forests and vast marshes covering much of the land. Apart from tendrils of smoke rising from the forests far to the east, there were few signs of the Morini or any indication the Menapii had come south to join the other neighboring tribes.

Strabo halted the decuria on a treeless patch of muddy ground to allow the cavalrymen to stretch and rest the horses. The terrain was unrelieved flat and, as far as he was concerned, completely inhospitable where boats were the primary means to traverse the sodden countryside. The hillock they were on was only slightly higher than the water-soaked ground they had spent most of their time on since leaving the legions several hours ago. Under less demanding circumstances, the decuria would have traveled 10-15 miles. He doubted they had gone half that distance in the time they'd been in the saddle. Occasionally, they were able to canter the horses. Most of the time, the wet conditions limited the horses to a slower gait.

Ursinus bent down and lifted the left foreleg of his horse, examined the hoof and muttered a stream of curses.

“Decurion, the horses need to get out of the mud and water for a few days. Longer would be better. The hooves are getting soft. The condition they’re in, they could be permanently lamed if we had to run them on rough, rocky ground.”

Strabo examined one of Aquilo’s hooves and found it was noticeably softer than it was the previous day. He didn’t have the experience Ursinus had so deferred to the truth of what he said. The challenge Servius made and he accepted would be an event for a place much dryer than this part of Gaul. It would take time for the horses to recover.

“I agree, this is as far as we go.”

Two hours later, the cavalrymen heard the recognizable, unmistakable sound of battle. Strabo urged a faster pace. A few minutes later, they saw the legions in disorganized confusion in close contact with the Gauls he presumed to be the Morini. He was reminded of the ambush by the Nervii when the legionnaires were spread out constructing the night camp more prepared to dig than fight. It had been a battle the Romans had come close to tasting the bitter taste of defeat.

The scene here was startling reminiscent. The legionnaires had left their shields, weapons and equipment behind as they started to entrench the encampment. The short-handled pickaxes were no match against long swords and axes wielded by the Gauls swarming out of a forested area 300 hundred paces away bordered by marsh. The legionnaires were slowly and relentlessly being pushed back to where they had left their swords and shields. The legionnaires rallied and began to force the warriors back. A chaotic defense rapidly transitioned to an organized offense.

The auxilia cavalry attempted an envelopment of the Gaulish right flank. It failed after a continuous barrage of arrows and spears were launched from the safety of the tree line. The cavalry withdrew out of missile range and concentrated on attacking the flank closer to the encampment.

Strabo spotted Tarquin and the troops from the other legions preparing to assault the Morini left flank. Without hesitation or concern what it would cost the horses, he signaled line abreast, and with swords drawn, the decuria joined the attack.

Slowly the Gauls began to give ground. Again, Strabo was reminded of the resolute determination shown by the Nervii so unlike most of the other tribes they fought.

The field was slippery, and the Morini infantry was struggling to maintain balance and footing, a disadvantage shared by the legionnaires but not by the sure-footed, slow-moving cavalry horses. The persistent movement of the cavalry on both flanks along with the advancing legionnaires began to compress the Gaulish ranks further impeding their effectiveness. With their casualties steadily mounting, the Morini broke when the rear ranks reached the tree line.

Tarquin led the turmae back to a safe distance where the cavalrymen waited and dreaded the order to follow the legionnaires into the forest where the cavalry was vulnerable and ineffective. The momentum of the legionnaires slowed perceptibly as they entered the forest. The Gauls began to slow the Roman advance. The centuries, less able to maintain disciplined order, revived the Morini, and the legionnaire advance began to falter.

Caesar regarded the tired generals and senior centurions and realized it was a mistake to have come this far north at this time of the year. The combination of poor weather and terrain favoring the Gauls required a practical reassessment of continuing a campaign with little chance of a successful conclusion. Unless a significant victory could be realized soon, the longer they remained here, the toll would likely not justify the gains. He chose his words carefully to project a balance of optimism and practical reality.

"This day has not gone as I expected. Even though their losses are greater than ours, I do not take consolation in the numbers. We're facing a determined adversary defending an environment hostile to us and friendly to them. We must adapt and deny them the advantage of terrain and weather which so far has encouraged them to believe the legions can be held at bay. We will take away the safety of the forest they are relying upon. Tomorrow we'll begin cutting down their safe haven foot by foot, mile by mile, as far as it requires to force them to accept defeat. Every tree cut down will be used to barricade our flanks."

The progress of deforestation over the next two days was impressive and aided by clearing skies and an occasional glimpse of a pale sun. Despite the improved weather, morale remained low in having to work and sleep in appalling conditions. The capture of a significant number of cattle promptly slaughtered brought a welcome if momentary relief from the usual repetitive diet.

That night it began to rain. Until then, the precipitation had been sporadic and mainly a light drizzle, uncomfortable but tolerable. The rain had become a constant downpour. Within a few hours, the water within the camps had risen high enough the leather tents of the legionnaires were flooded. By first light, Caesar had given the order to move south, a decision delayed too long with an army on the verge of mutiny. The legions departed two hours later to begin the 100-mile trip south to the valley of the Seine and winter quarters.

Chapter 29
55 B.C.E
Winter Quarters Valley of the Seine

"What do you think?" Strabo asked Ursinus who was bent over examining the last of Aquilo's hooves.

"Better than I would have expected. There's no sign of any softness. He can race."

It wasn't the answer he really wanted. He had reservations his agreement hastily made nearly three months ago was a mistake. If Servius did win, he doubted he was going to be satisfied. For weeks he avoided the race based first on the condition of Aquilo's hooves and the weather. He no longer had a reason to put it off with a sudden and welcome change in the weather. If he refused to race, Servius would be unrelenting in making him an object of ridicule. He had to consider how it would look to the decuria and particularly Ursinus. Ursinus had not been subtle in his expectation there would be a race.

The cavalryman saw Strabo's frown and correctly interpreted his reaction. "You don't want to race him?" It was more a statement than a question.

"No, it will be a race I'll lose even if I beat him." Strabo saw the perplexed expression on the other's face and explained what he meant. "I'm not worried about the possibility I'll lose. There's not a horse in any of the legions faster than Aquilo. It's what Servius will do if I do win. He's unpredictable, and I don't believe he will ever forget or forgive what I did to him at Visontio. I regret I let my anger get out of control. General Crassus and Tribune Setarius were right. I should have settled the matter privately."

"Ride another horse and don't win." There was a hint of condemnation in the remark, and Strabo was quick to respond.

"It won't work. Servius is an experienced racer. He'd know if I held back and let him win. The outcome could be worse than if he lost. It's against my principles to do that, and besides, I like to win as much as Servius."

"Then that's it, you're going to race him." Strabo knew the comment was nothing less than a challenge.

"Of course, I will." Strabo saw Ursinus smile for the first time in weeks. "I'll talk to Servius as soon as he gets back from patrol. In the meantime, we need to find a two-mile course with challenges similar to Visontio. It has to be far enough away the generals won't know about it. Servius and I were ordered not to race again while were in the legions. If we're found out, there would be consequences, and you'll have a new decurion to train."

Two days later, Strabo told Servius Aquilo was fit enough to race. "Here are my conditions. We race one week from today, the course will be two miles long over difficult terrain, we will not be armed, no riding crops of any kind will be used and we ride or walk the course only once before the race. I suggest Ursinus and whoever you choose look for a suitable place far enough away so the generals will have less chance to find out about it."

"So, you finally ran out of excuses to avoid a rematch. Maybe you've got some balls I was beginning to think you didn't have. I accept your conditions. I prefer delaying the race by a week to allow time to prepare." Strabo agreed even though he thought the additional week was unnecessary. "Traian will work with Ursinus to find a suitable place. Can I trust you won't ride the course more than once?"

"You can't, but I'm less likely to than you. Unlike you, I don't have a reputation for winning at all costs." Strabo paused before adding, "Although my experience in our previous race suggests I can and should adapt."

Servius laughed with genuine humor. "I may get to like you, although I still think you're a rich, privileged son of a bitch. Shit, we may have more in common than I thought."

"I doubt it. You're a capable leader, and I've seen that on several occasions. The battlefield is probably the one place where we have common ground. Servius, I intend to win."

"You won't, and I'll wager 20 denarii on it."

"You owe me ten denarii you bet during the race at Visontio. You put up 20 denarii and I'll match it with 10 in a purse to be held by Tarquin."

"Done. I wish you good fortune because you'll need it."

The confident look on Servius's face made him uneasy, suspicious. It would be surprising if Servius didn't have something in mind to improve his chance of winning.

Ursinus and Traian dismounted and walked their horses to where Strabo was sitting on a stump sharpening his spatha.

"Decurion, I think we've found a place for the course." Ursinus took a stick and scratched a U-shaped line with another line crossing the top of the U. He drew a wavy line down the middle.

"The line at the top is a bridge across a river. It's slow-moving and about six feet deep and 50 feet across flowing north to south. The course has two one-mile legs on either side of the river. The start line is on the west side, and for the first 300 paces, it's relatively flat. The terrain on the east side close to the finish line is even and suitable for a faster finish. It should do with a little work to clear brush near the start and finish lines."

"What does the ground look like on either side of the river where it isn't flat?"

"Rougher on the west side with more trees, hills and places where the river banks are steeper. Some of the hills have sharp, rocky drop-offs that can't be seen until you're at the top. By then, if you're in a gallop, you may not recover from a bad result. A few hills less precipitous, although higher, will slow the horses down on the way up. The east leg by comparison is easier with fewer dangerous obstacles."

Strabo said, "Traian, I'm going to take a look tomorrow. I invite you and Decurion Servius to come with me and Ursinus."

"Sir, Decurion Servius is gone and won't return until next week. He's given me authority to act in his behalf for all arrangements until he gets back."

"Where did he go?"

"He didn't tell me."

Strabo was certain the cavalryman knew where Servius had gone and why. For whatever the reason, it explained why he wanted to delay the race.

"Very well. I'll wait to look at the course until he returns. Meanwhile, I'll leave it to both of you to do whatever must be done to make the course safer."

If it wasn't for his stature and features, Strabo wouldn't have known Servius so changed from the hard-faced, edgy image he was accustomed to. His jocular disposition was enough to tell Strabo the decurion was too confident of a win and had another surprise for him.

A day before the race, Strabo was quietly speculating what Servius might be up to when Ursinus appeared in the doorway of the tent with an expression of bemused concern.

"Sir, everyone knows about the race tomorrow. I've already refused multiple offers of making a wager. I've heard even some of the officers are betting."

"Shit! I wonder who talked too much. It's too late to call it off without looking like I'm afraid of Servius or losing. Minutes after Servius and I cross the finish line, we'll be lucky if the consequence is only losing our rank."

"I think you worry too much. I'll bet General Labienus knew about the race days, maybe within hours after you and Servius agreed to race."

"Then why didn't he stop it?"

"After we finished with the Aduatuci, morale was good. We all thought we were going into winter quarters. Instead, we went north to fight the Venetii and morale went down and got worse after going after the Morini. The campaign ended with a victory Caesar and the generals claimed, and the rankers, including me, knew it wasn't. Since then, morale has improved some but not by much. The generals are looking the other way because the legions need something to lift them up. I've heard rumors winter games are being planned. Although unscheduled, I believe the race is going to be the first event."

"I hope you're right. For someone who came to the legions in protest, I'm reluctant to leave them."

Chapter 30

He thought about it, rationalized if he should do it and finally decided Servius was devious enough that he should take the dagger Ursinus had given him. He left the tent carrying the racing saddle he hadn't used since Visontio. In comparison to the heavy working saddle with multiple heavy double straps and a wide girth band, the lighter saddle was fastened to the horse with a thin breast and haunch strap looped under the tail and a narrow girth band. He didn't feel any regret not mentioning to Servius the lighter tack he was going to use. It was about endurance in the first mile and speed in the last.

Strabo's first surprise was the number of legionnaires from both legions lining both sides of the river and on the nearby hills. He looked across the river at the finish line and spotted Generals Labienus, Metellus, Crassus and a large crowd of officers. Ursinus was right about the unspoken approval to lift morale.

Servius was already there standing next to one of the ugliest stallions Strabo had ever seen. At one time, the brown horse may have looked better. From the look of the numerous scars on his face and flanks, time and too many battles had left their mark. The horse was a hand shorter, heavier and more muscled than Aquilo. It wasn't built for speed, and Strabo wondered why Servius would consider racing it against Aquilo with the additional disadvantage of a heavy saddle.

"Servius, where did you get him? Maybe I'll hold Aquilo to a canter to give you an even chance to win."

"That beast is going to cost you ten denarii," Servius replied with a confident smile. "Speed isn't going to determine who wins; it's whoever can finish the race, and the money is on Bellator. *Warrior* always fights to win. Strabo, it's not too late to forfeit and not risk your pretty stallion."

"If you're that confident, why not raise the bet another ten denarii?"

"I propose something bigger. If I win, I get Aquilo, and you can have Bellator as a consolation prize."

"Not today or any day."

Tarquin motioned for them to approach the start line. The muted sound of the watching legionnaires gradually increased in anticipation the race was about to begin. The horses were similarly affected and showed it by their immediate and mutual dislike. Before reaching the line, Strabo tried to keep distance between them after Bellator made repeated attempts to bite without discriminating between human or horse. Servius laughed and aggravated the situation by immediately closing the distance.

Tarquin held up a stick with a notch carved in the end. "Whichever horse the notch points to takes the position closest to the river."

With an underhand toss, Tarquin threw the stick in the air end over end. It landed and the notch pointed closest to Aquilo. Strabo momentarily considered giving up the advantage of the inside track and the slightly better chance to avoid humiliating Servius again. He decided against it — the bastard deserved what was going to happen, and he looked forward to it.

"Mount your horses and move to the line," Tarquin yelled. "The bugle will signal the start. Are you ready?" Both men nodded, and the decurion pointed to the bugler.

The first note was enough for Bellator to take a short lead. Strabo was confident it would be the last time and not for long. He held Aquilo to a cautious pace in keeping with the uneven ground.

Both riders maintained the same easy gallop through the open meadow until they reached the trees where the hills became steeper. Servius drew farther ahead and widened the distance to the river bank. Strabo urged Aquilo to a faster pace and easily caught up until they were briefly neck and neck. As he was starting to pass, Servius looked at him and smiled.

"Strabo, your first mistake," and abruptly turned his horse into Aquilo's left flank forcing the stallion toward the river bank.

Strabo pulled back on the reins to get the panicked horse under control. Servius slowed his horse and tried to push Strabo out of the saddle. Off balance, Strabo grabbed the left pommel in a desperate effort to keep from falling off. Leaning precariously to the right caused Aquilo to move closer to the edge, and the stallion struggled to keep from going over. For a brief moment, Strabo thought they would until Aquilo came to a halt, and Bellator moved on ahead.

Furious and shaken, Strabo calmed the nervous horse and watched Servius gallop off. By the time Aquilo settled down, Servius had gained a significant lead. Strabo wasn't too concerned. The race would not begin in earnest until they crossed the river where the river bank was shallow, and the flatter course gave Aquilo the advantage. Until then, he was willing to allow Servius to keep a length ahead.

Servius surprisingly turned away from the easier river bank track and gave up the lead by climbing a small hill. Strabo knew why. Servius was going up the small hill to gain the downhill momentum for another attempt to push him into the river. Strabo cautiously followed Servius up the hill.

"Strabo, you're learning."

"You're a good teacher. Too bad there aren't any steep banks on the other side."

"I have time. The race isn't half over, and much can happen before it is."

The two riders were nearly to the hilltop with Aquilo a half-length behind Bellator. Servius abruptly reined in. Strabo found himself in the lead and unprepared for Bellator's vicious attack. With a combination of pain and rage, Aquilo screamed from the bite on his flank. Again, Strabo found himself trying to control the stallion and keep it from going downhill too fast over the irregular surface. At the bottom of the hill, Aquilo was ready for Bellator.

Oblivious of the riders, the two stallions were on their hind legs kicking and biting. Strabo heard Servius laughing.

"Strabo, I think before this race is done, your horse is going to look like Bellator."

The decurion's laughter turned to angry curses after Aquilo bit him on the upper arm, and it was Strabo's turn to laugh.

"It looks like you will, too."

The two men finally got the two horses apart and under enough control to resume the race. For most of the remaining distance to the river crossing, they kept the pace slow enough to avoid injuring the horses over the rough course. On several occasions, the terrain caused the riders to come close enough both horses suffered nasty bites. In one such incident, Aquilo was equally satisfied to bite Servius on the leg causing Strabo to laugh again.

Strabo saw the river through the trees and briefly considered increasing the pace to get there before Servius. He changed his mind after considering how steep the bank was and took his time. The riders let the horses make their way down the steep bank to the river's edge. Aquilo was the first to reach the water, and Strabo waited until the stallion was swimming then slid out of the saddle. The shock of the cold water was almost unbearable. He heard a splash behind on his right followed by a loud curse as Servius slid off Bellator into the water. Concentrating on keeping a firm grip on the forward pommel and away from Aquilo's hooves, Strabo failed to see Servius catching up and guiding his horse close to his. The horses reached the shallows at the same time. It wasn't until Strabo tried to climb in the saddle and felt it sliding toward him that he realized something was wrong, quickly confirmed by the severed breast and haunch straps. He looked up and saw Servius mounted on Bellator holding up a small dagger shining in the morning sunlight.

"When you don't have the fastest horse, you find another way to win. Strabo, another day we'll race again. Until then enjoy the long walk ahead of you. If you're wondering how to explain the mishap, blame the gods for severing the haunch strap. All right, they had some help from a mortal willing to do their bidding." Servius tossed the dagger into the river. "It's time to return the instrument the gods told me to use so I would win."

Strabo contained his anger and focused on what he had to do. He reached down under his tunic, drew the dagger and held it up. "Servius the gods changed their mind."

Servius stared in open-mouthed astonishment. He finally managed to say with a cheerful expression not quite convincing, "I'm disappointed. You violated your condition for no daggers. Strabo, I think we're more alike than you think."

With one stroke, Strabo cut the left breast and girth strap. Grasping the reins in one hand and a fistful of mane in the other, he was on Aquilo's back before the loose saddle reached the bottom of the river.

'Shit!" Servius smacked Bellator's haunch without the slightest hesitation or concern for the possibility of injuring the horse on the slippery bank.

Strabo had to restrain Aquilo from following at a similar pace, confident Servius had no chance. He considered for a moment allowing Servius a narrow loss rather than being humiliated again. He rationalized being generous might reduce the enmity between them. The problem was he didn't feel the least bit generous. Evidently Aquilo didn't either and without any urging the horse was in a full gallop.

It had been a long time since he last rode bareback, and he'd forgotten the exhilaration of becoming bonded to the horse in a way a saddle couldn't equal. By the time he reached the half-mile mark to the finish line, the horses were neck and neck for a brief moment. On the side of the course where the *Claudia* legionnaires watched, the cheers were muted while the opposite side of the bridge, dominated by legionnaires from the Tenth, erupted in loud, sustained cheering.

He considered slowing down to cross the finish line at a trot. Servius had once again shown he was willing do anything underhanded and dangerous to win. He decided not to. It would be seen as arrogant and maybe a little too humiliating. Strabo let the stallion go. Servius crossed the line a comfortable distance behind.

Strabo relaxed after seeing the approving nods and smiles on the faces of the generals. General Crassus was the first to congratulate him.

"Marcellus, it seems you haven't forgotten how to win a race without a saddle. That you started with a saddle and finished without it might be interesting to find out why. On the other hand, it might be better if I don't know."

"I think the gods decided who would win, and I'm happy they favored me."

Servius heard the comment and silently passed by with an angry scowl.

Strabo shook his head resigned to what he expected would happen. Nothing had been settled except his resolve never to race him again. Another thought came to him. He had less reason to believe Servius's assurance not to worry about his back.

Chapter 31

Tribune Setarius smiled and motioned to the chair on the other side of the table. "You were surrounded by so many generals I didn't get a chance to congratulate you. It was quite a finish, possibly a bit one-sided and not quite as dramatic as the Visontio race. It will keep the legions talking about it for some time. I don't suppose you're going to tell me what happened to your saddle?"

"General Crassus asked me the same thing, and I declined to answer the question. I gave the credit to the gods."

"The gods are fickle and cannot always be depended upon. I think you, much like Caesar, are favored by them. It's been almost two years since you became a legionnaire. What you've achieved in that time is impressive. I said it before, your father would be pleased and proud."

The tribune cleared his throat and continued, "General Labienus has an answer to a request made by Diviciacus and wants you deliver it. It's an opportunity at some point for you to spend some time in Bibracte as circumstances allow."

The pleasant prospect of seeing Raven and Caturix was lessened by the tribune's last conditional words *as circumstances allow.*

"Diviciacus has further confirmation of what General Labienus suspected during his visit to the eastern and Belgae tribes. The unrest in the region is growing. There are signs the Suebi across the Rhine may be preparing for another incursion into Gaul. Worse, a few of the tribes west of the Rhine are rumored to be encouraging it with the promise of assistance if they do. General Labienus believes it's only a matter of time before we go back there and confront the Germani again. He's agreed to your uncle's request to send someone to him whose presence in the region will reinforce Rome's commitment to the Aedui. General

Labienus has another reason to support the request. He wants someone there who can evaluate and advise him as the situation develops."

"Sir, I think my uncle probably had someone experienced with higher rank than a mere decurion."

"True, and that's why I'm going. I need someone to assist me in talking with the tribal chiefs. You don't credit the capabilities you've demonstrated by your timely and incisive reports that caught Caesar's attention. He was the first to say you were worth more than carrying a shield and gladius in the ranks."

"When do we leave?"

"In two days. By the way, your decuria will be my escort. We're going to Bibracte. It's a long way. We'll need pack horses to carry supplies for the journey."

Strabo left wondering how eager Ursinus and the others would be to leave winter quarters in a better climate than farther east. He didn't care if it was snowing the whole time they were gone. The prospect of seeing Raven was worth it.

Bibracte
Six days later

The drawn look on his uncle's face followed by a warm but brief welcome did not bode well. Strabo sensed the situation in eastern Gaul might be worse than General Labienus believed. Diviciacus didn't waste time confirming it.

"General Labienus and I traveled together for much of his visit. We both concluded the Germani are likely planning another invasion which is not surprising. Of equal concern is the impression we both had some tribes on this side of the Rhine might choose to remain neutral if they do."

"Which tribes?" Setarius asked.

"To varying degrees most of the border tribes including the Treveri."

The tribune's eyes widened in surprise. "General Labienus did not speak of that. The Treveri have been staunch supporters of Caesar, and their cavalry has been indispensable," Setarius hesitated, "at least until we fought the Nervii, when they left before the battle had barely started."

"The Treveri left because they thought the battle was lost, and it ended their belief the legions are invincible."

"We won the battle decisively, and the Nervii were virtually annihilated."

"They learned that later; unfortunately, by the time they did, the damage was done."

"The Sequani were nominal allies of the Helvetii, and it didn't save them. The example should serve as a reminder for the Treveri not to depend on the good faith of any tribe across the border."

"I've said as much to Indutiomarus, the leader of the Treveri. What I did not know until I met with him recently is that he's not the supporter of Rome that Caesar thinks he is; he wants the legions out of Gaul. His son-in-law, Cingetorix, admires Rome, and thus far Indutiomarus has tolerated it by allowing him to provide cavalry support to Caesar. The sudden flight of the cavalry at the Sambre may indicate Cingetorix is rethinking his opinion and support of Rome. I don't believe Indutiomarus has entered into any formal agreement with the Germani, but I don't discount the possibility he will. I have my scouts moving among the Treveri to find out what their intentions are in the event the Germani cross the Rhine."

Strabo heard the last and hoped in the time the decuria would be in the vicinity, there would be a chance to see Corius. His uncle's following comments turned the hope into a certainty he would.

"Tribune, I asked General Labienus to send someone to see with Roman eyes what is developing along the border and among the tribes within Gaul since he was here. The Helvetii then the Germani by Ariovistus threat made the legions welcome, albeit cautiously so. If Caesar had not come, Gaul would look different than it did before.

"In a way, Gaul does look different. The legions remain and grow in number. Tribal alliances occasionally tested before the legions wintered here have become strained in the belief Rome will stay in Celtica Gaul forever as a pretext to defend us from invasion by tribes from Belgica and Germania. The Aedui are viewed as strongly allied with Rome as Caesar assumed the Treveri were. Other tribes here are showing interest in forming closer ties with tribes across the borders. As leader of the Aedui, I'm no longer certain how many of our tribes remain firmly affiliated. In part, Dumnorix has contributed to this, but not as much as Rome."

Exasperated, Setarius threw up his hands and said with an edge to his voice, "It sounds as if you want me to go back and tell General Labienus and Caesar everything would be better for Gaul if we took the legions out tomorrow."

"No, that would be unrealistic and not what I want. I knew it would be a risk when I went to Rome two years ago and asked Caesar for assistance in resisting the Suebi who were colonizing in the northeast. The risk being the Romans, once here, wouldn't leave. I accepted that risk. I believe a Roman presence in Gaul is not necessarily a bad thing. Trade and mutual defense against Germania are beneficial for both Gaul and Rome. Previous concerns for Rome's long-term intent have turned to conviction that Rome already sees Gaul as another province. The recent arrival of two more legions has increased this belief. The stability of Gaul is in as much danger from within as it is from across the borders. General Labienus was focused on the external threat. I asked for a senior officer to come here for longer than General Labienus was here to have a better understanding of the situation I described. A Roman officer will be listened to closer and believed more convincingly than a *barbarian* Gaul even if the barbarian is the tribal leader of the largest tribal federation in Gaul." The last was said with a combination of sadness and bitterness.

"My Lord, I accept everything you've said, and I'm willing to go back now and inform Caesar..."

"No, it wouldn't be enough. You must *see* and *hear* for yourself to be truly convincing. if you agree my concerns are justified, then you'll be persuasive in gaining Caesar's attention."

"Assuming I verify your concerns, Caesar is not going to take the legions out of Gaul even if the situation is worse than you've described. If it is, he'll bring in additional legions. I'm not sure what you expect him to do."

"I accept that reality just as I hope what you said does not happen. I am not asking Caesar to reduce the number of legions while there remains a threat from across the borders. I am merely offering advice against bringing in more legions and reduce the number of legions already here as soon as possible. The timing and the extent of the reduction is less important than the *perception* there will be a reduction. My worry is if these measures are not taken, the tribes will join together in common cause against Rome."

Strabo was shaken by the grim outlook his uncle was predicting. It wasn't as if he hadn't heard it before. Corius and Raven had said as much. Dumnorix was widely known to prefer any other cross-border power to rule Gaul than Rome. His dismay was in hearing Diviciacus saying the same thing. He looked at the tribune and thought he, too, was taken aback at what amounted to a gentle ultimatum no matter how artfully phrased. Caesar would still interpret it as an ultimatum. He felt he was an outsider listening to two potential adversaries objectively discussing matters which were going to profoundly affect him. Lost in his own reflections, it was the sudden silence that roused him. He saw the tribune sitting with his chin on his fist, deep in thought. His uncle wasn't looking at Setarius; he was regarding him with an expression of sympathy.

Setarius sighed. "My Lord, your words are not surprising. I confess to having similar worries prompted by your brother's actions in helping the Helvetii and recently King Galba. I'll tell Caesar of your concerns and ways to mitigate them. Having said that, I don't believe it will have any near-term effect for what he will do in Gaul. He envisions a peaceful

Gaul which can only be achieved by the legions and the confidence it will last because of the legions. After Gaul shows signs of a stable peace, I've no doubt some if not all legions will be withdrawn and deployed to other regions where they are needed. When and how many legions will leave cannot be foretold at this time."

"That is all I ask. The capability to foretell the future is the province of the gods."

"Where do you suggest I concentrate my efforts?"

"The Treveri is key to the safety of the Aedui. Indutiomarus has so far remained detached and allowed Cingetorix to support Caesar. How long that will be is the question. The Germani have shown they can cross the Rhine, and the Treveri are just across the river. I would not be surprised if Indutiomarus has an understanding with the Germani similar to what the Sequani thought they had with the Helvetti. I don't expect you'll be able to determine that; however, in talking to Cingetorix, you may be able to detect the possibility. When will you leave?"

"We'll rest the horses tomorrow and leave the next day. We'll need additional supplies to last a few weeks."

"I will see to it." Diviciacus turned his attention to Strabo. "You have a fine-looking son, and his mother is doing well. I've been pleased to spend time with both of them. They give me comfort and relief from affairs becoming increasingly challenging for an aging man."

Tribune Setarius stood. "My Lord, the time grows late for another aging man as well."

"You will stay where you have before. Your escort has been given quarters next to you. Marcellus, I believe there is someone who would be pleased to welcome you."

Outside the spacious dwelling, the two men followed the guide who was waiting. Setarius was the first to speak.

"Your uncle is troubled, and he has good reason to be. His brother's influence remains and may be getting stronger while his influence in

Gaul may be on the wane. The alliances the Aedui have are apparently not as strong as we believed, and he's afraid some of the tribes would prefer dealing with the Belgae and Germani without involving the legions. Finally, there's his concern Caesar intends to make Gaul another province of Rome. Your uncle has every reason to fear that outcome. He's caught in the middle. He needs Rome to help him maintain his influence with the Gaulish tribes, yet our support is seen as a necessary evil for which he is being viewed as being responsible for the legions being here."

Strabo hurried to Raven's conical, thatched dwelling. He was apprehensive. Given his abrupt departure several months ago, he wasn't certain his sudden arrival would be as welcome as his uncle did.

He approached the doorway and heard voices intermixed with the babbling, cooing of a child. He paused, listening, reluctant to intrude and doubting if he should. Raven surely knew he was in the settlement and wondering why he hadn't come to see her. He took a deep breath and walked in.

With Caturix beside her, Raven was sitting on the bed dangling a string of hollow nut shells that rattled softly and were visibly pleasing to the infant. He watched silently, hesitant to interrupt until Raven sensed he was there and looked up. He was relieved to see her warm welcoming smile. She picked up Caturix and speaking softly to him put him on the floor and took his hand. Still talking, she walked toward him. He was astonished to see the little boy walking although somewhat unsteadily. It wasn't until they had almost reached him that he realized she was speaking Latin, rudimentary, but understandable.

She saw his puzzled expression. "Diviciacus has been teaching me. He said if I and Caturix were going to live in two worlds, we must be able to speak in both as your mother did. At first, I wasn't willing then I decided he was right for the sake of our son and me. I want to be ready for whatever world we may live in."

Strabo knelt down shaking his head in disbelief. "He is so changed. Does he talk?"

"Caturix, how do you greet your father?"

The toddler looked at Raven then gave him a solemn look and responded in less than perfect but understandable Latin. "*Sahve, Pattay.*"

Strabo picked him up and with a broad smile replied, *"Salve, Filius meus.* Raven, you've done well. I'm proud and pleased with both of you." He thought of leaving tomorrow and regretted he was.

Raven noted his changed expression. "How long can you stay?"

"I leave the day after tomorrow to visit the Treveri and other tribes in the region."

When he said no more, she forced a smile and reached for Caturix who was on the verge of falling asleep. "Then we'll have to make the most of our time together."

Strabo awoke to the sound of voices. He opened his eyes and saw Raven with a blanket wrapped around her at the doorway talking to Ursinus, each struggling to understand the other and talking louder in the attempt. It was still dark outside.

"Ursinus, what's the matter?"

"Sir, Tribune Setarius wants to see you. I don't think we'll be leaving as planned."

"Why?"

"The Aeduan scouts arrived a short time ago and reported the Germani have crossed the Rhine in the far north."

Suddenly wide awake, Strabo dressed hurriedly while speculating what was going to follow. He was still wondering what the implications might be as he and Ursinus arrived at the guest dwelling. The murmur of voices from the large rectangular building farther up the hill told him the clan leaders had been assembled.

The two men entered and saw the tribune deep in thought sitting at a table, elbows propping his folded hands under his chin. A flickering oil lamp deepened the lines in his face making him look older.

The tribune waived them to chairs across from him. "Aeduan scouts arrived not long ago and reported two large tribes, the Usipetes and the Tencteri, crossed the Rhine ten days ago in the far northwest corner of Belgica and slaughtered the Menapi Tribe. Except for their mutual alliance, they are much like the Nervii, formidable and independent. Of the two, the Tencteri are the fiercest. For the time being, they've stayed where they are living off the winter stores the Menapi had. The Eburones south of the Menapi have encountered Tencteri patrols through their territory indicating a possible move south. This was all Diviciacus had time to tell me. He's been meeting with the tribal elders for several hours since we last spoke. We'll talk again after the meeting is concluded.

"Talk to the scouts and see if you can find out anything else. Your uncle's Latin is adequate, but there could be details he didn't mention or could not because of his language limitations. In all probability, I'll return to winter quarters to inform General Labienus after I'm satisfied that I have a full understanding of the situation. I haven't decided yet if the decuria will go on to the Treveri as planned, remain here, or return with me." Setarius smiled and added, "It's ironic had we been successful with the Morini and wintered there, the legions would probably be on the march with what's left of the Menapi happy to see them."

There was a tap on the hide screen, and Strabo went to see who it was. He pulled the screen aside and saw Corius looking at him in bewilderment.

"Marcellus, I didn't expect to see you."

"I came yesterday with Tribune Setarius. It appears coming here was providential considering the information you brought. The tribune is waiting until the tribal meeting is over to talk to Diviciacus."

"The elders have left, and Diviciacus wants to see the tribune."

"Sir, Diviciacus wants to see you."

Setarius stood and said, "Marcellus, come with me."

Looking more drawn than the day before, the tribal chief dispensed with the preliminaries.

"What is happening in Belgica is a surprise. We were expecting it would be the Suebi not the Usipetes and Tencteri. From what the Eburones learned and told the Treveri, the two tribes were forced to cross the Rhine to escape the Suebi privations they've endured for many years. What the Belgac tribes will do to resist the incursion is unknown. Caesar's recent successes there have weakened alliances and made the Belgae tribes vulnerable. Some Belgae tribes have made deputations to the invaders pledging any support required if they would leave and go back to Germania. The offer has been summarily rejected for the reason they fear only the Suebi and no other tribes including those on the west side of the Rhine.

"Their easy subjugation of the Menapi has emboldened them to remain where they are until they decide where they will go. The Eburones and Treveri believe if the two tribes migrate farther, they will go south based on the patrolling they've been doing along the border between the Eburones and the Aduatuci."

"What are the western tribes in Gaul planning to do?" Setarius asked.

"Observe and see what they will do. If they remain where they are, it is for the Belgae to decide. Should they come south intending to enter Gaul, we will fight."

"Will you ask for Caesar's help?"

The tribal leader's face was expressionless when he replied, "I doubt I need to. After you inform Caesar of what's happened, the legions will march with or without my request. And if he does march, who am I to do other than give thanks for his assistance."

Recalling their conversation a few hours ago, the tribune wasn't surprised by the tactful, realistic response.

"In view of what's happened, I'll return to winter quarters tomorrow and inform General Labienus. I'd like Decurion Strabo to remain with you to report any further developments in Belgica especially if the two tribes show any indication of coming south into Gaul."

The tribune did not notice Strabo's strained expression, but the tribal leader did.

"Marcellus is always welcome."

The two men remained silent, deep in thought for different reasons as they walked back to the tribune's quarters. Once there, it was Strabo who spoke first working hard to control his temper.

"Sir, I would like to clarify what my role is to be."

"I thought I made that clear. What don't you understand?" The tribune suddenly realized Strabo's concern. "You think you are here to spy on your uncle and the Aedui. I assure you that isn't the reason, nor did it cross my mind. On the contrary, if I were to consider you a spy it would be on behalf of Diviciacus. You will do as I told your uncle I was planning to do. Observe and report what happens in the north. If anything, your presence will benefit your uncle as it will Caesar. Diviciacus is as important to Rome as he is to the Aedui and the future of Gaul."

Mollified, Strabo relaxed. "Thank you for your assurance. I was reminded of last year when Dumnorix attempted to use my assumed influence to learn Caesar's plans for him, and Caesar, possibly you as well, assumed I was. Being part Aedui places me in a position where I can easily be accused of being something I will never be."

"I'm glad you spoke up. I confess I see you primarily as General Strabo's son and a Roman. In so doing, I don't take into consideration you are as much Aedui."

"And I admit, I am occasionally conflicted by being both. What do you think Caesar will do about what's happening in northern Belgica?"

"Caesar has made it very clear by his defeat of the Helvetii and the Suebi what will happen to any eastern tribe that crosses the Rhine.

General Labienus understands that and will prepare the legions to march by the time Caesar returns to Gaul. He'll want to convene a meeting with the tribal leaders to obtain Auxilia cavalry and logistical support. Before I leave, I'll tell Diviciacus to plan for this as early as six weeks from now. Assuming the Aeduan scouts will soon return to the northern border of the Treveri, will you have any difficulty in being allowed to accompany them?"

"Not at all. Diviciacus would expect it, and Corius, the leader of the scouts, is a close friend and brother of Raven. Corius would be surprised and possibly insulted it I didn't. I will make a point of seeing him before you depart probably before the day is out after he's had some rest. I'm certain Diviciacus expects them to go back to the border area as soon as they're rested and resupplied."

"If it turns out you're wrong, I'll leave half the decuria here with you. It's important we maintain continuous surveillance on the two tribes. Given what happened in the battle of the Nervii, we can no longer depend on the Treveri as we did before."

Chapter 32
Northeast Gaul four weeks later
Territory of the Eburones

The Aeduan and Treveri scouts had been patrolling continuously over the past two weeks following sporadic sightings of near-naked warriors south of the Aduatuci/Eburones border. The patrols focused their efforts within the Arduenna Silva, a large expanse of densely-forested terrain crisscrossed with deep ravines. The patrols found nothing to substantiate the reports, only small isolated Aduatuci enclaves taking refuge following the tribe's recent defeat by the Romans.

Corius and Katamorus, the Treveri scout patrol leader, agreed it was time to extend the range of the patrols across the Meuse River farther north into the territory of the Eburones. Strabo noted Katamorus's slight hesitation before agreeing and taking his patrol along the Rhine River.

The decision to patrol farther north was reinforced by Talos that morning who had just come from Bibracte with an urgent message from Diviciacus. Caesar was back in the Seine valley winter quarters and expected to take the legions northeast along the west bank of the Meuse to the border of the Eburones and the Menapi.

Corius halted the patrol on a steep bluff overlooking the Meuse River to rest the horses. The river below made a sharp turn flowing from the southeast to the northeast. The far side was tranquil except for a cluster of ravens perched in the trees or circling above the bluff. A tendril of smoke curling up through the trees indicated a settlement and the reason for several boats pulled up on the river bank below.

Corius looked in both directions and saw no way to get safely down to the river bank. He sent a scout in each direction along the bluff to find a way.

Strabo beckoned to Corius, and the two men walked their horses away from the others. "Corius, how much do you trust Katamorus?"

Corius was slow to answer. It was obvious by Corius's expression the blunt question had caught him by surprise. His response was equally brusque.

"I don't, what made you ask?"

"Katamorus didn't seem too eager to go farther north. Before we left Bibracte, my uncle told Tribune Setarius and me he had doubts about the Treveri and Indutiomarus in particular. He knows some tribes have sent deputations to the Germani encouraging them to go back across the Rhine and speculates the Treveri could have been one of them. The Sequani had an understanding with the Helvetii until Divico became their leader. It's possible Indutiomarus has come to a similar *understanding* with the Usipetes and Tencteri."

"Diviciacus said much the same to me, and I've been trying to find out if there's any truth to it. So far, I haven't, but I have suspicions. The cavalry still appears loyal to Cingetorix who on the surface is still pro-Roman although his influence with the Tribal Leader is not what it used to be. My suspicion is the Treveri neither want to help or provoke the Germani by patrolling too close to the Menapi border. Their preference is the Germani will stay where they are or go west without the Treveri giving them a reason to come south instead."

"So, it's possible Katamorus won't cross the river and risk encountering any Germani patrols?"

"Perhaps, and that's the reason we're going northeast after we cross over. The Germani aren't going to remain where they are after they're finished living off of what the Menapi have. Going west is not likely. The land of the Morini is even less abundant than where the Menapi live. The two Germani tribes are nomadic and will eventually leave. South is where they will go. It's only a matter of when."

The scout sent south returned and reported seeing no trail safe enough to get to the river. It took longer for the scout sent in the other direction to come back and report finding a well-worn trail down to the river. What he said next was even of more importance.

"There's a recent campsite where up to a dozen horses were picketed. Whoever they were crossed the river, camped one night and went back across the next day without going any farther south. From the human waste and horse dung found, they went back yesterday."

Strabo said, "It could be they were Germani looking for a way to cross the river. The boats and smoke on the other side may be a settlement located there because the river is shallower here than farther north or south."

Corius signified agreement with a nod. "We'll go down to the river the same way and follow their trail. The villagers can tell us whether they're Eburones or Germani. If they're Germani, we'll avoid them. We're too few to do anything except look around, assess what the Germani are doing or not doing and report to Diviciacus."

Once across the river, the patrol followed a well-used trail up the bank. At the top of the bluff, the familiar cloying odor of burnt flesh was overwhelming. Corius signaled a halt and silently pointed to Talos and waved him down the road where the breeze was coming from. The sudden cloud of squawking ravens and crows rising above the treetops showed Talos had found the source of the smell. The grim-faced scout soon returned.

Talos gestured over his shoulder and said, "A small settlement burned to the ground, and the villagers massacred sometime yesterday. A dozen or so adult men and women and about twice as many children. The men and women show signs of torture before they were beheaded. Some of the bodies were thrown onto the burning dwellings. It looks to me the ones who camped on the other side of the river did it. The trail goes right past the settlement and continues northeast. It looks as if they passed through toward the river without harming anyone then came back the next day and for whatever reason, killed them."

Strabo frowned. "Could be on the way to the river, the Germani purposely avoided any conflict until they decided there were no large Eburones settlements. Once they learned there weren't any and found a way to cross the river, they ransacked the village and left no survivors to tell who did it."

"They're going the same direction we're going," Corius said. "We'll take the same trail. Marcellus, you and Talos take the lead. We'll follow a few hundred paces behind. If possible, we'll avoid contact with the Germani. We're about fifty miles from the Menapi border. I doubt we'll need to go that far before we know if they're migrating south or remaining where they are. As soon as we can answer the question, we turn back and report it."

Strabo entered the clearing and saw at a glance Talos had omitted some of the gruesome details of the slaughter. He saw the remains of what had been a young child, and he thought of Caturix. By now, he was well used to the carnage of a battlefield and the brutality of legionnaires in the heat of battle making little distinction between warriors and civilians. This was worse. It was cold-blooded butchery. Corius had made a point of emphasizing they came across the river to scout and not to provoke. He would bear that in mind. It was after all what scouts were supposed to do until circumstances dictated otherwise. He looked forward to the opportunity they would do more than passively observe.

Close to dusk, Strabo and Talos found another small settlement ravaged in the same manner as the previous one. The burning dwellings were not yet fully consumed, and the dismembered bodies had not been dead long enough to attract predators. The two men turned back and stopped the patrol from going farther.

Strabo described what they had found and concluded by saying, "Corius, they can't be far ahead. This late in the day, it could be they may not have gone very far. If we keep following this trail, it's likely we could run into them. The alternative is head north and avoid the risk."

"I don't feel like wandering through the forest to find another trail, and if we didn't, it would take too much time to get near enough to the Menapi border to find out what we came here for. The bastards are in our way."

Corius slowly looked around at the scouts surrounding him. Strabo saw the beginning of a smile on his friend's face and returned by the scouts. He was reminded of the time the two of them were returning to camp, and Corius saw a Helvetii patrol with odds against them three to one. Corius attacked without telling him he was going to. Both of them were wounded, and it would've been worse had not Raven and the other scouts found them in time. He was reconciled to what Corius was about to say and smiled.

"All right, this is what we're going to do. We'll keep on riding until it gets dark then we walk the horses. Marcellus, Talos, stay a half mile ahead of us until you see or smell a fire or hear their horses. One of you come back and tell us where they are. The one left behind will try and locate the sentinels. We need to take care of them first. We'll leave the horses far enough away they can't be heard and go the rest of the way on foot. At the camp, we spread out and kill as many as we can while they're asleep. Having come this way before, I doubt they have any reason to be concerned about being attacked."

Strabo smelled smoke first then saw the reddish glow of burning coals. He tapped Talos on the arm and whispered, "We're too close. We need to get farther back."

The two men turned the horses around and walked them back down the trail. Talos agreed to go back and tell Corius. Strabo tethered his horse and walked back to the camp to take a close look and specifically to find where the guards were posted.

He heard heavy breathing before he saw the guard sitting on the ground with his back to a tree sound asleep. He drew his dagger and started to move closer but froze after hearing a noise on the opposite side of the clearing. He saw a shadowy figure approach the center of the camp. There was a thump followed soon after by a shower of sparks bursting in the air. The fire slowly grew brighter revealing a tall, burly warrior naked except for a cape tied at the neck reaching to the knees. A baldric over his right shoulder held a sheathed sword at his left hip. There was now enough light to reveal fifteen pale forms lying in a circle around the fire who appeared to be no more clothed than the warrior standing by the fire. The sleeping sentinel he planned to silence had roused and stood up to join the other warrior.

Strabo waited only long enough until the two sentinels were occupied in a low conversation then made his way back to his horse to wait for the scouts. He didn't have to wait long before hearing the faint sound of hooves. Strabo gathered the scouts in a close half circle and described what he had seen and the location of the guards. Strabo recalled Talos telling how he had managed to get through the Bellovaci lines at Bibrax without being challenged by wearing the clothes and helmet of a Bellovaci warrior. He volunteered to take out the sentinels by dressing or in this case, being undressed as the Germani were. Corius was skeptical but reluctantly agreed.

The scouts stopped a short distance away from the camp where Strabo removed his clothes, boots and left his shield. Wearing only his baldric and dagger belt, Strabo crept alone to the nearest guard sitting where he had been earlier. The guard was awake but starting to nod off. Strabo inched closer to the tree until he was standing behind it. He waited until the rhythmic breathing told him the guard was asleep before slitting his throat.

With the guard's woolen cape draped over his shoulders, Strabo strolled leisurely across the camp to where he thought the other guard was. He reached the edge of the clearing and saw the guard standing on the trail with his back to him. He was only a few feet away when the guard turned around and said something in a soft voice that sounded at first like a question. The guard suddenly started to draw his sword, and

Strabo knew it was time to act. His dagger was in the guard's throat before his sword was out of the scabbard. The guard's warning cry was stifled enough to keep from waking up the warriors sleeping nearby.

Across the camp, Strabo heard the scouts advancing into the camp followed by hoarse cries of alarm and choked off by slashing blades. Strabo shrugged off the cape and drew his sword in time to confront several Germani running toward him, two with swords and one with an axe. He was over-matched and made worse by not having a shield. The nearest Germani raised his sword with both hands for a downward stroke. Strabo stepped forward, blocked the blade and stabbed him in the stomach then pulled it upward. The two warriors coming up behind slowed down and spread out. Strabo was relieved to see Talos running up behind the one on the right and concentrated on the other warrior. A sudden cry of pain told him Talos had been successful. The warrior he was about to fight looked to see what happened and turned too late to stop the sword that killed him.

There was a sudden silence in the clearing. The brief battle was over. Strabo looked around and saw the scouts already occupied in taking the heads of the dead Germani. A custom that once repelled him had become inconsequential.

Three days later, near the north border of the Menapi and Eburones

The patrol reached the top of a hill overlooking the south bank of the Meuse River. Twenty-five miles west where Corius said the Meuse joined the Rhine, they glimpsed the blue waters of the North Sea beyond. A wider vista of the sea was obscured intermittently by a pall of smoke drifting southwest from an area across the river 10 to 15 miles away.

"It looks to me the Germani are on the move," Corius said to Strabo. "Where the smoke is coming from is the main settlement of the Menapi, or I should say *was* their main settlement."

"Which way do you think they'll go?" Strabo asked.

"It will depend on how successful Indutiomarus is in persuading the Germani not to come through Treveri lands by going down the west bank of the Rhine. If he is, they'll go south along the east bank of the Meuse through the Eburones and Aduatuci lands."

"Corius, we need to hear what Katamorus has learned before we go back. The legions may have already left winter quarters. Caesar will need to know which way the Germani will take to avoid engaging them in the densest part the Arduenna Silva."

"I agree. There's a place not far from here to cross the river where Katamorus and I planned to meet. We're a few days later than what we estimated, but he also knew our route was longer. There's a good chance we can be on the way south before the day is out."

Katamorus made it clear to Corius and Strabo his foul mood was not caused by the late arrival of the Aeduan scouts or the Germani. Rather it was the internal conflict within the Treveri leadership that disgusted him.

"The Eburones and what's left of the Aduatuci have convinced Indutiomarus to keep negotiating with the Germani. They want to persuade the Germani to transit their lands peacefully and avoid what they did to the Menapi. The smoke you've seen is their farewell to the Menapi. It will certainly be the same for any tribe once the bastards are through taking everything they have. They do not have livestock nor do they till the land. Their way is to live off other tribes, and after there's nothing left, they move on and do the same to any tribe in their way. I believe the Germani will soon be on their way somewhere south to pillage the Eburones or southeast to do the same with the Treveri. The one thing that seems certain is they are not going back to Germania. Cingetorix wants to fight them here and hopes Caesar will come and help."

"What is the warrior strength of the two tribes and where are they camped?" Strabo asked

"They claim their combined population is 400,000. If true, their warrior strength is expected to be about 85,000. Their camp is located between the Rhine and the Waal Rivers five or six miles west of where the Waal begins as a tributary of the Rhine. For the time being, Indutiomarus has managed to keep them from going farther pending the arrival of a delegation from the Ubii with an offer to settle in their lands. The Usipetes might consider such a proposal; however, the Tencteri have already said they won't go back no matter what is offered. They don't believe the Ubii are strong enough to protect them from the Suebi. If the Usipetes accept an offer, the Tencteri may have to reconsider remaining in Gaul with half the strength they had before."

"When is the Ubii delegation expected?" Corius asked.

Katamorus shook his head. "That's what the Germani are asking, too. They've said they won't wait much longer before moving on without indicating where they will go. Cingetorix believes they will go south through the lands of the Eburones to avoid the Arduenna Silva."

Corius looked at Strabo and said, "I think it's time to go back and tell Diviciacus and Caesar what we know and what we don't."

"I agree. I'm going back in the direction of the winter quarters where Caesar has gone. If he's already left with the legions which I expect he has, I hope to meet him somewhere in between. What about you?"

"We'll go together for wherever Caesar is now, Diviciacus is almost certainly close by."

Chapter 33

East of the Meuse, twenty miles from the Germani camp

Ursinus reined in and reported to Strabo. "Sir, there's about twenty Germani coming this way with a cavalry escort. They saw me, and the cavalry gave no chase after I turned back. From the way they're dressed, it looks like it might be a delegation."

"Ursinus, keep the decuria here while I find out what they want. If you see them coming this way without me, go back and warn the legions."

The cavalryman rode in closer to Strabo and said in a low voice, "With all due respect, that's not a good idea. If you were any other officer, I'd say it's a really stupid idea. I suggest *we* ride back and tell Tarquin visitors are coming. Besides, is your Germani good enough to ask them what they want before they take your head?"

Strabo tried hard not to smile. "I can get by although I expect they have someone who knows enough Gaulish or Latin to understand me. I won't be gone long."

He didn't get far when he heard the decuria coming up behind him. He looked back and wasn't surprised to see Ursinus leading with an angry scowl. Strabo couldn't hold back the smile any longer. Not surprising, the cavalryman expressed his disagreement further with an obscene gesture.

The Germani saw them coming and stopped. A single rider rode toward him and stopped. Similar to the other Germani waiting behind, he was heavily bearded, bare-chested and muscled. He was dressed in knee-high breeches with his hair tied on top and falling in a long horsetail behind. He spoke in fluent Gaulish close enough to Aeduan to be easily understood. His lips curved upward in what must have been an attempt a friendly smile. The result was a grimace closer to a wolf baring its teeth.

"I am Odoracar of the Usipetes and speaker for my lord, King Waramunt, and King Sigheri of the Tencteri. They wish to speak to Caesar on matters most grave and important to their tribes and those tribes on this side of the Rhine River. We come in peace. Will you take us to him?"

"My name is Strabo, and I'll take you to him. Which of those behind are the two tribal kings?"

"King Waramunt wears an eagle helmet, and he is much older than King Sigheri. King Sigheri is the large warrior on his left." Strabo looked past Odoracar and easily identified both men. Of the two, the Tencteri king was the most impressive with his scarred face and torso.

"Caesar is not far from here. I'll send one of my men ahead to inform him of your peaceful embassy. We'll ride slowly to give sufficient time for Caesar to prepare for your arrival. It will be for him to decide if he wishes to meet."

Odoracar rode back to tell the two kings, and Strabo took the opportunity to tell the decuria what had been discussed and arranged.

"Martinus, ride back and tell Tarquin I'm escorting the kings of the two Germani tribes who want to meet with Caesar. We'll come back slowly to give Caesar time to prepare."

With a wide grin, Tarquin was waiting a half-mile from where the legions had temporarily halted the day's march twelve miles from the Germani camp.

"Marcellus, I send you out on a routine patrol, and you come back with a couple of Germani kings. Too bad I wasn't there with the two other decuria. We could have bagged the lot of them, and without their leaders, it might have given the rest of them a reason to get back on their side of the river. Come on, Caesar's waiting and curious. He'll see them outside the fort. Good idea sending Martinus back here. Caesar is ready to see them with all the grandeur of Rome or at least as good as you can do out here in the wilderness."

Strabo saw immediately what Tarquin meant. Under the shade of a large tree, Caesar sat in a curule chair placed on top of a low dais. The *fasces* behind him were held upright by two large, immaculately accoutered legionnaires. The bundle of tied birch rods around an axe symbolized the *imperium* of a high official including province governors. Caesar wore his gold laurel-leaf circlet and his long red cloak draped across the right shoulder down to the right knee. The greaves on his legs matched the ornate, bronze cuirass he was wearing. General Labienus stood a pace behind with the tribunes of the Tenth Legion. Several hundred paces away buglers blew a fanfare and the first cohort came to attention. There was no question Caesar's intention was to make an impression. Strabo thought in the time provided, Caesar was doing just that.

Strabo didn't need to be told he was expected to make the introductions and translate the questions and responses.

After the introductions, Caesar didn't waste time but asked sharply, "Why have you come here?"

King Waramunt answered. "We do not want to fight the Romans. We came from Germania to escape the Suebi who have been raiding and pursuing us for a long time. Although we fear no one but them, they proved stronger. No one can defeat them, and with no other choice, we crossed the Rhine to escape their deprivations and find peace. We were without hope and had no other choice than to come here. If our entry was forceful, consider it was only after our friendly overtures were not received in kind."

Caesar frowned, and his response was biting, accusing. "Your overtures were not friendly. You ravaged the lands of the Menapi and the Eburones instead. I think there is reason and proof your motive for crossing the river is less peaceful than to gain land you could no longer hold in Germania. Your argument is not persuasive to grant you a sympathetic ear and acceptance for what you've done in Gaul. If you have come to seek asylum, it is not granted. You've shown only belligerence and battle to gain new land. As for your comment that no one can defeat the Suebi, I have done so, and King Ariovistus is no longer in Gaul.

"However, I'll consider what you've said to better understand your plight and consider ways we can come to a solution that satisfies the Menapi with acceptable reparations for their losses. Then there is also the concern Rome has your presence here impedes the mutual objective of Rome and the Gaulish tribes for achieving a lasting peace in Gaul. Peace here has so far proved elusive. Your presence and what your tribes have done here can only be viewed as disruptive and dangerous."

King Waramunt started to protest. Caesar interrupted impatiently. "Come back tomorrow after we've both had time to consider if there are any alternatives. Bring your clan elders and chieftains. I want a wider forum to discuss mutually beneficial solutions to our problems rather than solving them on a battlefield."

"Noble Caesar, we will do as you ask; however, we ask you in the meantime not to move your legions closer to our camp. We also request your cavalry to stay away from our camp lest their presence be interpreted as provocative.

"King Waramunt, I must move my legions four miles closer to your cantonment. The water here is insufficient to our needs. I'll advance no farther than that." The response was met by a quiet but heated conversation between the two kings. Odoracar spoke after the interchange ended.

"The conditions are acceptable; however, we request three days to send a delegation to the Ubii for the purpose of assessing their offer of land in exchange for assistance in resisting Suebi depredations. If the discussions are satisfactory, we'll consider returning to Germania."

Caesar avoided a direct answer to the request by saying, "I'll give you my answer tomorrow."

The two kings exchanged looks, and Waramunt muttered something. Sigheri responded with a non-committal shrug, turned his back on Caesar and walked to his horse. Waramunt at least gave a slight nod for a hint of cordiality before striding to his horse.

Caesar waited until the delegation had ridden far enough away to say with a broad smile, "Titus, if they're going to give me bullshit, I can respond in kind. In a few hours, our night camp is going to be four miles closer to their camp. Who knows, perhaps the water there might even be better. Their request for three days to meet with the Ubii is nothing more than a delay until their cavalry finish looting the Eburones."

"Do you really expect they'll show up tomorrow?" Labienus asked.

"I think they will if only to keep up the pretense. If they don't, we'll attack tomorrow with the advantage nearly all of their cavalry is on the other side of the Meuse. Waramunt is right though about warning the Gaulish cavalry not to get too close to their camp. I don't want to provoke a battle today. Send someone ahead and warn them." Caesar sighed and said, "Titus, from past experience with Gaulish cavalry, and most recently with the Treveri at the Sambre, I might be willing to trade all five thousand for half the number of Germani cavalry."

Caesar was incredulous after being told what happened. "Are you telling me our entire cavalry force was routed after being attacked by 800 Germani cavalry? The treacherous sons of bitches! And with a truce only three hours old. I have half a mind not to wait until tomorrow. I want to make sure the bastards don't live to see the sun come up!" He looked at the startled faces of the officers around him and sat back. "Relax, my other half says we won't. All right, tell me what happened."

General Cotta, commander of the Auxilia shifted uncomfortably. "The Germani initiated the attack and surprised our cavalry who, believing a truce was in effect, were unprepared. The manner in which the Germani cavalry attacked was unnerving and contributed to the defeat. Instead of remaining mounted, they fought like infantry and concentrated on killing the Gaulish horses. We lost almost a hundred cavalrymen." The general paused, swallowed and said, "They suffered a few wounded with none killed during the brief fight."

Caesar shook his head in despair and cursed. "Jupiter, did you mistake which cavalry belonged to me, or are you testing my patience? General Cotta, tomorrow the Gaulish cavalry will be in the rear. This is not out of sympathetic concern for their *unfortunate* defeat today. I don't think they are up to suffering another one tomorrow, and by the gods, neither am I. The legionary cavalry will provide lead and flank security."

Without fanfare, the legionnaires began to break camp the next morning. The legions were starting to form ranks as the large Germani delegation arrived consisting of what appeared to be the entire leadership of the two tribes. Caesar asked Jupiter to forgive him for his profane accusation the day before and gave thanks for the godly gift. He ordered the delegation to be taken under guard by the Fourteenth Legion remaining behind to protect the baggage train. Then he gave the order to march. Without the accompaniment of bugles and drums, the legions marched silently and quickly toward the Germani camp in columns four abreast Carrying only one day of rations, the legionnaires on the flat open terrain took less than three hours to cover the eight-mile march to the Germani camp. The route was a wide corridor between the Meuse and Waal Rivers curving from north to southwest.

The Germani only realized they were under attack after they saw the legionary turmae in front deploying to the flanks and the legions wheeling into three ranks across a one-mile front. The Thirteenth Legion in reserve took position in the center behind the forward legions. Tarquin led the turmae to the left flank to join the turmae of the Eighth and Ninth Legions to screen the left flank.

Terrified screams and shouts erupted as panic-stricken women and children fled to the rear of the camp and kept running. Absent their leaders, there was no organized resistance. Fighting bravely in small groups, warriors died in a hopeless attempt to overcome the disciplined legionnaires. An hour after the battle began, there were no Germani warriors left to fight. Still the legions pushed the survivors west in a corridor rapidly becoming a narrow funnel where the rivers converged from an 18-mile width at the camp to a half-mile wide bottleneck 15 miles west. The river banks were too far away from where the camp was located; consequently, the only escape was a long trek west with a better opportunity to reach one of the river banks and swim to safety.

The legionary cavalry remained on the flanks and ahead of the legionary ranks to prevent what was left of the desperate survivors from getting to a river bank and safety. Several hours later a few miles from the bottleneck, Strabo felt like a herder, but instead of livestock, the moving mass was a forlorn human tide of exhausted refugees desperately trying to flee the horror behind them. There was an eerie, prevailing silence broken only by subdued cries and groans of the wounded and the relentless tramp of the legions behind.

The river banks gradually came closer, and those still able tried to reach them. Initially, Tarquin had the turma stopping them. Not long after in disgust, he reversed the order. Of the few who tried to swim the cold and swift-moving river, most never made it across.

Strabo saw the bodies floating past and moving faster than the walking pace of the horses and refugees. He looked at Tarquin and asked, "What's the point of this? If Caesar's going to give them to the slavers, why not turn them back instead of going farther west?"

Tarquin shook his head. "I wish I knew. I've been waiting for an order to tell us what to do." He pointed ahead at the bottleneck they were approaching. "There's about five thousand Germani cavalry somewhere over there we haven't seen yet. It could be Caesar wants to find them. If that's his plan, these pathetic bastards are going to be in the way. It's also possible he wants to make sure they go back across the Rhine."

The conversation was interrupted by a bugle signaling a halt and recall. Tarquin smiled in relief. "About time. Now the only question is do we take them with us to the slavers or let them go?"

The answer came soon preceded by the thunder of thousands of horses coming from behind. Strabo and Tarquin looked at each other with puzzled expressions. The Gaulish cavalry appeared on both flanks and swept past them. A tribune following called to Tarquin.

"Withdraw by order of Caesar, the Auxiliary cavalry will finish here."

Bewildered, Tarquin started to question what the order meant. The tribune answered angrily, "You have your order, obey it."

Tarquin gritted his teeth and turned the turmae around. Strabo looked back and was speechless at what he saw. The massacre unfolding would be a lasting memory and question whether there was any difference between the Gauls and the Romans in committing needless brutality.

Caesar's Headquarters following the battle

Brow wrinkled in thought, Caesar said, "After we leave here, the five thousand Germani cavalry that escaped across the river could return with Sugambri infantry. Titus, the possibility is one I can't ignore. It's unfinished business, and I'm inclined to finish it by crossing the river to end the threat. What do you think we should do?"

"I don't agree. it's not a threat big enough to justify the time, effort and the risk of crossing into Germania. You want to go to Britannia; therefore, it is south we should be going not east."

"You have a point, but then if not here, we're still going to cross the Rhine." Caesar noted the shock on the general's face and smiled. "The Ubii representatives that left here several days ago met first with the Germani to offer lands for help against the Suebi. Afterward, the Ubii asked the same of me, and I'm inclined to give it. The Ubii are proving to be stronger allied with the interests of Rome than just about every tribe in Gaul including the Aedui. My intent is to take the legions southeast to the Treveri opposite the Ubii lands across the river, find a suitable place, build a bridge and take the legions into Germania."

If Labienus was surprised a moment ago, he was now thunderstruck and momentarily speechless. "Why do you want to do that? The Ubii may be friendly; however, any alliance with them is not going to materially help Gaul and implies we're going to provide more than moral support against the Suebi. Caesar, the Rhine is a mighty river. Does Marcus Mammura know about this and can he even build a bridge long and strong enough?"

"He will after I tell him. I've sent for him, and he should be here soon. Mammura is a talented resourceful engineer, and I have no doubt he will welcome the challenge of being the first to bridge the Rhine – and I'll be the first Roman commander to cross it."

Labienus remained skeptical. "Once built the bridge will have to be defended, and that would rely principally on the Treveri and the Ubii to guard it. I would not trust either tribe to stop the Suebi using it to cross into Gaul faster than they've ever done before on boats."

"There won't be a bridge left to secure. After I'm finished with it because it will be destroyed."

Exasperated, Labienus said, "In my opinion what you propose is a long and expensive endeavor for reasons that do not justify it."

"There's a larger, important reason to cross the river. It will prove Rome's capability to fight the Germanic tribes at any time and any place of our choosing."

Labienus concealed his misgivings and changed the subject. "What do you want to do with the Germani delegation – release them, take their heads or turn them over to the slavers?"

"Our prisoners told me they don't want to be released in fear they'll suffer a fate worse than with me. Their concerns are fully justified. There's been enough killing today, and Jupiter should be satisfied. I may have a better solution. We'll take them with us and offer them to the Ubii. Perhaps they could prove useful as hostages. If not, they can decide what to do with them."

Chapter 34
Near the confluence of the Moselle and Rhine Rivers

The air was permeated with the smell of freshly-cut timber lying in piles according to the depth of the river varying from 10 to 35 feet. Strabo and hundreds of legionnaires close to the bridgehead stopped whatever they were doing and watched the fabri below. The engineers were maneuvering two unwieldy rafts against the river current several feet from the riverbank. A similar effort was underway on the opposite bank 1200 feet away.

Each raft was a platform for a 45-foot tower used to drop a heavy, rectangular shaped rock down two slanted logs lashed 18-inches apart. The hammers drove two thick logs, two-feet apart into the riverbed to form a balk opposite the other. The balks were inclined 40-feet apart at the base; the downstream balk inclined upstream and the upstream balk was in the direction of the downriver flow. The balks were separated 36-feet at the top and joined by a transom to form a base for crossbars to connect the next pair of balks 30-feet away. The crossbars would be covered by a flooring of wattle-work. Strabo was skeptical not for the capability of the engineers to build it, rather for the ten days Caesar expected it to be finished.

Five days later, Strabo was again skeptical. This time it had nothing to do with Caesar's expectation for completion of the bridge which looked as if was going to be easily met. It was solving the problem of getting Aquilo onto the shallow draft barge to cross the river. The rest of the decuria was already on the other bank waiting for him. Even worse, so was Tarquin and the two turma from the Ninth and Eleventh Legions about to begin a three-day patrol in Germania.

He was less angry at the horse than for his obviously poor decision to take Aquilo instead of the more docile Secundus. The boatmen were staring apprehensively at the fractious animal. He saw their concerns and wouldn't have blamed them if they had slipped the moorings and left him. The oldest boatman who appeared to be in charge came ashore with a length of cloth and a reassuring smile. He pointed to the horse and wrapped the cloth around his eyes instantly making clear a blindfold was a better solution for solving the problem than a crop and harsh words. The crossing was uneventful.

Ursinus, never one to mince words, greeted Strabo in his usual laconic way. "We thought you might be waiting until the bridge was finished." It was enough to elicit chuckles and smiles from the other cavalrymen and Strabo as well.

"I considered doing that. I've decided I'm not going back across until the bridge is done and proven safe for a skittish horse. If not, I'll stay here and learn to speak Germani."

Strabo broke away and joined the other decurions surrounding Tarquin. The senior cavalryman wasn't one to let it go either. "Nice of you to join us."

Servius also had a comment. "You claimed you knew how to handle a horse. You were dead last to come over the *waterline.*"

"True, but as I've shown on occasion, I do better with a finish line on land." Servius clenched his teeth and scowled. The other decurions snickered.

After the byplay between Strabo and Servius, Tarquin thought it was time to focus attention on why they were there.

"The five thousand Germani cavalry we expected to fight a week ago returned to Germania. Caesar wants to know where they went. The concern is they may be coming south along the Rhine. Their presence this close to the crossing sight would be unwelcome for the next week especially if they're joined by the Suebi. The legions need time to cross and prepare for the battles to come without interference. This is what we're going to do. Initially, we will head north to see if they're following the Rhine to the bridging site. By early this afternoon, we'll begin curving northeast in an arc through the Sugambri lands in which we will make our first camp. From there we will gradually swing east then southeast into territory claimed by the Chatti. We'll make our last camp there before coming south to report what we found or didn't find.

"Our objective is a search for information not a fight unless we can't avoid it. We'll question herders and stop at select settlements along the way. I use the term *select* because both the Sugambri and Chatti, while friendly with the Ubii, that is not a guarantee we'll be welcome; consequently, we have three Ubii interpreters, one for each turma, who will help us determine who's friendly and those not so friendly. If we run into anyone that doesn't want to talk, we smile, wish them a long, happy life and leave. If we don't see the Germani cavalry, a trail may tell us where they're going. It will be difficult to miss what five thousand cavalrymen will leave behind traveling through the countryside.

"We'll travel abreast: I'll be in the center. Servius, you'll be on my left, and Caius, you're on the right. Keep your flankers in sight of mine and signal if you find a trail or anyone that knows where the Germani might be. If anything happens to me, Servius will command."

Soon after leaving, Tarquin's first attempt to talk to the interpreter in Latin ended abruptly, and the frustrated Decurion summoned Strabo. Strabo tried Aeduan, and the translator responded with a grin of relief. Thereafter, Fedde became Strabo's responsibility.

At mid-day there was no sign of the Germani cavalry, and the three troops began to swing northeast. The one herdsman they encountered knew nothing and was immediately alarmed by the possibility who they might be. The sun was late in the sky when the lead scout came back to report several thatched huts in a copse of trees. Tarquin halted the turma while Strabo went with Fedde to find out if they were hostile or inclined to be helpful. The curious villagers greeted them cautiously until Fedde finished telling them why they were there. Their reaction was similar to that of the herdsman. After a brief animated exchange during which the wizened village chief pointed northeast, the translator's face brightened.

"Decurion, he says they have not seen horsemen, but yesterday they saw a cloud of smoke in the direction he pointed and said there's a large settlement a day's walk from here. They believe the settlement was attacked; consequently, they've been hiding in fear the attackers would come this way."

The two men left the villagers encouraged by the possibility it might be the first tangible sign of the Germani cavalry. Tarquin agreed and changed course to an easterly direction.

The faint stench of rotting flesh kept getting stronger the farther they went. The burned remains of the settlement validated what the villagers suspected. There was enough daylight left to see charred bodies, dismembered limbs and heads planted on a long line of stakes. From the number of scorched foundations, Strabo estimated there may have been as many as a hundred people living there.

Strabo said, "It didn't take very many warriors to do this. I think it was a foraging party."

Tarquin agreed and said, "If I'm right, we're going to see more of the same. We'll go upwind a few miles from here and camp to get away from the smell. Tomorrow we'll see if we're tracking a lot of hungry cavalrymen or a rival settlement with a grudge."

The next day the turmae followed the trail left by the foraging party. An hour later, the cavalrymen spotted a flock of Ravens circling in the air a mile ahead and assumed it was another ravaged settlement. There was a very faint smell of rotting flesh; however, the dominating odor was shit, both human and horse. The cause was the abandoned Germani camp left to the raucous scavengers flocking on the far side of the campsite. A wide swath of trampled ground led northeast from the camp. The direction was perplexing. The trail was going directly toward Suebi territory, the tribes the Usipetes and Tencteri had crossed the Rhine to get away from.

Curious, Ursinus rode over to investigate what was attracting the birds. He was gone a long time and Tarquin asked, "What's taking him so long?"

Strabo came to his defense. "He's methodical and takes his time. It's always worth the wait."

The cavalryman was gone so long, Strabo was starting to worry until he saw him returning from the direction the Germani had come.

"They were here longer than a night – possibly three days from the amount of shit and trash. The ravens are eating what's left of butchered horses. I counted 50. They haven't been dead long, maybe the day they left. I found a dead horse in the trees on the far side of where the herd had been picketed. It must have been still alive and overlooked when they left. The horse was in bad shape and would have been butchered had they found it. Could be the rest of the herd isn't much better. I backtracked their trail for a mile or so. They're walking the horses because they were ridden too hard. The horses needed rest, and maybe the men did, too."

Strabo nodded agreement. "I suspect they left Gaul in a hurry without time to take enough food or forage. They've been living off the land which explains what happened to the settlement."

Tarquin agreed. "We'll follow a little farther to see if they're still going in the same direction. If they do, I wonder how welcoming the Suebi will be."

Cautiously, Tarquin led the three decuriae traveling slower than he expected for the reasons Ursinus and Strabo surmised. Tarquin wanted verification but not at the expense of catching up to an adversary that even in poor condition, its overwhelming strength would finish the legionary cavalry less than the time it took Jupiter to piss.

The first indication they might be closing in on the Germani was the not unpleasant smell of horses carried by the breeze coming out of the northeast. Tarquin signaled to the two flank turmae to close in.

"This is as far as we go. If we keep on going, we'll be close enough to ask them where they're going. We've gone far enough to assume with some confidence the Suebi tribes are the destination, and I see no reason to risk going farther. We turn south here and head back toward the bridge site. We should get there tomorrow and earlier than I expected. Since we're no longer looking for a trail, our formation will be the same but tighter and close enough for voice commands. I'll lead. Costa, your decuria will screen forward. We'll travel at a trot and canter when the terrain permits."

Less than two miles from the Germani trail, Strabo heard shouts ahead and the scouts were returning at a gallop with a horse without a rider – it was Costa's. Close behind was a score of Germani horsemen who hastily turned back after seeing the Roman turmae. Tarquin ordered an attack. The assessment Ursinus had given concerning the condition of the Germani horses proved accurate, and the turmae rapidly closed the distance. Strabo saw the lifeless body of the Tenth Legion's second senior decurion turma lying on the ground with an arrow buried deep in his chest. The arrow was also a warning it wasn't only swords they were going to face.

Accepting there was no possibility of outrunning the Romans, the Germani stopped in a tree-studded clearing, dismounted and formed a semi-circle in front of a dense stand of trees. In the trees, a dozen laden packhorses were being guarded by another twenty warriors. The location of the impromptu defense was well-chosen. Tarquin signaled to Servius and Caius to envelop the Germani flanks as far as possible. Strabo noted the defiant dismounted warriors and recollected the Auxilia cavalry were defeated by a significantly smaller and dismounted Germani cavalry force fighting as infantry. It was soon evident from the eager confidence shown by many of the Roman cavalrymen, they were either unaware of or underestimated the effectiveness of the Germanic tactic.

The first cavalrymen to reach the Germani realized too late they were too far ahead of the others leaving their shield side unprotected.

Operating in choreographed teams, one warrior engaged a cavalryman on his sword side, and another ran to the opposite, unprotected side to disembowel the horse. The riders were dead before the horses. The lesson was learned, and the three senior decurions pulled their decuriae back and dismounted.

The single archer between the line of warriors and the packhorses now proved to be the most formidable adversary by taking down two more Romans. Strabo regretted Raven or one of the other Aeduan archers wasn't there. He moved closer to Tarquin.

"Sir, unless the archer is killed, an attack is going to be costly. With your permission, I'll take my decuria dismounted through the trees behind them. Even if we don't kill the archer, the distraction alone may serve to improve our odds and with fewer casualties."

Reluctantly Tarquin understood what the rest of the turmae would do and gave his approval. Strabo withdrew the decuria farther to the rear in a shallow gulley and told the cavalrymen what he planned to do and why.

"After we get behind them, I'll give the signal to make enough noise to make them think we're after the packhorses. At the same time, Decurion Tarquin will order an attack. Ursinus, you're the best and most silent tracker. You are going to be far enough ahead of us the archer will concentrate on where the noise is and not the direction you will be. This may give you the chance to get in among the horses and close enough to silence the archer. What do you think?"

"I think it's a shitty plan, and if I could think of a better one, I'd say let's do mine. I can't so I suggest we get moving before the sun sets on our ass."

Strabo clinched his teeth and halted the decuriae. It had taken longer to get to the Germani right flank where Servius's turma was positioned than he thought it would, and Ursinus needed additional time to move closer to the archer. How much time was a guess for the gods to make. He silently pleaded with Jupiter for some help. He heard a packhorse snort and hoped it was Jupiter telling him it was time to go and not how *shitty* his plan was. He stood up and waved the men through the brush and trees. The sound of the shields was noisy, and they increased it with yells to sound like twice the number they had. The noise from the clearing indicated the battle had begun. He didn't see Ursinus and could only pray the sarcastic cavalryman, if not successful, would live to tell him why he wasn't.

Strabo came out of the trees to a tight, turbulent melee in which each Germani, with no hope of survival, fought to take as many Romans with him into the next world as he could. He stopped and leaned against a tree to catch his breath. He saw Servius bleeding from his shoulder and staggering as he fought two warriors. The decurion collapsed falling to his knees, stabbed upward and thrust his sword into the belly of the closest warrior. With both hands, the other one swung his longer and wider sword back for a fatal blow. Strabo was faster, and the Germani's head fell in front of the decurion.

The decurion looked up with a vacant stare that took a moment to register what had happened. "Servius, we're even for what you did for me at the Aisne River."

"The only thanks I have is I'll live longer to even the score between us."

"The odds you ever will are not in your favor. I don't intend to ever race you again."

Surprisingly the decurion's face softened when he replied with the hint of a smile, "Perhaps, you're right. I'll think of other ways to make me believe the gods don't always favor you."

Shaking his head, Strabo walked to where Ursinus was standing with a cluster of cavalrymen from the Tenth Legion's turma. They were clustered around a still form on the ground. He went over to see who it was.

Grief-stricken, Ursinus said, "I wasn't quick enough. The archer released the arrow before I had a chance to kill him."

Strabo went closer and made his way through the circle of cavalrymen and saw Tarquin's vacant eyes looking at the sky with an arrow protruding from his neck. He was numb with the sudden realization Servius was in command of what was left of the three turmae. Tribune Setarius told him *the gods are fickle.* They proved it when the archer's last arrow hit Tarquin instead of Servius.

Servius was brief and impersonal as he told Strabo what he wanted. "At least two of the bastards got away and headed in the direction of the Germani main body. Take your decuria," he stopped and amended, "I understand the other decurions of the Tenth have deferred to you to take command. So be it. Send one of your decuriae to stop them. We can't afford the chance they'll get back to tell what happened. If one of them does, we're going to deal with a lot more Germani than we fought here. In the meantime, I'm taking the wounded and dead along with the packhorses in the direction of the bridge site." Servius hesitated then said, "You and your decuria did a good job. Was it Tarquin's idea to get behind them?"

"No, I proposed it. At first, he wasn't in favor. He thought we didn't have much of a chance to get it done. I agreed although I thought it was worth a try."

Servius nodded and responded with a curt, "Well done," and immediately turned his attention to getting the wounded cared for and the turmae prepared to leave.

Strabo assembled what was left of the turma and told the cavalrymen what Servius had ordered. "It's critical the two Germani that escaped do not reach the main body; consequently, I'm taking Naevius, Domitius and Philo to go after them. Their horses are almost as fast as Aquilo. In my absence, Ursinus will command my decuria, and Cosmin commands the turma."

The four men hadn't gone far when it became clear they were following three horses not two. A mile later, a dead horse was lying beside the trail. The deeper hoof prints of one of the two remaining horses indicated it was carrying double.

Farther on, Strabo noted the cloud of dust ahead rapidly becoming larger. Strabo saw the hill ahead and shouted, "We can't get too much closer, or we'll be running for our lives. I'm going to risk increasing the pace for the horses capable. Anyone who can't keep up, slow down. Don't risk foundering your horse."

Domitius remained at the same pace while the other three moved ahead up the hill. Cresting the top, they saw the overloaded horse partway down on the ground with a warrior pinned underneath and struggling to get free. The other warrior was making a desperate run for a copse of trees. The third rider was a few hundred yards away and frantically lashing a horse that from its erratic gait appeared close to foundering.

Strabo pointed to the two warriors. "Naevius, Philo, take care of those two."

By the time he was halfway to the third warrior, the horse collapsed. Strabo slowed Aquilo to a canter and took his time after seeing the Germani remaining next to the horse holding a two-handed sword at the ready. Strabo stopped a short distance away and dismounted. He had no intention of risking Aquilo. The warrior's relaxed stance and confident smile disappeared after looking past Strabo and seeing two Roman cavalrymen closing at a gallop and a third one coming at a slower pace.

Strabo heard the hoof beats and saw the warrior's changed expression. He knew help was on the way. He drew his spatha, adjusted the shield and started walking toward the warrior.

Naevius reined in and shouted anxiously, "Sir, how about some help?"

"Only if it looks like I'm getting the worst of it. After seeing what these whoresons have been doing lately, I want all the pleasure of killing him."

The closer Strabo got to the warrior and saw how big and muscled he was, he was starting to reconsider Naevius's offer.

The warrior didn't give him time and made the first move swinging his heavy sword angling up and down from left to right. Strabo moved back looking for the best way to counter the wind-milling assault. His chance came when the sword started down on his left side. He stepped in and blocked it with the shield long enough to ram the spatha into the warrior's stomach. The Germani dropped his sword and fell to his knees clutching his belly with both hands. Recalling the brutality of the Germani over the past three weeks, he briefly considered leaving him to die a slow death. The thought sickened him as he recalled the recent cruel massacre at the Waal River. Had he come to the point where killing was not enough, that it had to include needless cruelty as well? He knew the answer as he pulled the dagger out and walked over to the warrior.

Strabo wondered why it was taking longer to catch up to the turmae than he expected. He assumed the pace of the weakened packhorses would slow the turmae down enough they would have caught up hours ago.

He found the answer at the first river they had to cross. Four packhorses without packs were cropping dried grass in a clearing. Near the bank of a narrow, swift flowing river, blood-stained wrappings were strewn about. The river had proven too much for the exhausted animals to cross and were released to survive as they could. The meat and grain in the packs were given to the fish and turtles.

The sun was close to setting before they finally reached the turmae camp tired and saddle-weary. Ursinus was relieved to see them. Servius was only interested to learn if they had been successful. After being assured they were, he had no interest in the details.

Epilogue

Strabo turned in the saddle and looked at the seven legions lined up stretching nearly two miles on the west side of the bridge waiting for Caesar to lead them into Germania. As usual, the Tenth Legion would lead with the legion's turma in front. The legionnaires standing at ease were unusually animated, excited at what was about to take place. Caesar had said to each of the legions the day before the incursion into Germania would be an historic event. Strabo looked ahead at the long wooden bridge stretching to the other side of the river and thought Caesar was right. The bridge was an unbelievable marvel doubted at first by almost everyone except for two men, the one who conceived it, and the one who built it.

His mind drifted back to the morning he woke up in a legionary training camp near Massilia half-drunk and outraged to find he'd been conscripted. Since then, he had changed significantly from privileged wastrel to becoming the senior decurion of the Tenth Legion. The change was motivated by the conviction he was serving both sides of his heritage in resisting an invasion of Gaul. Subsequently, his satisfaction for being a successful Roman soldier was offset by Raven's dislike of all things Roman. Then she began learning Latin so that she and Caturix could be with him, even if it meant living as a Roman. It was a revelation that left him no longer feeeling conflicted in having to choose to be either Roman or Aeduan. He could live and serve both worlds until circumstances dictate he may have to decide one side or the other. He smiled and felt free for the first time since being conscripted.

Ursinus noted his relaxed expression and said, "Sir, you seem to be enjoying yourself, and well you should. I remember not long ago the only thing you had in your favor was the *Strabo* name. At first, I had misgivings. You proved yourself better than most of the dumb shits I've trained over the years."

Strabo's throat constricted at the rough-worded compliment. It was better than the accolades General Labienus expressed after Servius related what happened before and after the battle. Servius credited Strabo and his decuria for the success of the patrol.

Ursinus interrupted again. "Decurion, why is it officers call a formation, and we wait around until they decide to show up? It's the usual hurry up and wait. One day, I'll ask the gods why they made me sign up to walk long or ride hard and fight some ignorant son of a bitch probably wondering the same as me."

Strabo couldn't help himself and responded with a laugh. "You just summarized after twenty years of service what I'm beginning to think after two years."

There was a successive wave of enthusiastic shouts faint at first growing louder as Caesar's entourage rode the length of the long column to the bridgehead. General Labienus was already there to greet him. Strabo called the turma to attention and waited for the bugles and drums. Aquilo reacted nervously with a skittish sidestep showing signs the bridge before him might be too far and dangerous to cross.

Caesar called out, "Decurion Strabo, are you ready to lead us to the other side of this muddy river?"

Strabo didn't answer. He was too busy controlling the stallion. The gray beast was showing signs he might prefer going down the river bank and swim across than trust something that looked worse than a boat.

Author's Notes

All the battles in the narrative follow Caesar's description in the *Commentaries* concerning how and under what circumstances they were fought. I've added details and characters to Caesar's otherwise high-level summaries which do not often mention participants by name. He was certainly sparse when it came to praising. A good example of the latter is he never once mentions Marcus Vitruvius Mamurra, his principal engineer (*fabri*) responsible for overseeing bridging including the Rhine River, construction of siege machines, extensive fortifications and even ship building without which Caesar would not have accomplished what he did so quickly and effectively.

Historians accept Caesar inflated the strength of his opponents. Tribal strength often included the entire population of the migrating or attacking force. He can be alibied in part for the exaggeration because women did often fight alongside the men. Even if the women did not bear arms, they were frequently present at the battle giving vocal support and aiding the wounded. Discounting the women and children and tribesmen not able to fight, Caesar's adversaries generally outnumbered him by roughly three to one. The odds were still in Caesar's favor. The tribal armies for the most part were conscripted farmers facing a professional, highly trained Roman Army that decisively defeated the Helvetii and Suebi the previous year. For two of the battle sketches, I relied on the research of Baron Eugene Stoffel, a French colonel in the 19th century and a noted scholar of Caesar's battles.

<u>Battle of the Aisne:</u> Caesar chose the battle site well. Considerably outnumbered (or so he believed), the marsh was key terrain in maintaining a strong defensive position. He hoped King Galba would attack through it and become hopelessly bogged down. Galba never took the bait. Galba's initial attack at Bibrax about ten miles away was a failure, and unknown to Caesar, Galba's coalition of Belgae and Germani tribes was not coming together. Galba stalled for

time. Caesar grew impatient and sent the cavalry out to provoke Galba to attack which he eventually did with disastrous results at the river. Following the battle, the dispirited Belgae Army melted away in the night. Caesar delayed following in the belief it was a trick. He finally realized it wasn't a ploy, and he sent two legions and the cavalry after the fleeing Belgae.

<u>Battle of the Sambre (Sabis):</u> Modern historians have recently concluded Caesar cited the wrong river. The details of the battle in the narrative and sketch accurately describe and show what happened. Normally, each legion had its baggage train following behind it. For some reason, Caesar combined the baggage trains into one with the two recently recruited legions following. It was unfortunate for Buodognatus who counted on the legions being widely separated.

This was a battle Caesar came very close to losing. The only reason he did not was the capability of the legions to react quickly to the ambush and organize a defense. General Labienus prevented the battle from becoming a disaster when he saw from across the river what was happening and aborted his attack. His return turned the tide in favor of the Romans. Caesar is not without credit for boosting morale and tenacity by moving to the front line with sword and shield. One of the few times Caesar mentions a centurion by name is when he saw Bucelus so badly wounded he could barely stand. The Nervii fought almost to the last man virtually surrounded by what was left of the legions and Auxilia. After the battle, Buodognatus was never mentioned again; therefore, I assumed he died in the final battle. Caesar avoided any mention of casualties which must have been unusually excessive. Historians concluded it was because the battle came close to being a Pyrrhic victory. To this day in the Benelux countries, the name Caesar is not held in high esteem; the one exception is in the vicinity of Brussels where his praise for the bravery of the Nervii following the battle is appreciated.

Battle of the Aduatuci: Caesar assessed the impressive fortified settlement of the Aduatuci and settled in for a long-term siege with a circumvallation. As it happened, the moving siege tower convinced the Aduatuci (I was never able to find out the name of the tribal chief and invented Drusalos) to talk. Caesar did not trust the sudden turnaround and planned accordingly. For their treachery, he enslaved virtually the entire tribe or at least those worth the effort. Historians believe it may have been the largest auction of a single tribe in Rome. The reference to the popular poet Cutullus and his semi-humorous and often rude poems about notable people, including Caesar and Mamurra, comes from other sources and certainly not from the *Commentaries*. Apparently both men had reputations for licentiousness and possibly as much envied as denigrated.

Massacre of the Usipetes and Tencteri: The battle developed and occurred as described in the *Commentaries* and as I present in the narrative. Where it occurred is near the vicinity of the town of Lith on the bank of the Meuse River just west of Nijmegen, Netherlands. In 2016, the actual site was convincingly narrowed down as shown on the sketch map. The precise locations of the Germani and Roman Camps are conjectured based on Caesar's comments on mileage distance. The battle is best remembered by what happened after the legions pushed the Germani west toward the bottleneck, the term I used to describe the location on the map. Caesar's cryptic comment *...and Caesar dispatched the cavalry in pursuit* is when the battle was over, and the massacre really began. Scholars have pondered why Caesar allowed the massacre to occur. Battles in the time were bloody, but apparently the aftermath was particularly so as reported by others. Possibly in defense of Caesar after releasing the cavalry, there were unintended results. When word reached Rome about the massacre, Caesar was widely condemned. Cato proposed that Caesar should be given to the barbarians.

Caesar recaptured his tarnished reputation by being the first Roman Commander to take legions across the Rhine River. The location of the bridge is believed to be a few miles north of the confluence of the Moselle and Rhine Rivers and close to the German city of Koblenz. Why did Caesar go 100 miles south from the massacre site to build the bridge instead of remaining where he was? Caesar doesn't say other than mentioning pursuing a Germani cavalry troop reported going south along the west bank of the Rhine — it's not very credible. I suggest he went for several reasons. The Ubii were regularly threatened by the Suebi, and they wanted to send a signal of Roman support. A bridge would be a very perceptible signal. Ubii territory included the bridge site and ensured security of the eastern side of the river during construction. The western bridge site was in the land of the Treveri which offered additional security. However, I believe Caesar's growing concern about Indutiomarus's continued support of Rome was the main reason for him to take eight legions south for a not so subtle reminder to stay in line. It wouldn't be too much longer before Caesar's concerns about Indutiomarus were fully justified.

Caesar doesn't mention what happened to the Germani tribal leaders and elders who refused to be turned loose for fear of what would happen to them. I decided to fill in the blank by having Caesar give them to the Ubii as hostages. What happened to the 5000 Germani cavalry raiding the Eburones that left the two tribes vulnerable to the Roman attack? They were too late to do anything but cross the Rhine where they probably remained in the territory from where they came. I imagined another scenario. They had lost their families and everything except the plunder gained from the Eburones and had no other choice but to try and make peace with the Suebi. Who knows? But it gave a causal reason for Tarquin and Strabo to cross the Rhine and find out where the cavalry went. It was also a way to continue Strabo's journey in Book 3 accompanied by his nemesis, Quintus Servius.

The Legion: A legion was commanded by a general who held the post for several years. Second in command was the senior tribune of the five tribunes. Tribunes were primarily staff officers and normally did not command except under circumstances when two or more cohorts were detached or if the legion separated into separate winter camps. If the commanding general was killed, the senior tribune took command, and if he was also killed, the *praefectus castrorum*, (camp prefect) was next in line to take command. The praefectus would probably have been a former *primus pilus*, First Spear.

The first cohort was commanded by the primus pilus, the senior centurion of the legion and had a strength of 800 men with 9 centuries instead of 6 in each of the other cohorts. The following graphic is intended to simplify and summarize the organization and structure of the legion.

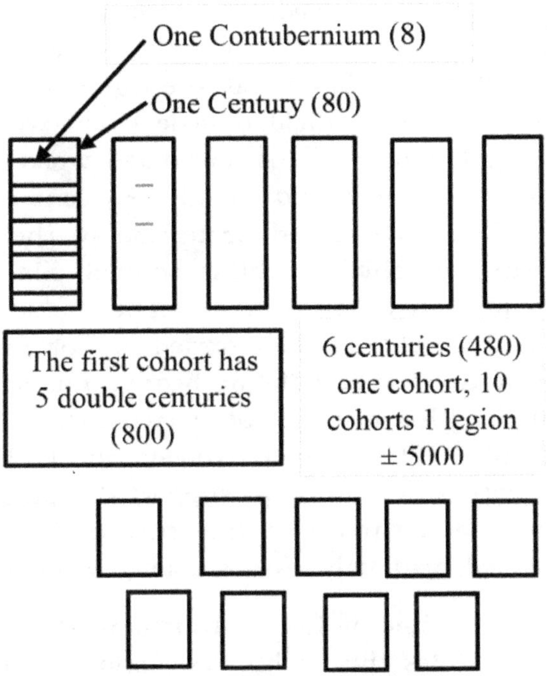

Cavalry: 3000 organized in 10 turmae (troops) consisting of 30 cavalrymen for each cohort

Legion Organization and Structure

The strength of a legion was plus or minus 5000 men, about the size of a modern-day army brigade consisting of ten cohorts with each cohort divided into three maniples. Caesar never mentions maniples, and for that reason, I don't either.

The legionnaire wore a linen undergarment beneath a sleeveless, woolen tunic stretching to the knees. Over the tunic he wore a metal cuirass that depending on the period would have been either chain mail or segmented armor. In cold weather, he wore knee-length breeches (bracae). His doubled-soled boots (*caligae*) were heavy hobnailed, leather shoe-sandals and tied with thongs reaching above the ankle. His helmet under which he wore a padded, metal skullcap was bronze with hinged metal cheek pieces and an extension in back to protect the neck. With the left hand, the legionnaire carried a rectangular, convex-shaped shield a little over two-feet wide and four feet long. It was made of laminated wood covered in leather and edged with a round metal boss centered on the facing side. The boss gave added protection to the left hand while weaponizing the shield in close combat. Since the left side was more protected, his armor might include a metal greave worn on the right leg. He carried one or more spears (*pila*) depending if they were light or heavy. The spears were over six feet in length consisting of a two-foot metal shank with a three-pointed tip held in a wooden shaft. Around his waist, a heavy leather belt (*balteus*) supported a dagger (*pugio*) on the left side and a three-foot (sword) on the right. The sword was intended primarily as a stabbing weapon.

The legions at the time of Caesar fought in three lines, and Caesar specifically states this in his descriptions of the battles he fought. The lines would vary in size according to the terrain, the tactics the commander might devise and the enemy's strength. The first line consisted of the heavy infantry, the second line was occupied by lighter infantry and the third was the reserve from the Auxilia or select cohorts from all or multiple legions. The cavalry was deployed as wings on both flanks. Lightly-armed skirmishers either infantry or archers or both might be deployed in front of the first line. Since the archers did not carry shields, they would take position behind the infantry for protection.

A Roman attack was initiated with psychological intent — a silent, ominous advance that on signal became a noisy, shield-banging, bugle-blowing thunderous noise designed to awe the enemy and weaken their resolve. The psychological effect merely added to the major advantage the Romans had, specifically, superb discipline and organization that compensated for the numerical strength the Gauls always had. I found it interesting Vegetius advocated the commander should be positioned on the right flank between the cavalry and infantry with his second in command in the center of the line and his third senior commander commanding the reserve. His rationale being he could see the length of his front line. It would seem this would make sense only if the terrain on the right flank was elevated sufficiently to give him a "bird's eye view" of the battlefield. I put Caesar in the center with the Tenth Legion (he looked upon the legion as his personal guard) in the belief it was more practical to be centrally located where the main attack would be launched and close to either flank in case a problem developed.

Vegetius defines seven basic formations the Romans used with advantages and disadvantages for each. The above description is general and a default description for how the highly-disciplined and trained Romans planned ahead and executed according to the situation, a concept unknown to their adversaries. The principal defensive position when circumstances required was the *testudo* (tortoise) formation in which the ranks behind the first raised their shields overhead and the right and left outside row of legionnaires locked their shields in a wall to protect the flanks.

I included Caesar's continued concern about grain for the legionnaires and forage for the livestock. It was a genuine concern for it frequently influenced where a battle was fought (Bibracte and Vosges) or postponed. The legions were not able to carry large amounts of supplies; consequently, they were extremely dependent on what could be obtained locally by paying for it, obtaining it by reason of helping a tribe (i.e. the Aedui) or by conquest. Roman army rations seldom included meat. Wheat (corn) or when it wasn't available, barley was the preferred ration. Barley was issued instead of wheat to a unit that by their actions or inactions did not deserve the food of choice. The actions of Dumnorix in delaying logistical assistance to the Romans while doing what he could to help the attacking tribes was both a tactical and a political threat because of his relationship to Diviciacus.

Cavalry: The Roman army relied principally on foreign tribes, including Gaulish Tribes, for large cavalry support. Cavalry support covered a wide range of missions: scouting/intelligence gathering, guarding the legion flanks, initial engagement of opposing cavalry and pursuit of a defeated enemy particularly fleeing infantry. Such missions are similar to armored cavalry in a modern army. In comparison to Legion Cavalry, tribal cavalry was not well organized or consistently dependable.

Caesar describes two occasions when his tribal cavalry failed him. At the Battle of the Sambre, his reliable Treveri cavalry bolted after one look at what the Nervii were doing to the legions. The second was the day before the battle with the Usipetes and Tencteri when 5000 Gaulish cavalry were routed by 800 Germani cavalry.

A legion had 10 turmae (troops) with a combined total of 300 cavalrymen. A troop consisted of three 10-man decuriae (squads) with each squad commanded by a decurion. The three decurions were not equal; the senior decurion commanded the troop when they were deployed as a single unit. When the troop was split up, the other two decurions commanded independently. The troop could be assigned as a unit or in separate units to support legion units deployed in multiple centuries or cohorts as dictated by circumstance and battle exigencies.

The Roman cavalryman wore an elaborate bronze helmet with a padded skullcap underneath. The helmet with cheek plates was embossed with decorations, small removable fur crests or feathers. On formal occasions and occasionally in battle, a metal face mask was worn less for protection to the face than to convey a menacing look. Over a padded tunic, he wore a chain mail or segmented cuirass. His leather knee-length breeches and ankle-high boots were similar to what were worn by a legionnaire. He was armed with a straight sword (*spatha*) about four feet long and carried a long spear (*hasta*) used for stabbing. Roman Cavalry did not use stirrups until late in the Imperial period; consequently, the spear could not be used as a lance. A quiver of smaller javelins was attached to the four-pommel saddle. His shield was oval-shaped and smaller than the legionary rectangular (*scuta*) shield.

Throughout the novel, I've emphasized the use of legionary cavalry and probably embellished their importance beyond historic reality. However, Marcellus Strabo and legionary cavalry are not given tasks nor do they fight battles unrealistic to what would be expected of a cavalry squad or troop.

Glossary of Terms and Place Names

Terms

Aquila (a qwee la): The legion standard represented by an eagle gilded in silver clutching gold thunderbolts

Aquilfer (a qweel fer): Legion's senior standard bearer ranking just below a centurion

Auxilia (owks eel e ah): Auxiliary refers to the non-Roman forces that frequently manned the frontiers or reinforced the legion, particularly with cavalry. It was common practice to relocate indigenous troops to locations along the Roman frontiers in other than their own tribal lands. The latter provided further assurance against internal rebellion. During the time of Julius Caesar and the republic, the Roman Army depended on foreign cavalry, placing its emphasis on heavy and light infantry to win battles. Caesar's battle experience in Gaul taught him the importance of cavalry, and gradually the Romans began to place increased reliance for their capabilities in reconnaissance, skirmishing, and flanking maneuvers. By the second and third centuries, the Roman army completely embraced the use of cavalry and had become proficient in its use. The cavalrymen were the highest paid in comparison to the legionnaires attesting to their increased value.

Balteus (ball tay oose): The Roman military belt was distinctive and prized by the legionnaire. Taking away the belt was both a severe punishment and a disgrace.

Breccae: The leather trousers reaching below the knee worn primarily in winter. Apparently, they were uncomfortable and grudgingly accepted only in cold weather.

Caligae: The hobnailed boot-sandal all Roman officers and legionaries wore. They varied in thickness if not in basic design according to the weather and terrain. Somewhat open around the upper foot they were laced to mid-calf or higher, depending on the weather. In winter and cold regions, legionaries wore socks and wrapped their legs in felt or wool cloth for additional warmth. The Emperor Caligula derived his name from the time he was a small boy and spent much of his time in uniform around legionary barracks. Because of that, he was given the nickname *Little Boots.*

Carnyx: A type of tapered trumpet used in battle by the celtic tribes. It was almost six feet long and held vertically when played to allow the sound to carry farther, and presumably above the battlefield. Only pieces from the top (animal or dragon heads) of the instruments have been found. Depictions on Roman coins and decorative objects give some idea of the size and shape. Modern reconstructions have been included in Celtic music ensembles. The sound, mournfully rich and not unpleasant, ranges from a deep bass to a high-pitched blast. The notes would have traveled a great distance and made them both effective for signaling as well as inspiring warriors to give it their best. Sample audios can be heard by Googling 'Carnyx' on the internet.

Castigato: For major offenses, punishment was administered by a whip consisting of multiple of leather lashes with or without lead balls attached to each lash. See fustuarium below.

Centurion: The rank of centurion was both prestigious and highly coveted. The role of centurion in the Roman Army has no direct counterpart in the U.S. Army today. It is fair to say, the centurion performed the duties with the commensurate responsibility of a modern-day commissioned officer, warrant officer or senior non-commissioned officer depending upon the centurion's seniority and specific position in the Roman military hierarchy. For example, the most senior centurion in a legion of typically 5000 strong could be legitimately compared to a battalion commander and normally in the grade of lieutenant colonel, while the most junior centurion was assigned duties in line with a first sergeant or sergeant major. The centurion above all represented the senior, combat-tested leadership of the legion, which represented the primary fighting unit of the Roman Army. Unlike the tribunes and even the legion commanders who normally served only brief periods in the army, the centurions were the professional backbone upon which legion and field commanders absolutely depended upon to maintain discipline and win battles.

Century: A unit of 80 men commanded by a centurion; 60 centuries to a legion. The century was divided into ten *contubernia* with eight men assigned to each *contubernium.*

Cohort (Cohors pl**):** A unit of 480 men; ten cohorts to a legion. The exception was the first cohort nearly double in strength and led by the senior centurion, the primus pilus.

Consilium: Military council.

Contubernium (contubernia pl) An eight-man unit that shared a mule (with or without a cart) to carry their baggage, a tent in the field and a room or space in garrison. The eight men were allocated rations as a small unified mess. See Century above.

Cornicin (ies): Horn blower(s).

Dignitas: The literal meaning meant dignity; however, the term conveyed more than the modern literal definition. It represented the sum total of a man's stature gained from political and military service to the state. In particular, Roman nobility and officers would seek death before the loss of dignitas, a loss of stature that could only be redeemed by suicide.

Decuria (e) Ten-man cavalry unit.

Decurion (aes): An officer commanding a ten-man decuria. A legionary cavalry turma (troop) consisted of three decuriae each commanded by a decurion. The senior decurion commanded the turma when two or all three decuriae were deployed together; the duplicarius was second in seniority and the sesquiplicarius was third in command.

Denarius (denarii): The largest Roman coinage denomination. It is estimated the legionary foot soldier was paid about 180 denarii a year with the combined infantry and cavalry legionaries earning more.

Dolabra (doe la bra) Dolabrae pl: Combined pick and axe the legionary used to dig trenches and fell trees for constructing fortifications, obstacles and roads.

Dux: Leader. The equivalent rank of a general but without a leadership position assigned to the staff of a Roman legion or army. Over the centuries, the title eventually became precursor to the title duke.

Epona: The horse goddess worshipped widely by Celtic tribes throughout Gaul and Britannia.

Fabri: Craftsmen: The fabri were similar to the modern-day military engineers responsible for technical supervision and construction of projects such as roads, bridges, even aqueducts. The legionnaire provided the bulk of the workforce as necessary. During the Roman Republic, there were no physicians (medici) except occasionally there might be a civilian doctor available to tend the sick and wounded. Most often the wounded were looked after by the fabri, likely because they were not required to fight as legionnaires and were available. The Roman practice at the time was to place the wounded in nearby villages where medical care was available. It was not until later during the Roman Empire the army brought physicians and medical orderlies into the army structure

Fasces: A bundle of tied birch rods around an axe that symbolized the *imperium* (authority) of a high official including the emperor and province governors. The fasces were carried by *lictors* walking in front of the official in a public event. The fasces continue to be used in modern day and are represented on U.S. coinage and as part of the formal seal of the U.S. Congress.

Ferrata: Legion name meaning iron

Flagrum: Also, *flagellum*. A whip consisting of three leather thongs and sometimes tipped with lead. Lighter whips without the lead were used for less severe punishment while the heavier version was reserved for major punishments and to scourge a victim prior to crucifixion.

Fustuarium: A harsh sentence reserved for particularly serious offenses such as sleeping on guard, cowardice or desertion during periods of active engagement with the enemy. The condemned man was set upon with cudgels, usually the wooden portion of the pilum with the metal shaft removed, by members of the individual's own unit, probably his century. The punishment was occasionally administered to an entire unit including a legion under a charge of cowardice. In such cases, lots were drawn and every tenth man was condemned. The term 'decimated' refers to this practice. In most cases, the individual or individuals died from the brutal beating. If an individual somehow managed to survive which was probably rare, he was summarily dismissed from the army in disgrace.

Gladius (glah dee oose): The short sword carried by officers and legionaries.

Gravitas: A derivation of 'gravis,' yet the word connoted something more than a 'grave' or dignified demeanor. Much like the oriental concept of 'face,' the individual who had gravitas commanded respect and authority far beyond the prestige accorded only by title or position.

Hasta: The long spear carried by legionary cavalrymen.

Hastile: The distinctive knobbed staff carried by an optio (see optio below). The staff was almost as tall as the optio. In addition to being a visible sign of authority much like the vine stick (*vitis*) of a centurion, it was used to "encourage" legionnaires forward into battle or to administer punishment for minor infractions.

Legatus: (le gah toose): Legate, a province governor and or a general.

Medicus: (medi coose) (medici pl): Medical doctor.

Mentula: Vulgar reference to the penis

Optio (nes): A rank below centurion equivalent to a junior officer or senior sergeant. The *optio* wore a crest on his helmet smaller than a centurion's or feathers on each side of the helmet. Unlike a centurion, he wore his gladius on the right hip as did the common legionnaire. The optio was generally positioned in the rear rank to prod legionaries who appeared to be ready to break ranks.

Phalorae: Military decorations

ilum (pee loom), Pila (pee la pl)**:** Spear. It's common for most to believe the short sword (Spanish sword, or gladius, was the weapon that most characterized the Roman legionary. The argument can be made it was the heavy javelin which defined the Roman Army. Slightly over six feet in length, it had a long pyramidal shaped point that took up almost a third of the total length of the weapon. The opposite end was encased in a short metal sleeve. The Roman Army depended on volleys of pila to deliver a punishing barrage before the front ranks charged. The metal shafts of each pilum were not tempered and bent easily on contact. The latter was an intended consequence and resulted in weighing down the shields of the opposing ranks to provide the opportunity to use a gladius.

Principia (prin sip e ah): The headquarters building or tent in a Roman fort.

Primipilatus (pre me pee lah toose): Former senior centurion.

Primus pilus (pre moos pee loose): It literally means "first spear" and was the form of address and title of the senior centurion commanding the first cohort in a Roman Legion. Prestigious and coveted, the position was the apex of the centurion's career. The position was usually held for only one campaign season before it was surrendered. There was no limit on the number of times an individual might hold the position. Serving multiple times in a career was rare. Once a centurion attained the position, he was automatically accepted into the equestrian class, a distinct step up in the social hierarchy of the Roman Republic and Empire. The vast majority of centurions never achieved the rank. See Primi pilatus.

Pugio (poo gee oh): The dagger each legionary wore on the balteus on the opposite side from the *gladius.* Centurions wore the dagger on the right side while the legionary wore his on the left.

Sacramentum (sahc rah men toom): The oath each legionary took to the emperor after recruitment and later during the empire to the legion commander to assure personal loyalty

Sagum (sah goom): Military cloak made of rough spun wool worn by the common legionary

Salve: Hail. Used as a greeting.

Scutum (Scuta) (skoo toom; skoo tah)): Shield; (plural)

Sesterce (ses ter chee) (pl- sestertii): A coin worth approximately a quarter of a denarius (see above) and two and a half 'asses,' the smallest of the three denominations.

Spatha: Cavalry sword much longer than the gladius

Testudo: A tight defensive formation named for the tortoise in which the inside ranks placed their shields over their heads while the outside ranks kept their shield facing outward. The formation provided protection from arrows and other missiles from above and the sides.

Torque (tor kwee): Military or tribal decoration worn around the neck.

Tribuli: (thistles) Thick stakes 5-6 feet long and sharpened at both ends used as part of the defense of a Roman fort or marching camp. Three stakes were lashed together at the center to form a large caltrop which were embedded in the upcast obtained from the forward defensive ditch below the low rampart walls. The stakes would have been a deterrent to any foot or mounted attack. When the camp was moved, the stakes were pulled up, untied, and loaded on mules or carried by the legionaries for use in building the next camp.

Turma (ae): Cavalry troop consisting of 30 men and led by a decurion. (See decurion above). There were 10 turmae assigned to a legion during the time of Caesar.

Via Principalis: One of the two main streets that crossed in the center of a Roman fortress at a right angle with the *via praetoria.* Near the intersection of these two roads is where the headquarters or principia would be located.

Vitis (vee tis): The distinctive twisted 'vine' stick a centurion carried symbolizing his rank. It was frequently used as an instrument for administering corporal punishment.

Place Names and Geographical Features

Aduatuca: The modern city of Tongeren, the oldest city in eastern Belgium near the Dutch border, northwest of Liuge and the Ardennes in the south. After the conquest of Germania, it became a Roman stronghold linking the route between Bavay, France and Cologne, Germany. There is some dispute concerning the exact location. The terrain Caesar describes is more rugged than where Tongeren is.

Arduenna Silva: The Ardennes, a rugged, heavily forested area covering southern Belgium and Luxembourg and extending across the Rhine into Germany. In WWII the Ardennes were considered by both the allied and German forces as impenetrable for any track or vehicular traffic.

Armorica: The land between the Loire and Seine including the Brittany Peninsula

Bay of Quiberon: A bay on the southwestern coast of Brittany, France (see Gulf of Morbihan below)

Bibracte: Near Autun, France

Bibrax: The main oppidum (fortified settlement) settlement of the Remi Tribe believed to be the town of Saint Thomas, France, located approximately 15 miles northwest of Reims and 8 miles southeast of Laon.

Genava: Geneva, Switzerland

Gesoriacum: Boulogne, France

Gulf of Morbihan: A 28 by 15 mile gulf in France south of the city of Vannes leading into the Bay of Quiberon on the south coast of Brittany

Sambre River: A tributary of the Meuse River in Northern France and southern Belgium

Hispania: Spain

Massilia: The port of Marseilles, France

Visontio: Besaɜon, located in eastern France in a near circular loop of the Doubs River, a tributary of the Saɸne River, approximately 50 miles southeast of Dijon and 60 miles west of the Swiss border.

CPSIA information can be obtained
at www.ICGtesting.com
Printed in the USA
LVHW041738040323
740939LV00003B/178

9 781952 439469